What Tomorrow Brings

Mary Fitzgerald was born and brought up in Chester. At eighteen she left home to start nursing training. She ended up as an operating theatre sister in a large London hospital and there met her husband. Ten years and four children later the family settled for a while in Canada and later the USA. For several years they lived in West Wales, northern Scotland and finally southern Ireland until they settled again near Chester. Mary had long given up nursing and gone into business, first a children's clothes shop, then a book shop and finally an internet clothes enterprise.

Mary now lives in a small village in north Shropshire close to the Montgomery canal and with a view of both the Welsh and the Shropshire hills.

Mary Fitzgerald

What Tomorrow Brings

arrow books

First published by Arrow Books, 2014

2 4 6 8 10 9 7 5 3 1

First published in Great Britain by Arrow Books, 2014
The Random House Group Limited
20 Vauxhall Bridge Road, London, SW1V 2SA

www.randomhousebooks.co.uk

Addresses for companies within The Random House Group Limited can be found at:
www.randomhouse.co.uk/offices.htm

The Random House Group Limited Reg. No. 954009

A CIP catalogue record for this book
is available from the British Library

ISBN 9780099585367

Typeset in Palatino by Palimpsest Book Production Limited, Falkirk, Stirlingshire

Printed and bound by CPI Group (UK) Ltd, Croydon, CR0 4YY

PART ONE

1937–1938

Prologue

'Don't go.' I tightened my hand around his arm and pulled him back into the doorway. 'Please,' I begged and didn't mind that I sounded pathetic, and that tears were beginning to run down my face. 'Stay. Stay with me.'

'No.' He shook his head. 'This is something I have to do. I believe in it totally and I thought you did.' He gently pushed me away and bent to pick up his bag.

I gazed at his hand. It was thin with long, smooth fingers. A hand that had never used an implement larger than a pen and which would be required quite soon, if what he had said was true, to carry and use a gun.

'But it was only talk,' I wailed. 'We didn't really mean it.'

'I did.' He smiled and bent his head to kiss me. 'Goodbye, my darling girl.'

That scene lives with me still. On days like this when the morning sun makes diamond patterns on the sea and the little half-moon beach is smooth and golden, washed clean by the gentle summer waves, I think of Amyas and how I loved him. I love him still really in memory because that feeling of utter adoration has never left me. Oh, it has modified, yes. The long years between then and now have left their mark on me as they have on everyone, yet if, by some miracle, he walked into this room today I would still see him as I did and feel the same.

Can you love someone and despair of him at the same time? I have to say yes. For I loved Amyas from the first moment I saw him on that summer day when he walked out of the sea and into my life. Later he found another life. Other lives. Other loves. But for me, he was the only life. The only love.

Chapter One

Cornwall, 1937

I was at the house by the sea with my younger sister, Xanthe. Poor Xanthe, always unlucky in love and this time so distressed by the callousness of her latest beau that my mother begged me to take her away from London.

'Go to Summer's Rest,' my mother had said. We had come into Father's study so that Xanthe wouldn't hear us discussing her. 'That's what you must do, Seffy darling. Take her on long walks, wear her out so she's able to sleep. That way she'll get over that despicable man very quickly.' She'd sighed and patted her immaculate iron-grey hair. 'How she gets into these scrapes I'll never know. After all, with her looks she should have no trouble in finding a suitable husband.'

'I can't,' I'd protested. 'I've only just started my job. What will they think of me if I clear off now?'

Mother had shrugged, bewildered by my objections. 'Darling, don't be silly. What job could possibly be more important than your sister's happiness?'

I looked to my father for support. He'd been the one who'd got me the job, via a friend of a friend, and I was loving it. Working on a national newspaper and being at the heart of everything was what I'd dreamed of and although at the moment I was a glorified tea girl I was positive that some day my talent would be recognised.

'Daddy,' I begged. 'I need to stay in London. Tell Mother.'

He was at his desk with a sheaf of notes in front of him and an open copy of the *Iliad* beside them. 'What?' He looked up, his eyes huge behind the magnifying spectacles, then back again at his work. 'Do what your mother says, child. She knows best.'

It was hopeless. Neither of them would be moved, and the sound of Xanthe's wails from her room on the half landing made my mother even more determined. So we were here at the house by the sea where we'd come every summer that I could remember.

Summer's Rest had been in the family since my grandparents' time, an Arts and Crafts house, built before the First World War by my father's father so that his family could get an August break from the grimy air in Manchester. He was a mill-owner and had plenty of money. They did in those days, some of the cotton kings. He ran his mills as sweatshops and had no time for the growing number of owners who had a more charitable attitude to their workers. I remember him as an old man in his grand house in Cheshire, constantly growling about the unions who had made him raise the wages and run the mills on shorter working days. 'They want something for nothing, those buggers,' he would shout to us, his puzzled granddaughters. 'Mark my words, revolution is in the air, a Socialist hell is on the way.'

'What does he mean?' whispered Xanthe. We were six and eight and it was the year before the old man died.

'I don't know,' I whispered back. 'It's to do with politics.' She looked at me blankly and then back to our grandfather who was now repeating, 'A fair day's pay for a fair day's work, aye, a fair day's pay for a fair day's work,' while thumping his gnarled fist on the arm of his leather chair. Our grandmother, fluttering her hands in their black lace half-gloves, would shush him and instruct the nurse to take him back to his room.

But for all his grumblings the old man liked to spend his money and had commissioned a wonderful holiday house. It perched on the hillside above a Cornish headland and had a view of the sea from the white veranda so all-encompassing that it took my breath away every time I came here. Steps led down from the house to a little beach. Our beach, a private beach where Xanthe and I had built sand castles and gone shrimping in the little rock pools on the periphery. I learned to swim, with help from my father, but Xanthe didn't. She would paddle in shallow water as it dragged across the sand but wouldn't venture any further and if a rogue wave splashed her above her knees she would squeal and run back to our nest of towels. But I loved to swim and would breaststroke the short distance from one headland of our little bay to the other, with never the least thought of danger.

'You're a tomboy,' Mother had said. 'You'll never find a husband.' That was all that mattered to her.

I was hoping to swim on the second morning that Xanthe and I had been at the house. 'Come down to the beach,' I'd said to her as we sat in our dressing gowns at the wooden table on the veranda. It was a brilliant day, warm and sunny at nine o'clock in the morning, and I'd put the coffee pot and a plate of toast in front of her.

'No, I don't think so,' she replied and lit a second cigarette. Her eyes were still red from sobbing and her pale blonde hair bedraggled and sticky from tears. 'I'm going back to bed.'

'Mother said I was to take you on walks along the headland,' I muttered. I was still furious about being forced to come to Cornwall, and Xanthe's miserable face didn't help.

'Why?'

'Because she thought it would do you good, you goose.'

'Look.' Xanthe stood up. 'I did what she wanted and came here with you. I'm not doing anything else. In fact, I'm going back to London as soon as possible. I might be able to make Clive change his mind.'

'Change his mind?' I reached for the pot and poured myself another cup of coffee. 'He's married. D'you think he's going to leave his wife for you? You were his "bit on the side". And only one of his "bits" so I heard.'

'Oh,' she gasped. 'I hate you.' There was more energy displayed in her stamping exit than I had seen for days and it gave me hope that she was on the mend.

'I hate you too,' I called after her as she went through the long windows back to her room. I didn't hate her, of course, that was just sister talk, but I did resent her. I resented the fact that I'd been dragged away from my job and that I would have to work hard to regain my editor's confidence. I knew he'd only taken me on as a favour and I was having to prove my worth daily. My English degree didn't cut much ice with him, and my colleagues on the newspaper didn't seem to think much of me either. In the pub, where everyone went after work,

I hung about on the edge of the crowd, usually quite unable to join in the conversations. On the few occasions that I tried I was generally shot down as an ignorant junior. Only a few days ago they had been discussing the Civil War in Spain.

'Why the hell are we constantly talking about it?' shouted Peter Spears from the bar where he was ordering his third whisky and soda. The pub was crowded and very noisy and you had to shout to make yourself heard. Peter was the cricket correspondent and did some gardening features as well. 'It's nothing to do with us. Let them fight it out.'

'Quite right,' agreed Monica Cathcart, the gossip columnist, with whom I'd been working for the last few weeks, sorting out the chatter and watching her decide which bit of poison to drip into the public ear. I couldn't bear her. She was a terrible snob and a hypocrite too. She drifted on the edge of the party set to which Xanthe belonged, seemingly friends with many, but always with an ear for something scandalous. 'General Franco has the right ideas,' she continued. 'He's fighting to get the country working efficiently again. Like Hitler and Mussolini. God knows, we could do with leaders like them in this country.'

'But they're dictators and if Franco wins he'll be one too.' I couldn't keep my mouth shut and regretted it immediately.

'Nothing wrong with that,' Monica snapped back. 'And who asked you anyway? You're just the office girl.'

Her acolytes, who were sitting beside her at the wooden pub table, grinned and dug each other in the ribs. In my couple of months at the paper I had quickly realised that it was ridden with factions. Unfortunately I'd been put to work with the queen of the most unpleasant one.

'She's got a point.' I looked round to see who'd made that remark. It was Greg Archer, the elderly political reporter. 'I've seen some of the reports coming out of Madrid,' he added. 'They don't make easy reading.'

'Well we all know where you're coming from.' Monica shook her head pityingly. 'Didn't you campaign with Attlee last time around?' She gave her cruel laugh. 'Not really in keeping with the politics of the paper, is it? I wonder what our owner thinks of that?'

'That's not fair,' I said hotly, upset with the way this argument was going.

'Don't worry, young lady.' Mr Archer smiled at me. 'I don't need defending from Monica Cathcart. Her grasp of politics is tenuous, to say the least.'

Monica's face darkened. She was angry. Her casual put-down had not shut me up and she looked to her best friend, Jane Porter, who wrote occasional cookery pieces, for support.

'I think you're being most disagreeable to Miss Cathcart,' Jane said to me in her whiny voice. 'After all she's been very kind, showing you the intricacies of her column. You should be grateful and not argue with her.'

'We're not arguing, we're debating,' I said, exasperated. 'The fact that she can't understand that there are two sides to the Civil War is her problem, not mine.'

There was a nervous round of laughter at that remark and Peter, arriving back with his drink, gave me a mocking look. 'I've heard everything now,' he grinned, glancing at the other journalists who were in a group around Monica. 'The tea girl instructing us on international affairs.'

'I've got an opinion,' I protested. 'And as this isn't a police state yet, I'm entitled to give it.'

Monica gave one of her spiteful little laughs. 'An opinion from a person barely out of the nursery isn't worth listening to,' she sneered, and the group around her fell silent, rather shocked, I now think, by her unpleasantness. At the time though I imagined that it was because I'd dared to speak up. But I was furious and, job or no job, I wasn't going to let her get away with that.

'I'm twenty-three,' I said evenly. 'I have a degree from a prestigious university, which I think is more than you have, and I might be learning my trade here but my opinion on the war in Spain is just as valid as yours.'

Her mouth dropped open and she quickly grabbed her glass of brandy and took a large gulp. 'You may be well connected, Miss Blake,' she said slowly, and I felt as though she was drilling holes into my face with her narrow muddy-brown eyes. 'But that doesn't entitle you to be rude to a senior reporter, of any newspaper, let alone ours. Trust me, you haven't heard the last of this.'

'Well said, Monica,' brayed Peter Spears. 'These juniors have to learn their place.'

My stomach was churning but I stared back at them until their faces were lost in the group of colleagues who had gathered around them. If they disagreed none of them said so. They knew Monica had the ear of the editor and, it was whispered, of the owner too. My face red from anger and embarrassment, I started to leave and was pushing my way through the noisy drinkers when my arm was grabbed and a voice spoke into my ear.

'Well done, young lady. It's about time Monica Cathcart was taken down a peg or six.'

I looked over my shoulder into the amused face of Charlie Bradford, the foreign correspondent who had recently returned from China. He was, at a relatively young age, fast becoming talked about in his field as the man to watch.

'Thank you,' I said shyly. 'But I think I've just lost my job.'

He grinned, his blue eyes crinkling up behind his rimless glasses. 'Don't worry,' he said. 'Monica isn't half as powerful as she thinks. In a toss-up between a keen young reporter and an old has-been, I know who I'd choose. Our esteemed editor would too.' He looked me up and down. 'You must have arrived at the paper while I was abroad. I'm Charlie Bradford.'

'I know,' I said. 'You were pointed out to me yesterday when you were walking through the newsroom.' I held out my hand. 'Persephone Blake . . . Seffy.'

He nodded. 'Well, Seffy Blake, scourge of dictators, how about us going for a *quiet* drink somewhere?'

For a moment I hesitated. The girl from the archives department who'd pointed Charlie out had also said that he had a bit of a reputation with women. From the catch in her throat I'd guessed she'd made up part of that reputation. But that didn't mean I had to be involved with him. Sexually, that is. Besides, I wanted to hear about China.

'Yes,' I said. 'I'd like that.'

I had imagined that he'd take me to a different, smaller pub somewhere around Fleet Street but he flagged down a taxi and told the driver to take us to Soho. 'D'you like Italian food?' he asked, quite casually.

'Yes,' I said eagerly. We'd been on holiday in Italy. Twice to Rome and once to Florence and although my mother and Xanthe almost starved themselves until they could get back to plain English food, Daddy and I relished the dishes of pasta and grilled fish that were placed in front of us at our hotel.

'Good.' Charlie grinned. 'I know a great little place.' That was the thing about Charlie. He knew so many great little places and I had some of the best meals of my life in his company. In those far-off days, before the Second World War foreign food was something of a rarity but with Charlie I tried everything from as many countries as he could find.

That night we went to Gennaro's in Dean Street where all the ladies were presented with a rose as they went in. That set the mood for the evening and while we waited for our meal we drank red wine from an earthenware carafe and talked about China and the recent Japanese invasion.

'What are the Japanese after?' I asked, keen to hear his explanation.

'Oh, it's power and money as much as anything. The Japanese economy is in a mess and they want to rape the Chinese of their agriculture and mining products. They're militaristic in Tokyo and bloody desperate to expand their empire. West into China is about the only place they can go, what with the Americans holding on to the islands in the south and east. They don't seem to care that it's costing them to keep armies in Manchuria.'

Manchuria and Tokyo. Even the names were exciting. 'Have you been to Manchuria?' I asked, breathlessly.

He shook his head. 'I tried but I couldn't get in, but I did get to the Marco Polo bridge south of Peking, where

there is a face-off. The Japs are pretending to do man-
oeuvres on their side but it's only a ruse. They're trying
to force the Chinese to react. It's going to be terrible.' He
smoothed his fair hair back from his face. He wasn't bad-
looking, I thought, but not my type. I didn't know what
my type was, really. I'd had a few boyfriends, intellectual
fellows at university with whom I'd debated politics and
rearmament and other matters of the day but none of
those friendships had come to anything. I didn't seem
to be able to give my heart easily.

'Are you going back?' We were eating pasta covered
in a marvellous creamy sauce which in my excitement I
kept dripping on to my chin. At one point Charlie reached
over and wiped my face with his napkin. 'Mucky pup,'
he smiled and I was embarrassed but his amused blue
eyes were gentle behind the glasses.

'Sorry,' I muttered and told myself severely to calm
down. This sort of conversation was what I'd been longing
for and I wasn't going to let the opportunity slip away.

'It doesn't matter,' he laughed. 'Gennaro would be
pleased that you are so relaxed and enjoying his food.
Me too.' Was he flirting with me? Yes of course he was.
Charlie liked to flirt but I wasn't ready for that.

'China,' I said. 'Are you going back?'

'No,' he said. 'I'm not going back to China for the
moment. I think Spain is calling.' He shrugged his shoulders. 'Another day, another war.'

'Which side do you support?' I asked, rather boldly I
suppose because I'd only just met him.

He turned the question back on me. 'Which do you?'
he said and held up his glass of wine to indicate to the
waiter that we wanted some more.

I paused before answering. Xanthe had come home a couple of months ago talking about Clive getting into a fight with some men in a bar. 'They were communists,' she said excitedly. 'People he'd known at school, from decent families, not common workers or anything. They were going to Spain to fight in the International Brigade. Against Franco, I think. I'm not really sure.' She put her finger to her red-painted lips and frowned. She was thinking, trying to remember the exact ins and outs. But I knew she wouldn't be able to. Xanthe generally only heard parts of a conversation. 'Anyway,' she continued, 'Clive was furious and said they were Reds and class traitors and words like that. He hit one of them.' Her eyes were sparkling. 'It was thrilling.'

But I had an utterly different take on the situation. Three years at university had given me ample opportunity for debate and I had made up my mind a year ago. I was scared of the rise of fascism in Europe. I was scared too of the rise of communism in eastern Europe but in Spain the Socialists seemed to have more legitimacy.

'The Republicans,' I said and waited for his face to fall. It didn't.

'I knew you'd say that,' he laughed. 'And I agree, although as a reporter and not a politician I have to be pretty neutral.'

'Yes,' I agreed. 'It's our job to put the facts out clearly and let our readers decide.'

'Is that what you do with Monica and the gossip column?'

I could feel my cheeks going red. I'd been getting above myself.

He leant back in his chair and stared at me. 'You

know, Blake, you're not bad-looking. I'm guessing that you're pretty intelligent and . . . mm . . . ambitious? Yes? You're probably made for the newspaper industry.'

I blushed even more. Nobody had ever told me I was good-looking. Xanthe was the pretty one in our family, a fact that was accepted by everyone, me included. She was petite and blonde with blue eyes and the regulation tip-tilted nose. Nobody could doubt she was one of my mother's glamorous family, the talked-about beauties who had all been photographed as 'girls in pearls' in glossy magazines. On the other hand, I was a twig cut from the northern mill family tree. I had red-brown hair in those days which bounced crazily away from my head unless it was held back with clips or a ribbon. My hazel eyes had flecks of green in them and I was tallish and thin with a flat chest and boy's hips. Worst of all, in the summer I had a scattering of childish freckles across my nose which everybody remarked upon. They were there now and I self-consciously put my hand up to my face.

'It's no good trying to hide those freckles,' Charlie smiled. 'I've already spotted them. Very Just William.'

I frowned at first and then laughed with him. It was odd. In only a few hours I felt as though I'd known him for ever and that we could say anything to each other. That never changed. Charlie Bradford was the best of men, kind and clever and almost honourable. Nobody is entirely honourable. That first night though he was quite keen on my coming to his flat for a coffee after we left Gennaro's but I shook my head. 'I must get home,' I said. 'My parents will be wondering where I am.'

'You still live at home? My God! That's no way to behave, Blake.' He helped me on with my jacket and

16

then picked up my rose from the table. 'Don't forget this. Now, you must find yourself a flat. That is if you want to be independent, which I'm assuming you do.'

'I am independent,' I said fiercely, but of course, I wasn't. And then the next day my mother proved it by forcing me to take Xanthe away and now I was stuck reading my newspaper while my erstwhile colleagues were writing it.

'Oh hell,' I groaned out loud as I sat alone on the veranda looking out across the village and harbour to the sea. It was cobalt blue this morning and flat calm, perfect for a swim. As soon as my coffee had settled I would gather my bathing things and go down the steps to the beach.

Mrs Penney, who did for us when we were at the holiday house, had brought the newspaper up with her when she came first thing and I had eagerly riffled through the pages. It was my paper; and I read the articles carefully instead of looking to see which of my colleagues had been published. There was a photograph of our new king and queen on the front and I studied it for a moment before turning to the inside pages.

Monica Cathcart had chosen three letters to reply to with her usual cloying false sincerity. I wondered who had actually done the choosing – it wouldn't be her, that was certain. Then I turned to Charlie's column, a thoughtful piece about how the Spanish bishops had come out in support of Generalissimo Franco. I read it avidly and found myself agreeing with his obvious distaste.

My reading was disturbed by shouting from our beach and I stood up and went to the edge of the veranda to look down. Three men were on the sand running about and laughing and while I watched, one of them started stripping off his clothes ready, I supposed, to go in for a swim. Couldn't they read the 'private beach' notices? I thought indignantly.

'I'm going down to the beach,' I called to Xanthe, who didn't reply and in a temper born not only from the trespassers but from my frustration at being here at all, I hurried down the winding steps which would take me directly on to the sand.

'Hello,' said one of the men who, with his pal, was lying beside the rocks. They looked startled, staring at me with puzzled and slightly embarrassed expressions. 'Where on earth did you spring from?' They were young, in their early twenties I guessed, with open friendly faces and sun-streaked hair. They were dressed in white slacks and white shirts. To my eyes they looked like members of a cricket team.

'I came from my house, up there.' I nodded towards the steps. 'And you are trespassing. This is a private beach.'

'Oh Lord,' said the first man. He was young, probably younger than I was and judging from the striped varsity tie that he was using as a belt, still in college. 'I'm sorry,' he apologised. 'We didn't know.'

'We came across the rocks from the other side,' said the other one, scrambling to his feet. 'We'll go.'

They seemed quite nice and I was sorry that I'd been so snappy with them. 'You can go up our steps,' I conceded. 'It'll be quicker. Turn left at the house and follow the road round. It'll take you into the village.'

I waited while they gathered their shoes and white

panamas, then a thought struck me. 'I saw three of you. I'm sure I did.'

They turned their heads towards the sea and I did too. Someone was swimming across the bay like I loved to do and, strangely compelled, I started to walk to the water's edge. The sun was dancing on the sea and making the rough water thrown up by the swimmer's arms sparkle in a million drops. He turned and struck out for the shore until he was able to stand up in the foam and shake the glittering beads of water from his black hair. And the world stopped spinning as I watched Amyas walk out of the sea.

Chapter Two

In the years after whenever I thought of summer it was of those idyllic weeks spent with Amyas. From my chair here on the veranda I can look down to the very spot where I first met him, that strange almost mythical figure who came out of the ocean.

He stood in the little waves of foam which were washing the beach, with his hands raised, squeezing water out of his hair, which hung below his ears, then wiping his face with his hand. I stared at him with my eyes screwed up, for the sun was behind him and he appeared to be in some sort of magical haze.

The vision spoke. 'The water is fantastic.'

I swallowed, closing my mouth, which I feared had been hanging open. 'Yes,' I stuttered. 'It always is.'

Now he was staring at me. 'You're a nut-brown girl, if ever I saw one,' he said. 'Do you know that Irish folk song? It could have been written about you. That hair' – he was looking at the wild locks blowing around my face – 'it's the colour of chestnuts. Glorious. Are you Irish?'

I shook my head. I seemed to be unable to speak. All I could do was stare at him; at his slightly olive skin and the fan of dark hair which covered his chest, and looking up I gazed at his face which now, as my vision cleared, I could see was the most handsome I had ever seen. It seems wrong to describe a man as beautiful, but Amyas was. His every feature was well formed: straight nose, firm chin, and dark brown eyes which in almost a flick of a switch could display every emotion from passion to amusement and even hatred.

My eyes trailed down. He wasn't wearing swimming trunks but had gone into the sea in his knee-length thin cotton underpants which clung to his body and left nothing hidden. He knew I was staring.

'I wasn't planning to swim when we set out this morning,' he laughed and looked down at his pants, where I could see the dark outline of hair and the bulge of his manhood. 'Am I embarrassing you?' It was bold and careless and I bit my lip. His arrogance infuriated me.

'Not in the least,' I replied sharply, finding my voice at last. 'But you'd better get dressed and leave. You're trespassing. This is a private beach.'

'Private?' He gave me an amused look. 'Do people have private beaches these days?'

'Of course they do. If they can afford them.'

'And you can?'

'The house and the beach belong to my family,' I said, now feeling awkward, 'not that it's any of your business.' My anger was returning and I turned my head and looked back to the rocks. The other two men were climbing the steps and as I watched one of them turned and waved.

'Look,' I said, 'your friends are leaving.'

'So they are.' He didn't move but then suddenly thrust out his hand. 'Amyas Troy. How do you do?'

I automatically took his hand and nodded my own greeting. 'Seffy Blake.'

'Seffy?'

'Persephone.' I waited for the raised eyebrows and nervous laugh which usually greeted the announcement of my name. But none came. He simply nodded.

I turned away and started to walk back towards the rocks and after a moment Amyas fell in beside me. I could see a pile of clothes close to where the other boys had been. 'Are those yours?' I pointed to them.

He looked around the empty cove. 'I suppose they must be,' he said. 'I don't see any other trespassers on your private beach.' He was laughing at me, making fun of my ridiculous outrage, and reaching the clothes I paused. God, I thought, I must sound like the most awful snob and was suddenly ashamed of myself. What was so wrong about these perfectly ordinary young men enjoying themselves on the beach? Only days ago I'd argued for the Socialists in Spain and here I was fiercely protecting our private property. I was as big a hypocrite as Monica Cathcart.

'Mr Troy,' I said slowly. 'You can stay here for a bit, if you like. I don't mind. Have another swim, perhaps.'

He bent down and finding his jacket on top of the pile reached into the pocket for a packet of cigarettes. He lit one and deeply inhaled the smoke. 'I might,' he said. 'I might if you stay with me.'

'Oh, I can't,' I said quickly. 'I have things to do.'

'You don't.' He grinned at me. 'You know you don't.'

'Don't I?' I felt helpless and overwhelmed and so unlike my normal self. It was as if I didn't want to leave him. Couldn't leave him. But this was foolish and I gave myself a mental shake. 'My sister is in the house.' I looked up the steps. 'I'm supposed to be looking after her.'

Amyas threw away his cigarette. 'All right,' he said

cheerfully. 'Let me strip off these wet shorts and I'll come with you.'

'No . . .' I started to say but he already had a hand on the waistband and was pulling down the underpants. I spun round and stood with my back to him, gazing out over the sea and the azure sky above it. I could smell the surf, the sharp ozone scent of the ocean, and wondered what beaches this water had washed up on before. Perhaps exciting foreign lands where coconut trees grew on white sand and half-naked men fished from palm leaf boats. Oh, the prospect thrilled my already heightened imagination and an unaccustomed tremor fizzed through my body.

Behind me Amyas was whistling quietly as he dressed and I ached to turn around and look at him again. What had happened to me? I wondered. Why wasn't I running up the steps and back to the security of the house and the annoyance that was Xanthe?

'Ready.' He spoke softly and I turned to find him dressed in white slacks like those of the other boys and an unbuttoned white shirt. 'You didn't embarrass me either,' he said with a mock serious expression.

I was puzzled. How on earth could I have embarrassed him? 'I don't know what you mean.'

'Well,' he tucked his jacket and canvas shoes under one arm and then picked up the wet pants. 'You were standing against the sun and you aren't exactly dressed in armour plate.' I looked down and realised with a horrified gasp that I was still in my thin nightdress covered only by the filmiest of peignoirs. Amyas must have been able to see straight through it.

'Oh, God,' I said and then burst into laughter. 'I'm as bad as you,' I giggled.

'Nobody's as bad as me,' he replied.

Back at the house, I made fresh coffee which we drank sitting on the veranda. Xanthe hadn't emerged from her room and Mrs Penney had gone home so we were on our own.

'I like your house,' said Amyas. 'Arts and Crafts, isn't it?'

I nodded. 'My grandfather had it built before the war. It's a holiday home.'

'So, I conclude that your family is wealthy?'

I squirmed a bit. My mother said that talking about money was vulgar, but then she'd always had plenty and couldn't understand that to some people talking about it was a vital daily need.

'Yes, I suppose so,' I answered.

'Titled?'

'Well, yes,' I said, with an embarrassed laugh. 'My grandfather had cotton mills in Manchester and made a lot of money. He gave some of it to the government of the day and they rewarded him with a baronetcy. But we're trade, really.'

Amyas nodded and turned his face away to look at the sea. He had the most perfect profile, not one feature wrong and everything in handsome proportion. I couldn't stop staring at him.

'What about you?' I asked. 'What are you doing down here? You and your pals.'

'Walking tour. Although to tell you the truth there hasn't been much walking and no bad thing, either. I hate walking.'

I laughed. 'Why did you join in, then?'

Amyas was silent for a moment then he said, 'I've

never been to Cornwall before. It was an opportunity.'
He turned and gave me the full force of his smile. 'And
now I've been rewarded.'

The moment was lost in a blare of dance music from
the wireless in Xanthe's room. She's bored, I thought.
Decided to give up crying and any minute she'll be out
here, demanding I drive her to the station. Amyas was
cocking his head towards the long windows where the
music was coming from.

'It's my sister,' I explained. 'I've had to bring her here
so that she can get over a love affair. He was a bad lot
anyway.'

'Who is he?' Amyas asked. 'Someone I might know?'

'I don't expect so. Clive Powell, son of the steel
magnate.' The words were scarcely out of my mouth
when Xanthe appeared through the windows. She was
dressed and made up, ready to travel.

'You were talking about Clive,' she said her voice shrill,
'I heard you. And to a stranger. It's not fair.'

'This is Mr Troy.' I glanced at him. He was standing.
'I invited him for a coffee.' I nodded to my sister. 'My
sister, Xanthe.'

Xanthe held out her hand for a brief shake before
sitting down at the table. All trace of the tears had gone
and she looked her normal pretty self. Oh hell, I thought.
This is the point at which Amyas's interest in me dies.

'I believe you've been going out with Clive Powell.'
He had resumed his seat and spoke to her in an almost
big-brotherly way.

'Yes,' she snapped. 'What of it?'

Amyas shrugged. 'He's a rotter. A rotter and a fascist.
And a married rotter and Fascist.'

'Oh!' Xanthe cried. 'That's a horrible thing to say.' She scowled at me. 'You told him that. I hate you.'

'No I didn't,' I snapped back. 'I just said his name.'

'How do you know him?' Xanthe demanded, glaring at Amyas. 'I've never seen you at any of the parties I go to. Who are you, anyway?'

He grinned. 'I'm Amyas Troy. And as for how I know Clive Powell, well, let's say I know everyone.'

Surprisingly, that shut her up and she sat for a moment annoyingly tapping a coffee spoon on the table. Then she said to me. 'You can drive me to the station. I'm going back to London.'

'No,' I argued wearily. 'You have to stay here.'

'I don't. And I'm not going to. If you won't take me, I'll get a taxi.'

She was quite right, of course. Xanthe didn't have to stay anywhere. She was over twenty-one and had her own money. We both had money, substantial amounts left to us in our grandfather's will. To all intents and purposes we were wealthy young women, despite the fact that we still lived at home.

'Oh all right,' I grumbled, 'but you explain it to Mother.' I was glad that she was going because that meant I could get back to the paper. The only thing was, I'd met Amyas. I looked at him. He was leaning back in his chair with his bare feet up on the veranda railing. He looked as if he owned the place.

'If you wait till tomorrow,' I said, turning back to Xanthe, 'I'll drive you to London. I can't go today, it's too late now. Besides, I'll have to close the house up.'

'No. I'm going today.'

In the end she agreed to wait and take the night

26

sleeper and I set about looking for something to make for lunch. 'Will you stay and eat with us?' I asked Amyas.

'Thank you,' he smiled.

Lunch was a jolly affair. He charmed Xanthe out of her bad temper, talking about people she knew and dropping seductive bits of gossip. I heard her say, 'No, not her, surely?' then screaming with laughter while I was in the kitchen making a crab salad.

'We've only got beer to drink with this,' I said taking the tray of salad on to the veranda table.

'What could be better?' asked Amyas, looking straight into my eyes and smiling.

I tried not to watch him as we ate our lunch but he fascinated me. He was using his fork to push the crab around the plate, eating the salad and bread only and pausing now and then to drink deeply from his glass of beer. Perhaps, I thought, he doesn't like crab and is too polite to say so. But I said nothing and when we finished I took his plate away without asking. He had no problem with the bowl of fresh strawberries.

'What do you do with your life?' he asked us when we had put down our spoons.

'Do?' asked Xanthe. 'What d'you mean, do?'

He shrugged. 'Do you have a job?'

She laughed. 'No, of course not. Why on earth would I want a job? Seffy's the one who works.'

'Yes,' he grinned. 'I thought she might.' He turned to me. 'What do you do?'

'I'm training to be a journalist.' I said this shyly and wondered if he would laugh. Xanthe was hooting with derisive mirth.

'Seffy imagines she will be the next great writer,' she laughed. 'She has ambition.'

'We all have ambitions,' Amyas said. 'You do, Xanthe.'

'No.' She frowned. 'I told you. I don't go out to work.'

'But you're looking for a wealthy husband. Isn't that an ambition?'

I waited for her to give him a sharp dismissive reply but I was surprised. She grinned. 'Yes, I am looking for somebody rich, preferably with a title. If you call that ambition, then yes I do and I think it's a damn sight better than Seffy's.'

'I should imagine that you're already quite rich.'

Xanthe reached for her packet of cigarettes and after taking one handed the packet to Amyas who took one also. 'Yes,' she blew out a lungful of smoke. 'I suppose I am and that should make it easier. Nobody could really call me a gold-digger.'

'And what about love?'

She shook her head. 'Don't be silly. Love isn't necessary.'

Amyas looked at her for a moment and then away to the sea. A boat with a red sail was tacking slowly across the bay, the sailor so expert that he hardly raised a ripple as he wove his way through the water.

'Love is always necessary.' Amyas spoke so quietly that at first I wasn't sure I'd heard him. Xanthe had got up and gone inside so we were alone.

I put my hand on his arm and leant towards him. 'What was that, Amyas? What did you say?' He didn't answer but instead suddenly turned his head and kissed me hard on the lips. It was the most wonderful yet alarming thing that had ever happened to me. When he drew back I was too shocked to say anything and sat gaping at him while he lifted his hand and gently pushed my hair away from my face. 'I said, darling girl, that love is always necessary.'

'Anyone want a gin?' Xanthe had come back on to the veranda with a glass in her hand.

'No, not for me,' I said, clearing my throat and standing up. 'I'll make some coffee.' I needed to get into the cool of the house. I shot a look over my shoulder at Amyas as I went through the long windows. He was smiling at me, his brown eyes full of desire and promise, and I nodded.

'You're smitten,' whispered Xanthe, following me into the kitchen. 'I don't blame you, he's absolutely gorgeous.' She went into the pantry to get some cream. 'Who is he? D'you know?'

I shook my head. 'He came out of the sea.' I could hear the note of wonder in my voice. 'Like something out of a story.'

'Who's the silly one now,' Xanthe smirked.

At about four o'clock Amyas pulled on his canvas shoes and grabbed his jacket. 'I'll go now and join my friends. We're staying at the pub.' He looked at Xanthe. 'I meant what I said about Clive Powell, but you must do what you want to.'

'I always do,' she answered, shaking his hand. 'And,' she screwed her eyes up and gave him a studied glance, 'I suspect you do too.'

He laughed. Turning to me, he took my hand in his. 'This has been a wonderful day,' he breathed. 'I'll never forget it.'

Later, in the car, as I drove to Truro to put Xanthe on the train, we talked about Amyas. 'What does he do?' she asked.

I shrugged. 'I don't know.'

'Do you know *anything* about him?'

'No.'

After a while she said, 'He's a bit of a mystery, isn't he, and I don't think Mother would like him. Not really our type, she'd say. D'you think he's foreign?'

A vision of Amyas's beautiful face swam into my head. Foreign? No, I was sure not. His English was perfect and there was an almost poetical quality to his voice, or rather, to the way he framed his sentences. 'No, he's as English as we are,' I said.

'Mm.' Xanthe pursed her lips. 'Did you notice that he found out everything about us but told us nothing about himself?'

I thought back. She and I had chatted all through lunch and afterwards. We talked about our parents and grandparents and Xanthe had been quite animated, telling him about the people who were part of her set. I thought I'd been quieter but now I remembered that I had told him about university and the newspaper and how I yearned to travel. I'd even recounted the argument I'd had with Monica and put forward my reasons for supporting the Republican side in the Spanish Civil War. Somehow he had encouraged us to talk while managing to remain silent about himself.

'Well,' I said as we turned into the station. 'It doesn't really matter. We'll never see him again. Now,' I gave her a kiss. 'I'll see you in a few days. Try and behave yourself.'

'You should talk,' she smiled sardonically, pulling her suitcase out of the back of my car. 'You're the one who picked up a man on the beach.'

I finally went for my swim when the sun was going down, crossing the bay with long, lazy strokes. Thoughts and images were chasing one after another through my mind, without ever settling into something I could understand. Ever since Amyas had walked out of the sea I had felt excited and unnerved as though something momentous had happened. I had been immediately attracted to him, but then I often got immediately attracted to something – a painting, perhaps, or a piece of music. Once, in Italy I'd visited the same church in Florence four times just to look at a triptych covered in gold leaf. And only very recently I had been attracted to Charlie Bradford, yearning to hear more of his life of travel and adventure.

But my feelings for Amyas seemed stronger than that. Could it be that I had fallen in love? Is that how love at first sight happened? I wondered. But if that was true for me, I wasn't sure he felt the same. Indeed, as he'd left, he'd said goodbye firmly, indicating that although he'd had a lovely day with me, it wasn't to be repeated. Oh, hell, I thought, and stopped swimming, treading water while I tried to calm myself. Eventually, realising that my excited state was wrong for swimming alone, I headed back to the shore and, reaching land, trudged slowly across the sand until I was by the steps.

Amyas was an experience, I told myself. A mysterious, magical happening which I could savour and remember while I got on with my life and career. I climbed the steps and went into the house to make tea, before packing my few belongings ready for an early start in the morning. It was a hot night and I lay in my bed with the long windows open and the net curtains blowing in the breeze coming off the sea. I could see the moon, a silver crescent in a velvet star-studded sky, and hear the deep rumble of the surf as it rolled on to the sand. The sight enchanted me, and I felt as though I was floating on a coral boat towards the wild shores of Illyria.

'Hello, darling girl.' Amyas walked in through the window and while I watched, enthralled, he took off his clothes and slid into bed beside me. I didn't cry out or urge him to leave or any of the entreaties I should have made.

'Hello, Amyas,' I said, and closed my eyes as he lowered himself on to me. It was the beginning of ecstasy.

Chapter Three

That night and the days and nights that followed, I existed only in the land created by Amyas. A land where passion ruled, where all sense of time or obligation was forgotten and where I gave myself utterly and completely to him. I was the abducted girl of myth, but, unlike her, I was a willing visitor to my lover's kingdom.

On that first morning I lay in my tumbled bed and gazed at the sleeping man beside me. He looked completely relaxed, his arms bent above his head, his chest and one leg exposed with only the sheet covering the rest of him. I felt that if I closed my eyes and then opened them again quickly, I would be alone in my bed. But it wasn't a dream. Amyas, whom I'd met less than twenty-four hours ago, was still beside me. I thought of the night that had passed, and smiled. How could this person who had cried out in savage pleasure be me, the so-called bluestocking of the family? I wanted to laugh out loud with the sheer joy of it all.

I turned away to look out of the open window on to a chalk-blue morning sky. The long net curtains wafted in the slight breeze, bringing in a distinctive smell of the sea and over it the pungent odour of the fish which would already be landed on the quay. Gulls swooped above the bay, squabbling over dropped fish from rivals' beaks and the choughs on the cliff tops pierced the air with their distinctive caw. Life was going on as normal in the village and everywhere, I supposed. I wondered briefly about Xanthe. She'd be in London, having breakfast at my parents' house and explaining why she'd decided to come home.

'Seffy was no help,' she'd grumble. 'More concerned with her stupid job than me. Anyway, she'll be here tonight. It'll take all day for her to drive up. You know what's she's like.' Mother and Father would be expecting me but I wouldn't be there.

Amyas moved slightly and I returned my gaze to him. I had been a virgin when he slipped into my bed but that act had burst a dam of passion and desire in me. Now, I was anxious to experience everything that lovers had ever known.

I propped myself up on my elbow. He was asleep, his face turned slightly to the side and his dark eyelashes resting softly beneath his closed eyes. Locks of his hair curled beneath his ears and lay carelessly over his forehead. He looked like a man in a Renaissance painting, a young god who stood guard over distressed mythological maidens. Was it his otherworldly beauty that fascinated me, I wondered, or was it his lack of moral rectitude? It was both, I decided and took a deep breath, thinking of the night that had passed and my own lack of morals. I had been abandoned, reckless and I felt no contrition. The passion that he'd generated in me was beyond my imaginings. Curious, I looked down at the sheet covering him and gently pulled it up, peering beneath to study the first entirely naked man I'd ever seen.

It lay before me, that important part of a man. Of course I'd seen it in paintings and in anatomy books, guiltily perused in the library when I was supposed to be studying. But, in the flesh, literally in the flesh, never. I stared, fascinated, longing to touch but not daring to.

'Come up to your expectations?'

'Oh!' Dropping the sheet I transferred my gaze to Amyas's face. His eyes were still closed but he was smiling. He knew that I was blushing.

'Shall I show you how it works?'

He rolled over in the bed and grabbed me, transporting me once again into the realms of ecstasy. 'Oh, Amyas,' I breathed when we were lying back, exhausted. 'I never imagined it would be like this. So, so wonderful.'

'Persephone,' he groaned. 'Strange, unworldly Persephone. How could you not know? You've studied English, did you not realise what the writers were saying? Poets have written about love. Bards have sung about it. What are so many of Shakespeare's stories about if not the delights of love?'

I considered what he said. The poets had written about love in the abstract sense. But I couldn't remember reading about the raw sex that I had just experienced. Or maybe I couldn't read between the lines. Then I realised that he had used the word love and held it to my heart.

While I was still thinking about it, Amyas slid out of bed and walked on to the veranda. He was naked but unconcerned. I was thrilled. Nobody could see him, unless they were on the beach, but it was something I'd never done. Now I followed him. The sea air bathed my body and I breathed deeply, exulting in the sheer pleasure of being alive and in love. Totally and completely in love.

The words 'I love you' were teetering on the tip of my tongue when suddenly he said, 'Christ, I'm hungry.'

35

'Me too,' I agreed, quickly going back into the bedroom to pull on my nightdress.

Later, we sat on the veranda drinking coffee and eating scrambled eggs, which I'd made, as Mrs Penney hadn't come up to the house this morning. I could hear the sound of the fishing boats chugging into the harbour and the occasional squeal from a joyful child on the public beach, but we could have been the only people in the world as far as I was concerned and I think Amyas felt the same. He kept smiling at me and had one hand on my thigh under the table. It was bliss and I wanted it never to end. Suddenly he stood up and grabbing my hand pulled me through the long windows into my room.

'What have you done to me?' he said after we had made frantic love. 'I can't get enough of you.'

I couldn't get enough of him either, and grinned stupidly through the tears that had welled up.

Afterwards, we went down to the beach and swam in the cold morning sea. 'Shall we race across the bay?' he asked. 'Can you beat me?'

I shook my head. 'No. I don't want to race. I feel too soft this morning, too relaxed.'

'Chicken,' he laughed and set off to the headland, leaving me to stroke lazily towards the shore.

Lying on the beach after our swim I thought idly about phoning my mother. I would have to tell her I was staying on in Cornwall for another few days so that she wouldn't worry. She'd be surprised, I was sure, and Xanthe would smirk and drop mysterious hints about me meeting a man. My mother would certainly not connect, 'meeting a man' with full-blown sex, but would ask, 'Do we know him? Has he connections?'

Amyas was drawing his finger down my body, tracing a line along my breast and on to my belly. 'You've got a fantastic body. So straight, so boyish.'

I couldn't believe he liked it. I'd always wanted to be like Xanthe. Petite and curvaceous with a peaches and cream skin. But it seemed that he preferred me, gawky, coltish me.

'I must go and phone my family,' I said, after a while. 'They'll be expecting me. Then I'd better go to the grocer's. Get some bread and things. We'll need to eat.'

'I thought you were going back to London.' He said it quietly and I froze. Had I taken him for granted? Was I simply a holiday fling and he was ready to move on? I swallowed. 'It's too late to set out today.' My mouth was dry and my heart was thumping.

Amyas rolled on to his back and closed his eyes. 'Good,' he said. 'Stay here, with me.'

The relief almost overwhelmed me. 'Your friends will be missing you,' I said. 'What about your walking holiday?'

'They won't care.' He grinned. 'Neither will I.'

For a week, Amyas and I drifted through the days and nights exulting in each other. He would pick up shells, the glistening ones that looked like mother-of-pearl, and present them to me as though they were precious jewels and pick pink thrift and sea lavender and thread the flowers through my hair. And in between making love we talked about everything – art, literature, music and politics. He had a breadth of knowledge that amazed me and sometimes I felt like a student lapping up the wisdom of my tutor.

'Amyas,' I said, early one evening, as we were sitting

on the veranda drinking wine. 'Where do you live and what do you do?'

He didn't answer for a moment and then said, 'I live in Cambridge.'

Of course, I thought. He's at the university. He'll be a junior lecturer and those two boys he was with are his students. 'Do you teach those two boys?'

He grinned. 'Yes. You could say that.'

I adored the thought that my lover was an academic. I could see him in the years to come as a respected professor, someone of note, whose opinion was sought after by the highest in the land. With his brains and looks he could be anything. But I needed to know more. 'Your parents? Where do they live?'

He stood up and leant on the railing, looking out over the ocean. There was a mackerel sky above us and I tried to remember the old saying about it. Did it mean rain?

'Where?' I repeated.

'They're dead,' he answered.

'Oh!' I said. 'I'm sorry.'

He picked up his glass and emptied it into his mouth. 'How about us going down to the pub,' he said. 'I want to see if Graham and Percy are still here.'

'Oh, all right.' Since he'd walked into my life, Amyas hadn't seemed to want to go anywhere. He had appeared as contented with our solitude as I was, but now I was thrilled at the prospect of walking with him through the village.

'Hello, Miss Blake,' said Alan Williams, the landlord of the Lobster Pot, when we walked in. 'I didn't know you were down here.'

'Yes,' I smiled. I glanced at Amyas, who was waving to the two boys sitting at a table by the fireplace. 'This is Mr Troy, a friend of mine.'

'Yes, I know who he is.' Alan frowned. 'He was staying here. I thought he'd gone.'

Amyas took over. 'Persephone, go and sit with my pals, they'll be pleased to see you. I'll bring the drinks to the table.'

Graham and Percy stood up when I went over. 'Hello,' I said. 'Seffy Blake.' We shook hands and they introduced themselves. When we sat down, Graham said, 'We're sorry about trespassing the other day. We hadn't realised.'

'It doesn't matter,' I answered and smiled at them. They were young, certainly younger than Amyas. I decided to ask him tonight how old he was. 'I believe you're on a walking holiday,' I said, and they nodded.

'We haven't done much walking,' admitted Percy, a blond-haired boy with nervous pale blue eyes. 'We've really come away to make our minds up about something. It needs a lot of thought, so here, away from all the influences of home, we felt that we could come to . . .' He stopped, his youthful face creased with concern.

'Percy's still a bit troubled,' Graham butted in. 'But I think we should go. It's the only right thing to do.'

'Go where?' I asked.

'To Spain. To fight. We want to join the International Brigade. Amyas believes in it utterly.'

'Does he?' I looked over to the bar where Amyas was picking up a tray of drinks. There were a few holiday-makers in the pub and I saw them looking at him. One girl whispered to her friend and the two of them giggled. I guessed what she'd said and grinned to myself. Yes he is, I wanted to yell to them across the room. He's fantastic in bed, better than you could possibly imagine and it's me he's doing it with.

'So, what are we talking about?' he asked, putting the tray on the table. He pulled over a chair and sat beside me. His hand rested casually on my thigh and a familiar thrill went through me.

Graham sighed. 'Spain. What else?'

'Have you made your decision?' Amyas took a sip of his beer and looked around. The two girls were still staring at him, and when he smiled at them they blushed and looked away. 'Going or not going?'

'Going, for me,' said Graham. He had stiff brown hair and a healthy round face. His broad shoulders looked like those of a farmer or a rugby player and I was sure that he would be a brave and competent fighter. But Percy was different. He was slighter and pale and his hands trembled when he picked up his glass of beer.

'I do believe in the cause, absolutely,' he said, looking almost pleadingly at Amyas. 'But I'm my parents' only child. It would be hard on them if anything, well . . .' he bit his lip. 'If I was to be killed.'

'Then you mustn't go,' I said. 'Let others take your place.' I looked to Amyas for confirmation, but he was gazing out of the window to the harbour and fidgeting with the coins on the tray that he'd received as change. He seemed restless this evening and the first tremors of concern trickled slyly into my brain. 'What d'you say, Amyas?' I asked. 'Percy should stay at home, don't you think?'

'It's not my decision.'

'It was your idea in the first place,' Graham spoke up,

robustly. 'You took us to the meetings, introduced us to the people who were organising the British end of the Brigade.'

'I did.' Amyas turned his head back from the view. 'And you were glad to be there. Both of you. But now, as I said, it's up to you.'

They were silent. What Amyas had said was logical. He reminded me of one of my lecturers who had put propositions to us and then left us to work out what was real and what was imaginary. But this was much more important than a line from *King Lear* or the actual meaning of *The Pilgrim's Progress*.

A tap on my shoulder made me turn around. It was Mr Penney. I'd known him all my life and I stood up and gave him a hug.

'Well, Miss Seffy, what are you doing here?' His weather-beaten, fisherman's face creased in a thousand places as he smiled at me. 'The wife said you'd gone back to London. She's been in Barnstaple, you know, but back now.'

'I decided to stay on for a few days. The weather was so good.' I was making excuses.

'It'll turn tonight. There's a storm coming in.' He looked over his shoulder to another fisherman, who was holding up darts and jerking his head towards the board. 'Aye, Fancy, I'm coming.' He turned back to me and grinned. 'You be taking care, now, Miss Seffy.'

I resumed my seat and prayed that Peter Penney would sink so much beer this night that he would forget about me and not tell his wife.

'Who was that?' asked Amyas. I hadn't introduced him or the boys. I don't know why, it just hadn't seemed appropriate.

'He's a fisherman. I've known him all my life. Mrs Penney, his wife, is our housekeeper when we're here.'

'Don't you live here all the year?' Percy seemed to be glad of the diversion.

'No, we have a house in Eaton Square. Summer's Rest is a holiday home.'

Graham gave a long, low whistle. 'I think we're mixing with the quality here, Percy.' He stared at me and then, narrowing his eyes towards Amyas, gave a small, rather sour laugh.

'What?' I asked puzzled. 'Why did you laugh?'

Percy touched my bare arm. 'Ignore him, Seffy. He's had too much beer.'

It was an uncomfortable moment and I wondered if Amyas would respond, but he was gazing out at the harbour again. When Graham and Percy went for more drinks I asked him if something was wrong.

'No, darling girl.' He turned and smiled his brilliant smile at me. My heart melted yet again. 'Nothing's wrong. I was thinking, that's all.'

'About the war in Spain?'

'That and something else.'

'What?'

He bent his head and gave me a quick kiss. 'I'll tell you when we get home.'

Before we left I told Graham and Percy that they were welcome to swim in our bay. 'And come and have a drink at the house,' I added.

'Thank you,' said Percy. 'We'd like that.'

Graham nodded, but remained silent. I couldn't get rid of the feeling that there was something difficult between him and Amyas. Perhaps he didn't like me and was angry that Amyas was staying at my house instead of helping him to persuade Percy to join up. Whatever it was, I felt the atmosphere acutely.

'Does Graham not like me?' I asked Amyas as we walked home.

'What?' he asked. 'Graham doesn't like you? No. He thinks you're fine. Probably too good for me. That's what it's about.'

'But how could I be too good for you?'

'You've got money,' he said and his voice took on a bitter note. 'I haven't.'

Poor Amyas. His lack of a fortune was the driving force of his life, but at that time I didn't realise it. All I thought was why would anyone as clever and handsome as him care about money?

'Don't be silly,' I said. 'I've got enough for both of us.'

He was quiet as we climbed the short hill back to the house and I wondered if I'd made another gaffe; showing off about how wealthy I was. I hadn't meant to, and squirmed with embarrassment.

I made coffee when we got in and we sat on the veranda with the cups in front of us. It was dark and moonless and the wind had got up, blowing in from the sea. Soon I felt a splash on my arm and then another as we sat in silence.

'I want to marry you.' Amyas spoke suddenly but his words were carried away on the wind and I wasn't sure that I'd heard him properly.

'What?' I asked, astonished.

'I can't imagine life without you.' He leant forward and took my arm. 'You are the one woman I've been looking for all my life. I don't know what it is, but there's something indefinable about you.' He looked deeply into my eyes and my heart did somersaults. 'You are utterly perfect, in every way.' He bent and kissed my hands, his lips hot as fire on my cold fingers. 'Marry me, darling Persephone. Make me a better person.'

It was only afterwards that I remembered that he had never said he loved me. He'd said I was perfect, utterly perfect and the woman he'd been looking for all his life. But he had never said love. I had. I'd laughed, entranced by joy and said, 'Yes, yes of course I'll marry you. I love you.' And in the lovemaking that followed I'd repeated it several times but all he'd done was grin and roll me over and over until we fell out of bed in gales of laughter. I had never been so happy – but then I woke, suddenly in the night, and remembered what Amyas hadn't said.

Rain was pouring the next morning, steady, soaking rain, and a blanket of mist had rolled in from the sea. It seemed ominous, almost as though it was the end of summer. I'd been in Cornwall often enough to know that it rained frequently, so I was being foolish, I thought, and told myself it would probably dry up by lunchtime and we could go for a swim.

Amyas was deeply asleep, lying on his face and I stroked a hand over his tanned back, loving the feel of the muscles beneath the skin. I was dizzy with passion, wanting him to wake up and take me in his arms, but he didn't move. So I got up to make breakfast. We ate eggs in bed, while we planned our wedding. I wanted it to be at the little church on the headland with its Celtic cross and the wild flowers which grew between the grave-stones. I would wear a simple white frock and only the family would attend. My mother's hopes of a society wedding would be dashed, but I didn't care.

If I hadn't had my head so full of plans I might have heard the noises from the kitchen and paused before bursting through the closed door.

'The kettle's just boiled, Miss Seffy.' It was Mrs Penney, plump and bustling, pouring boiling water into the teapot and humming a little tune.

'Oh,' I gasped. 'I wasn't expecting you.' I looked around the kitchen, anxiously, for signs of Amyas. His cigarettes were on the table and I stared at them. Mrs Penney looked at them too.

'I see your sister's still here,' she said, shaking her head. 'That girl smokes far too much, I'm sure it's bad for her. I've said to Penney on more than one occasion that it's his old pipe that causes him to cough all through the winter, and Miss Xanthe will be the same.'

I heard the lavatory flush and my heart nearly stopped. Mrs Penney took another cup and saucer from the dresser. 'I expect she'll go back to bed,' she said with a smile. 'I'll take a cup up to her.'

'No.' I could hear my voice squeaking in alarm. 'No.' I swallowed. 'I'll take it.'

'It ain't no bother.' And before I could stop her she poured tea into the cup, picked it up and walked to the door. It opened before she reached it and Amyas, looking more god-like than ever and wearing only a towel wrapped around his waist as gods always do, walked in.

I don't know how she kept hold of the cup and saucer, but it rattled in her hand and tea slopped on to the stone floor. 'Oh mygar,' she breathed, using a familiar Cornish expression, and looked back at me in my thin nightdress.

'Miss Seffy!' Her smile disappeared and her previously kindly face creased in shock. 'What have you done?'

'I know what it looks like,' I stuttered, my face scarlet. 'But . . .' I couldn't think of any excuse that would sound even remotely true. 'We're getting married. Soon.'

'That tea going begging?' asked Amyas casually, and took the cup and saucer out of Mrs Penney's hands. 'Good morning,' he smiled. 'I'm Amyas.'

I waited for her to melt and return his smile but she growled and walked back to face me. 'How long has he been here?' she said and jerked her head over her shoulder.

'A week,' I muttered. Thinking back, I realise that there should have been no need for my embarrassment in front of Mrs Penney. After all, she wasn't my mother, but . . .

'Seffy Blake, I can't believe what I'm seeing.' She put her hands on her hips and scowled at me. 'Carrying on with this . . . what is he? A jowster? I'm ashamed of you, your ma will break her heart and your pa, well he'll be so upset.'

I nodded. 'I know. But we are getting married.' I looked at Amyas, hoping that he would charm her, like he did everyone else, but he just stood there, an amused look on his face, watching as she wagged her finger at me. Suddenly she spun round to face him. 'You, get some clothes on. You should be ashamed of yourself. Standing there, half naked.'

I knew that she would phone my mother. I could have begged her not to, but what would be the point? They'd have to know, sooner or later, and when, that evening, the telephone rang and I picked it up to hear my mother's hysterical voice on the other end of the line, I was ready for her.

'I'm getting married,' I argued. 'Soon. There'll be no shame.'

'But who is he?' Mother sobbed. 'Who are his people?'

The fact that I didn't know almost sent her into a total breakdown. 'We're coming down,' she whispered finally, after exhausting herself with weeping and shouting. 'Your father and I. We'll put a stop to all this nonsense.'

Chapter Four

We were quieter in our lovemaking that night. Amyas shrugged when I said that my parents were coming down to Cornwall to confront us. 'That's all right,' he said, confident, I thought, that they would like him.

I was nervous. 'They're coming the day after tomorrow. They've an important dinner party to attend and Mother wants everything to appear normal. As far as she's concerned, this is a blip. Something that she can put a stop to.' I looked at him lying easily on the bed. 'She can't, can she?'

'No,' he murmured.

I was comforted by that and lay back beside him wondering yet again why he'd picked me. There must have been other girls, other loves. 'Have you loved anyone else?' I asked, half joking.

He shook his head. 'Not the way I love you.'

I wanted to believe him, so I did.

Mrs Penney came again the next day, banging around the house with her mop and bucket and following me into every room. Her anger and disapproval didn't stop her from making soup for us and she'd brought fresh bread. 'The village is scandalised,' she muttered, when I went into the kitchen to get a cup of tea. 'Alan Williams, at the Lobster Pot, says that man didn't pay his bill until the other night.' She gave me a fierce look. 'I hope you didn't pay it, Miss Seffy.' I shook my head, my cheeks burning.

I went down to the beach later in the afternoon, when the rain had drifted away and the warm sun had returned to dry up the sand and glitter on the blue-green water. Amyas decided not to come with me. He'd found a book on Father's bookshelf that he wanted to look at. 'It's a quite rare edition,' he said, turning the volume over in his hands. 'Too precious to be taken on to the beach.'

'All right,' I smiled. 'See you later.'

He grinned and kissed me and for a moment I thought he would drop the book and take me in his arms, but he didn't. His thoughts were elsewhere that afternoon. I didn't mind, really, because although I would have revelled in the lovemaking, I wasn't sorry to have time to myself. I needed to think, and I couldn't do that when I was with him. His presence swamped my brain with desire, leaving no room for anything else. And for over a week I hadn't wanted anything else. But now I needed to plan a way to handle my parents. To show them what a marvellous being Amyas was, and that if they would look beyond class and connections they would see that he could be an asset to our family. Anyway, for all I knew, his family was as good or better than mine and he'd be able to show them that. After all, he seemed to know the people that Xanthe mixed with and they were acceptable to Mother.

But when I walked on to the beach I found that I wasn't alone. Percy was sitting beside the rocks, with his head in his hands. He didn't hear me approaching until I was quite close and when he looked up I saw, to my dismay, that he'd been crying.

'Oh! I'm so sorry, Percy,' I murmured, embarrassed to have stumbled upon him when he was so obviously upset.

He wiped his eyes with the sleeve of his shirt. 'It doesn't matter. I've got over it now.'

I turned back to the steps. 'I'll leave you alone.'

'No. Don't.' Percy stood up. 'Come and talk to me. I need someone.'

We walked down to the shoreline and let the sea wash over our ankles, feeling that odd sensation of excitement and alarm when the sand beneath our feet was gradually sucked away and then returned. At first Percy stood quietly beside me, sniffling a bit, and I could hear the occasional shuddering breath. I decided he must still be upset about making the decision to go to Spain. But suddenly he turned to me and said, 'Graham's gone and I don't know how I'm going to live without him. I love him so much.'

I couldn't stop myself from giving a little gasp of shock.

'You must think that I'm a dreadful person,' he muttered. 'Saying what I've just said. But I can't help it.'

I was shocked; I couldn't help it. I had never spoken openly to a man who professed his love for another man. It was a crime, punishable with a prison sentence. We all knew it went on, but I felt awkward and confused and wished that Amyas was here with me to answer Percy's question. But he wasn't, and when I answered him it was from my heart and without guile.

'No,' I said. 'I don't think you're a dreadful person. I liked you yesterday and I still like you today. What you've said makes no difference.' I took his hand and gave it a squeeze to show I meant it, but at that gesture of friendship his face crumpled and the tears that he'd said were gone returned. It was awful to see this grown man wailing like a lost child and, without thinking, I put my arms around him and let him dig his head into my neck and weep.

While he wept I gazed over his shaking shoulders to the bay, where seagulls bobbed on the little waves and a cloud drifted over the sun making the water turn from blue to grey. That made the mood of despair heighten, but I held on to him until the shaking stopped and he was able to pull himself away.

'Thank you, Seffy,' he said, when his tears dried up and he was able to speak. 'You're a very kind girl, as well as beautiful.'

Beautiful? Percy thought me beautiful? As we walked back to the rocks and sat down again, I asked myself what had happened to me over the last few weeks to make men like what they saw. Even the cynical Charlie Bradford had said I was not bad-looking. I thought briefly about Charlie and wondered where he was. Had he gone to Spain? I remembered how envious I'd been of his life when we'd been in the restaurant; how I longed to travel to dangerous places and record what I saw. Being a foreign correspondent had been the pinnacle of my dreams. But that, of course, was before Amyas came into my life. And now I wasn't envious of anyone. Besides, there was nothing to stop Amyas and me travelling wherever we wished. The thought of the places we could visit was thrilling.

'Amyas knew this would happen.'

The sun was shining brilliantly again and the wind had dropped so that my imagining of foreign travel was accompanied by a climate to match.

'What?' I asked, dragging my mind away from Amyas and our future.

'He told me, ages ago, that Graham didn't really love me. That I was an experiment. Just to see what it was like.'

'That's awful,' I said, appalled. 'How cruel.' Did men behave like this? Trying out sex with a man, rather than a woman, just to see what it was like? It seemed incredible and I gave Percy a sideways glance. Was he imagining it?

'I didn't believe Amyas, then, you know. I thought he was simply saying it because he was jealous.'

Now I was totally confused. 'Jealous of what? Of whom?'

Percy turned his pale face to me. 'Of Graham and me. He hated us being so close.'

'D'you mean to say he didn't approve? Of your . . . relationship?'

'No.' Percy looked back towards the sea. The boat with the red sail was tacking across the bay again and we both watched it. 'No,' he repeated. 'I didn't mean that.'

Suddenly, I didn't want to talk about Graham any more. I was beginning to feel uncomfortable with the whole situation. 'Come up to the house,' I said. 'Have supper with us.'

Percy shook his head. 'Thanks, but no. In the mood I'm in, I'd just make you miserable.'

'Come on,' I urged. 'Come for a drink, at least.'

He was persuaded and climbed the steps, then allowed me to lead him across the terrace and on to the veranda. 'Wait here,' I said. 'I'll get us something to drink. Gin all right?'

I found Amyas in my father's study, still examining the books. There was a small pile of four or five old

52

volumes on the desk, which I supposed he'd picked out to look at.

'I've got Percy on the veranda,' I whispered to him. 'Graham's left him and it's breaking his heart. I've brought him in for a drink and a chat. Go and talk to him.'

Amyas looked up. 'Oh, God,' he groaned. 'Where is he?'

'I told you. On the veranda.' I looked over my shoulder to make sure I couldn't be overheard before adding, 'He says that you told him it would happen. I think he's angry with you. Be careful.'

Amyas sighed. 'Stupid kid,' and with a lingering look at the pile of books, he walked back through the house. I watched him stroll away, my heart throbbing with love. He looked so fine in his white shirt and buttermilk linen trousers. His belongings had been sent up from the pub, but truth to tell there wasn't much. Mrs Penney had washed his clothes along with mine, grumbling constantly under her breath but leaving two freshly ironed shirts on the table on the landing. She refused to accept that he slept in my bed. I smiled to myself and went to get the gin and glasses.

If I thought there would be a difficult atmosphere between Amyas and Percy then I was wrong. By the time I reached the veranda with the tray of drinks, Percy was sitting back in the wooden chair with a calm expression and all sign of the tears had gone. And as the evening clouds gathered over the sea, the fleeting looks of misery which had darkened the boy's face became more and more sporadic, as Amyas talked him back into control.

We didn't discuss Spain, it seemed too emotive a subject then, and instead we chatted about books. I was reading A. J. Cronin's *The Citadel*. At least, I'd brought it down with me but since Amyas had come into my life

I'd barely opened the covers. Percy had brought Orwell's *The Road to Wigan Pier* and was hugely impressed with it. 'I can't understand why so many people object to his ideas,' Percy complained. 'They seem so logical.'

'Logical, if you accept Orwell's underlying rationale,' said Amyas. 'But, if you don't?'

Both Percy and I stared at him. 'Read it again,' Amyas advised. 'And be more like Orwell; question everything. Get it into your head that he's playing devil's advocate.'

Percy frowned and pushed a trembling hand through his straight blond hair. I was scared that he might get upset again so I hastily changed the subject. 'They still haven't found Amelia Earhart. They think her plane crashed into the sea, although that area is dotted with islands and she might have been able to land. It's awful, isn't it. She was such an adventurer.'

Amyas gave me a private smile. He guessed that I envied her. At least, I envied her spirit, not her supposed sad death.

Percy stayed for supper; more of Mrs Penney's vegetable soup, then thick slices of pork pie with cold boiled potatoes and chutney. 'I needed this,' he said, sitting back after putting his knife and fork neatly on his empty plate. 'I couldn't eat any breakfast or lunch.'

'When did Graham go?' asked Amyas.

'First thing. About six o'clock.' Percy stared at the remains of the pie, just a few crumbs of pastry which Amyas was picking slowly off the plate. 'He said he'd been awake most of the night, thinking about what to do and once he'd decided, he couldn't wait any longer. When he woke me, his bags were already packed. It was awful. He wouldn't even discuss it; he said we'd talked enough.' Tears started welling in Percy's pale blue eyes. 'Then he went.'

'Where?' asked Amyas.

'His parents first, I think, in Yorkshire, and then Spain, I suppose.'

'You can't just go to Spain,' said Amyas. 'You have to make your way to Paris first, to an address in the 9th arrondissement. They organise your way into Spain. It's not like going on holiday.'

'Yes, I knew that,' Percy said, irritated, which was more than I did. I was surprised that Amyas knew, but then he seemed to know everything. Once again I despaired at my ignorance of how the world worked.

'It does sound exciting,' I said, forgetting that Percy had pulled out of Graham's plan. Amyas laughed. 'You'd like to go, wouldn't you?'

'Yes.' I smiled, surprising myself by realising that what I said was true. I yearned for adventure.

'They have women's brigades, you know. D'you fancy joining them? You could. It would suit you.'

I laughed, but inside I felt appalled. Didn't he care if I went away? Weren't we going to be together for life?

Telling myself not to be silly I got up and gathered the plates to take to the kitchen. There was cheese in the pantry and I thought it would do to finish off the meal. It was while I was in there that the phone rang. It'll be my mother, I thought, and, feeling slightly sick at the prospect of what she might say, I rushed into the hall to pick up the receiver. Amyas had reached it before me.

'It's your sister,' he called. I heard him laughing at something she'd said and answering, 'naughty girl', and that uneasy feeling increased. He chatted for another minute before casually handing the phone to me. 'I'll take Percy for a walk on the beach,' he said. 'I want to give him a few pointers. Join us when you've finished.'

I nodded. 'All right, I won't be long,' then watching him go, I spoke into the receiver. 'What d'you want, Xanthe?' I asked, irritated with her although I had no real cause to be.

'Goodness,' she giggled. 'You do sound angry. Aren't things going well in paradise?'

'They're wonderful,' I said, making an effort to calm down. 'I'm getting married to the most fantastic man and I'm happier than I've ever been. What could possibly be wrong?'

'Well, it could be the fact that Mummy and Daddy don't approve and have got private investigators in to find out all they can about your Mr Troy. Oh yes. Trust me. Money has changed hands. That's what I called to tell you, so don't you be mean to me.'

I gripped the receiver tightly, trying to control my furious reaction. That the man I wanted as my husband was being investigated by my parents was positively medieval. They wouldn't find anything bad, I knew that. You only had to look at Amyas and hear him speak to know that he was perfectly acceptable. Anyway, no matter what the investigator found, I would never give him up.

'Seffy? Are you still there?'

'Yes.' I gave myself a little shake. 'Yes, I'm here. I was trying to take in what you said. It seems a horrid thing for Mother to do. She's such a snob.'

'She is,' agreed Xanthe and gave one of her tinkling laughs, 'but I can't say that I blame her. After all, we don't want any riff-raff in the family, no matter how gorgeous they might be. Anyway, sis, I must fly. Johnny Blazer is taking me to the Café de Paris and we'll probably go on somewhere after that. I'll see you Thursday with Mummy and Daddy.'

'Are you coming down too?' I asked, aghast at the prospect.

'You bet,' she laughed. 'I wouldn't miss what promises to be the row of the century for anything. Bye.'

My mind was whirling when I went on to the veranda so I thought I would wait a while to calm down before I went to join Amyas and Percy but, to my surprise, I found Percy waiting for me.

'Is Amyas here?' I asked, looking back towards the house.

'No,' Percy shook his head. 'He's gone for a swim, so I'm going back to the pub. I've decided to go home tomorrow.'

'Oh,' I said, surprised. 'Was that Amyas's idea?'

It was now Percy's turn to look surprised. 'No,' he said, rather crossly. 'I do have a mind of my own, you know.'

'Of course.' I could feel my cheeks burning. 'Sorry.'

He touched my arm. 'Don't be, Seffy. You're the best person I've met for years. No, I want to go home and talk to my father. He's very understanding and I feel that he would give me good advice.' He paused. 'Better advice.'

I ignored the implications of that remark and smiled at him. I was glad he had someone who loved him. 'Well, I'm happy for you,' I said, and leaning forward I grasped his slight shoulders and gave him a kiss on the cheek. 'We must keep in touch,' I added, 'and I'll send you an invitation to the wedding.'

He sprang back from me as though he'd had an electric shock. 'Wedding?' He frowned. 'Whose wedding?'

'Mine and Amyas's.' I grinned, loving our names being spoken together. 'Didn't you know?'

He shook his head slowly. 'I didn't know. Oh dear.'

My grin faded. 'Oh dear? Why? Amyas and I are in love. He wants to marry me.' I looked at his concerned face. 'I love him, Percy. I want to be with him for ever.'

'Mm,' he said, then he picked up his jacket which he'd thrown across the railing. 'I'd better get going. Thank you for supper, Seffy. I've had a lovely evening. Goodnight.'

He started to walk across the terrace towards the lane which led down to the village and I stood on the veranda, waiting for him to turn back and explain. He had to. But he walked on until he was through our gate. I couldn't bear it. 'Percy,' I called. 'Wait.'

I ran after him, determined to ask him why I shouldn't marry my beautiful lover.

'Tell me,' I begged. 'What's wrong with me marrying Amyas?' I could hear the desperation in my voice. What Percy knew, my mother's investigator would find out. 'You must know him well,' I said. 'He's your lecturer at the university and you've come away on holiday with him. So you must know him.'

Percy gave a short laugh. 'I know him and he isn't a lecturer at the university. Did he tell you that he was?'

I thought back. Did he say that he was, or had I just assumed it? 'No, not exactly,' I muttered. 'But he knows so much.'

'Oh, he does,' Percy conceded. 'He knows everything and everybody.'

I was confused. 'Then what? What does he do?'

Percy shrugged. 'Nothing. He does nothing.'

I felt like crying. Everything was crumbling. My assumptions had been proved wrong and my parents would have an unassailable reason for rejecting Amyas. But then, I thought, he must have some money – he must have or he wouldn't have been able to come to Cornwall. Perhaps he's privately wealthy. Perhaps he doesn't need to work, his family supports him like mine do and he's no different from me. That's it, I decided. He has private means. And I felt happier.

'Ask him about Mrs Cartwright,' said Percy suddenly. 'That'll put an end to your marriage plans.'

'Who?' I asked, bewildered. 'Who is Mrs Cartwright?'

But he wouldn't say. He walked away, leaving me to stand helplessly in the lane.

When I got back to the house Amyas was talking on the telephone and I stood there waiting, with dread, to hear that my parents had already found out something so awful that I was going to be ordered to leave the house that night. However, after a moment I realised that Amyas was talking to someone he knew and that the conversation had nothing to do with me, with us. I walked on into living room still confused, but relieved that there was at least one more night of reprieve.

Later, in bed, I plucked up the courage to tell Amyas that my parents were having him investigated, and would be here on Thursday. 'They're determined to find out everything about you,' I said. 'I'm so sorry, it's awful.'

He said nothing at first, then stroked my face. 'Do you love me?' he asked.

'You know I do.'

'Then it doesn't matter.'

I switched off the light and lay listening to the rain, which had returned. I had to ask. 'Who's Mrs Cartwright?'

'Christ!' Amyas sat up in bed. 'You've been talking to Percy.'

'Yes,' I said, sitting up too. 'Who is she?'

'She's my landlady, in Cambridge.'

'Is she more than that?' Why am I doing this? I wondered. Surely he would have told me if he was involved with someone else.

He got out of bed and pulled on his slacks. 'You're spoiling everything.' He sounded angry. All at once I was frightened. He's hiding some terrible secret, I thought, and remembered that he'd told me nothing about himself. Then the terrible thought came to me that perhaps he was married already and that this Mrs Cartwright was really his wife. Oh, God.

He'd left the bedroom and I threw myself out of bed and dragged on my nightdress. I found him in Father's study, sitting at the desk, looking for all the world as though he owned it. For some reason that made my fright dissolve into anger. How dare he sit there, I thought. Keeping himself so secret.

'Tell me,' I demanded. 'You have to.'

Idly he turned the page of the book in front of him. 'I don't have to,' he said slowly. 'But as you're insisting, I will. Mrs Cartwright rescued me when I was in difficulties. She took me to live with her in her home, which, I might add, is very beautiful and always full of the most interesting guests. Is she more than a landlady? Well,' he looked up at me and grinned. 'I have to say, yes.'

I gasped. 'Does she know about me?' My voice was tiny. 'Have you phoned her?'

'No.' He shook his head. 'It's none of her business.'

'But of course it is.' My tiny voice had grown. 'If you're sleeping with her and sleeping with me then it is her business.'

He shrugged. 'I don't remember saying that I was sleeping with her.'

That was Amyas in a nutshell. Always mysterious, never ever giving a straight answer. Charlie said once that it was a defence mechanism and that he couldn't help it, but I was never sure. I thought later that much of his life was an act, but if it was, he gave the most perfect performance.

'But you're close, you and . . . Mrs Cartwright,' I said, and an uncomfortable lump was growing in my throat. Tears were beginning to well into my eyes. 'More than friends.'

'More than friends,' he agreed. 'But you are the one I want to marry. You're my girl, with the chestnut hair and freckles. My brave adventurer. Somehow, dearest Persephone, you have found the door to my heart and whatever happens it will always be open to you.'

He got up then and walked towards me and even though I was angry and close to breaking down, I let him take me into his arms. I couldn't speak; the host of different emotions racing through my mind overwhelmed me and all I could do I was let him hold me close and listen to him whisper into my hair, 'Trust me, darling girl. Just trust me.'

Chapter Five

We walked on the headland the next morning, strolling through the coarse grass towards the little church of St Mary of the Sea. The sun had returned and now shone down generously on us. My white cotton dress with its inserts of broderie anglaise wafted in the breeze which blew my hair into tangles. I should have tied it back, I thought despairingly. I'll never get a comb through it and I need to look composed and adult this evening.

I was thinking about my parents' imminent arrival and the row that would ensue. Mother would be crying her disapproval, while my father would agree with her, take her side completely and then disappear off to his study. That would leave Mother to continue her rant plus – and here my heart sank – Xanthe, elegantly smoking and with a gin and tonic in hand, would be sniping little bits of poison from the sidelines. I was in for a horrid evening.

Amyas walked quietly beside me. We hadn't mentioned Mrs Cartwright again since last night but her invisible presence lay heavily between us. Mother's investigator would have found out all about her, I was sure of that, and I would be the only one who didn't know the whole truth. It was an impossible situation. I had to know more.

'Amyas,' I started, meaning to tackle him again, but he stopped walking and put a finger to my lips.

'Don't,' he said. 'Don't let's talk about anything now. It's a wonderful day and a stunning place. I want to drink in all this beauty so that I can remember it.'

So we walked on until we were in the graveyard, where wild flowers grew between the leaning headstones, and butterflies, tossed by the breeze, flitted purposely between the plants. I could smell the sea and that hot metallic scent of old granite that I always noticed when I came to St Mary's. The church was open and we walked inside.

'This is where I want to get married,' I said, smoothing my hand along the polished oak back of a pew and looking up to the simple leaded window which lit the east end of the church. There was only room for six rows on either side of the aisle and the unadorned stone altar was a projection of the wall, but I loved the atmosphere and the knowledge that generations had worshipped here. I could imagine them, sitting on these very pews in their sixteenth- and seventeenth-century clothes. Fishermen and their wives and children, ignorant of life beyond this district but assured of their presence in God. It was so romantic, I thought, and I wanted to be part of it. 'It's small,' I said, 'and not many people will be able to come but that's what we want, isn't it?'

'It's what you want,' Amyas smiled. 'Register office would be fine for me.'

I held my breath. I'd presumed too much, again. 'Sorry,' I muttered. 'We don't have to have a church ceremony. I don't care, honestly.'

'You do.' He grinned and walked out through the studded oak door. I lingered for a minute in the quiet building, looking at the dust particles dancing on shafts of sunlight, at the brass memorial plaques on the walls and at the stone font beside me, covered now in a circular wooden lid. My children will be christened here, I thought. Mine and Amyas's. Surely he wouldn't refuse that.

He was waiting for me, leaning against the wall, smoking a cigarette. 'Shall we go back to the house?' he suggested. 'Things to do, you know.'

I nodded. We had got things to do. Amyas would have to move out, back to the pub. I couldn't possibly have him in my bed, not with my parents in the house, and I needed to ask Mrs Penney to prepare some sort of a meal for us all. Then I would have to go and collect them from the train. What a journey back that would be. I dreaded it and felt myself give a shudder as we walked along the lane back to the village.

'I wonder where Percy is,' said Amyas. We squeezed into the hedge as a tractor rumbled by pulling a trailer loaded with hay. The farmer at the wheel of the tractor tipped his cap to me but gave Amyas a long, hard stare. I realised that Mrs Penney's remarks about us being a scandal in the village was true. Amyas smiled at the farmer, seemingly unconcerned that he was being scowled at, before adding, 'D'you think he's already back in London?'

'No.' I shook my head. 'He left too late to get the night train. But he'll be on his way.' I thought of Percy's tears on the beach and how distraught he'd been. 'I do hope his father will be able to comfort him.'

'Maybe he will.' Amyas shrugged. 'But I doubt it. Percy is a boy who doesn't really know what he wants. I despair of him. He should grow up and be more like Graham.'

'That's not entirely fair,' I protested. 'Percy's got obligations to his family. He can't simply drop everything and go to a war. That's understandable, isn't it?'

'No. It isn't. If one is convinced by the rightness of a cause then everything else should be set aside.'

This was the first time he had said anything so positive about conviction. I'd thought that his opinion of the war in Spain was ambivalent, that if you believed in a cause, you should carry it through, but that he wasn't particularly keen on going himself. Now I wondered whether he'd been inspired by Graham's resolve and was planning a similar expedition. I sneaked a look at him, strolling along with that half-amused expression on his beautiful face and his normal relaxed demeanour.

Then I realised that this was an instruction to me. That I must not be afraid of my parents and must hold firm to my convictions. Of course, that's what he meant. Relieved, I took his hand and held it all the way back to the house.

Mrs Penney made us omelettes for lunch and afterwards, before she left, she took me into the pantry to show me the platter of seafood she'd prepared. 'Everything came off the boat this morning,' she assured me, 'and is quite fresh, so don't you worry. All you need to do is boil the new potatoes and make a salad. Can you do that?'

'Yes, of course,' I said crossly.

She jerked her head towards the veranda where Amyas was sitting with his feet up on the railing. 'He going? Before your ma and pa arrive?'

That was an order as much as anything and I frowned, but nodded again. 'Mr Amyas will be staying at the pub for tonight and I'll introduce him tomorrow.'

'Hmm!' She shook her head. 'That'll be a sight to see.'

I was glad when she left. I wanted to be alone with

Amyas for another few hours. 'Shall we go down to the beach?' I asked, when I joined him on the veranda.

'Yes,' he said. 'We'll swim.'

It was warm and the water was soft on my skin as I waded out into the blue afternoon. Amyas was beside me and held my hand as we dipped into the sea only letting go when we struck out into deeper water. I was confident that I'd be able to convince my father, at least, of Amyas's worth. After all, he was clever and well read and seemed to know everyone. Mother would be the difficult one.

Amyas swam over to me and put his arms around my body. 'Kiss me,' he demanded and treading water I surrendered to his touch and felt myself floating back into his dream world. My bathing costume was gently pulled off as we let the tide draw us to the shore. Abandoning all thoughts other than those of desire, we made reckless, joyous love in the surf, while the water surged over us and the gulls swooped figures of eight through the cobalt-blue sky.

'I love you, Amyas,' I breathed, my hands running across the muscles on his back.

'You are mine, darling Persephone,' he replied tenderly. 'And I'll never let you go.' Back at the house I showered and dressed, putting on my white broderie anglaise frock again. I looked in the glass at my unfashionably sunburnt face, the freckles scattered across my nose and my hair with streaks highlighted by the sun. Xanthe would make fun of me, and my mother would be alarmed at how abandoned I appeared. 'Oh, Seffy, darling,' she would say. 'What on earth has happened to you?'

'I've made tea,' I called to Amyas. He had gone into

Father's study to have a last look at the books, I supposed, and then into the bedroom to pack his holdall.

I was on the veranda when he came out. 'Have you phoned the pub,' I asked. 'To book a room?'

He shook his head. 'No.'

'It'll be busy,' I said, suddenly nervous. 'It's July. Tourists are in the village.'

'It doesn't matter.' He was looking directly at me. 'I'm not going to the pub.'

I knew then. Knew that he was leaving me. But I kept up the pretence. 'But, Amyas,' I was gabbling now, 'where will you stay? I think Mrs Penney's sister has a boarding house on the quay. You could ask if she has a room . . .' My voice faded away as I watched him lift up the holdall. He was looking past me to the panorama of the bay and to the sea where only an hour before I'd drifted, yet again, into that world of deep desire which he'd created.

He turned his face back to me. 'I'm going to Spain,' he said. 'I've made up my mind.'

My heart stopped. I grabbed hold of the railing to steady myself. 'But what about our plans? Us marrying?'

'It will probably happen,' he said. 'Some time.'

The sun continued to shine above us and I could hear the waves slapping on to the sand below but my world dimmed and Amyas began to fade out of it. I reached out, trying desperately to keep him with me. 'Was it because I took you to the church?' I cried. 'I'm sorry. I'm so sorry. We don't have to marry there. I told you.'

'No, Persephone. It's got nothing to do with that.' He walked through the house until he was at the front door and, dropping his bag with a small thump, grabbed his white panama hat from the stand. Placing it carefully on his head he turned back to me and smiled. He'd never looked so handsome.

'Don't go.' I tightened my hand around his arm and pulled him back into the doorway. 'Please,' I begged and didn't mind that I sounded pathetic, and that tears were beginning to run down my face. 'Stay. Stay with me.'

'No.' He shook his head. 'This is something I have to do. I believe in it totally and I thought you did.' He gently pushed me away and bent to pick up his bag.

I gazed at his hand. It was thin with long, smooth fingers. A hand that had never used an implement larger than a pen and which would be required, quite soon, if what he had said was true, to carry and use a gun.

'But it was only talk,' I wailed. 'We didn't really mean it.'

'I did.' He smiled and bent his head to kiss me. 'Goodbye, my darling girl.'

London

I'd been alone for nearly four months. Summer had gone, taking Amyas and any chance of happiness with it. After his departure I had been so heartbroken and sick that I thought I could sink no lower. Until the morning when I realised, as I rushed yet again to the lavatory, that Amyas had left me with a legacy, and I wasn't sure whether to clutch it to me in joy at still having a part of him with me, or terror at how I would cope. Terror won, and my mother took charge. In my weakened state, I could not fight her insistence that I get rid of the baby. But nothing went according to plan, and in the terrible aftermath I was weaker both physically and mentally than I had ever been, and I just couldn't summon the courage to get over it.

I heard the knocking on my door but ignored it. Whoever it was would soon give up, just as others had, leaving me alone with my thoughts. 'Go away,' I whispered wearily, not moving from the wooden chair where I sat and looked out on to the London square. Autumn leaves scudded past my window, some momentarily pasting themselves against the glass before flying away to join those littering the grass of the communal garden. They were driven on a raw gusting wind with the sharp spells of rain which rapped against the panes and wouldn't allow me to relax. I looked across to the houses opposite and to the enclosed garden below, where the trees were reluctantly giving up their foliage and the squat grimy hedges stood patiently, buffeted by the gale but scarcely moving. It was a miserable scene, but it suited my mood. In the months since Amyas had left I'd become a shadow of my former self. And then, last week, I'd been in hospital.

Life was hopeless. I was hopeless. I didn't know what to do.

The knock came again, more insistent this time and then a voice I vaguely recognised called, 'Blake! I know you're in there. Open this bloody door.'

Who called me Blake? I frowned, trying to think, then suddenly I remembered. Charlie Bradford. Of course. Oh hell, I didn't want to talk to anyone, least of all somebody as perceptive and insistent as Charlie. I bit my lip, waiting for him to go away, but to my dismay he hammered on the door again, calling, 'Come on, Blake, I haven't got all day.'

I could hear a door opening opposite mine. It would be old Mr Weiss, who always came out of his flat to talk to me, on the very rare occasions that I left mine. 'I think you're a woman of mystery, Fräulein . . . I forget, what is your name again?' he would chuckle. '*Ein Geheimnis*. Isn't she, Willi?' His little dog, a dachshund, stared at me mournfully from the protection of his master's arms. I would give them a brief smile and hurriedly head for the lift or, if I was returning from a brief visit to the shops, open my door. I couldn't be bothered to make a new friend, however harmless. Now he would be standing at his door wanting to know what was going on.

Damn!

'All right,' I sighed, getting up. 'Stop knocking!'

'Good girl, Blake. Let me in.'

When I opened the door, Charlie stood there, full of life and purpose, one hand resting on the door frame and his blue eyes crinkling a smile behind the rimless glasses. Over his shoulder Mr Weiss beamed at me and lifted Willi's paw in a little wave. I nodded to him and stepped aside to let Charlie into the flat.

For the first few seconds we stared at each other. Charlie, despite his wet trench coat and his fair hair plastered to his head, looked the same as I remembered him. I'd liked him and that feeling hadn't changed, even though I didn't really want to see him, or anyone at all.

'Christ,' he said, looking me up and down. 'What in God's name has happened to you?'

I didn't know how to answer. So I just shrugged and went back to my chair at the window. He followed and looked down at me. 'You've lost weight and you look like hell. Are you ill?'

I shook my head. 'No. I'm all right. What d'you want?'

'Well,' he said, taking off his mac and sitting down on the only soft chair in the room, 'I wanted to see you, of course, and there was something else.'

'What?'

He frowned. 'I'm not sure, now. Looking at you, I mean.' He got to his feet again and walked back to the window. 'I see you took my advice and got yourself your own place to live. Nice area, this, but not cheap.'

Those were the exact words the house agent had used when I'd gone into his office to enquire about an apartment. 'I have a very good first-floor flat,' he'd said cautiously, 'but it may be a little out of your price range. It's in a very nice area, very central. But not cheap.'

It was empty and I took it straight away. I bought a few pieces of furniture, not many really, but enough for me. It was a bolt-hole, where I could be on my own and nurse my shredded heart. Of course, Mother and Father had made a fuss, but I was determined. I told them the address, then told them not to visit. After what they'd done, what Mother had done, I could hardly bear to look at them, let alone live in the same house.

Xanthe had visited once, elegant in a fine tweed suit and matching side-tilted beret. Her heavy perfume almost choked the air. She made fun of the badly decorated rooms and my few sticks of furniture, but she approved of the location.

'It's quite smart here, actually,' she'd said. 'Freddie Machin's people live in this square and most of the better embassies are around about. As it happens, I'm going to a cocktail party tonight at the German Embassy, which,' she looked out of the window, 'I'm sure is not too far from here. One of the attachés was a guest at Jane Delacourt's wedding and Clive introduced us. He and this German, Count something or other, are great pals. Clive's going to Germany soon to stay at the Count's castle. Isn't that a scream? Anyway, he invited me to go to this party. He's quite a dish.'

'Clive?' I said. 'Clive Powell?'

'Yes,' she pouted, 'and what of it? I don't think you of all people are in any position to tell me what to do.'

I had no answer to that, but Xanthe didn't visit again. She knew that I blamed her as well as my parents. She sent a note a few weeks later to say that the count had invited her to visit him in Germany, and she was so looking forward to it. 'Will have to buy lots of new clothes,' she'd scrawled: 'apparently he's well known in society.' That was a month ago, so she could be home by now.

'Well,' Charlie Bradford looked at me. 'On your own now?'

What did he mean by that? I wondered and glanced up angrily. Did he know too? 'I've taken a flat,' I said evenly, 'if that's what you're getting at.'

'What else?' He narrowed his eyes. 'Look, Blake, I need to talk to you and you look as if you could do with a square meal. Go and get your hat and I'll take you to lunch. I know a great little place round the corner.'

I almost laughed. Charlie and his great little places. 'No, I don't think so,' I said slowly. 'I've . . .'

He wouldn't have it. 'Come on. You don't get out of it that easily. Go and get your hat, powder your nose, do what you have to. I'll wait.'

I was going to refuse, but somehow his enthusiasm broke my resolve and I nodded. 'All right. Give me a minute.'

It was a Russian restaurant, dark and smoky, with heavy chandeliers and embroidered tablecloths. The place was busy and the waiters sped from table to table bearing trays full of aromatic dishes. The maître d' grasped Charlie's hand when we went in. 'Mr Bradford,' he grinned. 'So good to see you, again.' And he clicked his fingers, sending two waiters into a frenzy of arranging a table for us and then helping us into our seats. 'A drink, while you consider the menu,' he said, thrusting two large cards into our hands. I wasn't asked what I wanted to drink or eat. A bottle of iced vodka and small glasses arrived almost immediately, followed by a platter of salami on circles of black bread surrounded by tiny pickled mushrooms.

'We'll eat shashlik after this and a vinegar beetroot salad. All right?' Charlie said. I nodded. I didn't care really. Food hadn't been of interest to me for weeks.

'Cheers,' he knocked back his small glass of vodka in one gulp and waited for me to do the same. It burned my throat and made me cough. Tears came to my eyes, and that almost set me off again.

I'd been crying for weeks.

'Perhaps you shouldn't have drunk that,' Charlie said anxiously. 'After all, you're not long out of hospital.'

'What?' I said nervously. 'How did you know that?'

He had the grace to blush. 'I am a journalist,' he answered, for once embarrassed. 'I notice things. There was a letter from the hospital on your table. I read it while you were getting your hat.'

I was horrified and tried desperately to remember the exact wording on the invoice from the private clinic. I looked up at him, hoping the agony wouldn't show in my eyes.

'It was a hefty bill,' he said. 'What was wrong?'

I swallowed in relief. He didn't know. 'Appendix,' I lied. 'Had to have surgery.'

'No wonder you look so pasty,' Charlie laughed. 'You need building up.' He handed me a piece of bread and salami. 'Eat up, Blake. That's an order.'

Later, when we were eating the delicious plum dessert, Charlie asked where I'd been for the last three months. 'The word at the paper was that you had to look after your sister and that was why you had to leave so abruptly. However, Monica Cathcart was putting it about that Xanthe – is that her name? – had been seen about town. Then someone else heard that you'd had a nervous break-down. Apparently that came from your sister. And now I discover that you've been ill with appendicitis.'

'Yes,' I licked my spoon. The dessert had been delicious and I'd eaten more in the last hour than I had all week.

Charlie raised his hand and ordered tea for us. I loved the sight of the samovar being placed on the table, with the glass cups in their fancy metal holders and the dish of lemon slices.

'Of course,' Charlie said carefully. 'Appendicitis is an acute illness, as I understand it, so that doesn't really explain the last three months, does it?'

I took a sip of tea and considered my reply. I could easily tell him to mind his own business, which is precisely what I intended to do. After the terrible row I'd had with my mother, I swore I'd never talk about it again. But when I opened my mouth I found that I was telling him about Amyas. 'I fell in love,' I said. 'Suddenly, totally, and in the end, it devastated me.'

Charlie leant forward. 'So who was the lucky man?' he asked.

'Oh, you wouldn't know him. He lives in Cambridge. Amyas Troy.' I savoured his name, remembering the first time he'd said it, on the beach on that brilliant day.

Charlie frowned and tapped his finger against his chin. 'What happened?'

'He left me. Went to Spain to join the International Brigade.'

'Very noble of him. But it sounds as if there was more.'

Strangely, I didn't feel like crying now, while talking about Amyas. Perhaps I was coming out of the other end of grief, or it could have been that Charlie was a good listener. 'There is more. He was living with another woman, a Mrs Cartwright. My parents had him investigated, because he'd asked me to marry him and they, well, my mother, didn't approve. Anyway, this Mrs Cartwright is an older woman, an actress and she kept him. My mother said that he was nothing but a gigolo.' I rested my chin on my hand, remembering the dreadful scene at Summer's Rest after the almost silent drive back from the station.

'A gigolo and a thief. My father found that several of his valuable books had disappeared.'

'You think he took them?'

'I know he did.' I remembered him going into Father's study just before he left; that, and the noise that his holdall made when he dropped it on the floor.

Charlie reached his hand across the table and took

mine in his grasp. 'Think of it as an experience. We all have unhappy love affairs. You'll get over it.'

'I won't,' I said. 'I'll love Amyas until I die.'

I couldn't understand why Charlie's face took on such a bleak look. It was only for a fleeting moment, but I saw it and wondered if he too had had an unhappy love affair and was, therefore, able to sympathise with me.

'Well, Blake,' he sighed after a minute. 'I think it's time you went back to work.'

'My job's gone,' I shrugged. 'I made a mess of that.'

He raised his eyebrows, then taking off his glasses rubbed his eyes. 'How about working for me?'

'Doing what?'

'Being my assistant. I'll pay you. Not much, I'm afraid, but, for now, you could be freelance and then, if you prove yourself, the editor will probably take you back.'

I stared at him. The restaurant was now almost empty and when I spoke I could hear my voice echoing around the room. 'Are you going abroad?'

'Oh yes. And it's we: we're going abroad.'

'To Spain?' My heart was beating very quickly. If we went to Spain, maybe I could find Amyas.

He laughed. He knew what I was thinking. 'No, Blake,' he said. 'Not this time. We're going to Berlin.'

Chapter Six

Berlin 1937

My room at the Hotel Adlon was on the fourth floor, a small single, but big enough for me and my new acquisition. It sat proudly on the table in front of the window and I felt excited every time I looked at it.

'Get yourself a decent portable typewriter, Blake. The Remingtons are good,' Charlie had said after lunch, when we discussed the details of our journey to Berlin. We were walking through Belgravia in the rain, and despite it being mid-afternoon on a working day, the streets were pretty empty. 'I've got one but I'll need it and it's as well for you to have one too. You can type up my reports and pretend that you're a real foreign correspondent.'

That made me angry and I considered telling him to go to hell; that I wasn't interested in his offer. I scowled at him. 'You sought me out,' I snapped. 'You must have thought I could do the job. But if that's what you think . . .'

He laughed. 'A thin skin is a terrible curse, Blake. Now, I presume you've got a passport, so we'll leave on . . . er . . . how about Friday?'

'Where will we stay?' I asked, calming down. 'D'you want me to . . .' Did my job as his assistant include arranging accommodation?

'Stop fussing. I've booked us rooms at the Hotel Adlon on Unter den Linden.'

I must have looked blank because he added with a grin, 'That's the best street in Berlin and the hotel is excellent. It's in the heart of the city, opposite the Brandenburg Gate. And anybody who is anybody stays there. Charlie Chaplin and Franklin Roosevelt have been guests, amongst others of that ilk. Don't worry, Blake. It's well up to your standards.'

He left me at the door to my flat, with a swift kiss on the cheek. 'Four days until we go, and I've work to do, arranging contacts and all that, so get yourself moving. You'll have to carry your own luggage, so don't bring much.'

'I hadn't planned to pack my ball gown,' I answered, with a dismissive laugh.

'Good.' Charlie refused to rise to my sarcasm and turned to go. 'I'll pick you up Friday morning. The boat train goes from Victoria at seven, so be waiting for me at six. Bye.'

While I was standing at my door, staring at his departing figure, Mr Weiss came out of his flat. 'Good afternoon, Fräulein.' He nodded kindly. 'Ah, you are looking better today. I can see colour in the cheeks.' The little dog in his arms gave a tiny yelp and Mr Weiss smiled. '*Ja*, she's a pretty girl. Don't you think, Willi? *Ein shaineh maidel.*'

For once, instead of darting through my door to safety, I stopped and smiled at him. 'Thank you, Mr Weiss. I do feel better today.' Then, as I heard the lift mechanism working and knew that Charlie was on his way out of the building, I said excitedly, 'I'm going abroad at the end of the week, on an assignment. I'm a journalist.'

'A journalist? But not working recently, I think. You have been sick, yes?'

I nodded and was about to go into my flat when a thought struck me. 'You're German, Mr Weiss, aren't you? That's where we're going. Do you know Berlin?'

To my surprise, his face fell. '*Ja*,' he said slowly. 'I know Berlin. It is my home.'

Oh dear, I thought, I've made him homesick. 'Do you visit often? Maybe you can tell me where the good restaurants are.' The notion that I could surprise Charlie by finding a 'great little place' before he did tickled me.

Mr Weiss shrugged. 'I don't know now. Things have changed since I was last there. I don't visit because I would not be welcome. It has become a cruel place for people of my faith.'

I must have looked shocked, because he reached out and patted my arm. 'You will be fine, Fräulein. No harm will come to you and you will learn many things.' Waving Willi's paw he turned and went back into his flat, leaving me sorry that I'd mentioned my forthcoming trip.

The four days passed in a flurry of activity. I bought my typewriter: not a Remington, but an Imperial Good Companion. Named, said the salesman, after the book by J.B. Priestley, and guaranteed to bring fame to those who typed on it. I didn't believe him, but bought it all the same; the idea appealed to me. Then I bought clothes, a neat tweed suit, which had a similar weave to the one Xanthe had worn, but with a longer, belted jacket and large pockets. Comfortable brown shoes and a trench coat completed the outfit. I had a squashable brown hat, which would do. It wasn't flattering, but then, I wasn't going to Berlin to flirt with anyone. Trying them on the night before we left, I was pleased with what I saw in my long mirror. I looked the part, smart but businesslike. I would wear the outfit the next day and put a pair of slacks and a couple of blouses along with my underwear in the small suitcase I'd chosen. I had a shoulder bag and the typewriter to take, and I practised carrying them around my sitting room.

A knock came at my door and for a moment I wondered, with a sinking heart, if it was Charlie, come to tell me that the trip was off. However, when I opened the door I almost cried in relief. It was Mr Weiss and Willi.

'I wonder, Fräulein, if I could request of you a small favour.' He was holding a rather bulky envelope and a piece of folded paper.

'Of course, come in, Mr Weiss.' I held the door wide and cautiously he stepped inside. I was surprised at myself. Only last week I would have rudely rejected any overture from a neighbour, but Charlie's intervention, with his exciting job offer, had knocked a bit of sense into me. I thought of Amyas constantly, wondering where he was and if he was safe and why he had left me. At night I still cried, grieving for what I had lost. But I was young and my life had to go on, so I remembered my good manners and smiled at the old man. Taking off my silly brown hat I said, 'Would you like a drink? Whisky?'

'Thank you.' He sat down heavily in the armchair and Willi curled up on his knee. 'You are packed and ready to go?'

'Yes,' I nodded. 'Mr Bradford is coming for me in the morning, early.'

'He is, perhaps, your young man?'

'No,' I smiled and handed him a glass of Scotch. 'He's

my boss.' I dragged the wooden chair from its place by the window and sat down beside the old man. I looked at him properly for the first time. He had a ring of white fluffy hair around a bald head, and kind eyes. His grey cardigan and white shirt were scrupulously clean and I was amused to note his floppy black silk bow tie. He could have been from another age; a musician maybe or an artist. But not from England.

'So,' he said, 'you have someone else who is a boyfriend?'

Did my face give me away? I think it did, for he watched me intently when I said, 'I used to, but he's gone now.' I didn't want him to feel sorry for me, so I added brightly, 'He's gone to Spain, to fight the Fascists.'

Mr Weiss nodded. 'That is good,' he said. 'The Fascists must be fought, everywhere.' He sighed. 'They have taken over my homeland. The people there are mad for them.' He paused and then said wearily, 'You will see it, dear Fräulein, when you are in Berlin. I think there is an insanity sweeping over my country.'

Rain beat heavily against the windowpanes and despite the warmth of my room I gave a little shiver. I wondered what I would find in Berlin. I took a sip of my drink and turned back to the old man. 'How long have you been in London?' I asked.

'Leah and I bought the flat in 1930. I came and went constantly for my business and then we decided to settle here. Leah had family in London, cousins of a sort, although they're all gone now. My business is importing furs which I buy all over Europe and from across Russia. It has been a successful enterprise, although in the last few years, since Leah died, I haven't travelled. An assistant, Emanuel, he travels for me.' He smiled.

'Emanuel's a clever boy, a boy who likes to learn. He chooses the best pelts and gets them at a good price and I, who have the connections, sell them on. We work well together and I enjoy his company when he is in London.'

Listening to his story I found myself feeling sorry for him; he seemed so lonely. 'Have you children, Mr Weiss?'

'Fräulein, you must call me Jacob. I would like that. We are friends now, are we not?' I nodded, smiling. 'No,' he sighed and stroked Willi's smooth little head. 'No, I have no children living. We had a good boy and a gentle little girl, but they died of the flu in 1919. Leah and I were spared, but our poor children were taken. There were no more after that. But still, we had each other, until . . .' He reached into his cardigan pocket and withdrew a large handkerchief. I looked away while he wiped his eyes and blew his nose. After a moment he said more brightly, 'But, I do have a sister and niece in Berlin, and this letter,' he held up the envelope, 'is for them.'

I looked at it. It had her name, Sarah Goldstein, but no address.

'This is her address.' Jacob showed me the piece of paper. 'I would like you to take the letter to her. The mail . . .' He shrugged. 'The mail doesn't always deliver to that part of Berlin. Sometimes the letters are opened; they look for money, you know. The postmen. They have no morals now. My letter to Sarah does contain money. Money for her and for Kitty to come to England and to live with me. Here, they will be safe.'

I didn't know what to say. It seemed such a small request and I couldn't see why I shouldn't do it, but there was something, just a feeling, that all was not right. I'd read enough newspaper reports to know that Jews were being persecuted in Germany and it was obvious that this was the problem.

'Is this address in the city?' I asked cautiously. 'I don't think I'll have time to go further afield.'

'*Ja*, it's in the city.' The old man frowned. 'Where are you staying?'

'At the Hotel Adlon.'

'Ah, the best. So, it is about two kilometres away. A walk for you, on a nice day. Or the bus if it is raining. You must cross the river. My sister lives by the girls' school and her building is easy to find.' He looked down at the little dog, settled and gently snoring on his lap. When he looked up his eyes were again full of tears. 'It would be a great kindness, dear Fräulein, if you could do this for me.'

How could I refuse? We sat quietly together and drank our whisky. He was looking at the luggage tag on my suitcase. 'You are Persephone?'

I nodded. 'My friends call me Seffy. That's what you must call me.'

'Thank you,' he smiled. 'I am honoured to have such a fine new friend.' He watched as I put the letter and the piece of paper with his sister's address in my handbag and then rose to his feet. 'I wish you a safe journey, dear . . . Seffy, and I will watch over your flat. Shall I take the spare key or have you arranged for someone else?'

I hadn't even thought about it and now I realised that living alone had its responsibilities. 'Here,' I said, taking the key out of the drawer in the table. 'Thank you, Jacob.'

So, now I was in my room at the Adlon, where from the window I could look across to the magnificent Brandenburg Gate and down the broad street that was Unter den Linden. Sadly, the great lime trees after which the street had been named were gone, cut down recently to facilitate the building of the new subway, but saplings had been planted to replace them and in time they would grow to be just as magnificent. There was a picture of how it had looked before the trees were cut, in the Berlin travel guide I'd bought from Hatchards in Piccadilly. I'd studied this book all through the journey, on the ferry and on the train across Europe.

Charlie had grinned when he saw what I was reading. 'Very good, Blake,' he'd said. 'Background knowledge is always useful. However, there's nothing like being there and talking to people.'

'So why are we really going to Berlin?' I was sitting opposite him in the comfortable compartment which we had to ourselves. The diesel train travelled smoothly with barely a jolt and we had the services of a smartly uniformed steward. The food in the dining car had been excellent and we had enjoyed our lunch and a glass of wine. Now, back in our compartment, Charlie had spent half an hour writing in his flip-over notebook and I, while reading my book, had lectured myself about my foolishness in not buying a similar pad. It was the most basic journalist equipment. I'll get one in Berlin, I promised myself. Thinking that, I fished out the English/German dictionary from my handbag, to look up the correct words. I had remembered to buy that.

'Why Berlin?' Charlie repeated my question. 'Because it's the most important place in Europe, at the moment.'

'Surely not more than Spain?'

'Spain is horrible. Bloody and evil. But Germany is about to blow up. Hitler is taking the country into hell and he'll take the rest of us with it.'

His words were bleak and terrible and I sat back and stared at him. I'd followed the news, of course. I knew about the rise of the National Socialist Party, the Nazis, and had heard vaguely about the suppression of dissenters, particularly of the Jews. I thought about Jacob telling me that he was no longer welcome in his own country. Poor Jacob, I thought, and felt afraid for Sarah and Kitty. 'My neighbour,' I said slowly, 'says that there is an insanity sweeping the country.'

Charlie nodded. 'Good words, and I might well steal them.' He pencilled them quickly into his notebook. 'We shall see when we get there. I have some contacts in Berlin who will tell me more, but you keep your ears and eyes open, Blake. Honest reporting is what's needed.'

'I don't speak much German,' I admitted, feeling stupid. 'Practically nothing.'

'Doesn't matter. I have some, and anyway the atmosphere about the place is what's important. That will reinforce any true information we can gather. Our esteemed government imagines that they can sit on their hands and do nothing and, somehow, everything will come out all right. They are so terrified of recreating what happened in the trenches that they've blinded themselves to the danger creeping up on us. In my opinion, they're wrong. But we shall see.'

I was quiet then, hating myself for being so ignorant. I thought of Amyas and knew that if he'd been asked he would have had all the facts at his fingertips. Why had I let so much about international affairs pass me by?

'I've been asking around about Amyas Troy,' said Charlie.

I gasped. How did he know I'd been thinking about

him? Did it show on my face? I took a deep breath. 'Why?' I asked. 'Of what possible interest could he be to you?'

Charlie shrugged. 'I don't know. I suppose it's because he's important to you, and you are now part of my team. From what I gather, he let you down.'

'He may have.' I wasn't prepared to criticise Amyas. Simply mentioning his name made my insides collapse.

'He is known. One or two people I've spoken to have met him and met his friend. What did you call her? Oh yes, Mrs Cartwright. She's well fixed, I believe, got a house in Cambridge and a flat in London. All left to her by her late husband. She was on the stage, but not an actress. Vaudeville, whatever that implies.' He laughed. 'Probably a stripper. Anyway, she keeps your friend, Amyas, in some style.'

I looked out of the window at the flat countryside rushing by and remembered that day when Amyas had walked out of the sea. If I closed my eyes I could be back there, allowing that magical feeling to wash over me again. Sometimes, I felt as though I'd taken a drug which would leave me addicted to Amyas for ever.

'Of course' – Charlie was still talking – 'that's what I know about him at present. Who he is and where he came from are a mystery.'

I dragged my eyes away from the window and looked at him. He had taken off his glasses and was polishing them with the corner of his paisley tie. 'Leave it, Charlie,' I said. 'Just leave it.'

'All right.' He replaced his glasses and picked up his notebook and pencil. 'I'll tell you one last thing, though. Amyas Troy is not his real name. It couldn't be. It's too . . . too romantic. He has chosen it, deliberately.'

Amyas was not mentioned again for the remainder of the journey and I was able to calm down and take in the sights that flashed by the window.

We crossed Holland, a flat peaceful land where canals ran alongside the railway lines and people on bicycles, waiting patiently at level crossings, waved to the train as it sped by. I wondered what they thought of their aggressive neighbour. Were they as alarmed as Charlie patently was, or did they accept that Germany had merely reinvented itself and it was nothing to do with them?

We were stopped at the border for about half an hour, when the green-uniformed German guards came on the train to examine our passports. They were not unpleasant, but not particularly friendly either.

'You are a tourist?' asked one of them, holding our passports in one hand and examining the names and photographs.

'Yes,' said Charlie immediately. Why didn't he say that we were journalists?

'And you, Fräulein. A tourist also?' The guard was frowning, and I don't think he believed Charlie. I decided to be brave.

'Yes, partially,' I said. 'I work for a travel company and I'm here looking for holiday destinations. I believe some of your countryside is very beautiful and, after the publicity of the Olympic Games last year, many people in England are interested in visiting Germany.'

The guard translated my words into German for his companion, who, to my relief, gave a big grin. He spoke rapidly to me and I waited for the explanation. 'My friend, Fräulein, says that you must visit the Harz mountains. They are magnificent.'

'I'll make a note of that,' I smiled and, satisfied, the two guards left.

'Well done,' said Charlie, looking rather surprised.

'Why didn't you tell them we were journalists?' I was watching the platform out of my window and saw two men being bundled off the train. I supposed they hadn't got passports. A guard with a dog approached them, the dog lurching forward on his lead and barking horribly. The train started moving, so I didn't see what happened but it left me with a cold feeling.

'Because they would have passed my name on to the SD, the secret police, that is, and we'd have been followed before we'd even got to the hotel, let alone had a chance to meet any of my contacts. They wouldn't speak to me if they knew I had the SD on my heels. Get it into your head, Blake. This is a police state.'

'Those are the Harz mountains,' said Charlie after an hour, pointing to the wavering outline. 'From what I've been told, there is a lot of industry building up in the area. I'm betting the factories there are part of Hitler's rearmament programme.' He sat back and gazed at the wooden ceiling of our compartment. 'D'you know, I seem to remember that there are legends and fairy tales about those mountains. I think Goethe wrote about the place.'

I had to bow to his superior knowledge and promised myself once again that I would read more, about everything, and make myself better informed. Later, as the afternoon wore on and the sun became a red ball in the autumn sky, we drew into Magdeburg station. There were soldiers and armed police on the platform and I wondered if some disturbance had happened, but it was the same at every major station we went through.

'Germany has become entirely militarised,' Charlie said, staring out of the window. Red and black flags and banners were everywhere, most of them emblazoned with the swastika, but the people on the platforms didn't seem to resent the attentions of the police. They hurried on and off the trains, walking purposefully and lining up to have their papers checked as though it was the most natural thing in the world. I found it chilling and some of my excitement started to drain away. I wondered if it would be the same in Berlin.

We went straight to the hotel when we arrived that evening, and later ate dinner at the very glamorous restaurant at the Adlon. Looking round I noted the elegance of the diners, and wished I'd brought smarter clothes; perhaps I'd have the opportunity to buy a dress while I was there.

'Tomorrow, after breakfast,' Charlie said while we ate, 'I'll take you for a bit of a walk, a sort of orientation exercise. In the afternoon I've got a meeting with a contact. I'd better go on my own to that one, so you can wander about or have a look at the shops. Get an idea of the place, the price of things and what's available. It'll all be good background stuff.'

I nodded. I was looking forward to becoming a real reporter in a foreign country. This was what I had longed to do. Excitedly I started to tell him which shops I thought I should go into and whether I should take a stab at the theatres and cinemas, but he cut across me.

'Your sister,' he said, 'she's mixing with a funny crowd.'

'In what way funny?' I asked. 'They're not my type, certainly. Idiots most of them. And her particular chum, Clive Powell, is a bad lot.'

'I believe she's been invited to parties at the German Embassy.'

My mouth must have dropped open. 'How did you know that?' I asked.

Charlie grinned and tapped his nose. 'Ear to the ground, Blake. You've got to be aware of everything, it's the only way.'

'Well,' I was determined not to be outdone in the information exchange, 'did you know that she's been in Germany recently? She told me that she'd been invited to visit some count or other. I didn't catch his name.'

'She's still here, actually,' Charlie said, his eyes twinkling behind his glasses. 'The count is Wolf von Klausen, and he is a very important man.'

I frowned. Charlie must have known that she was here before he invited me to join him on this assignment. 'You knew,' I said angrily. 'You knew she was here. That's why you asked me to come. You've used me.'

'For God's sake, Blake. Calm down. I didn't know, not until a couple of days ago. Your friend told me.'

'What friend?'

'Monica Cathcart. She's a hanger-on in that group and was at the party where Xanthe met von Klausen. She told me on Wednesday when I was in the office getting my final briefing. Somebody she knew had just come back from Berlin and said that Xanthe was doing the rounds of all the better soirées. I thought you knew.'

I shook my head. 'We're not a close family, these days.' I left it at that, still not sure that I was being given the entire truth.

Chapter Seven

Charlie and I walked along the pedestrianised centre of Unter den Linden, looking at the swastikas that flew everywhere. Not just on flagpoles and the tops of buildings; huge banners depicting the symbol soared fifty feet above the road. It was an announcement to the world that this was, indeed, a Nazi state.

Behind us was the Brandenburg Gate, which, with its giant statues, seemed to embody the confidence and power of the government. Ahead, Unter den Linden was a wonderful thoroughfare, where shops, restaurants and cafés jostled for business. To the right and left of us cars and buses passed by and people walked purposefully on the broad pavements. Berlin was a city on the move, and I couldn't tell then that this colourful, vibrant atmosphere masked a brutal, vicious hatred for all things outside its perfect Aryan world.

We passed a cinema showing posters for *Mutiny on the Bounty* with Clark Gable and Charles Laughton, which I'd seen in London the year before. I laughed. 'I thought the state wouldn't approve of mutiny.'

'No,' Charlie grinned. 'But I suppose they allow it because it's historical and anyway, that's what the Nazi party did a few years ago to the previous government. Turfed them out.'

'I suppose so,' I agreed, looking back at the poster.

'Let's go and get a coffee,' Charlie suggested, and we crossed the road.

'It's too cold to sit outside,' I said and he nodded and led me into the crowded, dark wood interior, where small tables dotted the room and waiters with white shirts and long black aprons expertly carried loaded silver trays in one hand.

'Instead of coffee,' Charlie said, ignoring the menu, 'try the hot chocolate.' It came in a tall glass with a metal holder and had a dollop of cream on top with a cinnamon stick poking out. I loved it, and every day for the following week I came to this café and ordered one. I learned the right words and the charming waiters always welcomed me warmly.

So too did the woman in the small boutique where I bought a petrol-blue wool crêpe evening dress. She spoke some English, so we could chat a little and she persuaded me to buy black high-heeled shoes and a metal necklace with a Greek key pattern worked into it. As I left the boutique, I felt almost happy for the first time since Amyas had left. Berlin was a wonderful city, I decided. Charlie was wrong about Germany.

That evening we went to the Borchardt restaurant, in the city centre. I was glad I'd bought the dress, because although it wasn't as formal as the dining room at the Adlon, it was smart. Wealthy-looking diners sat at the tables, talking loudly and waving to their friends; it was plainly a place where the elite of the city went to dine. We were shown to a table beside one of the great marble pillars which dominated the room and were joined by Dieter and Rachel, a couple in their forties who spoke excellent English.

'What do you think of our city?' Dieter asked me while we were eating. He was a reporter on one of the national newspapers and someone that Charlie had known for several years.

'It's magnificent,' I answered. 'I love the grand buildings and the broad pavements. There is an awful lot to see and everyone I've spoken to has been very pleasant.'

'They would be. To you,' Rachel said, not looking up from her plate. Her dark hair covered her face and I couldn't see her expression. I glanced quickly at Charlie and then back to Rachel.

'Why?' I said. 'Why wouldn't they be nice to you?'

'Many reasons.' She shrugged, and I watched as Dieter put his hand over hers. I'd made a mistake, I knew, and looked to Charlie for help. He changed the subject.

'What's the plan?' he asked, turning to Dieter. 'Are you getting out?'

'Yes,' Dieter nodded. 'We've got visas. We'll go to France first and then England if we can get on the quota.' He heaved a sigh and glanced, sympathetically, at his wife. 'It's just that Rachel's parents haven't got their visas and she's reluctant to go without them.'

I must have looked confused because Rachel gave me a sad, little smile. 'I'm a Jew, Seffy, and my poor husband, who is not, has had his life and work made so difficult because of it. I know that we have to leave but I can't bear to leave Mamma and Papa behind.'

I didn't know what to say. I thought of Jacob and the mission he had given me and began to feel more nervous about it. 'I have a friend,' I began, 'who wants me to take a letter to his sister. They're Jewish. She lives on a street called . . .' I fished the piece of paper from my bag, 'Auguststrasse.' I looked up. 'Do you know it?'

'Of course,' Rachel said. I was about to ask her if she would accompany me there but Charlie butted in.

'What on earth do you think you're up to, Blake?' He snatched the piece of paper from my hand and glared at it. 'You didn't tell me about a letter.'

'It was none of your business,' I replied, snatching the address back. I was cross and embarrassed that he should shout at me in front of his friends. 'I was doing a small favour, that's all.'

'Which might turn out to be not so small.' He was in a temper.

'Hey, Charlie.' Dieter grinned. 'Calm down, old friend. Seffy will be all right going to Auguststrasse. She can be a tourist who has lost her way, if questioned. But I don't think she will be. And it might be useful for her to look around that area to gather information for your article.'

I scowled at Charlie. 'There, see?' I was furious with him and looked around the busy restaurant to see if anyone had noticed our raised voices, but the other diners were more concerned with their food and friends and not looking at us.

'I suppose so.' Charlie refused to look at me and swigged his wine. Now I was even more determined to take the letter to Sarah and Kitty.

When we were eating dessert, Rachel turned to her husband and said something in German and he laughed. 'Rachel doesn't want to embarrass you, Seffy, but she says you remind her of the actress Katharine Hepburn. Both in looks and . . .' he frowned. 'I do not know the word in English . . . in German it is *resolut*.'

Charlie leant forward. 'What she means, Seffy, is "feisty".' He sighed. 'It's probably the best way to describe you.'

There was still a frosty atmosphere between us as we walked back to the Adlon. 'In future, Blake,' he said, when we entered the grand foyer, where the extravagant elephant fountain splashed water into an exquisitely ornate basin, 'you mustn't keep anything back from me. It could be dangerous.'

'Then,' I said, 'you must damn well do the same.' I stopped and turned to face him. 'I need to know where you are and who you're meeting. I'm not saying that I should come with you, although I'd like to, but you've got to tell me.'

He was thoughtful for a moment and then said, 'All right. So, tomorrow I'm going with Dieter on a little trip out of the city. We're going to Brandenburg where there is a mental hospital. Dieter says there have been rumours that the government is planning something there. I don't know what, exactly, and neither does he, but we have permission to visit. The authorities are keen to show it as an example of their excellent care. But we've only got two passes, so I can't take you with me. Sorry.'

'It's all right,' I said, as we headed for the lift. 'As long as I know. While you're away I'll try to absorb some more of life in Berlin and then I'll type it up.'

'Good girl, Blake.' He left me at my door. 'Be careful, though. These wide, well-lit streets and polite Berliners are only half the story.'

That night, in my comfortable bed, I considered all that had happened during the day. My thoughts were confused. I hadn't liked what I'd seen on the station with the guards, but they had been all right with me, and I'd found the same with the people I'd encountered in the city. Dieter and Rachel had made me think again, particularly Rachel. She had looked so sad when she was talking about leaving her parents. Could things be as bad as she said? I decided there and then that I would go looking for Sarah and Kitty tomorrow while Charlie was away.

As I was dressing the next morning I realised that I hadn't thought of Amyas for hours. Why did that feel as though I was abandoning him? Were all those torrid emotions empty illusions to be chased away by a change of scene and a few bright banners?

Dieter arrived in his Mercedes roadster to pick up Charlie at half past nine and after I waved them goodbye I hoisted my bag on my shoulder and set out for Auguststrasse. It was another sunny day and the wind was lighter. I had a map and the Leica camera I'd bought in the four days that Charlie had given me before we left.

Berlin was as bustling and beautiful as I'd expected, even when I walked across the bridge into the Mitte district. But after a few more blocks the streets became quieter, shops were boarded up and defaced with horrible graffiti. *Juden* was the most frequent word I saw. I knew what it meant and even if I had been in doubt, Star of David symbols were scrawled alongside the word and I could suddenly see why Jacob, and now Rachel, was so afraid.

The few people I saw stared at me, making me feel uncomfortable, an interloper. I looked at the graffiti and wondered how I would describe it, then I reached into my bag for my camera. Before I got it out, however, a black car drew up beside me.

'Fräulein?' A man in a green uniform got out of the car and approached me. I began to feel quite frightened.

'Yes?'

He spoke in German and I shrugged. 'English,' I said, my stomach churning. 'Tourist.'

His compatriot got out of the driving seat. They were both young. 'You are lost?' he asked, and remembering Dieter's advice from yesterday evening, I nodded. 'Yes.'

'You are in bad area,' the man, who I assumed was a policeman, said. 'You go back.' He nodded at the graffiti. 'This district for *Juden*. Not a good place.' He paused and looked at my bag. 'You have papers?'

They watched as I reached into my bag and produced my passport and then passed it between them. I was scared that they might ask to search my bag. If they did they would find the letter and the address to which I had to deliver it. I hoped my smile would convince them that I was indeed just a lost tourist, as they examined the document and then compared my photograph to my face. The first policeman laughed and muttered something in German. From the expression on their faces what he'd said was unpleasant. Eventually the driver pointed down the road which led back towards the bridge. 'You go that way.'

'Thank you,' I said, with a dry mouth, trying to sound grateful, then turned around and started walking. I walked until they had got back into their car and crawled past me. I could see them laughing, and knew that they'd enjoyed frightening me, so when they were out of sight I thought, to hell with them, and turning, darted into an alleyway. I waited, trembling a little, for the sound of the returning car, but hearing only distant traffic I walked on towards Auguststrasse. My heart was beating fast and I felt a little sick. Nothing had happened really, but I knew I wouldn't get away with the lost tourist excuse if the same car came back.

At the corner of the block I looked around to see if there was anyone who resembled an official, but the street was quiet, so I got out my camera and took photographs of the graffiti. A photograph would be far more dramatic than anything I could write.

Following the map I turned on to Auguststrasse and paused. It had been quite a long walk and I was thirsty and hoped to find a café. A woman accompanied by two teenage girls stopped beside me She spoke first in German and then when I shook my head and said 'English' she smiled and spoke hesitantly, 'Can I help you, Fräulein? You are lost, yes?'

I shook my head. 'Not lost, really. I'm looking for this address.' I showed her the piece of paper.

'Ah,' she smiled. 'Frau Goldstein. You are a friend?'

'No. Her brother, in London, is a friend. He asked me to visit her.'

She smiled again. 'I remember Jacob and dear Leah, who I believe has passed away.'

I nodded. 'He's on his own now.'

'So,' said the woman. 'Sarah lives in that building –' she pointed across the road to a large stone apartment block. Next to it I could see another building, which seemed newer than the rest of the street. It was brick rather than stone and in a rather stark, modernist style. The woman nodded at it. 'That's the girls' school, where my daughters and I are going. Sarah is a teacher there and she'll be in the school now. Will you walk with me?'

She introduced herself as Miriam and her two girls as Elisabeth and Lotte. The girls curtsied to me and then ran on towards the school entrance.

'I'm Persephone,' I said. 'From London. Jacob lives in the same building as me.'

My new friend held the door open for me and as we walked up the stairs she told me that she had been taking her daughters to the doctor for a medical certificate. 'We have permission to leave and visas for Canada. My husband is a doctor but they have told him he can no longer work at the hospital. It is sad but exciting to think of a new life.'

'Can't he get work elsewhere?' I regretted the words as soon as they were out of my mouth. Miriam gave me a pitying stare. 'Do you not understand, Persephone? We are Jews. We are not allowed to offer medical help to Christians or teach them in the schools or act as lawyers for them. Our businesses are being closed down and people feel free to spit at us in the street. Why would we want to stay here?'

The knowledge that Berlin was a divided city was being reinforced with every person I spoke to and I resolved there and then to stop being so wilfully ignorant. It would have been easy to simply enjoy the grandness of the hotel and the ability to wander around the beautiful shops and cafés and, in truth, I hated being here, in this distressed part of the town. But if I was to be a reporter and find out the reality of life here or anywhere else I went, I would have to work at it and go to places that others refused to acknowledge.

'If you wait here,' said Miriam, showing me to a chair in a corridor, 'I'll see if I can find Mrs Goldstein.'

I sat on the hard chair and sniffed the familiar scent of floor polish and listened to the faint buzz of voices coming from behind the closed doors which lined the corridor. It took me back to my own time at school, in London, which I'd loved. I'd been a good pupil, eager to learn and to go on to university, although I was only one of two girls in my year who had done so; it had seemed a natural progression. It was only after university that I began to have doubts. Mother and Xanthe made fun of me constantly for wanting to pursue first academic study and then a job. 'There's absolutely no need, darling,' Mother had said. 'Go out and enjoy yourself now, while you can, before you get married and bogged down in domestic concerns.' This last had seemed heart-felt and I'd given her a quick glance. What kind of life had she been missing? I wondered.

Then I thought about Amyas and those nights in my bed at the house by the sea. I could feel his hands on me, his mouth on mine, and my breath caught in my chest. Oh God, did that really happen? That week was beginning to take on a unreal quality and I could easily have believed that it was a dream, if it hadn't been for what had happened after. Without my bidding, my eyes began to fill with tears and I reached into my bag for a handkerchief.

'Fräulein!' I was startled by the near-silent approach of an older woman.

'Yes.' I scrambled to my feet and in my rush dropped my bag. The contents spewed out on to the polished wooden floor. 'Sorry,' I said and crouching began to gather up my hankies, the new notepad, my wallet, my camera and the host of other junk that I usually carried around. Most importantly, the envelope that Jacob had given me.

'You wished to see me?' the woman continued.

I straightened up and looked down at her. Sarah Goldstein was younger than her brother, quite a lot, I thought, but she had the same round face and kind, brown eyes as he did and she was now giving me a rather sweet smile.

'I surprised you, yes? You were having a . . .' She thought for a little and then said triumphantly, 'A daydream. Yes?'

I smiled. 'Something like that. Mrs Goldstein, your brother Jacob asked me to visit you and to bring you this.' I handed her the envelope, then watched as she turned it over in her hands and when she looked back at me her smile was gone.

'Do you know what this envelope contains?' she asked quietly.

'I do.' I lowered my voice. 'Mrs Goldstein, your brother Jacob is very anxious that you and your daughter come to London to live with him. He is worried about the situation here and knows that you will be safer there.' I looked around. The corridor was empty. 'He has sent you money,' I said.

She was quiet for a moment and then asked, 'How is it that you know Jacob? You are not of our faith, I think.'

'We live in the same building,' I answered. 'My flat is opposite his. And no, we are not of the same faith, but as I was coming to Berlin, I agreed to bring you this envelope and his message. He is a friend.'

The envelope seemed to be almost red-hot, the way she was turning it over and over in her hands and for a moment I thought she was going to hand it back to me, but suddenly she said, 'You will come to my home, now, yes? I will give you coffee and you shall meet Kitty. She is not too well today so has not been at school. I don't have a class until after lunch so we can go now.'

Sarah's flat was full of old, dark wooden furniture. The round table in the middle of the main room was covered in a red cloth with a pretty porcelain vase, empty of flowers, in the centre. Bookcases lined the walls and an old-fashioned gramophone stood in the corner. I liked the pictures hanging on the one wall without a bookcase. They were more modern than I would have expected. One in particular caught my eye. Sarah followed my gaze.

'Do you like that?' she asked.

'Yes,' I nodded. 'Very much.' It was a painting of a woman sitting on a narrow bed, looking as though she was waiting for someone. The background was the most compelling blue and the bedcover red. It wasn't the type of art my parents collected, pictures that could have been photographs, so accurate and defined. No, this picture gave an impression of what the woman was feeling, thinking. Her loneliness, perhaps.

'It's a Charlotte Salomon.' Sarah smiled. 'She is a friend. Now, sit down. I will make coffee.'

I longed to take out my notebook and record all that I saw. This charming apartment could be the background to an interview, but, at the same time, I knew I could never name Sarah. It would be too risky.

'Hello.' A pretty dark-haired girl came into the room. She was about thirteen, taller than her mother and with her hair cut in a fashionable bob.

'Hello,' I said, standing up. 'I'm Persephone Blake and

you, I think, are Kitty. I'm very pleased to meet you.' We shook hands very formally, but the girl grinned at me.

'I like your name,' she said. 'It is not usual.'

'My friends call me Seffy,' I said. 'And that's what you must call me.'

'I have a long name too,' she said, with a little giggle. 'I am Katharina but, always, Kitty.'

We sat around the table, drinking coffee and eating delicious apple and cinnamon cake. The envelope, unopened, lay on the cloth in front of Sarah but she didn't look at it. Instead she asked about my trip and what I was doing in Berlin. When I told her she nodded her head slowly.

'You do a good thing,' she said. 'The world must know what happens here.'

'The world does know,' I said. 'But I don't think they quite believe it. My boss, Charlie, who's here with me is a real reporter, he'll make sure they believe. He's brave and very honest and has reported on wars and crimes all over the world.'

'Open the letter, Mamma,' said Kitty, reaching over and pushing it towards her mother. 'Please.'

Reluctantly, Sarah tore open the bulky envelope and gasped as a handful of notes fell out. They were hundreds of pounds. I thought I must have been carrying close to a thousand. A letter was enclosed and Sarah read it quickly. 'Jacob says that we must go to him in England. Leave our home and all our dear things and live with him. He is most insistent.'

'He is right,' I said.

'How can I?' she said angrily. 'I have my teaching, my girls. They need me.' She looked around the room. 'And

103

I have this lovely home with its memories of my dear Felix. No, it is impossible.'

'I would like to see England,' said Kitty tentatively. 'I would like to travel.'

'All children want to travel and you will one day,' Sarah sighed. 'You will want to leave me. It is natural.' She stared at the pile of money, and then gathering it up shoved it back into the envelope. 'Here,' she said, pushing it towards me. 'Take it back to Jacob. Tell him, thank you. But we will be all right. Things will change. They always do.'

I was shocked. 'I can't take it back,' I said. 'Poor Jacob would be so upset. He's very lonely, you know. It's just him and Willi in the apartment.'

'Willi?' said Sarah with a frown. 'Who's Willi?'

'It's his little dog. He dotes on him.'

Sarah tutted. 'The old fool,' she whispered, but her angry expression softened.

'Look,' I said, getting up, 'I have to go now, but I'm staying at the Hotel Adlon. If you change your mind, or want me to take a message to Jacob, you can get hold of me there.' I had a sudden thought. 'May I take a photograph of you both? Jacob will be so pleased to see it.' They posed, smiling, by the window and I snapped their picture.

Then I shook hands with both of them and as she showed me downstairs into the lobby, Kitty said, 'Thank you for coming, Seffy. I know you are right about us leaving. My friends Elisabeth and Lotte are going but Mamma is stubborn. She feels that she is needed at the school. I will talk to her.'

'Good,' I said. 'I hope she will be persuaded.' And

waving to her, I walked away, past the graffiti-scrawled buildings and the closed businesses, until I crossed the river and was back in the vibrant part of the city. I had so much to think about and after a quick lunch in what had become my favourite café, I went to my room at the Adlon and typed up my impressions of Auguststrasse and of the people I'd met. It took me time to get my thoughts in order, because even then I wasn't entirely sure of what I'd seen and heard, and when Charlie knocked on my door at about four o'clock I was still sitting at my typewriter, going over what I'd written.

'Come in,' I said. He looked excited and was obviously bursting to tell me something, but at first he kept it to himself.

'How was your day?' he asked. 'Had a wander around the sights and the shops?'

'Er . . . not exactly. I went to Auguststrasse to meet my contact.' I loved saying that. I loved showing Charlie that he wasn't the only one who had contacts.

He frowned. 'Didn't I say not to do anything dangerous?' he grumbled.

'I didn't. It wasn't nice, the buildings are defaced with graffiti, but I found Mrs Goldstein and handed over the letter. I talked to her and to another woman and, Charlie, things are bad for the Jews in Berlin.'

'Well, we knew that already. But . . . did you get more stuff, more information?'

'I think so,' I said. 'I certainly got what would be a human interest story. And photographs.'

'Great! I knew you would be useful. I'll look at your material tomorrow.'

'What about you?' I asked. 'What about the mental hospital?'

He lifted his shoulders in a rather disappointed shrug. 'It seemed all right. The wards were clean and there were lots of staff on duty.' He sighed. 'But it was all a bit too efficient. I know there's something wrong there.' He shook his head and then, looking up and grinning, said, 'You know that when we discussed this visit to Berlin, you were very sarcastic and told me that you wouldn't be bringing your ball gown.'

'Yes,' I said cautiously.

'Well, you'll need one. Tonight.'

'What?' I almost shouted out. 'Why?'

'We've been invited to a do at the Kaiserhof hotel. Dinner and dance, and most of the guests will be members of the SS. Time to see how the ruling class lives. So, Blake, can you dolly yourself up for this evening?'

This was no time to ask questions. 'Watch me,' I said and, grabbing my bag, made for the door. 'What time will you pick me up?'

'Eight thirty, in the lobby?'

'Fine.' I went to the lift, then through the lobby and out on to Unter den Linden and soon I was back at the boutique where I'd bought my dinner dress.

'Fräulein?' said the same shop assistant. 'Can I help you?'

'I need a dress, suitable for a dinner and dance at the Kaiserhof hotel.'

'Oh!' She sounded almost faint. 'How wonderful. All the best people will be there.' She ushered me into the salon. 'I know I can find you something special. You have a wonderfully slim figure.'

106

Blushing, I waited while she brought dresses into the changing room and pulled them on and off me, until I knew that I had found the one. 'Oh, Fräulein, you look lovely,' she breathed. 'It is absolutely the correct colour for you.'

And when I stepped out of the lift at half past eight to meet Charlie in the lobby, I was conscious of a few heads turning.

'Wow!' said Charlie. 'You look stunning.'

'Thank you.' I smiled and took his arm as we went out to the cab. I knew I looked good. The long sea-green silk sheath dress fitted perfectly and the colour brought out the chestnut highlights in my hair. My shop assistant had found a paste diamond slide to hold back my wild curls and sold me a tiny black jewel-studded bag to match.

'Are you cold?' asked Charlie.

'No,' I lied. I was, but I would never have admitted it. Just wearing that fabulous dress was enough heat for me and I smiled with pleasure on the short journey to the Kaiserhof.

We walked through the hotel lobby and into the crowded ballroom. Tables had been set in a horseshoe arrangement around a circular dance floor with a bar at the far end. The band was playing Cole Porter's 'Night and Day' and I excitedly hummed along to it, looking at the people on the floor and comparing my dress to those of the other women. I thought mine looked as good as any of them. 'Who's giving this dance?' I asked.

'Not sure,' said Charlie. 'But I'm told that the senior officers of the SS will be here.' He adjusted his bow tie and smoothed down the lapel of his hired dinner jacket.

'Should be useful for background information and we can try and muscle in on some conversations because, sadly, we won't know anyone.'

But that wasn't entirely true. For there, in the centre of the room, surrounded by black-uniformed officers, was Xanthe.

Chapter Eight

'Oh my God,' I said, staring at Xanthe.

Charlie turned his head away from the dance floor, where he'd been tapping his foot in time to the band. 'What?' he said absently. 'What's the matter?'

'My sister. She's here.'

'What? Your sister? Where?'

I nodded towards the group that surrounded her. 'She's in the middle of that bunch of officers. I just saw her.'

He concentrated his previously wandering gaze on the centre of the dance floor. 'I can't see a girl,' he said. 'It's all men. You're imagining it.' But just then the group parted and Xanthe reappeared, her cheeks slightly pink with excitement, laughing at something one of them had said.

'There she is. Look.' I didn't need to point. Xanthe was a magnet to men's eyes and Charlie wasn't the only one in the room who was staring at her. I knew that she was loving it. Her arm was held protectively by a tall, aristocratic-looking officer, a man as blond as she, with a narrow, slightly tanned face and the bearing of a natural leader. They were the most compelling couple in the room.

'Good God!' Charlie breathed. 'So that's the famous Xanthe Blake.'

I closed my eyes and sighed. If Charlie had even

109

vaguely fancied me before, he wouldn't now. It was always the way.

But I was wrong.

'Christ,' he said. 'She's terrifying. How could anyone keep up with her?'

I laughed. 'They do, Charlie. They do. Perhaps they're braver men than you, or more foolish.' I stood for a moment and watched her. She was wearing a black, figure-hugging dress with bands of sequins around the bodice and tiny shoulder straps. It must have cost a fortune. But then, all her clothes cost a fortune.

'Are you going to introduce me?' Charlie asked eagerly. 'She's with a crowd that would be useful for us. I'd like to hear them talking about Herr Hitler and get an idea of what makes them tick. Why they're so devoted.'

I sighed. I knew I would have to go over and speak to her and put up with the patronising scorn that would be my fate, but I wanted a few more moments to keep that feeling of allure which had been buoying me up, so I stood and watched my sister while Charlie hovered impatiently at my side. I didn't have to wait for long. A piercing squeal, which stopped everyone in their tracks, announced that Xanthe had spotted me.

'Jesus!' said Charlie. 'What was that?'

'Xanthe,' I giggled. 'I'd know that screech anywhere.' And in a moment, trailing her entourage, she was by my side.

'Seffy!' she cried. 'What the hell are you doing here? And who's this?' She gave Charlie one of her seductive pouts. He was, for once, dumbstruck.

'Hello, Xanthe,' I said and gave her a sisterly peck on the cheek.

She kissed me back and I was enveloped in her heady aura of perfume and confidence. Again she asked, 'What are you doing here?'

'I'm working,' I said. 'Reporting on Berlin life.' I turned to Charlie. 'This is my boss, Charlie Bradford.'

'Boss?' simpered Xanthe with an arch expression. 'He doesn't look like a boss.'

'What would you know?' I said, combative once again, as I always was when faced with my sister's combined beauty and stupidity.

'Oh, Seff,' she laughed. 'Don't be horrid.' She turned to her companions. 'This is my sister,' she said. 'You'd never guess, would you?'

The officer who had been holding her arm smiled at me. 'Xanthe, *meine Liebe*, please introduce us correctly.'

Xanthe grinned. I knew she was about to show off. 'Wolf, may I introduce my sister, Persephone Blake, and her boss, Charlie . . . Bradford.' Her eyes were dancing as she smirked at me. 'And this officer is my friend, Count von Klausen.'

The count clicked his heels in an almost exaggerated way, and taking my proffered hand, raised it to his lips. 'Fräulein Blake. I am so very pleased to meet you.'

'How do you do?' I said and waited while the count clicked his heels and shook hands with Charlie. The other officers clicked their heels too and gave slight bows.

'I can't introduce them properly,' giggled Xanthe, 'because I only know their Christian names, but they're all jolly good fun.'

I smiled and nodded to the group of officers who, after a moment or two, drifted away, leaving the four of us together. 'Come, sit,' said von Klausen, 'let me get you some champagne.' He looked up and immediately a waiter appeared. We were shown to a table on the edge of the dance floor and champagne and glasses arrived within a minute. The count seemed to be the most important person in the room.

'So, Mr Bradford,' he said after we'd all taken a drink. 'What did you think of the facility at Brandenburg today?'

If Charlie was surprised, he gave absolutely no hint of it and replied, 'Impressive. The patients we saw appeared to be cared for excellently and the clinic is wonderfully clean and well equipped.'

Von Klausen smiled, flattening his lips over even white teeth. He and Xanthe were a striking pair and I wondered how deep their relationship was. He was obviously keen to show her off and she gazed at him with what was close to devotion. 'You wonder perhaps,' he continued, clearly irritated that Charlie hadn't risen to the bait, 'how I knew you'd been to Brandenburg. Is this a surprise to you?'

'Not really.' Charlie put on his deadpan face. 'I should imagine that everything I've done since I came into your country has been noticed. My newspaper has a large circulation and my name is hardly unknown. The editor and the owner are keen for me to shine a light on world affairs. You would want me to report the good things about Germany, and I will.' He took a sip from his glass of champagne. 'And, of course, any bad things I come across.'

Von Klausen ignored that last remark. 'You must have seen that Berlin has changed for the better. The decadence of the twenties has largely gone, is that not so?'

Charlie nodded. 'It has become a less exciting city,

certainly. And while it is perhaps more organised, there do seem to be fewer freedoms. Is that a good thing? Surely there should be room for some individualism.'

Our German host smiled, but his eyes remained cold. 'Freedom to do what, Herr Bradford? That is a tricky problem, is it not? Should the happiness of the people be disturbed by a few dissidents? No, I don't believe so.' Then without giving Charlie the opportunity to reply he turned to me. 'Your presence here has come as a surprise to me, Fräulein Blake. Until dear Xanthe introduced us I hadn't connected Mr Bradford's companion with her beautiful sister.'

'I suppose there's no reason why you should,' I said lightly. 'I'm a very junior member of Charlie's team. Here to look at the shops and the museums. That sort of thing.'

'Yes, we noted that you were walking around the city today. You got lost, I believe.'

My stomach was rapidly turning to water. Had I been followed to Sarah's flat and would she be in trouble because of it? Although I kept smiling, my mind was searching desperately for a suitable reply. Beside me I could feel Charlie sitting forward and knew he was going to answer for me. That's when I became angry. For one thing, I was furious that Charlie thought I couldn't answer for myself and, more than that, how dare this German secret policeman question me? How dare he have me followed?

'Goodness,' I said, my voice cold. 'However did you know that?' I pretended to think for a moment and then said, 'Of course. I was stopped by two policemen who looked at my passport. They said I was in a dangerous part of the city and should turn back.' I shook my head in a way that I'd always despised, that of someone who was part of the ruling class. 'I have to say that they were rather rude, making salacious remarks,' I continued. 'I got a very poor impression of your forces of law and order and I can't imagine a London policeman behaving like that. Our bobbies have much better manners.'

Von Klausen's smile disappeared and a nervous tic worked in his cheek. 'I apologise,' he said. 'On behalf of our police force. Those officers will be disciplined.' He wasn't giving up, though. 'So, did you turn back?'

I tried not to make my sigh of relief audible. He doesn't know, I thought gleefully. They didn't follow me afterwards. 'Of course,' I said lightly. 'I always do as I'm told.' I felt Charlie's hand giving my knee a squeeze. Well done, he was saying.

Xanthe butted in, obviously bored with a conversation which didn't include her. 'Seffy,' she said. 'Do the parents know you're here?'

'No,' I said. 'Do they know where you are?'

'No!' She giggled. 'Aren't we naughty?'

I laughed with her, while I looked around the room and waited for my heart to stop beating so energetically. The Kaiserhof wasn't as grand as the Adlon, but was still an important hotel and the guests mingling in the room looked every bit as wealthy. Most of the men were in uniform, many of them dressed, as was von Klausen, in black with silver braid and the death's head badge on the collar. There were others in different uniforms, but although they mixed with each other they stayed away from von Klausen's men. I decided I must ask Charlie about the different factions. And then there were civilians I guessed were government officials, who trailed little coteries of hangers-on. Their small fair-haired wives looked nervous, as though finding the grandeur of their surroundings terrifying.

'The women here aren't very fashionable,' said Xanthe loudly. 'Where on earth do they get those dreadful clothes?'

Abruptly, Von Klausen stood up. 'Herr Bradford. Would you like to meet some of the guests? There are people here that I know you would like to mention in your article. I shall introduce you.' He smiled down at Xanthe and me. 'I'm sure the ladies will excuse us. They must have family matters to discuss.'

Charlie leapt to his feet. 'Thank you, Count. I'd like that very much. I think I spotted Major Heydrich over by the bandstand. I should like to meet him. His organisation of the Olympic Games was most impressive.'

'You shall meet him,' von Klausen smiled magnanimously. 'Come.'

We watched them go over to a group of what were clearly high-ranking officials and there was much clicking of heels and bows as Charlie was introduced.

'Is he your new boyfriend?' Xanthe asked me. 'He's not bad-looking and quite well spoken.'

'No. He's my boss. I told you. I'm only here as an assistant. Anyway, what about you and this von Klausen?'

'Count von Klausen,' she corrected me and took a deep sigh. 'Isn't he absolutely gorgeous? I met him in London and he invited me to Germany. I've been to his hunting lodge in some forest or other, I forget the name, anyway it was so fantastic. Lovely parties, and servants everywhere. They all speak English, you know. The upper-class ones, I mean.'

'So, is he the one?'

'Well.' Xanthe lowered her voice. 'The thing is, Seff, he's married, but they don't live together and he's said that he'll get a divorce. Just imagine. If I married him I'd be a countess. Mother would love that. Then she wouldn't worry about the divorce thing.'

'Oh yes,' I agreed. 'She'd love that.' I looked at her, so pretty and so stupid, and the protective older sister in me came to the fore. 'Xanthe,' I said, putting my hand over her exquisitely manicured little paw, 'there's going to be a war between England and Germany. If you stay with this man, you'll be on the wrong side. You must think about it.'

'Don't be silly.' She held up her glass and a waiter rushed forward to refill it. 'There isn't going to be a war. The government at home will soon come to their senses and see that Herr Hitler is right. We can't let communists and Jews run everything like they are now. That's what Wolf believes and anyway, most of my set at home agree. I've told them here, whenever it's been discussed, that we all think that they're right and that our government is wrong.'

I shouldn't have been surprised; I knew that Xanthe mixed with a group of people who were fascists in all but name, but it appalled me just the same. What could I say to her? How could I show her she was wrong? I was still contemplating it when she said, 'That's not a bad dress you're wearing. Quite suits you, actually. Where did you get it?'

I swallowed the words I'd planned. What was the point in haranguing her? She'd never understand. 'I bought it here,' I answered with a sigh. 'In a little boutique.'

'I bought mine in Paris,' Xanthe preened. 'It looks it, doesn't it?'

'Yes.' I capitulated. 'It's lovely.'

She smiled, nodding to the people who seemed to recognise her and giving fluttering little waves to others. I looked around the room, wondering who Charlie was meeting and wishing I could meet them too. Suddenly Xanthe turned to me. 'God, I forgot. I've got something to tell you.'

'What?' I asked, looking at her excited face.

'You'll never guess who's here. In Berlin, I mean.'

'Who?' I asked idly, not at all interested in which of her unpleasant friends had joined her in Berlin, and transferred my gaze to the people mingling beside the bar. I could see Charlie being introduced to someone who looked important and to others who were being beckoned over to the group. Should I get up and walk over to them? It would be much more fascinating than listening to Xanthe. But she leant forward and grabbed my arm.

'Oh, you know, Seff. That man.'

More people were joining the group where Charlie stood. I watched them: smart, important people who looked as though they owned the world. 'Which man . . .' I started to say but got no further. I didn't need to. I was looking directly at Amyas.

For a moment I thought I might faint. My world crashed around me and I struggled to breathe.

'Oh look, Seffy. There he is.' Xanthe was squeaking with excitement. 'Shall I wave?'

'No,' I managed to whisper. 'Please don't.' I turned my head away and hoped, so hoped, that he wouldn't see me. I wanted to escape, to leave the hotel, leave Berlin and return to the safety of my flat and sit by the window, where I could look out at the autumn rain drenching the city garden square. I wanted dark and dreary days so that I couldn't be reminded of Amyas and the summer's magic which had left me for ever.

'My God.' Xanthe laughed. 'You look as though you've seen a ghost. For goodness' sake, Seffy, he was over months ago. Time for you to move on.'

How could I tell her that, for me, Amyas would never be over? I said nothing and prayed that Charlie would return quickly to the table and I could persuade him to take me back to the Adlon. I longed to turn and look at Amyas but I knew that the intensity of my gaze would cause him to look back at me.

'Oh!' Xanthe squealed. 'Here's Wolf and your "boss" coming back – and guess who they're bringing with them?'

Do I remember von Klausen clicking his fingers so that another table was drawn up to accommodate the extra people? Of course I do. Every detail, no matter how inane, was etched in my memory. That meal at the Kaiserhof, with the dizzying swell of the music and the rushing back and forth of waiters with plates of food which I couldn't taste, was imprinted on my brain.

'We have brought friends to join us,' von Klausen said, his cold blue eyes flitting from Xanthe to me. 'I believe you know them.'

'Yes, slightly,' Xanthe said, giving Amyas a glance. 'I have met this person once, although I'd say he is more a friend of my sister. However, you must introduce us to this lady.' She transferred her gaze to the middle-aged woman who stood beside Amyas. Until then my eyes had been fixed on Amyas, on his amused, beautiful face and unconcerned brown eyes, but now I flicked a quick look at her. Was this Mrs Cartwright? His . . . protectress?

'Of course, *meine Liebe*. Miss Persephone Blake and Miss Xanthe Blake, I present Mr Amyas Troy and Mrs Elvira Cartwright. Like you, they are visitors from England.'

'How do you do?' said Xanthe briefly, making no secret of her dislike, and then smiled at Charlie who was standing behind Amyas. 'Mr Bradford,' she said archly and patted the seat of the gilt chair beside her, 'do come and sit here.'

While von Klausen gallantly pulled out a chair for Mrs Cartwright, Amyas sat down beside me. 'Hello, Persephone,' he said and at the sound of his voice my heart did somersaults.

I swallowed, my mouth dry, and took a gulp of champagne before answering. 'Good evening, Amyas.' The words I really wanted to say were stuck in the back of my throat. Why are you here, you bastard? Why aren't you in Spain fighting for a noble cause? But, of course, I couldn't say them. All I could do was smile inanely as the chatter went on around the table until my jaw got tired and I had to drop the mask. I looked down, but that was hell too because Amyas's hand was there on the cloth in front of me and once again I could feel his fingers touching my naked body.

'Seffy!' Xanthe's high-pitched voice penetrated my brain. She was obviously repeating herself and I looked up to find that all eyes at the table were on me.

'Sorry,' I said. 'What?'

'Mrs Cartwright wants to know where we met Mr Troy. It was Cornwall, wasn't it?'

'Yes,' I said.

'In the summer?' Mrs Cartwright broke into the conversation. She was small and dark, with heavy eyebrows and her long, obviously dyed, black hair was held in a low bun at the back of her neck. That neck was circled by diamonds, real ones, I thought, as were those in her ears and around both her wrists. Her kingfisher-blue dress was too full of material to make it fashionable, but it might have looked wonderful on stage with lights catching the flash of colour and the swishing of the taffeta. She frowned at me. 'This summer?' she asked.

'Yes.' I could feel Amyas's leg twitching beneath the table and knew, without any doubt, that he was begging me to help him. Why should I? I thought. After what he did to me. I should just dump him in it and let him find his own way out. But I couldn't.

'Yes,' I said again. 'He was on our beach with his two friends. I invited them up to our house.'

'It was Graham and Percy,' Amyas said. 'You know, those boys I was tutoring.'

Mrs Cartwright's frown eased. 'Oh, them two. I know.' She had a strong northern accent. 'Aye,' she continued. 'They went to Spain, to fight. Silly little beggars.'

'Both of them?' I asked, surprised. 'Percy said he wouldn't go.'

'Well, he did.' She sniffed and looked at von Klausen. 'D'you get anything to eat in this place?'

At von Klausen's clicked fingers, menus were swiftly brought to the table and orders taken. 'There is something about you, Frau Cartwright, that reminds me of the English singer, Gracie Fields.' Von Klausen poured more champagne into her glass. 'Perhaps you come from the same area in England?'

'Not far away. She's a Rochdale lass, I'm Bolton. I knew her years ago. Her name was Stansfield as a girl, when we toured the halls.'

'So, you are an actress, yes.'

Mrs Cartwright smiled, showing teeth yellowed by too many cigarettes. 'I was once, love. A sort of an actress, mind. More revue, like. That sort of thing.' She wagged her head from side to side and gave him a knowing glance. He looked alarmed and I saw Charlie's eyes twinkling behind his glasses. But von Klausen persisted, determined to get as much information as possible.

'And now you have retired from the stage, yes?'

'Aye. I was luckier than Gracie. I married a rich old devil who left me very well fixed. I do what I like now.' This last was followed by a proprietorial look in Amyas's direction.

It all felt rather surreal, sitting in this ballroom with Amyas and Mrs Cartwright, surrounded by Nazi officers, with Xanthe chattering and Charlie patently taking mental notes. In the gap between courses, Charlie asked Xanthe to dance; after a look that amounted to a plea for permission from von Klausen, she agreed. A second later von Klausen stood up. He's going to ask me, I thought, my heart sinking. He'll start asking me questions again, about my walk in the city, where I went and what I saw, but to my relief he turned to Mrs Cartwright and as they walked out on to the dance floor, Amyas and I were left alone.

'You look absolutely beautiful, my darling Persephone,' he said and caught my hand in his under the table. 'Just seeing you is heaven.'

'Don't,' I said, snatching my hand away. 'How can you say that, after what you did to me? How can you be so casual?'

'I have to, darling girl.'

'Why?' I tried to keep the whine out of my voice, but I knew it was there. We weren't looking at each other, but watching the couples on the dance floor. Mrs Cartwright kept turning her head to stare at us. 'Is it because of her?'

He gave a short laugh. 'Not entirely.'

I was, once again, bewildered. 'What are you doing in Berlin? You said you were going to Spain.'

'Mm.' Amyas inserted his fingers between mine and I felt that same rush of desire. 'We're in Berlin because she has business here. She's put money into armaments. A lot of money.'

'She'll lose it in the long run,' I said spitefully.

Amyas grinned. 'I know.'

The band was playing the *Merry Widow* waltz and I looked at Charlie, who was falling over Xanthe's feet as he attempted to dance. He was so decent. I knew he'd asked her to dance so that there would be a chance for Amyas and me to talk in private. The trouble was that I didn't want to talk. I wanted to rage and scream and cry buckets over him and the effort to keep in control was making my whole body tremble.

Biting my lip, I said, 'So what happened to Spain? You got cold feet?'

'No.' Amyas shook his head slowly. 'It just wasn't possible, but I did go to Paris, to the 9th arrondissement. I took Percy.'

'But he said he wouldn't go,' I said, turning to face him. 'He had obligations to his parents.'

Amyas shrugged. 'He wanted to be with Graham. That mattered more.'

'Oh God,' I said bitterly. 'Love mattered more. How very nice for them.'

'Love does matter, darling girl,' Amyas said, almost under his breath, his eyes on the dance floor. 'But sometimes other things get in the way.' He stood up as von Klausen led Mrs Cartwright back to her seat. 'Did you enjoy that, Elvira?'

'I did, lad.' She fanned herself with the pudding menu. 'It's a long time since I enjoyed a whirl around a dance floor and this young man has excellent footwork.'

'Oh he has,' said Xanthe, who had returned with Charlie. 'I love dancing with him.'

Von Klausen gave her a careful smile. 'Thank you, *meine Liebe*.' He picked up the menu and studied it carefully. 'Now, what shall we have for dessert?'

I'd had enough, both of the food and the evening. There had been too many shocks and I needed to be alone in my room to think about them. 'I'm sorry,' I said, 'I have a dreadful headache. Would you mind if I went back to the Adlon?'

Charlie stood up. 'I'll take you.'

'No,' I said, 'I'll get a taxi. You stay and talk. I'll be all right. I probably walked too far today.' I didn't look at Amyas when I said my goodbyes, but Xanthe got up and followed me as I headed towards the lobby.

'Seff,' she said, grabbing my arm. 'If Mummy and Daddy ask about me, tell them not to worry, and if Wolf divorces his wife and we marry, speak up for me. Please.'

I nodded. 'I probably won't see them, but if I do, I will. But, Xanthe, you must do something for me first.'

'Anything!'

'Don't talk about me and Amyas. Don't tell von Klausen or Mrs Cartwright what happened in Cornwall. Promise!'

'I promise,' she said, and gave me a kiss on the cheek.

The taxi ride lasted less than ten minutes, but it felt like hours. I almost ran through the lobby to the lift and once in the privacy of my room, I threw myself on my bed and sobbed. I was in despair. I still wanted him, still felt the same and knew that I always would. But he didn't care. He had moved on. I was a summer's fling.

I was still lying on my bed, in my beautiful sea-green gown, two hours later when the knock came on my door. It'll be Charlie, I thought, wearily. Come to see if I'm all right. Maybe, if I don't answer, he'll think I'm asleep. But the knock persisted and dragging a hand across my tear-stained face I got up and went to the door. 'I'll see you in the morning, Charlie. I'm all right,' I said as I opened the door.

'But you're not,' said the man waiting in the corridor. And while I stood with my mouth open and my heart fluttering, Amyas walked in and took me in his arms.

Chapter Nine

'What d'you want,' I said tremulously.

'I want you.' His voice was heavy with desire as he led me to the bed and tore off my dress. 'I will always want you, Persephone. Don't doubt me on that.' And we made love; serious, passionate love, which left my whole body tingling from the feel of his hands and his beautiful body. I didn't hold back. Why would I when this was what I'd yearned for, all these months? I was as abandoned as I'd ever been, touching and holding and guiding him into me as though I was sucking the very life out of him.

And afterwards, when we lay back and gazed at the smooth plasterwork ceiling of the Hotel Adlon, I permitted myself a smile. He wanted me. That's all I needed to know.

'God, Persephone, you are wonderful.' He said it as though he meant it.

'Yes,' I said, feeling suddenly that our roles had irrevocably changed. 'I am.'

He laughed. 'I thought you'd throw me out.'

Did he sound sorry? No. Amyas never admitted that he'd done anything wrong. I looked at him, lying naked on my narrow hotel bed, with me squeezed up against the wall. Moonlight shone through the window on to his body and he was just as I'd remembered. Utterly perfect. Skin wonderfully smooth, without any blemishes, and his torso flat and impeccably muscled. And then there was his film star face and his thick, black hair, now tousled and lying untidily over his forehead. In the Kaiserhof it had been brushed smoothly back, which had given him a gaucho look, as though at any moment he would break into a tango. Now, in my bed, he was the Amyas of Cornwall. My lover who'd come out of the sea. My pirate king.

'I might throw you out, some time,' I said, though part of me simply refused to believe that.

'Good.' He pulled me to him. 'I like you tough. It suits you.'

'Can you stay?' I asked, after a while.

'Until the morning.' He rolled over. 'The injection will knock her out for quite a while.'

I wondered about that, but only briefly, and, exhausted by passion, I was soon asleep. But when I awoke at dawn, with the pale light sneaking through the small windows, I thought about the drugged Mrs Cartwright and her relationship with Amyas.

'What are you thinking of?'

His voice made me jump. I'd thought he was still asleep. 'What d'you think,' I said and he laughed softly and, pushing his knee between my legs, lowered his mouth on to mine. Later, sitting up in bed, while Amyas lay with his head turned towards the window, I asked him about her. 'Do you sleep with her?'

'I have,' he said. 'But not for some time.' He gave a short laugh. 'She likes to show me off. Like an expensive pet.'

'How can you bear it?'

'Easily,' he answered. 'She's very generous. I'm a kept

man, and kept very well most of the time. Now and then she can be mean and sometimes, when the mood takes her, she leaves me short. Then I have to rely on my own devices.'

'You stole my father's books.'

'Yes, I did.' The lack of concern in his voice shocked me and I turned my head to look at him. He was lying with his eyes open and a faint smile on his lips. 'They're quite rare volumes and the bookseller on the Charing Cross Road was thrilled to see them.' Amyas broadened his smile into a grin. 'We struck a good deal.'

'But that makes you a thief.'

'I suppose it does, my darling, but at the time it was necessary. I had no money and I needed to get away.' He frowned, thinking. 'The books were still in the shop last time I was there. Your father could easily buy them back. The amount would be nothing to him.'

I'll buy them back, I thought, and send them to Father and that would be one less thing for the parents to have over me. An unsuitable lover was one thing but a lover who was also a thief . . .

'You were lucky that my father didn't go to the police.'

Amyas said nothing. He knew as well as I did that my parents would do anything to avoid scandal. He looked at me. 'What have you been doing since the summer?'

Should I tell him? Should I cry and say that I spent three precious months carrying our unborn child and then tell him about the abortion forced on me by my mother? And how the surgeon bungled it and about how a few days later I nearly died of blood loss. Of the blood running out of me which wouldn't stop, and having to crawl on my hands and knees to the telephone. How to explain about the ambulance men running up the stairs and hammering on my door and then breaking in because I was too weak to open it? What could I tell him about the starchy disapproval of the nurses in the private hospital where I had the blood transfusion and spent my time weeping? No. I couldn't tell him any of it.

'I bought a flat,' was all I said. 'In Belgravia. I live there now.'

He nodded. 'I thought last night that you seemed to have grown up. You are a lovely woman, Persephone. Don't let anyone tell you otherwise. Particularly your silly little sister.' He sighed. 'She's swimming in dangerous waters.'

'Xanthe can't swim,' I said, thinking back to our childhood. 'She's never been able to.'

'Then she'll drown.'

A clock struck somewhere in the city and then another one. 'I have to get up,' I said. 'I don't know what Charlie's got planned for today but I want to go with him. I need to get in on this assignment properly.'

'Are you sleeping with him?' Amyas got out of bed and stood, naked, looking out of my small window at the view down Unter den Linden.

'No,' I laughed, dragging on my dressing gown and getting my wash bag. The bathroom was down the corridor. 'Obviously not. There's barely room for two in this bed, let alone three.'

'I like him,' Amyas nodded. 'He's one of the good guys.'

We ate breakfast in the dining room, Amyas oblivious to the other guests staring at his dinner jacket. Indeed, when he leant over to the next table to ask for their glass dish of plum jam, the woman fluttered a smile and the man beamed, 'Of course, sir,' and gave a deferential little bow. I shook my head and laughed to myself. He gives off an air of nobility, I thought. How does he do it?

'What d'you think of Berlin?' he asked, while the waiter poured more coffee into his cup.

I waited until he had gone before answering in a lowered voice. 'The buildings are magnificent and most of the people seem to be healthy and happy, but I think it's a different place for some. The uncertainty is all a bit frightening.' I looked around the dining room at the stout, cheerful people tucking into large breakfasts of sausage and hard-boiled eggs and at the friendly waiters for whom nothing seemed to be too much trouble. 'If you based an opinion on what you see here, you'd think Berlin is a wonderful city, but yesterday I went to an address off Auguststrasse . . .'

Amyas put his cup down so quickly that some of the coffee slopped into the saucer. 'Auguststrasse? Why the hell did you go there?'

'I had a message to deliver. From my neighbour at home.' I frowned. 'Not that it's any of your business. Anyway, he wanted me to take some money to his sister so that she and her daughter could leave Germany and come to London to live with him.' I looked over my shoulder to see if anyone was listening before saying, 'They're Jewish.'

'Of course they are,' Amyas said angrily. 'You shouldn't have gone. It's a wonder you weren't stopped.'

'I was.' I couldn't resist gloating. 'By the police. Or, at least, I think they were the police. I gave them the slip.'

I thought back to yesterday morning and gave an involuntary shiver. 'But, Amyas, it was frightening. The place is horrible, with boarded-up buildings and dreadful words written on the walls. And Mrs Goldstein says she won't leave. She says it will all blow over and that because she's a teacher she must stay with her girls.'

'She's mad.' He said the words bleakly as if they were a fact, not an opinion. 'It will get worse.' He picked up his coffee cup. 'Don't go there again.'

'I won't. I've promised Charlie.'

'Is that my name I hear taken in vain?' Charlie joined us at the table. He was dressed for work in his dusty grey suit with his trench coat slung over his arm. He nodded to the waiter, who brought him a cup and poured coffee. 'I've already had breakfast,' he said, giving me a quizzical look. 'I thought you'd join me but I see you've got more exciting company.'

Was I being reproved? I didn't know, but I did feel my cheeks beginning to glow.

'We've been catching up on old times,' Amyas said. 'And I've been hearing about Persephone's activities here in Berlin.'

Charlie changed the subject rather abruptly. 'What are you doing in this city, Mr Troy?'

'Oh, this and that. Mrs Cartwright has contacts here whom she needs to meet.'

'What contacts?' Charlie leant forward.

Amyas laughed. 'Quite the newshound, isn't he, Persephone?' He wiped his mouth with his napkin and stood up. 'You'll excuse me. I have things to do and I know you have too.' He bent and kissed me on the cheek. 'Goodbye.' The rest of the farewell was muttered in my ear, for me alone. 'I'll see you tonight, darling girl.'

Charlie and I watched him walk out of the dining room. People turned to stare, and Amyas smiled at one or two and stopped to shake hands with a rather plump man in uniform who was just coming in through the door. 'My God,' said Charlie, 'that's Hermann Göring. How the hell does he know him?'

'You met Heydrich last night,' I shrugged. 'Some might ask, in a year or so, how the hell do you know him? What's the difference?'

'I don't know, Blake, but there is one.'

In the taxi on the way to a press conference, Charlie said, 'So is it all on again with Troy?'

I shrugged. I didn't know the answer and even thinking about it made me uncomfortable.

'Well?' he insisted.

'We're ships that pass in the night,' I muttered, trying to seem casual, but as soon as the words were out of my mouth I knew how stupid I sounded.

Charlie laughed. 'From the look of you both,' he said, 'I'd hazard a guess that those ships docked last night.'

I blushed again and my face stayed like that for the short distance down the Wilhelmstrasse where we entered the Propaganda Ministry to listen to Joseph Goebbels extolling the virtues of the Third Reich. However, the Reich Minister's message wasn't all sweetness and light.

'The dissidents and terrorists who burned down the Reichstag have been dealt with and over the last few years we've brought law and order to the Fatherland.' Goebbels's words were chilling, as was everything else about him.

I craned my neck to get a better look at him: a small, narrow-faced man, who had limped when he walked into the room and who seemed to command the obedience of his staff with the slightest turn of his head. He was the most important man in Germany, after Hitler, and, from what I'd read, the most devoted to the elimination of dissidents. When questions were invited from the floor, I prayed that Charlie wouldn't speak. I didn't want the spotlight to be turned anywhere near us. But, of course, Charlie did.

'Dr Goebbels,' he called out, 'does the German air force intend to bomb any more towns in Spain?'

There was a collective gasp around the room as the journalists acknowledged the impoliteness of Charlie's question.

Goebbels was never going to answer.

I watched his face darken and he put up one finger to summon an aide. A short, whispered conversation ensued before the minister looked back to the gathered journalists and to Charlie in particular. 'A more relevant question please, gentlemen.'

A succession of polite and desultory questions were proffered about the new buildings, and why was the Klosterstrasse underground station partially closed? 'We're constantly updating our infrastructure,' was the reply. What I learned later was that Hitler, already with all-out war on his mind, had demanded that air-raid shelters must be built and the underground stations were the obvious choice.

As we walked out of the building at the end of the meeting, I noticed that we were being watched by the official that Dr Goebbels had spoken to. I pointed him out to Charlie.

'Yes, I can see him,' he said. 'I expected it and I know I should have kept my mouth shut. But that man is a reptile and I wanted to make him uncomfortable. It was stupid and unprofessional of me and that might make what we have to do this afternoon more difficult.'

'What?' I was excited.

'Come on,' he said. 'Let's get some lunch and I'll tell you.'

Over Wiener schnitzel and beer, he told me what he'd planned. 'I've arranged to meet someone at the university, but at the same time I've made an appointment to interview one of the professors. We'll start off talking to her together and then I'll excuse myself to go to the lavatory and you can carry on talking to her. She speaks excellent English, by the way.'

'And you'll meet your contact?'

'Yes, I hope so. Our watcher might stay with you, he'll think that I'm only going to be away for a moment and that will be true. My contact will be handing over a dossier of information. How we get it out of Germany is another problem, but we'll think about that later.'

At two o'clock we walked down Unter den Linden to the Humboldt University. 'It was from here that the books were taken for burning four years ago,' said Charlie, as we walked across the plaza in front of the grand building. 'Since then they've sacked all their Jewish professors and students. It's a haven for Nazis, but there are a few lecturers left who've kept their sympathies quiet. This fellow I'm hoping to see is leaving soon, but he wants the world to know what's going on. It's our duty to report it. Having evidence will be so much better than simple hearsay.'

'And who am I meeting?' I asked. I felt nervous.

'Oh,' Charlie grinned, 'she's a doozy. Professor Helga Waldorf. She has the chair of ethnic studies. And, from what I've read, she's quite mad.'

That last didn't reassure me and I could feel my feet dragging as I followed Charlie up the stairs to the professor's department. I looked down as we turned on the half-landing and I could see our watcher coming up the stairs on the floor below.

'He's still with us,' I muttered.

'Yes, I guessed he would be,' Charlie sighed. 'This is going to be difficult.'

The professor was waiting for us when we were shown into her office, standing, hands on hips, beside her enormous oak desk. 'Good afternoon to you, Mr Bradford.' She looked at me with piercing blue eyes. 'And this young woman is . . . ?'

I stepped forward before Charlie could introduce me, I determined not to be intimidated, and said, 'Persephone Blake, Mr Bradford's assistant. How d'you do?' For a moment she looked rather taken aback, at my boldness I suppose, then she nodded and indicated a chair against the wall where I was to sit. Charlie sat in the chair opposite her.

'So,' Professor Waldorf opened the interview. 'You wish to know about my research. Yes?'

'Indeed,' said Charlie. 'I've read something of your work, on eugenics and the like. I'm interested in how you came to your conclusions.'

She smiled, showing large, horsey teeth, and slapped her hands down on her desk. 'It was easy,' she whinnied. 'Look around the world and you can see which are the inferior races. They have made no progress in a thousand years. They remain Stone Age peoples.'

'And you take no account of climate, availability of food, water or natural resources?' Charlie's question, though mild and delivered gently, received a decisive shake of the head.

'It is not necessary, Mr Bradford. We have done experiments on some of our subjects. Submitted them to tests and brain examinations. My theory is proved every time. Let me explain further.'

I sat quietly, taking notes as they continued with the interview, not only on what the professor said, but on her appearance. She was the very epitome of German womanhood; her thick, faded blonde hair was severely parted along the centre of her large head and wound into plaited circles beside her ears. She wore a brown skirt and jacket over a cream blouse, which almost looked like a uniform, right down to her laced-up brown shoes. I gazed around the room and was struck by the large framed portrait of the Führer. She had draped a red cloth over the frame at the top and put a little laurel wreath above it. It looked almost like a shrine. There could be no doubt where her allegiance lay.

Suddenly Charlie stood up. 'I'm very sorry, Professor, will you excuse me for a moment. I need to find the toilet.'

She looked surprised but said, 'Of course, Mr Bradford. It's at the end of the corridor.'

I stayed in my chair and gave her an embarrassed little smile. 'Mr Bradford has not been too well this week,' I said. 'I think it was something he ate on the train here.'

She shrugged her hefty shoulders. 'It happens, Fräulein,'

she said, rearranging the papers on her desk into neat piles, and looked at me again. 'So. What is it that you do in London?'

'I'm training to be a journalist,' I answered and allowed a breathy quality into my voice. I hoped I sounded eager, although still at a learning stage. 'This is my first foreign assignment.'

'And your education?'

'I read English at London University.'

'Good. Young women should be educated.' She gave me her horsey smile. 'You come from an academic family?'

'No,' I laughed. 'Not really. My father studies Ancient Greece, but that is his private occupation. My mother and sister don't have the slightest interest in learning.'

She nodded. 'Many women are the same. You have to fight to get anywhere in this world, even in Germany. It is a man's world. But I hope you've been able to see something of our wonderful city?'

'Oh yes,' I said. 'I'm hugely impressed.'

'And had some fun, yes?'

'Mr Bradford and I went to a dance at the Kaiserhof hotel last night. That was fun.' I thought of Amyas and how I'd seen him across the dance floor, and then I thought of him in my bed at the Adlon. I almost laughed out loud. Now *that* had been hugely enjoyable.

'Ach, yes. I think some of the most prominent people in the government were there. I didn't attend. To me this ballroom dancing is decadent. The music is written by inferior races, is it not? I would, instead, prefer to encourage folk dancing. It combines healthy exercise and a display of our culture . . . but my views are not always followed.' She sighed and settled her muscular rear end more firmly in her chair. 'At the Kaiserhof, did you meet anyone important?'

'I met a Count von Klausen. He seemed to be quite important.'

To my astonishment Professor Waldorf gave her whinnying laugh. 'Ach, young Wolf. He's very well known. He was my student you know and quite a naughty boy! None of my ladies was safe.' She calmed down. 'He's grown up now. Married into old Prussian nobility and is a rising star in the SS.'

I decided to pretend to confide in her. She obviously liked to gossip and it would cover the lengthening time that Charlie was taking. 'I'm sorry to hear that he's married, Professor. He brought my young sister as his guest and she seemed quite struck on him.' I bit my lip. 'Oh dear,' I whispered in mock despair, 'I don't think she knows that he's married.'

'Well,' said the professor severely, 'you must tell her immediately that he's only having a bit of fun with her. He will never leave his wife. Oh, no. The countess is part of the establishment and her family is very close to . . .' She nodded towards the portrait of Hitler. 'I won't say more. Now,' she looked at her watch. 'I have a seminar very soon. Where is Mr Bradford?'

'Shall I go and look for him?' I stood up and edged towards the door.

'No. I will.' She heaved herself up and, reaching the door in a few strides, flung it open. The watcher who was standing in the corridor looked up, startled by the abrupt noise and at her sudden, emphatic appearance. Professor Helga gave him a withering stare. 'Who are you? What do you want?' she demanded. At least I thought that was what she said, because the conversation was held in German and I only gathered a few words.

'Herr Professor Braun,' the man stuttered. 'I'm looking for him.'

'Chemistry or Law?'

'Chemistry,' answered the watcher. I knew from his face that he'd hazarded a guess.

'Wrong building. Go down the stairs and across the *Platz*.' She pointed to the staircase. 'Off you go.'

He had no choice and I watched as, with a last look down the corridor towards the closed door, he walked reluctantly down the stairs and out of sight.

'Now, we find Mr Bradford,' the professor said, but at that moment Charlie appeared through the door at the end of the corridor. His face was pale, I thought, and rather grim-looking.

'My profound apologies, Frau Professor,' he said.

I butted in quickly. 'I told Professor Waldorf that you haven't been very well.'

She frowned at him. 'You should go back to your hotel, Herr Bradford, and lie down. And sadly, I can give you no more time. My students are expected directly.'

'Thank you,' Charlie said gratefully. 'Despite its being curtailed, our discussion has been very useful. I'll make sure that your position is explained fully in my article.'

'Good.' She shook his hand and then as I followed him she caught my arm. 'Tell your sister to go home. It is wrong for her to divert Count von Klausen from his duty.'

'Yes,' I nodded and closed the door behind me as we left. A group of students were waiting in the corridor as another group emerged from another room. I noticed a small middle-aged man come out of the door from which Charlie had emerged earlier and mingle with the students who were going downstairs. In the veritable scrum he vanished almost instantly. We followed more slowly.

'Are you all right?' I asked. 'You looked awful when you came out of the toilet.'

'You'd look awful if you'd heard what I just have. About concentration camps and sudden arrests. Medical experiments on live patients without anaesthetic. God, it's disgusting.'

The sun had come out as we walked back up Unter den Linden and the city glowed. I could smell coffee and cinnamon buns in the air. What Charlie had said seemed almost unbelievable. 'Have you got any proof?' I asked. 'Without it . . .'

'I've got names and dates and places,' said Charlie, patting his jacket. I could see a bulge. 'I can check it, but I don't think I've been given duff information. It's red-hot stuff.'

We walked on further, past the dress shop and I looked in the window. The helpful girl was there, arranging a midnight-blue evening gown on a dummy, and when I smiled at her she gave me a cheerful wave.

'What was that about Xanthe?' Charlie asked as we walked into the lobby.

'I'll tell you later,' I said. 'At supper. Where are we going, by the way?'

'I don't know,' he said. 'Let's meet in the bar here, at about seven thirty, and go on from there. Will that do?'

'Fine,' I said.

'I'm going to phone the paper.' Charlie walked towards

the bank of telephones which stood in the corridor beside the reception desk. 'I need to find out what our esteemed editor thinks of what we've done so far.' He grinned at me. 'I'll tell him you've been brilliant. Couldn't have managed without you.'

'Thanks,' I said, and went towards the lift. The door was just closing when a young girl slid in. It was Kitty Goldstein.

Chapter Ten

'Kitty!' I was astonished and at the same time concerned that she had come into the centre of Berlin.

'Please, Fräulein Blake, do not be angry with me for disturbing you at your hotel. I have to speak with you.' Her young face was creased with worry and I took her hand and gave it a squeeze.

'I'm not angry, Kitty. But isn't it difficult for you to come here? Does your mother know?'

Kitty shook her head. 'I got a lift in with Isaac, the baker. He makes bread for this hotel. It is not talked about but his bread is the best. He will come back for me in an hour. I waited for you in the lobby, only ten minutes. Mamma thinks I am having supper with my friend, Rakel.'

The lift stopped at my floor and I held Kitty back while I looked out to see if there was anyone watching. The corridor was empty and I led her to my room where she immediately went to the window and looked out. 'Oh,' she said excitedly. 'I can see so much. Look!'

'I've seen it,' I laughed. 'And I've walked down Unter den Linden several times.'

'You are . . . fortunate, is that the word?'

'Yes, I suppose I am fortunate, here in Germany. But in England everyone can go where they want to. London is a wonderful city with as many museums and galleries as there are in Berlin. And you would be able to go into them whenever you wanted. You and your mother would be so much happier.' I smiled at her. 'Your Uncle Jacob is a nice man. He would make a good life for you both.'

'I know, but . . .' Kitty's smile had faded and she heaved a sigh. 'Mamma, she has doubts. We should stay here, she says, we will be all right – but I don't think so. I am frightened.'

I was quiet for a moment, then I took her hand. 'You must try again, Kitty. You must persuade your mamma to use Jacob's money to leave Berlin. You're already in danger and it'll only get worse.'

Tears welled up in the girl's eyes and she held a small, embroidered handkerchief to her face. 'I have tried, Fräulein Blake,' she sobbed, 'but she will not hear me. Only you can tell her. I beg you. Please, come to our flat again.'

Oh God, I thought, dismayed with the whole situation and guiltily wishing I hadn't got involved in the first place. I can't go to that district again. I've promised, not only Charlie, but Amyas as well. But the girl looked at me, her brown eyes large and full of pleading, and I knew that I wouldn't turn her down. 'I'll try to get to you, Kitty,' I said cautiously. 'But I'm being followed most of the time by the police, I think, or the SS. I might bring more danger to you and your mother if I come to your home. Let me think about it and decide what I can do, but it will have to be soon, because I've only got one more day here in Berlin.'

She nodded and wiped her eyes, while my mind worked furiously to try and engineer some sort of a plan. We'd need to meet in a neutral place.

'Is there a park you know, here in the city? One that you and your mother would be allowed to go into?'

Kitty was looking out of the window again. She seemed fascinated by the view but she turned her head. 'Sometimes,' she said. 'We go to Monbijoupark. It is near the river and near the synagogue and there is a museum. It is very nice.'

'All right,' I said, making up my mind. 'Tell me a place at the park where we can meet.'

'By the museum steps?'

'Fine,' I answered, with a smile, although I didn't feel like smiling. 'You be there, with Mamma, at three o'clock tomorrow afternoon and if I can get rid of the men following me, I'll join you. But, Kitty, if I'm not there, it's because I think it's too dangerous. For both of us, I mean.'

She smiled, lighting up the room with her pretty, girlish face. It is all too cruel, I thought, and went over and gave her a hug.

'Thank you . . . Seffy.' She said my name shyly and as I pulled away she buttoned her green cloth coat and pulling out a knitted beret from her pocket, placed it on her dark curls. 'Now,' she said, 'I must go.'

I went to the door first and looked out. The corridor was empty. 'Be careful,' I said, and she smiled.

'I will go down in the service lift to the kitchen. Isaac will be waiting for me. Do not worry, I will be all right.' And with a kiss on both my cheeks she ran lightly down the corridor and round the corner, to where the big double-door service lift halted.

I did worry though and was still thinking about the plan I'd devised when I met Charlie in the bar later on.

'Here you are at last, Blake,' he said and pushed over a Martini. 'I've been waiting for you.'

'We said half past seven.' I looked at my watch. 'I'm on time.'

'Yes, I know.' He looked over his shoulder and moved closer to me. We were sitting on high stools next to the bar and the room was crowded with early evening drinkers. A pianist in the centre of the floor was playing hit songs, but it was difficult to hear the music properly because of the loud chatter and clinking of glasses. Charlie lowered his voice and muttered, 'It's that stuff I got this afternoon. I've been going through it and, I have to say, it's dynamite. Places, names, dates. If we can get it back safely, it must go straight to the government. They'll have to take notice.'

'Aren't they taking notice now?' I asked.

'Some of them are. But those out of government are more interested. Churchill has been warning about this for ages. D'you know? I think I'll take this dossier to him instead. He won't shove it under the carpet.' Charlie swigged back his drink and nodded to the barman, indicating that he wanted another. 'You?' he asked.

I shook my head. 'Not yet. I've only had a sip.' I shot a glance at him. 'Go easy, Charlie. How many have you had already?'

'Telling me off, Blake, eh? I don't remember telling you that it was part of your job.'

'Well, you seem a bit high this evening.'

'Mm, maybe.' Charlie nodded. 'You're right. I got excited when I was reading what that bloke gave me. I'll calm down now. I don't know what it is about this trip, I keep losing my normal control.' He gave me a grin.

'It's having you with me, Blake. There's something about you . . . don't know what it is. You seem to make things happen.'

I shook my head, dismissing what he said, but my plans for meeting Kitty and her mother were sitting uncomfortably in my mind. I knew I should tell him, but I also knew what he would say. Charlie, although usually mild in temper, had been furious with me for going to Auguststrasse and hadn't held back in letting me know. 'What are we doing tomorrow?' I asked, praying that he had set up a meeting with someone in the afternoon.

'That's the thing, Blake, I spoke to Geoff. I couldn't say a lot to him because I'm not sure how much is being overheard. But our editor was pleased with what I was able to tell him and he said that if we take photographs he'll give the article a double-page spread. So, you've got your camera and I thought that tomorrow we could have a wander around the city and take some snaps. It will round off the assignment nicely. What d'you say?'

What could I say? Absolutely nothing. I nodded 'Yes,' and momentarily closed my eyes. Poor Kitty and Sarah, I thought. They'll wait for me in vain.

A voice intruded on my musings. 'Darling! What the hell are you doing here?' It was Xanthe. She was exquisite, in a black and white sheath dress with a tiny black cocktail hat perched at a slant on her blonde curls.

'We're staying here,' I said impatiently. 'I told you last night.' She was almost the last person I wanted to see, but I gave her a sisterly kiss.

'Of course you did. Silly me,' Xanthe cooed and moved closer to Charlie. 'Hello you,' she giggled and pecked at his cheek. He looked as though he'd been bitten, but, remembering his manners, asked, 'Can I get you a drink?'

'Thank you, darling. Gin and It, please.'

'So, what are you doing here?' I returned the question. 'Are you alone?'

'God, no,' she laughed. 'I'm here with Wolf. He's over there.' She pointed to the other end of the bar, where I could see him, immaculately smart, chatting with a middle-aged man. 'He's talking to the Minister of War.'

Charlie looked eagerly in that direction, thinking, I knew, about whether he should go over and introduce himself.

'I saw you, and Wolf said I must come over. He'll join us in a moment.'

'Where are you staying?' I wondered why I hadn't asked that question last night and rather berated myself for being so uninterested in my sister's affairs.

'I'm at the Kaiserhof. It's quite good, you know, but not as smart as the Adlon. I might transfer.' Xanthe gazed at the well-dressed people who were sitting and standing in groups and gossiping loudly over drinks. 'Yes, I think I will.' She didn't bother to lower her voice when she said, 'Some of the guests at the Kaiserhof are not what we're used to, you know. Wolf says they're all very loyal but,' she twitched her shoulders, 'they're a bit, well, provincial, I suppose.' She gave me a smirk. 'Your particular friend is on the same floor as me at the Kaiserhof. Him and that common little person he travels with. My God, you should see her in the dining room, gobbling her food and waving her knife and fork around in a way that would have made our nanny faint.' She giggled. 'Your friend doesn't seem to mind her, though. He's very

attentive. Of course they're always surrounded by officers and government people. Wolf says that she's a good
friend of Herr Hitler and will bring us more friends from
England.'

'Us?' I questioned.

She had the grace to blush. 'I'm only saying what Wolf
says.' She gave a little pout. 'Don't be mean, Seffy.'

Charlie, sensing a row brewing, butted in. 'How long
are you staying in Berlin?' he asked.

'Oh, I don't know.' She gave a smile. 'Wolf doesn't
want me to leave, but I was thinking about joining Binkie
Durham's house party in Suffolk. I'm going to try and
persuade Wolf to come with me. And then, Christmas is
coming up and the parents will want me home for that.'
She bent her head towards Charlie and cooed. 'Now that
Seffy has blotted her copybook, there has to be one
daughter they can rely on.'

Bitch, I thought, but pretended that I wasn't listening.

I let my eyes wander about, but it was only after a
few seconds of peering about that I realised I was looking
for Amyas. Would he come here? Would he come to my
room later? The pianist was playing 'The Very Thought
of You', and as the strands of music floated across I almost
laughed out loud. How could he know?

I could see von Klausen making his way across the
room to join us, and turning to Charlie, I said, 'Have you
thought about where we can eat dinner?' Suddenly, I
wanted to get away from this noisy place and most of
all from Xanthe and her frightening friend.

'Oh,' Charlie sounded surprised. 'Er, all right. Let me
see.'

But it was too late. Von Klausen had arrived and within

seconds had invited us to dinner with him and Xanthe. 'We will go to Horcher's. I booked a table when I saw you were here. You have no other plans?'

I wanted to say yes, but Charlie looked eager and I remembered that I was here on an assignment. I gave myself a little shake. I was letting my personal life interfere with my job and I had wanted this job so much.

Horcher's was small. Beneath the heavily beamed ceiling there was only room for about eight or ten tables, and after the crush in the Adlon's cocktail bar it was quiet. The maître d' greeted von Klausen as a welcome and favoured customer and, on our short way to our table, several people got up to shake the count's hand.

'This is good, yes?' Von Klausen smiled at us, flattening his lips over his perfect teeth, but his chalk-blue eyes remained cold.

'It's very nice,' I agreed. 'Very intimate.'

'A good word,' von Klausen agreed. 'Herr Horcher is very careful about his clientele.' He examined the menu. 'Now. What shall we have?'

The meal was excellent, but it soon became apparent that we had been invited so that von Klausen could find out more about Charlie and me. 'I have read some of your articles, Mr Bradford. You are a much travelled man.'

'It's the nature of my job,' answered Charlie casually. He was tucking into medallions of beef.

'You have been twice to Spain, recently.'

Charlie frowned. 'Yes, earlier in the year. And I was in China and France and Romania. I go where there is a story.'

'So. There is a story in Berlin?'

'Oh yes.' Charlie's frown changed into a broad smile. 'I'd say.'

'And you will tell it truthfully?' It sounded more like an order than a question. As always, in the presence of von Klausen I felt uncomfortable. I shifted in my seat and looked around at the other diners. They were working their way steadily through each delicious dish set in front of them, and only at the table where four SS officers sat was there any laughter. One of them called for another bottle of wine and his voice was so loud that von Klausen glanced away from his polite interrogation. Excusing himself, he stood up and walked across to them. I don't know what was said, but the laughter stopped, and from the careful smile on his face as he returned, it was clear that he'd enjoyed throwing his weight about.

'I apologise,' he said, 'for that display of bad manners.'

I felt reckless. 'They weren't bothering me,' I said. 'I like to see people having fun.'

'And having it yourself, Miss Blake, so I believe.'

I shot a quick glance at Xanthe. Had she told him about me and Amyas after she promised not to? I was ready to kill her, but the rather vacant look on her face assured me that she wasn't the guilty party. That left Amyas. It must have been him. Oh God. How could he?

'You're quite wrong, Wolf,' said Xanthe pityingly. 'My sister doesn't approve of fun. She likes reading and going to museums and all that sort of boring stuff. She never goes to parties.'

'Ah, perhaps I've got it wrong, *meine Liebe*. Fräulein Persephone is the good girl in the family? Yes?'

Xanthe laughed and wagged her finger at him. 'Does that make me the bad girl?'

He smiled. 'No, *Liebchen*. You are good, in a different way.'

We had chocolate torte for dessert, but I couldn't eat more than a couple of forkfuls. I was thinking about Amyas telling von Klausen about us and determining that if he dared to come to my room tonight I would throw him out. But three hours later when the knock came at my door, I did let him in.

'Don't come near me,' I hissed.

'Why? What's happened?'

'You told von Klausen about us.'

He shook his head and casually took off his dinner jacket and threw it over the chair in front of the small dressing table. 'I told no one about us.'

'You must have,' I wailed. 'He knew, but not from Xanthe. I'm certain she hadn't told him. So how else could he have found out?'

Amyas sat on the bed and started to pull off his bow tie. He was frowning, his handsome face creased and his usual half-smile gone. 'I think,' he said slowly, 'it was Elvira. She's had her suspicions about me and it would be typical of her to bribe your mother's private detective to discover why I was being investigated. She generally finds a way to corrupt. Money, or lack of it, is a great inducement.'

I couldn't look at him. 'That's why you stole my father's books.'

He nodded. 'She cut off my allowance. The money from the books got me to Paris and I could have carried on but,' he shrugged, 'only in a poor sort of way.'

'What about principle?' I asked. 'You told Percy that it was more important than his obligations to his family.

You gave the impression that it mattered more than anything.'

Back to his normal relaxed self, he was unbuttoning his shirt. 'Well, darling Persephone, it seems that I haven't quite enough. I like to eat well and sleep in a bed.'

'God! You are a bastard.' I stood by the window, not going near him. He was worthless, unprincipled; everything that I normally despised. But when he walked over to me and kissed me I was lost again and allowed him to take me to bed, where I sank into that blissfully addictive magic of passion.

Later, we talked. First, about Percy and Graham. 'Do you know what's happened to them?' I asked.

'I knew a few months ago, though now I have no idea. Graham was already in Spain by the time Percy and I went to Paris. We met the organisers at a small hotel and signed up for the International Brigade.' He laughed. 'You wouldn't like them, Persephone. They're communists, anarchists and all sorts of odd people. Although, they probably do have an abiding principle, which you would like. Our organiser introduced us to a girl who was tasked to get us through France and on to a boat at Marseilles. Elena, that was her name.' He shook his head, remembering. 'She couldn't have been much more than seventeen and was so very pretty. But, my God, she was devoted to the cause and fierce in her hatred of the Nationalists. Percy was scared of her.'

'Were you?' I was stupidly jealous.

'No.' He sounded surprised at my question. 'I knew I could tame her.'

I lay in the curl of his arm and thought about him

'taming' the pretty Elena. I knew how he'd have done it. 'So you left Percy with this wildcat girl?

'I did,' he replied casually. 'When they got on the train to Marseilles at the Gare de Lyon I left that station and went to the Gare du Nord and took the boat train for home.' He chuckled. 'I bet Percy went looking for me through all the carriages.'

'God, you're cruel,' I said.

'Am I? I took him to Paris. That wasn't cruel. He wanted to go on. He believed, as I do, in the cause.' Amyas turned his head and stared at me. 'Would you rather I was there or here?' he asked.

'That's not fair,' I said.

'Nothing in life is fair. Not from the moment you're born. You have to even it out in the best way you can.' The words came out heartfelt, but bitterly, and I was lost for an answer. He was right, of course. Life for some wasn't fair. I thought about Kitty and her mother; their life was already hellish and would get worse.

'Amyas,' I whispered. 'I'm going to meet Kitty and Sarah Goldstein tomorrow afternoon.'

He sat up. 'No. You can't go to Auguststrasse again. It's too dangerous for you.'

'I know that. I've arranged to meet them at Monbijoupark at three o'clock, by the museum. That is, if I can get away from Charlie. He wants us to spend the day taking photographs for a picture spread.' I thought for a moment. 'It's important, Amyas. I must try and persuade Sarah to leave for England. Can you see that?'

'I can see that you would put them in even more danger if you were followed. Which you most likely would be. It's madness. Promise me you won't go.

Promise.' He had turned and was gripping my shoulders.

'All right,' I whispered miserably. 'I promise.' And he lowered his mouth on to mine and the conversation was ended.

At dawn he got up and started dressing. 'Where does she think you go to?' I asked, rubbing the sleep from my eyes. 'Your Mrs Cartwright.'

'She doesn't wake up before I come back,' he smiled. 'The morphine keeps her well sedated.'

'Is she a drug addict?' I asked, shocked.

'Oh yes,' he grinned. 'Part of my role in her life is finding a constant supply for her.' He noticed my frown. 'Not very edifying, I agree. But one does what one has to.'

I watched as he pulled on his trousers and fastened his shirt buttons. 'I won't see you tonight,' I said. 'We're getting the evening train. We'll be back in London tomorrow.'

His face fell and I could see that he was genuinely upset. 'I'll miss you, darling girl. Life is empty when you're not around.' He came over to the bed and kissed me.

'You could come and see me at my flat,' I said. 'I told you the address.'

'Yes,' he said, 'although . . .'

'Although what?'

'Nothing.' Gently he stroked my face and I could feel the enchantment sweeping over me. 'We'll be together again, Persephone. I don't know when but we will.'

'Yes,' I nodded, my heart bursting. I wanted to grab hold of him and cry that he mustn't leave. I wanted to take him back with me to the house by the sea and abandon myself to the careless bliss of passion, but I knew it was only a hopeless dream. Amyas marched to a different beat, only sometimes in step with me; so, instead, I bit my lip and watched him finish dressing.

'Amyas,' I called as he walked to the door. 'What's your real name?'

He shook his head and grinned in his devastating way. 'Too soon to tell you that, my darling.' And he shut the door behind him, leaving me alone once more.

I joined Charlie for breakfast and he could see from my face that I was upset. 'You'll see him again,' he said kindly, and I nodded. 'I know. It's just that . . .' Then I shook my head. 'It doesn't matter.'

So I drank my coffee, and drawing air into my lungs with a slightly shuddering breath, bent my head to study the map that Charlie had laid out on the table. All the sights that he wanted to photograph were marked and while I was taking the snaps, he would try and interview passers-by to get a flavour of what the man on the street thought.

'All right,' I said cautiously. 'D'you think they'll speak to you, especially when we've got an SS man following us?'

'Don't be defeatist, Blake. You'll never get anywhere with that attitude.'

Reproved, I entered fully into the day's activities. We admired the magnificent Brandenburg Gate and while I shot pictures from different angles, Charlie chatted to people who were on the Platz in front of it. Most shook their heads when he asked questions and hurried on their way, but he got more luck with an old flower seller, who

154

had nothing but greenery on her stall. Surprisingly, she was doing a roaring trade, as customers paid for small branches of pine and fir, some of which had decorative cones hanging from them.

'How is it for you?' Charlie asked her. His German was good. 'Wonderful,' she answered. 'We were starving before these good men took over. My grandsons will have a happy life. Better than me and their father.'

'Write that down,' he said to me, after translating her words. 'We have to make a balanced report.'

I was weary, even before lunch, because we had walked and talked all over the city. As we sat down to eat at my favourite café, he said, 'We need shots of the river. It's the artery of the city.'

I remembered that Kitty had said that Monbijoupark was by the river. 'Good idea,' I answered eagerly, 'and perhaps one or two of a park. I've seen a park on my map near the river.' It was madness, I knew, but there might be just a chance.

The afternoon had become quite murky, with low cloud and rain threatening by the time we reached the park. I looked at my watch, it showed five to three, and as we walked through, I wondered if I should just tell Charlie what I had planned. He'd shout at me, but so what? It was the right thing to do.

'Charlie,' I started, when he interrupted me. 'Look,' he hissed, 'we've gathered another watcher.' Pretending to look for interesting shots of the trees and the river, I swung my camera around and looked through the viewfinder. Two men were walking slowly behind us but, as my lens rested on them, they stopped, turned their faces away and conjured up a conversation. It would be impossible for me to escape them, I knew that now, and looking around I realised that my imagined plan of slipping between the trees was stupid too. Most of them had lost their leaves and stood stark and bare and, even through the rain that was falling now, I would have been easily seen.

'What's that building?' asked Charlie, pointing to what looked like a little eighteenth-century palace.

'I think I read in my guidebook that it's a museum.'

'Well,' said Charlie. He was turning up the collar of his trench coat. 'We'll get a couple of shots of that and then a taxi back to the hotel. I think we've got enough copy now.'

While I was taking photos, I looked for Kitty, but there was no sign of her or her mother. In fact the whole park was almost deserted and I couldn't help feeling relieved. If they hadn't come, it was because they probably thought it too dangerous, and they would have been right. Our followers watched every move we made.

'Let's go,' said Charlie. 'D'you know, Blake, even though I think we've got a good story to tell, I'll be glad to get out of this place.'

In the night as the train hurtled through the fields and forests of northern Germany I finally told Charlie of my plan to meet Kitty and her mother. 'It was supposed to be by that museum in Monbijoupark, but they weren't there.'

'Thank Christ someone saw sense,' he said. And that was all. 'Now, Blake, where's that dossier?'

I sighed. 'Under my clothes. Next to my skin and getting a little sweaty. Must it stay there?'

'Yes, it must. Until we get out of Germany. Then it can go into my bag. It does matter, you know. It might help your friends if what is being done to them is revealed to the world.'

Chapter Eleven

London, spring 1938

'I need to talk to you,' Charlie said one morning, perching on the corner of my desk. We were in the newspaper office where I now had my own corner in the foreign news department. Much to the annoyance of Monica Cathcart and her clique, I had been taken back on staff. Not as Monica's slave, but as a bona fide junior reporter and Mr Bradford's special assistant.

'Well, we all know how you got the job,' Monica had sneered one day in the pub, but though the spite in her voice raised a few giggles, it was not as many as she might have hoped.

'Oh yes,' I answered, more confident now. 'The same way as you got yours?' That shut her up, but not for long. She was a constant source of bad feeling and I think she once even went to the editor to demand that I be fired. She got a mouthful in return, and that added to her nastiness. After a while I learned to ignore her and got on with my job, and I loved it. Scouring the foreign press for snippets of news and reading dispatches from the press agencies was the stuff of my dreams. I had to collate them, then hand them over to the senior reporters, more often than not to Charlie. He went away again after Christmas, to Washington, DC, and I begged to go with him.

He shook his head. 'Not this time, Blake. I think you'd better stay in the office and learn your trade. Put together some small articles and see if Geoff will publish them. You know what to write, human interest based on solid information. The sort of stuff we did in Berlin.'

Our Berlin report went down brilliantly and I was thrilled to see my name added, albeit in smaller letters, below Charlie's byline. The photographs came out well, particularly the ones I'd taken of the graffiti and smashed-up shopfronts in Auguststrasse. They contrasted starkly with the magnificence of the Brandenburg Gate and the charming riverside scenes. I was proud of it and, knocking at his door, took the article to show Jacob.

'Come in, come in,' he said, holding wide the door. He had a lovely flat, which always made me feel that I should take more interest in mine. Jacob's was comfortably furnished, with deep carpets, plump, brightly coloured sofas and chairs, and small tables hosting elegant lamps and *objets d'art*. Paintings in gilt frames covered every wall; more traditional than the ones in Sarah's flat, but equally displaying the family's love of art.

'I brought the newspaper to show you,' I said, rather nervously. 'It is an impression of life in Berlin today. I hope we got it right.'

Jacob smiled. 'We have seen it, dear Seffy, have we not, Willi?' The little dog gave a yelp and thumped its tail against Jacob's belly. It seemed to approve. 'Your article was much talked about at the synagogue the other day and I was so happy to tell them that you are my friend. You did well.'

'Thank you.' I smiled and then I said, 'Oh, Jacob, I wish I'd been able to persuade Sarah and Kitty to leave Berlin.

It's not a good place for them any more. You can't imagine how horrible it is close to Auguststrasse. Many people are leaving and Kitty would love to, but Sarah . . .' I shrugged. 'She thinks things will get better. I'm sure they won't.'

His face was sad as he stroked Willi's smooth little head. 'No, they won't, Seffy. But my sister has always been a stubborn girl and her memories of Felix are still so very strong. I tell her, remember him, of course. He's there, in your head, already. You don't need the place.'

'They kept the money, though,' I said, trying to cheer him up. 'So, when she's ready, they'll be able to come.'

'I hope it's soon enough.'

He drew me into his flat and made me sit while he prepared a cup of coffee for me. It tasted so like the coffees I'd had in Berlin that I was back there, looking at the grand buildings and watching out for the SS. I thought of Amyas, who had been there too, and wondered where he was.

'So, dear Seffy. How are you, now?'

I smiled. 'I'm well. I've got my job back and I'm happy. I love being at the newspaper.'

'Good,' Jacob nodded. 'We were worried for you, before, Willi and me.'

'I'm fine now,' I reassured him.

I was. I'd got over the terrible grief of losing Amyas and our child. I knew that I would always love him, but now I could be more rational about it and accept that he wouldn't love me in the same way. We had a connection that would never be broken. In a way, I was almost happy with the situation. I had a life now, a working life, and that's what I'd always wanted. So I meant what I said. 'I'm fine,' I repeated.

I'd spent Christmas alone in my flat except for having Jacob and Willi for dinner on Boxing Day. Jacob talked about the old days in Berlin while I told him about our house in Cornwall. 'You can wake up in the morning and the first thing you see when you get out of bed is the Atlantic Ocean. It's glorious.' Then, I half whispered, 'I fell in love there.'

'And he let you down.' Jacob reached across the table and patted my hand.

I blushed. I hadn't meant to say it out loud. 'Yes, I suppose so, but . . .' I shrugged. 'That's over.' I got up and took a bottle of brandy from the sideboard. 'Let's have a drink, Jacob and remember the good times.'

In the new year, I'd met Xanthe for tea. She'd come home with von Klausen for the Suffolk house party, but he'd gone back to Germany after that. 'He had to join his wife in their schloss for Christmas,' she said. 'Isn't it tiresome of her? It seems she put her foot down.' She squealed a giggle, causing the other people having tea at the Ritz to look round. 'I bet that foot is a size ten.'

I gave her a 'be quiet' scowl and she returned to delicately pulling apart a cucumber sandwich, rejecting the tiny amount of bread in favour of the tiny amount of cucumber. Then she gave up eating altogether and lit yet another cigarette, putting it into a tortoiseshell holder. After taking a deep lungful and blowing out the smoke, she looked around to see if she could see anyone she knew.

'How was the house party?' I asked.

'Oh, fun, darling. Such fun. Wolf fitted in wonderfully and made great friends. Binkie's cousin, can't remember his name, is at the Foreign Office and he took Wolf there for the day to have a look round. They became good pals and Wolf said he'd enjoyed himself enormously.'

I bet he did, I thought, and prayed that Binkie's stupid cousin hadn't shown von Klausen too much. 'So what are you up to now?' I wasn't really interested. Xanthe's comings and goings were always an endless round of events so outside my realm of interest that we could have been born on different planets.

'I'm going back to Berlin next month. I've taken a suite at the Adlon. Then Monte in June. Binkie's taken a villa there for the season and I'm to be his special guest.'

'What?' I asked, almost shocked. 'Are you sleeping with him too?'

Her tinkling laugh echoed across the room. 'Don't be silly, darling. We're friends, good friends. And I'm not sleeping with him. Not really. Anyway . . .' she adjusted her little mink pillbox hat and stood up. 'I have to go. I'm meeting Mummy for cocktails at the Savoy. Shall I give her your love?'

'No,' I said. 'Don't bother.' Although I was curious; it wasn't like Mother to have cocktails. What had come over her?

The maître d' clicked his fingers and Xanthe's mink coat arrived, which she shrugged over the shoulders of her cream wool suit. She looked exquisite, as always. 'Oh, by the way,' she added, pulling on her gloves. 'There was a bit of a to-do in Berlin before I left. That Amyas friend of yours disappeared and that common little person was all over the place looking for him.'

'Really? What happened?' My stomach was rising into my chest but I tried to give the impression that I didn't care. I think she bought it.

'No idea,' Xanthe said. 'I left the next day. Bye.'

I sat alone at the table for five minutes, trying to calm down. Where was he? Why had he left? Had something dreadful happened to him? Xanthe had been talking about an event that had happened two months ago and it was quite possible that he was back with Mrs Cartwright now, for if Amyas had wanted to come to me here in London he knew where to find me.

And he hadn't.

A few weeks later, on a Saturday morning, there was a knock at my door. When I opened it I was confronted by the small, overdressed figure of Elvira Cartwright. While I was still gaping at her she pushed past me into my flat.

'I know the bugger isn't here,' she said flatly. 'Because I've had you watched these last two months. Everything you've done's been reported back to me. But you might have had a letter or a phone call. And I want to know.'

'How dare you have me followed.' I was spitting with fury. 'I'll report you to the police.'

'Tit for tat, young woman.' She wagged her finger at me. 'Your mam had me watched, didn't she, eh? Elvira Cartwright never forgets. Where is he, then? Where's my boy?'

'If you mean Amyas, I don't know. Why should I?' My heart was beating fast and I struggled to keep the wobble out of my voice. 'Maybe he's had an accident?' I could hardly bring myself to say those last words.

She scowled. 'He's had no bloody accident. He's gone, hasn't he. Taken all his clothes and the money and the jewellery I had in the hotel safe. The bugger's done a flit.'

162

I stared at her, not knowing what to say. It was typical Amyas. So completely without morals that he took what he wanted, whether it was love or property. Unable to stop myself I burst out laughing: the thought of him emptying the safe and making off with this horrible woman's money and jewellery was utterly delicious.

Mrs Cartwright went white with fury and raised a hand as though to hit me, but instead grasped the heavy gold chains about her neck, her eyes looking daggers at me.

'I haven't seen him or heard from him,' I said, and tried to keep up the pretence that I'd only met him briefly. 'There's no reason why I should have.'

'Come off it,' Mrs Cartwright snarled, and for the first time since barging in took a moment to glance around my living room. 'By God,' she said. 'What a dump. I can see why Amyas wouldn't come here. Whatever else he is, he knows a bit of classy furniture. I spent good brass on my house and it looks it, too.' She directed her malevolent gaze back to me. 'I know what went on in Cornwall. You're a bit of a trollop when all's said and done and he's nothing more than a randy tomcat.' She reached up and adjusted the fur tippet draped around her shoulders, so that the fox's evil face was staring at me. It was not unlike her own. 'But listen here, young woman,' she spat, 'he's my tomcat and even if he did pinch my stuff, I want him back. And I'll get him. Make no mistake.'

'I think you'd better leave.' I'd had more than enough of Mrs Cartwright.

'Aye, I'll go. But if you see him, you tell him that the jewellery is paste. The real stuff is in the bank.' She laughed sourly, showing her small yellowed teeth. 'He'll get nowt for it.'

After she'd gone I sat in the chair by the window and thought about Amyas. He was such a bastard, but I didn't care. And I laughed again. He would know as well as she that the jewellery was fake. The thing was, would the person he sold it to?

Over the next few weeks, I waited for him to come, listening for the late night knock at my door and answering my few phone calls with a thumping heart, in case it was him. Once, on a rainy afternoon, I thought I saw him walking on the opposite pavement in Fleet Street and I dashed across the road, but the man disappeared into a building and was lost.

Stop it, I told myself. He'll come to you in his own time. Get on with your life. And so I did.

I loved my job and worked hard to learn all that I could and when Charlie perched on my desk one day, I was ready for whatever he wanted.

'I'm going back to Spain,' he said.

'Good,' I replied, my mind working overtime with the organisation of tickets, press passes and getting myself geared up to do any research he required. 'What d'you need from me?' I asked.

'Well,' he said, his eyes smiling behind his rimless glasses. 'Let me see. First, I need you, Blake. You're coming with me.'

I was excited and struggled to keep a cool head. 'Oh,' I said. 'Shall I get tickets for Madrid?'

'Hold hard, Blake.' He slid off the desk and pulling over a chair, sat beside me. 'We're going a different route. I was thrown out last time I was there, my reports got back to them and they didn't like it. Either side. So this time my plan is to follow someone who is joining the International Brigade. That means we go to Paris first. I want to discover something about the organisers – who they are, what makes them tick – and that means I have to get close. What d'you think?'

'I think it's a splendid idea, but where do I come in?'

'Well, think about this. We go to Paris together, you rent a room or something and I join up for the Brigade. I'll get information out to you and you can dispatch it back to the paper, or maybe collate it for an article . . . I haven't worked it out entirely, yet.'

'But what happens when they send you to Spain?'

'I'll go along with it. I'll go on whichever route they send me and you can follow, as a reporter, of course. I want you to go as far as the border and then hang around for my dispatches, if and when I can get them out. You'll have your press pass so you'll be safe in France.' He gave me one of his twinkly-eyed smiles. 'You up for it?'

I grinned. 'Of course I am. When do we start?'

Over the next few days, Charlie and I planned our expedition. 'Look,' he said, 'the war in Spain has been going on for nearly three years now and, from what I gather, the Brigade are beginning to wind down. I might not be accepted but I'm going to try.' He frowned. 'I should have done this before, but better late than never. I must find out about the people and the organisation, so . . . when we get to Paris, we'll part company. Apparently the taxi drivers are mostly left wing and know where the recruitment office is so will take men who ask there. I've done a bit of research . . . yes, I know that's your job, but anyway there is a bar very close to the Gare Saint-Lazare, where some of the recruits and the recruiters go. If you can get a room nearby, then we could meet and I'll give you what I'll have learned.'

When we arrived in Paris I watched him go and then made my way to the rue Saint-Lazare, where I took the room in the bar that Charlie had mentioned.

Monsieur Heulin, who owned the bar, was curious. 'An Englishwoman wanting to stay here? It is strange.'

'I want to tell the readers of my paper about the real Parisians. Everyone's written about the artists and the poets, I want to write about the people, the ones who actually live and die in the city. My editor is looking for something different.'

He rubbed a hand over his blue chin and pursed his lips. I knew he didn't believe me, but he didn't really care, so he reached in the till and took out the key to one of his upstairs rooms. 'You will have Antoinette and Simone as neighbours. They're quiet girls and they won't bother you. They work at night.' This last was accompanied by a wink and a suggestive waggle of his hand.

As I went up the greasy back stairs to the room I smiled to myself. I was living above a cheap bar with a couple of prostitutes for neighbours. What would Mother think? It couldn't have been more different from my previous foreign assignment in the Hotel Adlon. The room was tiny and smelled of the rubbish that was piled in bins beneath the window. I had a bed, a lamp and a couple of hooks on the wall to hang my clothes, and behind a bead curtain there was a lavatory and a shower cubicle. But, sitting on the bed with the typewriter on my knee, I was happy.

I'd been there only a day when Monsieur Heulin knocked on my door. 'I need a waitress, someone to watch the place when I go out. I can pay just a few francs. Are you interested?' he asked.

I was going to say no, but then I realised that if Charlie came in I'd be able to talk to him without a problem. 'All right,' I said. 'I'll have a go.'

Fortunately the bar wasn't very busy during the day, so I was able to learn about serving the drinks and the few meals we did, which were mostly baguettes, sandwiches and omelettes. I didn't mind it and the next evening, Charlie turned up.

'What the hell are you doing here?' he asked, looking amazed.

'I'm a waitress, isn't it obvious?' I winked and looked over my shoulder at Monsieur Heulin, who was leaning on the bar talking to a friend. 'And I've got a room upstairs. It was advertised in the window, so I took it.'

Charlie nodded. 'Coffee,' he said out loud and later as I put the cup in front of him, he muttered, 'Meet me round the back in fifteen minutes.'

Monsieur Heulin called, 'I'm going out. You all right for half an hour?' I nodded. It couldn't have been better, we didn't need to go outside, and I ran upstairs for my notebook and came back to sit beside Charlie.

'The recruitment centre is run by a Polish colonel,' he said. 'I haven't seen him yet but I have seen someone called Josip Broz, a Yugoslavian. He's a communist and seems to have all the connections. He has control of the money and he's arranging our journey south.' Charlie leant back and rubbed a hand over his badly shaven chin, while I got up to give a couple of railway workers who were leaning on the bar, more drinks. When I came to sit down again, Charlie continued. 'There are three of us at the moment. Recruits, I mean. An American and a Welsh miner and me. We're going by train to Perpignan next week, and then across the border, somehow. The American says that the border is guarded by anarchists and they can be bloody difficult. We'll see.' He yawned and twitched his shoulders and I noticed that he looked grubby and tired. In two days he seemed to have lost weight.

'Where are you staying?' I asked.

'In some little worker's house not far from here. The French communists have taken over housing the volunteers, but the place they've given us is dirty and full of fleas and the food is terrible.'

'Oh God,' I said. 'Are you hungry? Wait.' I went into the kitchen behind the bar, grabbed a baton, sliced it and filled it with ham and cheese. 'Here,' I said, a couple of minutes later, putting the napkin-wrapped sandwich into his hand.

'Thanks.' He took a bite and then stopped and said, 'I'll share this with my two comrades.'

'Eat it. I'll make another for your pals.'

'Mademoiselle!' I looked up. Customers had come into the bar and I was busy for the next ten minutes, but I managed to make another two sandwiches and gave them to Charlie. I put my own money in the till so that Monsieur Heulin wouldn't suspect.

'Everything all right?' Monsieur Heulin walked in as I was serving the customers.

'Yes,' I nodded. 'Quite busy.'

He looked over to where Charlie was sitting by the window. 'That Englishman is still here, I see. Friend of yours?' His eyes narrowed, he gave me a calculating look.

I countered. 'How d'you know he's English?'

Monsieur Heulin shrugged. 'His jacket, his haircut, what can I say? He's English and a volunteer. They come in from time to time. The office is up the street.'

I pretended to be ignorant. 'A volunteer for what?'

'The war, girl. In Spain.' He stubbed out his thin cigarette and lighting another gave Charlie a sour look. 'They're all communists.' The distaste in his voice was patent.

'You don't like communists?' I asked.

'No, I don't. Why should I? If they took over I wouldn't be able to run my bar, they'd make rules and take all my money.'

'Oh,' I said and then grinned at him. 'But that doesn't stop you serving them.'

He grinned back. 'That's business. Anyway, they're all going to be killed as soon as they get to Spain.'

When I looked back to the window Charlie had gone.

I didn't see him again for a week. I occupied my time with working in the bar and getting to know some of the regular customers. They were mostly men who worked at the railway station, who came in for a brandy before, as well as after, work, and the working girls, who seemed to survive on cigarettes, coffee and as much pastis as they could afford. They were a quiet bunch, never apparently drunk, but always exhausted. I met my neighbours, Antoinette and Simone, both of whom were older than me; indeed I thought that Simone might not be far short of fifty. They would come into the bar every evening for an omelette and a few drinks, before heading out to work. I don't know where they entertained their customers because I never saw any men on the premises and I was glad of that.

'You are English?' Simone had asked on the first evening.

'Yes,' I nodded.

'I've met some Englishmen,' she said, putting her empty glass on my tray and pointing for another drink. 'They are polite. Better than some others.'

Antoinette nodded. 'Polite, yes. But shy.' They smiled at each other and I smiled with them. Amyas wouldn't have been shy, but perhaps Charlie would. That brought a new thought. What sort of love life did Charlie have? I'd been so wrapped up with Amyas that I'd never considered Charlie, but I remembered him making a pass at me, that first time at Gennaro's, before I'd even encountered Amyas. He hadn't tried again. Perhaps he didn't fancy me. I glanced at the two women and at the other girls sitting with their drinks. Did Charlie go with them?

On the Wednesday lunchtime of the following week he came in. I brought him a coffee and an omelette. 'We're getting the eight forty train to Perpignan this evening. It leaves from the Gare de Lyon. You'll have to get on it too.' He gave me a smile. 'Still up for it, Blake?'

'Of course,' I said.

He lifted an eyebrow and gave a pretend sigh of relief. 'Good. I wondered if you might have become enamoured of the waitressing life and not want to carry on with this reporting lark.'

'Go to hell,' I laughed.

I went up to my room at six o'clock and packed my small case. 'I'm off,' I told Monsieur Heulin. 'I've got all

I need for my article and now I'm moving on. Thanks for the job, I enjoyed it.'

He didn't look shocked, or even surprised. 'The train goes from the Gare de Lyon,' he said. 'Though I expect you know that already. I knew what you were up to all along . . . going as a nurse to join the Communists. Well, good luck. But you'll probably be killed.'

And with those words ringing in my ears I left and found my way to the station. I saw Charlie in the distance, standing on his own. Looking around the passengers waiting to board the train I noticed two other men who looked as lonely and as nervous as Charlie. I waited until he'd seen me and had got on the train before finding my carriage and settling down to the overnight journey. That night I dreamed I was back in Cornwall, being held by Amyas, as the surf rolled in.

Chapter Twelve

Cerbère, France, 1938

Once I arrived in Perpignan I made my way to Cerbère. It was the town Charlie and I had decided would be a good place for me to wait for him or, if possible, a good place from where I could cross into Spain. It was a small town right on the border, about twenty miles south of Perpignan and the railway terminus for the French trains. Before the war, Spanish trains would also come into this terminus and goods and passengers would be transferred for their onward journey, north or south. But now the border was closed and the only trains were the ones from the north. Shortly beyond the station the tracks disappeared into a long railway tunnel, which had been blasted through the mountains into Spain. I'd been told that people escaping the war walked through this tunnel, arriving in Cerbère dusty, desperate and bewildered. Those were precisely the people I needed to interview but, so far, I hadn't seen any of them.

When I first got there the nights were cold. It was the end of March and although in the daytime I could walk about in short sleeves, loving the feel of the sun on my bare arms, the temperature plummeted as night fell. But as March turned into April and April, May, the evenings became delightfully warm and I would have my supper in one of the cafés overlooking the sea.

My new home was the Hotel Belvedere. It was only ten years old then, a strange, white concrete building, long and narrow with a curved prow making it look for all the world like an ocean liner picked up by some wild wind and deposited in the town, on a promontory above the sea. The bedrooms were on the second floor, oddly arranged around an internal courtyard, which had a glass ceiling through which you could see the sky. If you were given a room on the west side, you would look out on to the railway lines beneath but also to the last dark crags of the Pyrenees, which rose up against the clear southern sky. On the east side, the view was of the coastline and the blue, shimmering waters of the Mediterranean. I took a room with the sea view and settled myself in for a wait, but I hadn't imagined how long it would be. Six weeks had passed which I'd spent gathering copy for articles and taking photographs of the coastline and the pretty villages. I sent some pieces home to our editor and I heard that they went into the travel section. I was thrilled at that, but the travel section really wasn't where I wanted my articles to be.

'I don't want you to cross the border,' Charlie had said when we were still in Paris. 'It's too dangerous. Several journalists have been killed . . . by both sides. Accused of spying, which is what, in effect, I'm doing.'

'Should you be going?' I'd asked. I began to feel seriously worried for him.

'Absolutely,' Charlie answered. 'How else can I gather the information I need? Now, you take a room somewhere close to the border and let Geoff know where you are.

I'll try and get through to him and he'll transfer the information to you. It'll be a three-way contact, but I want you to get the feel of the place and to interview likely people for your articles. I think you're very good at that. It's one of your strengths, along with having a good style of prose. You seem to attract contacts, and you know what, Blake, we make a good team.'

I was foolishly pleased to hear him say that. We had become real friends, as well as working colleagues. I trusted him with my life, and it seemed that he was prepared to trust me with his.

He'd reached into his pocket and pulled out a letter. 'If anything happens, I want you to make sure that this gets to Diana.'

'Diana?'

'Yes,' Charlie frowned. 'My wife, Diana.'

I must have sat and stared at him for at least thirty seconds. It felt like an hour.

'What is it, Blake?' he said, smiling. 'Don't you want the responsibility of telling her that I'm dead?'

'I . . . I didn't know you were married,' I said finally. 'You've never mentioned it.' I could hardly believe it. Charlie Bradford with a wife? Did everyone know except me?

'Haven't I?' He shrugged and, gulping down the coffee I'd brought him, pushed his chair back and stood up. 'We have a house in Dorset. She lives there. Diana doesn't do town.'

I followed him out of the café. It was beginning to rain and he turned up the collar on his jacket. 'You made a pass at me, when we first met,' I said, stupidly annoyed.

'Why wouldn't I?' He laughed. 'I'm a red-blooded man

and you're not a bad-looking woman. It would have been a crime not to have a go.'

I shook my head, trying to decide if I was flattered, or furious. 'Charlie,' I called as he turned to walk away, 'have you got any children?'

He raised two fingers as he walked down the street.

That letter was in my bag now, nestled close to my passport and wallet. I knew that, if necessary, I would take the letter to Diana, but I did wonder about their relationship and why I was so uncomfortable about it. Was I jealous? No, of course I wasn't because I was in love with Amyas. My thoughts turned to him. What was he doing? Enjoying himself on the Riviera, in and out of the casinos, gambling with the proceeds of the stolen jewellery? Or had he run out of money and gone back to Mrs Cartwright? I could picture him, black hair curling at his neck, maybe wearing a new Savile Row suit, jauntily turning up at her over-furnished mansion, grinning like a fool and not showing any remorse. She would take him back of course, calling him for everything, no doubt, but glad to see him. I laughed to myself, sitting on my bed looking out at the sea and didn't blame him. That was how he lived, how he survived. It was a job, like any other. Well, perhaps not like any other.

The image of Amyas was strongly with me as I wandered down to the hotel bar for a drink before I decided on dinner. He'd like it here, I thought, because it was a little like Cornwall with its miles of rocky headlands dropping down into small coves of golden beaches. And the beautiful sea was warm, clear and sparkling. Amyas loved the sea.

'Mademoiselle?' It was Paul Durban, another journalist

who was staying at the hotel. He was French and young; my age, probably, with a bony, rather clever face under a mop of dark wavy hair. He constantly had a cigarette hanging from his lips, the smoke from his Gauloise curling into the air around him. We had smiled at each other at breakfast and later, when I'd walked into the village, I'd bumped into him again and we'd introduced ourselves. 'Mademoiselle.' He grinned. 'Will you join me for a drink?'

'Thank you,' I said. We took our drinks to the balcony and sat gazing at the view of the rugged coastline as it wound itself into Spain.

'You are in Cerbère to look for refugees?' he asked.

'Yes,' I answered. 'I'm interested in gathering their stories but, so far,' I took a sip of the red, rather fruity wine and sighed, 'I haven't been able to find them. Apparently the flow of people coming out of Spain has dried up. In the meantime, I'm waiting for my boss.'

It was eight o'clock in the evening and the sun was going down over the mountains that loomed dark against the lilac sky and spoke of the cruelty and barbarism which was going on beyond them. I yearned to go into Spain. I wanted to find out for myself what was happening and, with my press pass, I was sure I'd be let in. God knows, it was an easy walk from the village to the border and I'd done it a couple of times and looked at the soldiers leaning aimlessly against the barrier, but, faithful to Charlie's instructions, I had never crossed over.

'Your boss?' Paul asked.

I nodded. 'Charlie Bradford.'

'Ah,' Paul grinned. 'The famous Charlie Bradford. I know him. He is in Spain, yes?'

'I think so,' I said. That bit was true. I only thought Charlie had got across the border, because I hadn't seen him since the station at Perpignan where I'd hung around and watched him and his two companions being collected by a couple of men and led out of the station. I'd followed them and was just in time to see them bundled into a vehicle and driven off. Charlie had looked back as he'd scrambled into the lorry and although he didn't acknowledge it, I knew he'd seen me.

'How did he get in?' Paul looked at me, curiously. 'He must be known to the authorities and it seems to be impossible for journalists at the moment. I have walked to the border every day but I am not allowed to cross.'

'Charlie has his ways,' I said, not willing to give details. However pleasant this young man was I didn't intend to endanger Charlie's life any further by opening my mouth.

'He was in China,' said Paul, 'when I was there. We travelled together. I felt fear many times, but Charlie . . . He was amazing.'

I nodded. I was discovering every day that I was apprenticed to someone who was a star in his field. It was up to me to do him justice.

'Mademoiselle Seffy.' Paul stood up. 'Will you accompany me to a restaurant? I would like that.'

'Yes, I'd like that too,' I said and we walked out of the hotel and down to the village. We found a small restaurant that overlooked the sea and sat on a pretty terrace under a pergola of vines and scented hibiscus. The sun had gone down, but the small glass lanterns which hung between the vines gently lit the terrace with a soft glow. After the white concrete severity of the Hotel Belvedere this little place was heavenly.

Paul brushed a hand through his curly hair and studied the short menu. 'This tells us what they serve tonight. There is no choice.' He looked concerned. 'This is bad for you?'

'No. Not at all,' I smiled. 'I'm sure it will be good.'

We had chilled pepper soup with crayfish tails, mopping it up with chunks of crusty bread, then duck eggs with a warm broad bean salad and, finally, tiny lamb chops on a bed of sliced garlic potatoes, grilled to perfection and flavoured with aromatic sprigs of rosemary. It was exciting food, brightly coloured and with a touch of fire. It was utterly delicious.

'Why are you in Cerbère?' I asked Paul, when our plates had been taken away and a wooden board of purple grapes put in the centre of the table. Coffee had been brought to us, so black and strong that it burst through the wine and food languor which had followed the meal and urged me back into investigative mood.

He shrugged. 'The same as you. My paper thinks that the war is nearly over. I am to go into Spain if I can. There will be reprisals and I'm to try and cover that.'

'You must have a press pass,' I said. 'Why can't you get in?'

Paul laughed. 'As I said, the border guards have refused me. My name is known, like your Charlie. I was expelled last year. I think I was fortunate not to be put in prison. A second time and I might not be so lucky. A colleague was shot last year and I know of an American who disappeared while on assignment.'

His words were chilling. How on earth would Charlie get away with it?

'So,' I said. 'You have a plan?'

We were almost the last of the diners. A man sat by himself at a table in a corner. He had a newspaper which he'd read assiduously throughout his meal. Paul jerked his head slightly in the man's direction and lowered his voice before replying, 'I'll tell you when we get back to the hotel.'

'Was that man following us?' I asked, as we walked back through the town. Since Germany that was a question which came far more naturally to my mind. A train had just come in and bursts of steam filled the air, bringing an odour of burning coal. I could see people walking off the platform and into the village and a taxi picking up a mother with several children. For all its small size, Cerbère was an active place.

'Yes,' Paul nodded. 'He follows me. Not you, I think.'

I resisted the desire to look behind me to see if the man was still there when we walked across the road, but as we went in through the doors, I managed to sneak a look over my shoulder and there he was, leaning against a railing opposite the hotel.

The reception area was full of holidaymakers from all over Europe, attracted by the unusual hotel and the beautiful scenery. Music from a gramophone filled the air, the records changed diligently by the youthful receptionist. We sat down on a banquette by the window, listening to Charles Trenet.

'So,' I said to Paul, after looking around to see if the man had followed us into the lounge. He hadn't. 'Your plan?'

The young journalist, satisfied that we weren't being watched, pulled out a folded-up map from his inside pocket. He spread it out on the table in front of us. I could see that it showed the local area, with roads and railway lines and all the small villages on both sides of the border. Some of the roads were tiny, with many hairpin bends and others came to a dead halt and after that there were no roads.

'These are the mountains,' said Paul, pointing to the blank areas on the map, 'and the roads finish, but you can walk. There are . . . how do you say . . . *chemin ou piste*, I do not know the word.'

'Tracks,' I said, 'paths.'

'Yes. Paths. So, you walk over the mountain and you are in Spain. They do not guard the whole border. I might try going west of Cerbère, to this place.' He pointed to a dot, indicating a small town and I leant forward to read the name. 'Tarascon-sur-Ariège,' I said out loud.

'Yes. It is a small town. I would not be noticed, perhaps. It is in a valley, but there are trails going up into the mountains. I think I can get from there across into Spain. People have come out that way. I have met them.'

'How will you get there?'

'Ah. My car is here. I will drive to Tarascon and then get as far up the road as it will go. I will park it somewhere and go on by foot.' He shrugged in a typically Gallic manner. 'I will collect it some time. It might be a week or a month. If they capture me, it might be never.'

He said it matter-of-factly, but I couldn't help the cold shiver that those words brought. It was a frightening prospect, going illegally into a war zone, but, at the same time, I envied him. I wanted to prove myself too as a foreign correspondent. A waiter came to our table and asked if we would like a drink. 'Let me get these,' I said, and ordered a couple of brandies. 'It's a dangerous plan,'

I said, after the waiter had delivered the drinks and we'd had a sip. 'But I'd go.'

We laughed together, sitting in the white concrete hotel, looking out at the tiny distant lights from the fishing boats glittering on the navy blue sea and the beam of the lighthouse sweeping across the bay. I could have been back in Cornwall, with Amyas.

Another thought occurred to me. 'Paul,' I asked, 'who is it that's following you?'

He lit a cigarette and blew smoke rings into the air. I remembered Xanthe doing that when she first learned to smoke. 'I'm not sure,' he said. 'I saw him in Perpignan by the newspaper office and then he was here again. Maybe it is nothing.'

'Republican or Nationalist?' I asked. It would have to be someone connected to the Civil War.

'I do not know. They are each as bad as the other about our telling the truth of what they do.'

'I was followed in Berlin,' I said.

'That would be the Nazis,' Paul said with a certainty that could not be doubted.

I sighed. 'I know. It is horrible there.'

'We do live in difficult times,' Paul said. 'Another war is coming. It will be terrible, far worse than this one in Spain.'

I thought again of Xanthe, with her Nazi boyfriend and her absolute denial of what was happening. I had to protect her, somehow.

The next morning the hotel manager came to my table at breakfast. 'There is a telegram for you,' he said. It was from our editor. BRADFORD COMING OUT OF SPAIN STOP NEEDS TO CONTACT YOU SOONEST STOP.

'There is a reply?' asked the manager. He was curious, I could see that.

'No,' I said and gave him a casual smile. I was cautious. He looked too interested. Finishing my breakfast, I went out and got on to the train to Perpignan, where I telegraphed back to Geoff. AM READY TO HELP STOP TELL ME WHAT HE WANTS STOP TELEGRAPH THIS OFFICE ONLY STOP.

It took hours for the reply to come, giving me time to have a nervous lunch at a pavement café across the river from the post office. It was another glorious day, perhaps even some sort of local festival, for the red and yellow striped Perpignan flags were flying everywhere and people were laughing and jostling in the street. I was lucky that the telegraph office was open. When I went back at half past two, the reply was waiting for me.

GET TO SORT IN SPAIN STOP HE'S WAITING STOP TAKE CARE STOP DON'T BE CAUGHT STOP.

I stared at the piece of paper and bit my lip. The telegraphic instructions were, of necessity, brief, but I knew what I had to do. I went straight from the post office to a bookshop where I bought a map. Where the hell was Sort? I sat on a bench beside the river and studied the map until I found it. It appeared to be a small town about thirty miles across the border into Spain, roughly in the direction that Paul had planned to go, and as I sat on the train back to Cerbère the inkling of an idea started to form.

He was in the reception area when I walked in and he jerked his head to me to follow him towards the lifts. I had passed his watcher as I'd walked up from the station; he was lingering at a cigarette booth and hadn't yet reached the hotel.

'What number is your room?' Paul asked, after the lift doors closed.

'Number eight, sea view.'

'Good. I meet you there. Two minutes.'

I waited, pacing around my room, my mind whirling. What did Paul want and how was I to get to Sort?

'I go tonight,' he said, after I'd let him into my room. 'I came to say goodbye.'

'Paul,' I hesitated, wondering how I could word my request. 'Have you got room for a passenger?'

He looked astonished and then grinned. 'Who? You?'

'Yes,' I said. 'I have to get into Spain now. Charlie is coming out and needs help. I don't know why. But he's at a place called Sort.'

'Yes, Sort. I know that place but . . .' he shook his head. 'It is where many people have come through. It will be well guarded. I thought not to go that way but, perhaps, one of the mountain passes before that.'

'Then take me with you as far as you go, please. I will try and get to Sort when we've crossed the border.' He frowned and I knew he was going to refuse. He would say the same as the others, that it was too dangerous, not a job for a woman, nor for someone as inexperienced as me. But to my amazement, all he said was, 'Yes. If you are sure?'

'I'm sure,' I said, delighted, and gave him a kiss on his cheek.

'Oh!' He smiled and rubbed the spot where my lips had been. 'What would Charlie say about that?'

'Charlie?' I answered, laughing. 'He would say nothing. He isn't my boyfriend.'

'But you do have a boyfriend, yes? A lover?'

183

The doors to my balcony were open and I looked out on to the sea. I remembered Amyas and me swimming across a bay not unlike the one before me and making love as the surf bubbled around us. 'Yes,' I murmured. 'I have a lover. But I don't know where he is.'

'I the same.' Paul's voice had dropped and his eyes were sad. 'I have someone I love but where . . .' he shrugged.

We smiled at each other. How odd life was. It had thrown us together and dumped us, like two pieces of flotsam, in this strange hotel.

Paul got himself together first. 'Now, I tell you what we do.'

The plan was to set off after dark. 'We try to get away from the man who follows me.'

'I saw him,' I said. 'Just now when I came up from the railway station. I expect he's outside the hotel.' Saying that, I stepped out on to the balcony and looked down. He was there, a thin, blue-chinned man in a dusty beige suit and a brown hat. I particularly noticed his two-toned shoes. Co-respondent shoes my sister used to call them, in a tone that implied 'common'. He was looking up at the same time and saw me. Quickly I backed inside.

'He's there,' I said. 'It's going to be difficult to shake him off.'

'Yes, but he is on his own. He must sleep some time. If he thinks I am in bed, he'll leave.'

We walked down to the village after the sun had set and sat in the pretty restaurant. I felt too excited to eat, but the waiter placed a platter of seafood in front of us and, enticed by the salt-water aromas of mussels, shrimp and octopus and the wonderful garlic mayonnaise, I found myself digging in with gusto. I even ate the mató cheese and honey dessert.

'I think we do not drink much tonight,' said Paul, and I nodded. We had to be sensible and aware of the danger ahead.

When we got back to the hotel, the night manager was on duty. 'Your key, Monsieur?' he asked.

'And the key of Mademoiselle Blake, if you please.'

'There is a telegram for Mademoiselle Blake,' the manager said, and I stepped forward to take it.

As I walked ahead to the lift I looked back over my shoulder and saw the cheerful manager give Paul a conspiratorial nod of his head. My eyes flicked towards the door where the man in the co-respondent shoes stood watching. He'd noticed the by-play and I knew that as soon as we had got in the lift he'd be asking the night manager about us.

'He'll tell him we are in your room. In for a long time,' laughed Paul. 'I would like that, Seffy. We change our plan, yes.'

'No, idiot.' I laughed too and opened the telegram. It was from the editor and contained one word, 'Llavorsí'. I held it out to Paul. 'What does this mean?'

'It is a town or a village. We look on the map.'

It was a tiny mountain village, north of Sort and I guessed that was where Charlie was waiting. But I had seen the look that passed between Paul's follower and the manager.

How much money would have to be paid before the contents of the telegram were known by the man? Perhaps he already knew. I said nothing to Paul. I didn't want to put him off taking me, which was selfish perhaps, but, I reasoned, he had latched on to me initially, hadn't he. Not the other way around.

Before supper, Paul had brought his holdall to my room and I had stuffed a few clothes into the large canvas bag I'd bought in the village. I'd changed into slacks and a shirt before dinner, so I was ready to go, but Paul said no.

'Wait, Seffy, ' he cautioned me, so we sat in the room until ten when he stood and turned off the light. 'If he is still watching, he will think we've gone to bed.'

We sat in the dark room for an hour before he nodded at me and said, 'Now, we go.'

I grabbed my bag and a jacket as we left the room, heading for the fire escape. We waited at the bottom for a few tense seconds, hoping, desperately, that no one was watching the road between us and Paul's car. We were in luck: a train came in at that moment in a cloud of steam and smoke and, using that for cover, we ran to the open-topped Citroën.

'Shall we put the top down?' I asked.

'No. We go now.' And we sped away, following the beam of the headlights as they cut through the darkness of the road west.

Chapter Thirteen

Spain, 1938

Despite my excitement and the adrenalin and the cold, I somehow managed to sleep as Paul drove through the night. Dawn was creeping over the mountains behind us when he braked the car at the side of the road and I woke up.

'God,' I said. 'I'm sorry. Have I been asleep for long?'

'No. An hour, maybe. It is of no matter.'

I sat up and looked around. We had stopped at the edge of a road which ran through a high valley. To the left of us the dark mountains rose majestically. Their topmost granite ridges soared into the pale morning sky, glinting white with snow and ice. They looked magnificent but formidable.

When I turned my head to the right of the small road, my eyes took in a softer scene: lush, rolling farmland, which fell gently into cow pastures and wild flower meadows. It was comfortable and beautiful. I sighed and gave a quick nervous glance back to the mountains. Somehow, we'd have to cross them.

Ahead of us I could see a village, white buildings with red-tiled roofs and the pointed tower of a medieval church.

'Is that Tarascon-sur-Ariège?' I asked, getting out of the car and stretching my legs.

Paul shook his head. 'No. It is a bigger town than that. I have been there before, when my father took me to walk the mountain trails.' He shrugged. 'I stopped now to make pee pee.' He blushed a little and I grinned. 'I could do with one too.'

Paul nodded towards the opposite roadside. 'Go to those trees. I keep watch.'

When I returned to the car Paul was examining the map. 'We are here,' he said, pointing to a dot of a village a few miles east of Tarascon. 'I think we not stop, but go on to the larger town. It will be easy to hide if the man still follows. Yes, we go there, eat breakfast and decide what must be done.'

I looked over my shoulder, suddenly concerned that the man in the co-respondent shoes had worked out where we were. It seemed impossible. It was only just after dawn and he would think we were still in bed. The road behind us was reassuringly empty and, apart from the twittering of birds as they awoke to a new day, silent. I turned back to my companion who was now climbing into the driving seat. I tried to remember why he'd said he was being followed, but it seemed that he had never explained it properly. And suddenly a small worm of doubt began to nudge my stomach. Maybe trusting Paul Durban was not such a good idea.

Tarascon-sur-Ariège was a pretty mountain town set on both banks of a river and was just coming to life as we drove in. A smell of bread and coffee wafted through the air and my stomach, so lately full of apprehension, began to growl.

'We eat breakfast here?' Paul suggested and stopped the car at a café, which overlooked the river. An avenue of pollarded trees lined the road and flowers bloomed merrily in pots all around us. It was a peaceful scene, but I didn't feel peaceful. I was nervous again. It took a few mouthfuls of the aromatic coffee, which was served in small white china bowls, and a chunk of warm bread roll, before I felt more settled and I was able to think clearly.

Paul, on the other hand, was even more twitchy than before. He kept glancing over his shoulder and once stood up to look back along the road in the direction in which we'd come.

'You know who's following you,' I said, now certain that he hadn't been telling me the whole truth.

'Do I?' he said, his eyes narrowing. 'How can you be sure?'

'Because you're frightened. Because you need to get away. Because . . .' here I stopped and looked down at my plate. 'Because you have done something bad.'

For a moment I thought that he would deny it and return to his youthful, amusing self, but, when he finally spoke, it was to the air. He didn't look directly at me, as one colleague explaining something to another, but instead gave the impression of a child admitting a crime to a priest or a parent. 'Yes, Seffy,' he said softly. 'I have done something bad. I have killed a man.'

My stomach lurched. 'What?' I said, appalled. 'Who? Who have you killed?'

Across the road from the café, the blue and white river tumbled noisily by and old women, in black cotton blouses and skirts, walked past us to the bread shop. It was such an ordinary scene, so quiet and peaceful, but I knew I was about to hear something terrible, and when

189

Paul spoke it sounded almost as if his voice was coming from far away. A narrator, on a wireless that wasn't properly tuned.

'It was in Perpignan, three weeks ago,' Paul started. 'He was a man who deserved to be killed and I have no regret. Except, I come from a Catholic family. I cannot tell them. They would not understand. I haven't told anyone, yet. Now, I tell you, Seffy. I want to. But first, there is a story to say.'

I swallowed nervously. I didn't think I wanted to hear his story and I looked around the café, wondering if I should just get up and leave. But he was already speaking.

'The last time I was in Spain, I was reporting from the battle front. I was with the Republicans when they overran a small town.' He stopped and looked across the road to the houses and shops and the men and women opening shutters and hanging out lines of washing. 'An ordinary town, like this one. The people there supported the Nationalists and the fighting was very fierce. When they had no more ammunition and many of their fighters had been killed, they surrendered, hanging out sheets as white flags from their windows and throwing the few weapons they had left into the main square. The Republican commander, Guisando, would not accept this surrender. He wanted to fight on, to destroy all the remaining buildings and kill all the people. But he was persuaded by some of his men, who were exhausted, to stop. So instead, he rounded up a group of people who, he said, had supported Generalissimo Franco. They were to be executed, as an example to other towns and villages.'

His eyes were full of tears when he turned his head

and looked at me. 'Oh, Seffy, they were terrified. Old men, pissing in their pants and young women huddled together, demented with fear. They had been grabbed from their homes and pushed into the square for no reason other than to make up the numbers. The commander told his soldiers to take aim and we reporters were to simply stand and watch.'

Silent tears were dropping on to the table now and his face contorted as he struggled to continue his story. 'I couldn't believe what was happening. I shouted, "No! This wrong! This is murder!" and I would have run forward to stop the slaughter, but friends, other reporters, held me back. We are neutral, they said. We report. We do not interfere.' A bleak look washed over his face. 'And the people were shot. All of them, even the baby that one of the young women was holding. I will hear that girl's screams until the day I die.'

I put out my hand and covered his. I couldn't think of anything to say.

He grasped my fingers, squeezing them until the blood almost stopped flowing. His distress was such that I thought he might howl out loud and I slid an anxious look to the few other people who had come for an early breakfast, but they were reading newspapers or, in the case of a young couple, staring into each other's eyes. 'What happened?' I asked.

Paul swallowed and, picking up a paper napkin, wiped his face. When he'd regained control, he continued, 'The commander arrested me and threw me into a stinking prison. I was there until my comrades persuaded him to let me out but I was taken to the border and pushed across. They told me if I go back I will be shot. When I got back to Perpignan and told them what had happened, the editor refused to let me publish my account of the massacre. He, and the owner, were both fierce sympathisers of the Republicans and feared what this story would do for the cause.'

It was a dreadful story, and I sat back for a moment to take it in. What I had planned to do in the next few hours, find my way, illegally, into Spain, frightened me. I could have gone across the border easily with my press pass, but I would be noticed, possibly followed, and that would bring Charlie into more danger. I looked back at Paul. He was leaning his chin on his hand, gazing into space. Poor boy, I thought, and then I remembered how the conversation had started.

'But the man, the man who follows you. Who is he?'

Paul squeezed the paper napkin into a tight ball. 'I do not know, but I think he is a friend of Guisando. From Perpignan.'

I looked at him, astonished. 'Why would he be following you?'

He started to speak, but a waitress came to ask if we wanted more coffee. I shook my head and pushed some francs on to the table. 'No, thank you,' I said. 'We're leaving,' and we got up and walked outside, still holding hands, and stood looking at the fast-moving river.

'I haven't told you all, yet,' Paul sighed. 'You see, after I'd been back in Perpignan for a few months, I had an assignment to cover the elections in our city. To find out about the different parties. I went one evening to a bar in the city, which I knew was popular with the Fascists, and, to my shock, Guisando was there with two of the men who had been in his command. He was there in

France! In a Fascist bar! I knew then that he'd left Spain because he could see where the war was going and he didn't want to be on the wrong side. He would be able to go back, claiming that he had seen the light.' His voice echoed contempt when he spat, 'The man was a murdering coward, a filthy disgusting coward! I wanted to go up to him and tell the others in the bar what he'd done, but, you see, Seffy, I am a coward too. I kept thinking about being neutral and reporting and not acting. It is very hard. Your Charlie can do it without losing his principles. But I can't.'

'What did you do?'

'I waited until he came out. It was late, the street was empty. I went up to him. Oh, he knew who I was, he even gave me a sneer and looked behind him to remind his friends about me.' Paul gave a sour laugh. 'They were not there, because they were still in the bar, picking up girls, maybe. He was on his own; laughing at me. I thought of the people screaming and I knew that he could not be permitted to live. I picked up a piece of broken stone and hit him on the head. Even at the last, he was laughing, he could not believe that I would actually do anything. So he fell and died, but not immediately. It was justice. I do not regret it.'

'Oh my God.' There in that small street, with passers-by looking on curiously, I took him in my arms and held him close. He was a murderer, yes, but I didn't care. I thought of Berlin and the wickedness I'd seen there. I knew that I would be capable of the same emotion, the same desire for justice.

'Do you hate me, Seffy? Now that you know,' he whispered the words into my neck.

'No,' I said, and looked up to the clouds hovering over the mountains I would soon have to cross. 'Of course I don't hate you. I understand.'

He took a long, shuddering breath and after a moment stepped out of my arms. 'Thank you,' he said. 'Thank you. I have wanted to tell someone for so long.'

I smiled and then remembered something. 'But the man? Why is he following you?'

'I think he is a friend of Guisando. He must have said my name before he died. This man. He waits to get me on my own, but I am careful and then you were there. You stood between him and me.'

How strange, I thought. He has been using me so why am I not angry? I looked at him, at his pale face and troubled eyes. He was my age and had covered terrible events in a terrible war and yet I felt older than him. Like a sister who needed to give a young brother protection. I should stay and help him. Then sense kicked in and I remembered what I'd promised my editor. 'Yes, I am here, standing between you and him, but Paul . . .' I gave him a direct look. 'Not for much longer. I have to get into Spain. One way or another. And today, if possible. I don't think Charlie can wait.'

He nodded and was quiet as he climbed into his car. I waited on the pavement, wondering if he might leave me there and go on west, or even return to Perpignan. Wherever it was that he felt safest.

'Just take me as far as you can,' I pleaded. 'I'll try and make my own way across the border.'

He started the engine. 'No. I take you, Seffy. Get in the car. We go into Spain together, but first we have to go to a shop I know.'

'To a shop?' I was astonished.

'Look,' he said, all trace of tears gone. 'We do not walk in a park. The mountains can be very dangerous. We need supplies.'

We headed south and the road rose higher and higher and narrowed until, by ten a.m., it was a single track and we were driving on scrubby grass and rocks, and eventually even that petered out into a footpath. It was not the sheer drop from the road which I'd feared, but the ground was wickedly uneven and we were bumped and rocked about. When Paul finally turned the steering wheel and drove on to a patch of flat ground beside a shepherd's stone hut, I was more than ready to get out. Ahead of us the trail filtered through rocks, a passage for sheep most likely, and looking up I could see them, white dots on the hillside moving from one patch of thin vegetation to another. My eyes scanned higher to the granite crags. Beyond them was Spain and Charlie.

'We leave the car here,' Paul said. 'Now we walk.'

At the shop I'd bought a pair of soft suede boots, which, although new, were totally comfortable. Those, with a padded jacket and a rucksack, had been my purchases, but Paul had also bought a pistol and some ammunition. I was surprised.

'There are bears and wild boars in the mountains,' he said. 'We must be prepared.'

'All right.' I didn't look at him as I transferred clothes out of my bag into the new rucksack, along with a tin box containing sausage and biscuits and a canteen of clean water. He had much the same and then, when we were kitted up, he locked my canvas bag in the back of his car.

'Here,' he said, and put the car keys in my hand. 'Keep them safe and then, when you bring your Charlie out, you can drive back to Cerbère.'

'What about you?' I asked. 'You'll need it.'

He grimaced. 'I think I come out of Spain a different way. It is of no matter.' He looked at the sheep track ahead of us and hoisted his rucksack on to his shoulders. 'Come, we must go.'

It took us nearly two days to cross the mountains, the worst two days of my life, up until then. At another time, in different circumstances, I would have enjoyed the trek, for the scenery was beautiful and dramatic. Hawks mewed in the clear sky and I watched them flying in ever upward circles on the thermal currents. I envied them. How easy it would be to fly across the mountains and get to Charlie within an hour. But we walked and scrambled and inched carefully along terrifyingly narrow paths, clinging to the rocks as the ground fell away on the other side.

After a couple of hours, we stopped for a breather. 'Do we have to go higher?' I asked, looking at the craggy barriers ahead of us, my eyes searching for a route.

'No,' said Paul. 'Now we go down. Do you see?' He pointed to a thin gushing waterfall, which leapt and sparkled down a hundred feet, until it reached a pool far below and then ran into a swift winding stream. 'That becomes a river. A river which will go through a valley and take us across the border. That is our way.' And he pointed to one side where the track curved out and down a steep hillside.

Oh God, it was hard getting to that pool. The track disappeared in places and we had to get down the hillside as best we could. My feet slipped constantly and, to keep my balance, I had to keep grabbing at tufts of grass and tore my palms on the jagged rocks. Eventually, I gave up trying to remain upright and resorted to inching down on my bottom, before, trembling with the effort, I reached the pool at last and was able to stand up once again. Paul wasn't so lucky. Three-quarters of the way down he fell, tumbling over and over, flailing hopelessly with his hands to try and gain purchase and not finding any until he came to rest, with a thud, winded, eyes closed, against a huge boulder.

'Are you all right?' I asked, breathlessly, when I eventually reached him. He had a smear of blood on his forehead and was clasping his right wrist.

'Yes,' he grunted. But I could see that he wasn't. He looked dazed, his eyes wandering, and I unhooked my canteen. Unscrewing the cap, I put the canteen to his mouth.

'We'll wait a moment,' I said, taking over. 'Until you feel better.' I was scared. Was he concussed, and if he was, what was the best course of action?

'We go on,' he said, groaning as he got to his feet. 'We get as far as we can while there is light.' We forced our way through rocks and scrubby vegetation, sometimes even walking through the dancing shallow waters of the stream as it slowly broadened out into a small river.

When it got dark, we stopped. Paul, indicating a cave in the rock face, said, 'We go there.' I hated the prospect of a dank cave, but, trying to be resolute, followed him in.

'How are you feeling?' I asked. He looked a bit better, his eyes focusing and the blood dried into a crust in his black curls.

'My head is all right,' he answered. 'But, this is bad.' He held out his wrist. It was swollen and mottled.

'My God,' I breathed. 'Is it broken?'

'No. I think not. Twisted. Is that the right word?' He gave a slight gasp as he used his other hand to lift the swollen arm on to his lap.

I stared at it, wondering what I could do. It needed binding up, I was sure of that. But what to use? Then I remembered, I had a pair of stockings in my rucksack. Why I'd put them there I had no idea. I hadn't worn stockings since coming to France, but they were mixed up with my underwear and I had transferred them from my case without thinking. 'Wait,' I said, and opening the drawstring neck of the rucksack, delved about inside until my hand fell upon the rolled-up silk stockings.

With Paul watching me nervously, I took one stocking and wound it tightly about his wrist, and then used the other as a sort of sling. 'There, that's the best I can do.'

'It feels better,' he said, and grinned at me.

I nodded, leant back against the rock wall of the cave and closed my eyes. I was exhausted. 'Where d'you think we are?' I asked.

'I am not sure,' he said. 'I think we have crossed the border. We will see a village tomorrow, a Spanish village. And I do not believe that there will be soldiers there.'

God, I hope not, I thought, but didn't say it.

'We should make a fire,' Paul said. 'It will get very cold.'

I collected dry twigs and bits of moss and then, because he couldn't do it with his left hand, I flicked the lighter to set them on fire. I added larger twigs as it caught and then more wood, until we had a decent blaze which both warmed and lit the bare cave.

'Now, we eat,' said Paul. I helped him get out his tin of food and opened the lid for him. He ate a biscuit and then stopped and had another drink of water. 'I have no hunger tonight,' he said. 'I will sleep.'

I opened my box and ate a piece of sausage and a couple of biscuits. They tasted like cardboard and even after all the walking, I wasn't hungry either, too exhausted, I think, but I persevered. I knew that I had to keep up my energy levels, because tomorrow would not be any easier than today had been. My arms and legs ached, and I could feel them stiffening up. After eating I went outside and breathed in the cold mountain air. It was dark and the night-time creatures were coming out to feed and play. The scrubby bushes on the track rustled and glints of curious eyes flashed, then disappeared. I remembered that Paul had said that bears and wild boars roamed these mountains and I went back inside the cave.

He was asleep. In the gloom I could make out the mound of his body and hear his deep rhythmic breathing, and I lay down beside him on the bare rocky floor. I thought I would never sleep because the ground was so hard and unyielding, but my eyes drooped shut. Once, in the night, he cried out, shouting 'No, no!' and I knew what terrible dreams he was having. Still half sleeping, I moved closer to him and put my arms around his shaking body, holding him closely. He calmed down then, and even though he remained asleep, he pulled me to him until we were wrapped in a strange but necessary embrace.

When I woke he wasn't there, and I lay for a few minutes, adjusting my eyes to the half-light of a new day and remembering the previous one.

'Good morning.' Paul stood at the entrance to the cave, his body black against the daylight, and I sat up and looked at my watch. It read just after six. 'I think we must get going,' he said.

'Yes. Give me five minutes to have a pee and to clean my teeth in the stream.'

'You can have longer than five minutes,' he laughed. 'You must eat, too. Have you food, still?'

I nodded. I could see that he felt better today. His grin had returned. He was still wearing the silk stocking sling, though.

By seven o'clock we were walking downhill, beside the fast-running river. It had broadened out yet again, after leaving the narrow pass where we'd camped overnight. Now, I could see sheep on the hillside, although the mountains beyond were as high and craggy as before. It was cloudy this morning and colder. After the heat of the Mediterranean I shivered and the sharp air cut into my throat and chest, making me cough as I scrambled over rocks and scree and through scrub.

We had been going for three or four hours, walking silently in single file, when Paul stopped and said, 'Look,' and jerked his head to the right.

I turned my head and searched the bare hillside, until my eyes fixed on a boy, sitting on a rock, watching us.

'He is a shepherd,' said Paul. 'We must be close to a village.'

'Will he go and tell on us?' I asked, scared.

'Probably. These villages are so small that we will be noticed. Anyway, they will guess what we are. People have been getting in and out through these mountain passes for centuries.'

The boy suddenly stood up and waved his arms. He was too far away for me to see his face clearly, so I didn't know whether he was pleased or angry to see us, but I waved back. Once, after we'd continued walking, I looked back over my shoulder. He was still on the rock.

In the distance I could hear a bell and, for several minutes, I thought I was imagining it, but then Paul turned and grinned. 'A church bell, do you hear it?'

'Yes.' I was excited and scared at the same time. Then, as we breasted a small hill, I saw below us a church in the centre of a tiny village of stone houses, nestling in the valley basin. 'Are we in Spain?'

Paul nodded. He was looking at his map. 'Now, we must be careful.'

Chapter Fourteen

Many curious eyes watched us as we walked into the village, and I was conscious of what a peculiar sight we must be. Paul, with his arm in a sling, and me in muddy trousers with my wild and uncombed hair hanging over my shoulders.

Paul spoke in Spanish to an old man who was sitting on a wooden chair outside one of the houses.

'What is the name of this village, señor?' he asked.

For a few moments there was no answer as the old man sucked on his pipe and gazed at the mountains. And then, when he finally spoke, it was in a different language. I was bewildered.

'He's speaking in Catalan,' Paul said. 'It's local to the area.'

'Do you understand it?'

Paul nodded. 'It is spoken on both sides of the border.'

He repeated his question and the old man replied. 'Ribera de Cardós.'

Paul looked at me. 'Did you get that?'

'Yes.' I was relieved and mentally scanned the map that Paul had shown me at the hotel. 'That's where we're supposed to be, isn't it? Ask him how far it is to Llavorsí and if there are any soldiers about.' I smiled at the old man and, politely, he struggled to his feet and swept off his black beret. We shook hands and he gave me a gap-toothed grin.

'There are strangers at Llavorsí. My son told me. Do you go to join them?'

When Paul translated this I wondered what to do. Should we shake our heads and pretend that we were on our own?

'I think we say yes,' said Paul.

So I nodded and said, 'Tell him we work for a news-paper. That we want to show the world what is happening.'

'We had soldiers here last month.' The old man spat on the dusty ground. 'Fascists! We, this village, are loyal to the King and the Church.'

'And now? The soldiers?'

He shrugged. 'Gone, I think. And our fighters have given up. We are left in peace.' He said something else and I waited for Paul to translate it. Although my French was good and I had some Spanish, I understood nothing of Catalan. Paul was smiling.

'What did he say?' I looked at the old man and then at Paul.

'He said I was very lucky to be with such a beautiful woman.'

I could feel my face reddening. 'I think his eyesight's failing,' I muttered.

Paul laughed. 'False modesty,' he said. 'Don't you realise? You are lovely.'

I laughed. Despite Charlie saying that I wasn't bad-looking, and Amyas being prepared to take me to bed, I was still unable to accept the compliment as genuine.

But it was nice to hear it. The old man was speaking again and I looked at Paul for an explanation.

'He says your hair is the colour of life. That you are a spirit of the mountain.' Paul shook his head. 'I would not agree. You are better than that. A companion, a colleague.' He looked down at his arm. 'A nurse. That is what you are to me.'

I smiled at the old man and shook his hand again before we walked on another few hundred yards into the heart of the village. The café was open and we ate a dish of butter beans, potatoes and fried egg loaded with garlic and chilli, and washed it down with a carafe of rough red wine. Every mouthful was delicious and I was embarrassed by how greedily I was eating. Paul though, only picked at his food.

'How far d'you think it is to Llavorsí?' I asked, wearily sitting back from the table and looking at the little stone street outside the open door of the café.

'Not very far,' Paul murmured. 'Three, four kilometres, perhaps. And on a road. It will be easy.'

Three or four kilometres, I thought, gazing up at the mountains. The cloud had lifted and the sun had come out, and was beaming down on the dusty, grey stone village. It was warm, and I turned my face to the glow. Just three or kilometres, then I will have to find Charlie. Somehow I didn't think that it would be difficult. In these small villages everyone was aware of a stranger. But I wondered again why he couldn't come out on his own. He was fitter than I was, and if I could make it across the mountains then so could he. I knew he was in danger of being arrested if he was found, having previously, like Paul, been thrown out of the country. And I also knew that the Nationalists had overrun this part of Spain, but that Madrid was still in Republican hands. He could have got there and flown out. So why hadn't he? It was only then that I realised he must have been injured. There was no other explanation. I started feeling anxious again. I had to find him.

'It's time to go,' I started to say, turning my head away from the mountains to look at Paul. To my alarm, his face was contorted with pain and beads of sweat lined his temples. He was nursing his arm, holding it close to his body and rocking slightly in his chair.

'What's the matter?' I gasped, shocked by his appearance.

'I don't know,' he groaned. 'I feel . . . strange.'

'Where? Your arm?'

'Yes. And my head.' I looked at his eyes: they were not focusing again, and after a few moments, he closed them.

'Oh no,' I wailed. Jumping up, I looked for help from the café owner, who was sitting at another table with a glass and uncorked bottle in front of him. 'A doctor!' I shouted in French. 'Is there a doctor anywhere? My friend is very sick.' He gaped at me and shook his head and I shouted again, 'A doctor!' Now, he stood up and edged warily over to Paul and stared at him. He muttered something and then shrugged.

'Paul!' I shook his shoulder. 'Wake up!' He opened his eyes.

'Yes. What d'you want?' His voice was slurred and his eyelids drooped.

'Please, Paul,' I cried, 'try to keep awake. I'll get help.' I ran out of the café and looked up and down the dusty street. There were very few people about, only an old woman who was carrying a rolled-up bundle of sticks and a man sitting on cart behind a bony horse.

'Is there a doctor?' I shouted. 'Can you help me?' They both looked at me in amazement, and the old woman held her sticks closer to her bent body, as though I was about to take them from her.

A priest was walking down from the little church, so I ran to him. 'Father. Is there a doctor? My friend is ill.'

The old priest answered me in French. 'No, mademoiselle. We have no doctor. At Sort, there is a doctor. Where is your friend?' I dragged him back to the café, where he looked at Paul who was slumped on the chair. 'What is the matter with him?'

'He fell, yesterday. He hit his head and his arm. We have walked since then, and I thought he was better.'

The priest bent down and spoke to Paul. 'You are sick, my son?'

Paul opened his eyes and tried to focus on the priest. 'Yes, Father, I have a headache. I think . . .' His voice trailed off and his eyes closed again.

I grabbed his shoulders and propped him up, for now he was in danger of falling off the chair, and I looked wildly at the priest. 'What should I do?' I cried.

The old man took charge. He said something rapidly to the café owner, and then shouted outside to the man with the cart. Reluctantly, both men came to the priest's aid, and between them they carried Paul outside and put him on the back of the cart.

'I will take him to the church. I have a mattress in the vestry. He can lie there.' The priest jerked his head to the carter, who clicked up the horse, and the cart slowly moved across the road. 'Come, mademoiselle.' The priest urged me to follow him, and I offered some francs to the café owner for our meal, then picked up both rucksacks and crossed the road.

Paul lay on a feather mattress in a stone room behind the church. The smell of incense bathed the air, and dust particles danced in the narrow shafts of sunlight which shone through small, arched windows. He wavered in and out of consciousness, and I fell to my knees beside him to wipe the sweat from his head with the damp cloth that the priest had given me.

'The carter will go for the doctor, if you give him some money, mademoiselle. I tried to get him to take your friend on the back of the cart but that he won't do. The responsibility is too much. So, instead, he will go and tell the doctor of your friend's injury. The doctor, Professor Gonzalez, has a car, and will come here.' He paused, and frowned as Paul started muttering and shouting sudden swear words. 'Your friend has a troubled conscience.'

'I don't know,' I lied. 'He is a reporter who has seen many dreadful things. They prey on his mind.'

'Ah,' the old priest replied. 'I understand. And you, mademoiselle? Have you seen terrible things also?'

'Not in Spain,' I answered, making an effort at conversation, although not really wanting to talk. Getting help for Paul was all I could really think of. 'I am new to this work. But,' I added, 'I was in Germany, horrible things have happened there.'

The priest shrugged. 'That is only to the Jews,' he said. 'It is not the same.'

I looked up, shocked at his callousness, and was ready to get into an argument. But Paul lay semi-conscious on the floor between us so I bit my tongue, and lowered my eyes. I bent over him again, and wiped his forehead. His eyes opened. 'Seffy,' he said. 'Go on to Llavorsí. It's only a few kilometres. You can do nothing for me here.'

'The priest has sent for a doctor,' I whispered. 'He will make you better.'

'Yes. Now go.'

I was torn. I knew I must get to Charlie, but I didn't want to leave Paul. In a stupid way I felt responsible for him. 'Go,' he whispered again, and, as I stood up, he added, 'Take my pistol.'

Why? I wanted to ask, but his eyelids had dropped shut again, and I stood, uncertain what I should do.

'The carter will go when you pay him,' the priest reminded me, and I made up my mind.

'I must go too,' I said. 'I leave my friend in your charge. His name is Paul Durban, and he comes from Perpignan, and,' I took out my wallet, 'this is payment for the doctor, and some for the church. I am grateful for your care.'

He took the money, and nodded. 'You are generous, my child.' And while he was putting the notes in a wooden box on a little side table, I opened Paul's rucksack and took out the pistol, transferring it to my bag.

With a last look at Paul, and a thank-you nod to the priest, I left the church and went outside into the hot afternoon.

The carter wanted to haggle over the amount he needed, jabbing his finger at me and speaking in heavily accented French. At another time, the old me would have weakly given in, but I was worked up with a mixture of anxiety and anger. 'I will give you this much,' I said, noticing a new edge of steel which had crept into my voice. 'And no more. It is enough.' I wasn't surprised when he accepted the money. He knew I wouldn't be argued with. 'I will come with you as far as Llavorsí,' I added. 'And,' I said firmly, 'the priest will know if you don't go for the doctor. And, what is more, so will God.'

The road to Llavorsí ran beside the river. It was a good surface, hard-packed dirt, smoothed by generations of travellers. A car could have made the distance in less than ten minutes, but the bony old horse only walked at about three miles an hour, and I sat beside the carter, baked by the blazing afternoon sun, while my mind whirled with events past, and the possibility of those to come.

The carter didn't speak, and I was glad of it, I needed to think. What would be my best course of action once we reached Llavorsí? Was it a bigger village than Ribera, with policemen, and other officials? And, most worrying of all, where was Charlie?

I looked down the road. It ran between steeply wooded hillsides and curved this way and that around bends, all the time at a gentle downhill gradient. Beside the road, the river gushed and tumbled its way through rocks and gulleys, heading for the softer lands beyond the Pyrenees. Indeed, almost the only noise I could hear was the river, for everywhere around us was silent. Except for the muffled clop of the horse and the occasional grunt of its master, I could have been alone in the world.

Suddenly the horse pricked up his ears, and, in the next moment, another cart came round the bend in the road to face us. It was pulled by an equally ancient animal. The driver stopped, and after giving me a curious glance, greeted us. My carter spoke to him in Catalan, while they both looked at me, and the new driver, frowning, jerked his head back over his shoulder.

'What is it?' I asked.

The carter cleared his throat, and spat over the side of the cart. 'There are soldiers in Llavorsí,' he growled. 'They have come an hour ago. Fascists.'

Oh, Jesus! My heart began to pound. I didn't know what to do. 'Is there a back road?' I asked, feeling breathless. The carter gave a short sarcastic laugh, and shook his head. The other man said something else. The two carters chatted for a moment, and then my man turned to me. 'You could get out now, and go through the trees.' He nodded to the steep slope beside the road. 'My friend tells me that strangers were in a house in the village, but have left now. Is that why you are going to Llavorsí?'

I nodded cautiously.

'He believes they are on the hills somewhere. Perhaps in a shepherd's hut.'

'Are the soldiers looking for them?'

'He does not think so.' He narrowed his eyes when he looked at me. 'Is there a price on their head?'

'No,' I said quickly, not wanting to offer him any opportunities. 'My friend is a reporter. An Englishman. I don't know about any others.' This was translated, and I heard the word *Anglès*. Which meant English, I supposed, and I didn't know whether they thought that this was good or bad. But with a lugubriously muttered farewell, the other man clicked up his horse and went on his way, and I was left sitting in the cart trying to make a decision. It didn't take me long. I hoisted my rucksack on to my shoulders, and climbed down. The carter watched me, then pointed with his short whip to the hillside. 'Go through the trees,' he repeated. 'Someone will know where your friend is.'

He clicked at the horse, and would have left but I grabbed the reins. 'Remember,' I warned. 'The priest, and God will know if you don't get the doctor.' He scowled, and, jerking the reins, urged the horse to move on, leaving me alone on the empty road.

My legs were still aching from the last two days, but I turned my face to the hillside and set off. It was hard, climbing up through oak and silver fir and struggling through rhododendron and Pyrenean broom. Startled birds flew out of the canopy above me, giving away my position to anyone watching, but I didn't think that anyone was, and I pushed on. My legs were even more scratched, and felt like jelly, but soon I was high above the road, and had rounded the bend. Through the trees I could see Llavorsí in the valley below me. It was larger than Ribera; the houses similarly built of grey stone, but there were more of them, and they spread further out beside the river and up on to the hillside. I could even see a barrier which had been put across the road. It was manned by soldiers.

I leant against a tree, and wondered in which direction to go. Should I go down into the village, or wander aimlessly around up here to try to find Charlie? As I scanned the hillside my eyes picked out what looked like the wall of a stone building. It was surrounded by trees, and probably not visible from the road below. It was a small house or a shepherd's hut, perhaps. Was that a likely place? I hitched up my rucksack. It was worth a try.

The best way to approach it would be from above, I decided, and climbed higher up the hillside. The trees didn't grow as close here, allowing me to make better time, but now and then spurs of granite rock stood in my way, which required an extra effort to get over. I knew that if anyone looked up I would sometimes be visible, a figure standing out and moving across the valley, up, away from the road. With binoculars they would see I wasn't a shepherd. With that realisation in mind, I kept low and crawled through the bushes, and over rocks, until I could see the roof of the hut about thirty feet below me.

There was no sound, nor any movement from the building, and I sat with my back against a rocky ledge, gathering my breath and staring down at it. Was anyone there? Was Charlie there?

I had to find out. I looked down at the village and saw the soldiers lazily leaning against the barrier, enjoying the late afternoon sun. I moved deeper into the trees, in the direction of the hut. It was in a clearing, a flat patch of scrubby ground surrounded by saplings and small rocks. A sheep path led away from it, down into the village. Standing in the trees, with the door of the hut only about a few feet away across the grass, I took a deep breath. I was scared at what I might find. Suppose Charlie was sick, like Paul, or even worse . . .

Just go, I told myself, and stepped out of the trees into the clearing.

'Hello, my darling.'

For a moment I didn't move. It couldn't be, could it? I spun round and there he was, behind me. Amyas, as beautiful as he'd ever been. My Amyas.

'Amyas,' I breathed, disbelieving. Was this figure standing in the trees something dragged out of my imagination? A god come to rescue me? For a moment I thought that I was going slightly mad, exhausted by the trek over the mountains and upset by Paul's sudden collapse, but there could be no doubt. The figure in front of me was real. 'Amyas?' I whispered his name again. 'Is that you?'

He nodded, and smiled, and I threw myself into his arms. All the questions that were forming in my head were put aside as I simply revelled in his presence. His arms felt strong as they held me close to him, and when he lowered his face and his lips pressed against mine, they were as firm and passionate as they'd ever been.

'You are a tease, Persephone,' he said, when we stopped kissing. 'I've been looking for you for the last two hours. I've been all over this damn hillside.'

'How did you know I was here?' I was gaping at him, almost wanting to cry with relief.

'The carter told me. I met him in the village. His description of you was so accurate that I didn't have a moment's doubt.'

'The carter?' Oh, Christ, I wondered. Who else has he told?

'What about the soldiers?'

'They're in the village. They're looking for deserters.'

I bit my lip and looked back over my shoulder to the hut. 'Charlie? Have you seen him?'

'He's in there.' He nodded towards the hut. 'I brought him this far, but he's got a fever and can't get much further. He was shot a couple of weeks ago in some sort of skirmish south of here. I found him at a field station and spirited him away before he was discovered for what he was. The Republican commanders don't take kindly to being played for fools. They know that if he gets out he'll report honestly, and some of their practices are as bad or worse than those of the Nationalists.'

'Where was he shot? I mean, where on his body?'

'Shoulder. He's lost a lot of blood, and I think the bullet might have chipped a bone.'

'I must go to him.' And I turned, and started to hurry to the hut.

Amyas kept up with me. 'There is somebody else in there,' he said, his voice unnaturally hesitant, but I wasn't interested. I needed to see Charlie.

He was lying on a trestle bed, which was pushed against the stone wall of the hut. In the gloom of the interior it was hard to see him clearly, but I could make out enough to know that he was damaged, and sick. He had lost an awful lot of weight, and two red spots flushed his sunken cheeks, the colour continuing down into his neck. A dirty bandage was wrapped across his naked shoulder and chest, and a dark patch of dried blood indicated the location of his wound.

'Well, Charlie Bradford,' I said lightly. 'What have you been up to?'

He opened his eyes. 'Blake?' he said and gave me one of his sweet smiles. 'You've taken your bloody time. What kept you?'

'Fool,' I laughed, and gave him a kiss on the cheek.

Amyas had followed me into the hut, and stood watching. 'He's been waiting for you ever since I sent that telegram.'

'You sent it?' I asked.

Amyas nodded. 'Well, as you see, he wasn't exactly able to.'

There was a movement on the other side of the room, and I turned sharply. A woman was sitting on the dusty floor, watching me. The room was dim, with only the twilight coming in through the glassless window, but I could see that she was young, with long black hair and a pretty, heart-shaped face. She struggled to her feet, grunting with the effort, and at first I thought that she must be sick too, but when she straightened up, I saw that she was heavily pregnant.

'This is Elena,' said Amyas. 'She is a deserter, like Charlie. I've brought them both out.'

Chapter Fifteen

Silence lay like a heavy blanket over the stone hut, and the four figures within could have been actors in a mimed tableau. Charlie, lying helplessly on the trestle bed; the girl, Elena, standing to the side, her dark brown eyes flashing with what seemed like suppressed anger; me, now slumped exhausted on the floor beside Charlie, and Amyas, looking as calm and as amused as ever, leaning against the frame of the open door.

He was the first to speak. 'Well, that's another fine mess you've got me into.' His Laurel and Hardy impersonation designed to lighten the atmosphere didn't work with everyone. I was too tired to respond, but Elena snorted her disgust and spat '¡capullo!', a word I didn't know but assumed was an insult. Amyas laughed at this and from his bed Charlie gave a weak chuckle.

I yawned. 'What are we going to do?'

'Nothing, tonight,' Amyas said. 'It's too late, too dark and too dangerous. Tomorrow, we'll get out of here.'

I nodded and looked around the hut. My eyes had adjusted to the gloom and I could see a fireplace, empty save for a pile of grey wood ash and, apart from the trestle bed where Charlie lay, no other furniture. It was simply a hut, where a shepherd and possibly, judging by the smell, his sheep could spend a night; nothing more. I peered at the shadowy stone walls and at the bare rafters above. 'Is there a lamp or something?' I asked. The hut was very gloomy, the last ray of sunlight having dropped behind the mountain. I could see a section of sky through the open door; a triangle of exhausted pale blue, painted with ragged streaks of red and purple cloud. Soon this exquisite light would disappear too and then complete darkness would descend.

'We could make a fire,' Charlie murmured. 'It would give both light and heat.'

'Are you cold?' I asked, concerned. Turning, I put out my hand to feel his.

'No. Not really.' He rumbled a cough and then gave an involuntary groan. I knew that his wound must hurt.

'A fire would give us away,' said Amyas. 'But then, does it matter? I'm sure the locals know where we are, and I think that the soldiers have left by now. They won't want to stay here overnight.' He straightened up. 'I'll go down to the village to check and try and get us some food, too.' He started to walk across the grass towards the sheep track, then stopped and called over his shoulder, 'Persephone. Come with me.'

Oh, I wanted to go. No matter how tired I was, I wanted to be alone with him, to hold his hand and perhaps to stop on the sheep track, hidden in the trees and slide into his arms and feel his body next to mine. He was like a drug that had been denied me and now he was here, emitting the same fascination and still utterly desirable. But I could hear Charlie breathing heavily behind me. 'No,' I said. 'I'll stay with Charlie and . . .' I peered at Elena's angry face, 'this girl.'

'All right.' I felt a small pang of disappointment at the ease with which he accepted my refusal and frowned as

I watched him through the open door, until he disappeared from sight.

'You should have gone with him,' said Charlie.

'Should I?'

'Of course. You know you wanted to.'

'I'm working,' I said. 'I should be with my boss.'

He smiled at that and made an effort to sit up. 'Christ, I need to pee,' he grunted. In the ten minutes I'd been with him I thought he'd started to look a bit better. More in control. Perhaps it was the responsibility of being a boss.

I got up. 'I'll take you outside. Can you stand?'

Elena moved from her place by the wall. 'I help him, too,' she said and between us we gently lifted Charlie upright and walked him outside.

'Lean me against that tree,' he muttered, 'and have the grace to turn your back.' I did, but Elena, not caring about the niceties, watched his every movement. She was a striking girl, young, still not twenty, I thought, and not as tall as me, but lithe and strong-looking. Even the bulge that was her unborn child seemed in proportion and she carried it easily, without a hint that it was a burden.

'When is your baby expected?' I asked. I spoke in French, sure that she would understand me. She did.

She shook her head. 'He comes today, tomorrow, I don't know. I think, this month or next.' Looking at her, I thought, that's all we bloody need. But I was determined to be positive and I stuck out my hand. 'I'm Seffy Blake, Charlie's assistant. How do you do?'

She looked surprised but took my hand. 'Elena Beltrán. I am lead recruiter for Spanish Republicans in Paris. But now, I am fighter.' She paused, her face angry and sad. 'That is, I *was* fighter – now I am deserter.'

'You can't fight with a baby so close to being born,' I offered, trying to be kind, but she snorted.

'I can fight. It is men who will not let me. They say I must make food for people in the hospital. The priest says I am wicked for having baby without husband and must go home.' She gave a dismissive laugh. 'I do not care what the priest says. I have no home and my parents are dead. Besides, I am communist. I am for the people, not the Church.'

I should have found her amusing, and if I had been Xanthe I would have given a tinkling laugh and disregarded her as common. Elena's opinions were so fixed and so extreme and they did sound odd coming from the mouth of such a pretty young girl. Instead of being amused I found that I felt sorry for her. She was alone and expecting a child, but facing her future courageously.

'Well, good luck,' I said and smiled at her. She frowned. Perhaps she wasn't used to people being nice to her, or perhaps she doubted that I would be.

'I don't believe in luck,' she snapped.

'I'm done,' Charlie muttered. Glad to escape this impossible conversation, I turned and took his arm. Elena, still simmering with rage, grabbed his other one, but he winced in pain and she snatched her hand away. 'I'm all right, thanks,' he said. 'Seffy can manage me.'

She nodded and walked further into the trees as I helped Charlie back to the hut. 'She's a bit feisty,' I said with a smile.

'Christ, yes. She's a holy terror. They picked the wrong person to upset and once she's had that kid, she'll go straight back to the fight . . . if there's any fighting still to be done.'

Back in the hut, with Charlie sitting on the bed, and me on the floor beside him, I asked about his experience with the Brigade.

'Christ, it was hell,' he started. 'At first, when we got to Albacete, we were locked in the barracks while we had weapons training and political lectures.' He gave a short laugh. 'As far as I could see the lectures were as important to the leaders as the training. It was really tough, though, and the people who ran the camp were quite harsh. They were always looking for infiltrators and I was scared most of the time. I think they suspected me right from the start. But they drafted me into an English-speaking battalion and I was sent up north to fight. It took days, in the back of lorries and marching through back roads and we were short of food, too. We ended up here in Catalonia, I can't remember the name of the place, but it will be in the records for when I come to write about it.' He gave an involuntary shiver and with a shaking hand tentatively rubbed his injured shoulder. His eyes were wide with pinpoint pupils when he said, 'And, Blake, guess what? I was shot on the first day of action. My terrible war was over in one day and d'you know? I was glad.'

I put my hand over his. I had no words of comfort, but he held on to it as if he'd never let it go. The normal controlled person that I knew Charlie to be, the twinkly-eyed chief reporter, internationally regarded and respected, seemed lost and beset by his memories. I searched for something to say that would cheer him up, bring him back to the man I knew, but I couldn't think of anything sensible. So I smiled at him and muttered, 'I'm just happy to see you here.'

There was a noise at the door as Elena came back inside and we watched her as she sat again by the empty fireplace. Why did Amyas come into my head as I looked at her? I swallowed and asked quietly, 'What happened next? How did Amyas rescue you?'

Charlie gave an astonished laugh. 'Now we come to the strange part. I was lying in a filthy field hospital and she,' he nodded to Elena, 'was there. Bringing water and bits of food to the patients. Then these political commissars turned up and started asking who I was, what did I do in civilian life and where I'd come from. I fobbed them off as best I could and thought I'd got away with it, but that night, out of the blue, Amyas appeared. "They're on to you," he said. "We'd better get you out." And with that, he pulled me out of bed, slung me over his shoulder and walked out of the camp. He had a car outside and to add to my amazement, Elena was sitting in it, waiting for him.' He lowered his voice. 'I think that her being there was a surprise to him too, but you know how he is, he pretends it's all a game.' He took a deep breath, groaning with the effort, and it was a moment before he got over the pain.

I sat quietly, taking it all in. Strange things do happen in war, but even so, Amyas? In a war zone? It was so unlikely because, with Mrs Cartwright's money, he could have gone anywhere. Enjoyed himself at the casinos, latched on to a more attractive, wealthier, widow. Or come to me. He knew I'd have taken him back, any time. I'd have given the world to have him back and I closed my eyes, remembering those magical nights in Cornwall. I could almost smell the salt coming in on the wind and see the stars twinkling in a midnight-blue sky.

I was brought down to earth when Charlie spoke again. 'We drove to Sort and holed up there. It's not very far from here. Amyas sent the telegram to Geoff for me, but while he was at the post office, Elena heard that the army was on its way, so we decided to move here – well, to this village. That's when he sent the telegram for you to come and get me. I thought it would be easy for you to get through the border, no problem, hire a car or something.' He looked at my exhausted face and at the scratches on my legs which I was examining. Some of them were turning septic. 'Not so easy, eh?'

I shook my head. 'The border's closed. I came over the mountain but I don't think you will be able to go back that way. It took us two days and there was some climbing involved.'

'Us?'

I realised then that I hadn't thought about Paul for hours and my stomach curdled, remembering how dreadful he'd looked when I left him. 'Yes,' I answered, hesitantly. 'I came with Paul Durban. D'you remember him? He said he knew you.'

'Yes, I remember him. He's very young, very driven. Gets involved too easily but he's a good reporter.' He paused for a moment. 'Where did you leave him?'

I sighed. 'He's in the last village. Oh, Charlie, he fell yesterday when we were coming down the mountain. He seemed all right afterwards and then, suddenly, a few hours ago, he started going unconscious. I've left him in the care of the priest at Ribera de Cardós. They've sent for the doctor but . . . I don't think he's going to make it.' I sighed, thinking of his young face and tear-filled eyes when he told me his terrible story, and then all at once I remembered the man with the co-respondent shoes. Where was he? Had he persuaded the hotel manager to reveal the contents of the telegram telling me to go to Llavorsí? I was sure that he had. And that meant he was here, somewhere, waiting for Paul.

Charlie must have noticed the sudden stiffening in my back for he said, 'What is it, Seffy? What's up?'

'Nothing.' He didn't need anything else to worry him. 'Nothing,' I repeated. 'Goose walked over my grave, that's all.'

Elena got up and walked to the door. 'He comes,' she said and went outside.

I got up too. 'I suppose she wants to get to France, so that she can be with the baby's father,' I said.

Charlie gave a sarcastic chuckle. 'She doesn't have to go that far. Sorry, Blake, but from what I gather, the father is right here.'

It wasn't such a shock, really. As soon as I'd heard her name I remembered Amyas talking about her when we were in bed in the Hotel Adlon. How she'd scared Percy, but not him because 'he knew a way to tame her'. And this was the result. He'd spoilt her life.

I should despise him, regard him as not worthy of my love, but the truth was, I didn't feel any of those things. I just accepted it, as I did everything that was to do with Amyas. In my head, the high standards I had for myself and for everyone else I encountered simply didn't apply to him. So when he walked in a few minutes later, with an orange box containing bread, cheese, grapes and a couple of bottles of wine, I smiled at him. Happy to see him, as always.

'The soldiers have gone,' he said. 'The village knows

we're here, so yes, we can light a fire and I've brought a couple of candles.'

It was a strange evening, sitting in that hut, with the greeny-yellow flames from the pinewood fire making shadows dance on the walls. Hungrily, we tore chunks from the bread and Amyas pulled out a flick knife from his pocket to cut up the cheese. He also had a folding corkscrew and opened the bottles of wine. It was one of the best meals I ever ate.

I told them about coming over the mountains, how hard it had been, and that we'd stayed in a cave overnight. And as the wine and exhaustion took hold, I found myself blurting out to them about Paul and the village massacre. Then I told them what he'd done.

Charlie frowned. 'That's not good,' he said. 'No matter what had been done, his action was indefensible.'

I looked at Amyas for his opinion, but he was silent, his face relaxed and amused, as though everything I'd said was unimportant.

'I think that man followed us all the way from Cerbère and I'm pretty sure that he knew we were coming to Llavorsí. You haven't seen a stranger hanging about in the village, have you?'

Amyas spread his hands. 'They're all strangers in the village. I've never been here before.'

'I know,' I said. 'But someone who looks out of place.' He shook his head, reaching again for the bottle of wine, and we sat, now silent, staring at the fire. As night fell it had grown colder and I took off my jacket and gave it to Charlie, for he had neither a shirt nor a coat, having been snatched from his hospital bed.

'Ah,' said Amyas, watching me helping Charlie. 'I

forgot.' And from the bottom of the orange box he produced a blanket.

'Where the hell did you get this?' I asked, as I draped the pink and yellow striped bedcover over Charlie's shoulders. 'And the food, for that matter.'

'I think, my darling, it would be better if you didn't ask.' Amyas raised his eyebrows and I grinned back. I knew he was a thief and for once I was glad of it.

We talked after Charlie had gone to sleep and Elena had walked outside. She seemed restless and fidgety and had barely eaten anything. I thought she was probably upset because I'd turned up and she had seen Amyas and me kissing at the edge of the clearing. Had she linked up with him again in the hope that he would marry her, or at least take care of her? It was not an unreasonable hope and I had to speak of it to Amyas. 'That girl is having your child,' I said, trying to make it a statement rather than an accusation.

'Yes,' he answered, looking at the fire. 'She is. Is that difficult for you, Persephone?'

I shrugged. 'Not really. It isn't as if we're married or even, "a couple".'

He was quiet for a few seconds and then said, 'No, I suppose not. But there is something between us. Something . . . magical. You put a spell on me in Cornwall which I've found impossible to escape.'

'Do you want to escape?'

He smiled and shook his head. 'No.'

'Neither do I.' And he took my hand and raised it to his lips.

It was one of those moments one lives for. Sitting next to him on the floor of the hut, with the heady scent of

225

pine resin as it oozed out of the burning wood, I felt as close to Amyas as I had ever done. I looked at his face, noticing for the first time that he had a healing scar on his temple. 'Amyas,' I asked. 'What on earth are you doing here?'

'What?' he said. 'You mean what am I doing here in this hut, or what am I doing here in Spain?'

'Both.'

He raised an eyebrow. 'What does anyone do when they come to Spain these days? You know I said I would, remember? But it had to be in my time. And after seeing you in Berlin, I knew it was the moment. So I flew to Madrid and joined up.'

'And did you fight?'

He nodded slowly. 'I fought, Persephone. Just the one battle. I killed men and men tried to kill me, but I was lucky. I survived. Then I came to my senses and left.'

'You're a deserter then?'

'Oh yes,' he nodded.

I almost laughed out loud. Here I was, illegally in the country, and I'd compounded my sin by sharing my illegality with three deserters. What a ridiculous situation. I thought back to the pub in Cornwall where Graham and Percy had discussed coming to Spain and Amyas had encouraged them. It had all sounded so romantic then, so noble. And now?

'What about Graham?' I asked. 'What has happened to him? Did Percy find him?'

Amyas shook his head. 'Graham was killed six months ago, before Percy ever got to the front. We only found out from another Englishman who'd been with him. He was shot through the head and died instantly.'

'Oh dear,' I said. 'Poor Percy. However will he get over that?'

Amyas gave a brief laugh. 'You'd be surprised. Percy has turned out to be a good soldier. He has nerves of ice and is a brilliant tactician. If he was upset about Graham, he kept it to himself. He's been made an officer, you know.'

'Does he know you've deserted?'

Amyas shrugged. 'I expect so. And he'll give me no quarter if he catches up with me.'

'So,' I continued, anxious now to hear everything, 'what were you doing at the hospital? How did you find Charlie?'

He shrugged. 'I needed an excuse for not being at the front.' He touched his temple, where I could just see the red line of a two-inch scar. 'I cut my head on a rock while I was getting away from the battlefield. Everyone thought it was shrapnel and that gave me a reason to go to the hospital. They were transporting injured men to Madrid and that was a good way for me to go. But, fate, as it so often does, intervened. Who should be the first person I saw but Elena. She guessed immediately what I was up to. "That is a scratch", she said, "not a wound. You are a bastard, and a bastard's son. Look what you have done to me," and she lifted her apron and showed me.'

I giggled and Amyas, putting an arm around my shoulder, chuckled too. 'I'll bet that gave you pause for thought,' I said.

'Yes. It was an . . . interesting moment.' For once, Amyas looked a little rueful. 'Quite a surprise. Anyway, she said that if I helped her to get to Paris she wouldn't give me away.'

'Why Paris?' I asked.

'Apparently she has friends there. Members of the party, I suppose. She planned to have the child there and give it to a couple, some other devoted followers of the hammer and sickle who have no children. She doesn't want it . . . it would be nothing but a nuisance to her, but she wanted to ensure that it would be brought up in the correct belief.'

Poor little baby, I thought. No mention of affection and care in those plans. 'But Charlie? How did you find him?'

'It was Elena. She told me that there was another Englishman in the ward who the commissars believed was a spy. She thought they were going to shoot him. I went to have a look and found it was Charlie. As soon as I saw him I knew that you wouldn't be far away. So I took him out.'

'And Elena came too.'

Amyas's face hardened. 'I was going to leave her, you know. She would only have held me back but I think, quite rightly, she didn't trust me.'

'You are an untrustworthy bastard,' I murmured. 'Mrs Cartwright can attest to that.'

He laughed. 'Did she contact you?'

I nodded. 'She came to see me, told me what you'd done. She'll have you back, you know.'

'Of course she will. But,' he smiled, 'I think that won't be necessary. There are other ways to make money. Besides, even I can't take any more of that old trout's friendship with the Fascists. They're even worse than the Communists.'

At that instant I wanted to say: marry me. I'll give you money. I'll set you up in a legitimate business if you want.

Or even, don't marry me, just ask me for money, be obligated to me. But I didn't. That wasn't how we were together; we were lovers. I turned my face to his. 'I want you,' I said, unabashed at my boldness. 'I want you to make love to me.'

'Just what I was thinking, my sweetheart. Let's go outside.'

Was it the same silver moon in the velvet sky and were they the same stars that shone on us at the house by the sea? Those twinkling pinpoints of light that watched as we tore at each other, starving for the ultimate satisfaction of desire. I know they were, I know too that nothing could have kept me from him that night. I wanted him, I needed him and he felt the same. He grabbed at my clothes with the same reckless urgency that I used on his, freeing my body from the constraints that prevented him from being at one with my willing flesh.

The damp grass beneath a scented, silver fir tree was our enchanted bed and it didn't disappoint. At the height of passion I called out my pent-up craving and afterwards burst into hot tears of relief. 'Oh, God,' I wept. 'I've missed you. So much.'

He held me close, kissing the soft skin behind my ear and running his hands down my back. 'Don't cry,' he whispered. 'Be happy. Nothing has changed. Between us, darling Persephone, love is paramount. Only death will stop it. And even then perhaps we'll continue on, like those stars above us.'

It was true. We would float on our coral boat into the velvet sky. Lovers for ever.

After a little while I eased my body from under his and, sighing, pulled on my clothes while he dressed too.

'We have to get some rest,' he groaned. 'Tomorrow might be difficult.'

'I know,' I said and started to get up. Suddenly, a low scream broke the stillness of the night and I froze. 'God,' I breathed, 'what's that?'

'I don't know.' Amyas stood up. 'It sounds like an animal in pain.'

I shivered. I thought of the wolves and the wild boar that roamed these mountains. Something had been caught and was being killed. And it was close by. 'We should get into the hut,' I said. 'It might be dangerous.'

Amyas nodded. 'All right', but then the scream came again and I clutched his arm, terrified. 'Come on,' I urged, but he didn't move.

'That's human,' he said and then called, 'Elena!'

We found her, only ten yards from where we'd made love. She was lying on the ground and in the moonlight I could see a spreading patch of dark fluid beneath her. Her body was contracting spasmodically and her clenched fists were crossed on her chest. 'It comes,' she grunted, when we knelt beside her. Her eyes were glittering with pain and anticipation when she whispered, 'The child of revolution will be born beneath the stars.'

Chapter Sixteen

It was like something from an ancient age. An age of stone and wood; raw and almost feral; when creatures crept out, away from the pack to bring new life into the world. And like them, this young woman had chosen to give birth on her own in the woods, a wolf maiden, snarling at modernity. Kneeling beside her, I couldn't help admiring her courage and I pushed my hand into her clenched fist and let her squeeze it tightly.

There was a sudden patter of rain and the wind rustled through the branches of the surrounding trees. 'She can't have her baby out here,' I whispered to Amyas. 'It's raining and too dark to see what we're doing and too cold for a baby. We'll have to get her into the hut.'

'Yes,' he nodded and without another word he bent and picked her up.

'No!' she wailed. 'Leave me. My child shall be born here, under the stars.' She struggled and fought with him as he carried her across the clearing, crying and swearing at him as though her heart would break, but Amyas, countering her fury, directed a stream of Spanish invective back at her. I wasn't surprised that he could speak Spanish. After all, I'd discovered that he was fluent in German and he probably spoke French as well. His ability with languages was just another facet to his personality.

Charlie's body was outlined by the light behind him

as he stood leaning against the door frame of the hut. 'What's happened?' he asked anxiously. 'I heard a scream.'

'She's in labour,' I answered, nodding towards the struggling girl in Amyas's arms. 'Her baby's coming.'

'Jesus!' he groaned. 'That's all we need.' He was echoing exactly the thought I'd had earlier.

We followed Amyas into the hut and watched as he laid Elena on the floor. Now he was surprisingly gentle with her, even though she was spitting out what I could only assume were more swear words.

'You should have put her on the bed,' said Charlie. 'I don't need it as much as she does,' but Amyas shook his head.

'The bed's too narrow. She's better here.'

Charlie dragged off the blanket he was holding around his shoulders. 'Then take this. Cover her.' I took the blanket and put it over the girl, but she threw it off, getting on to her hands and knees and growling with each contraction.

I felt helpless. I had no idea what to do, but as the only other woman in this bleak hut I thought I must take charge. 'Water,' I said. 'We ought to get water,' and I picked up the two empty wine bottles. 'Amyas,' I said. 'Can you fill these from the stream?' He took them and went outside while I surveyed our meagre provisions and equipment and wondered if we had anything useful. There was nothing. 'Where's her bag?' I asked, and looked by the wall, where Elena usually sat. It was there, a striped canvas carrier bag, and I rooted through it. To my relief I found a couple of baby vests and a pretty cobweb knitted shawl. A pile of cotton squares was wrapped around a feeding bottle. She had made some preparations.

'We need a doctor or a midwife,' Charlie muttered, looking down at the girl who, in the midst of another agonising contraction, was writhing, lips clamped together, on the floor.

'For God's sake,' I snapped, worked up by his feeble response. 'There isn't a doctor here in this village, and it's nearly midnight. How can we possibly find a midwife?' I knelt down next to Elena and offered her a drink of water from my canteen. She shook her head and looked again at the door, as though all she wanted to do was escape into the night. But Amyas was standing guard and she moaned out her dismay.

Charlie sat down again on the bed, his shoulders painfully hunched. I was sorry I'd snapped at him and gave him what I hoped was a confident smile. 'We'll do the best we can,' I said.

We tried to do useful things. Amyas brought water in the wine bottles and we stood them close to the fire so that they could warm up. I took a clean pair of pants from my rucksack and, soaking them in water, I wiped Elena's face whenever she'd let me near her. Even Charlie stumbled about outside in the dark, collecting sticks to keep the fire going. But mostly we watched, unable to help, as the labour dragged on.

'How long d'you think it's been going?' asked Charlie. Amyas shook his head, 'I think longer than we realise. She didn't eat any supper and was difficult most of yesterday.'

'We should have left her in the village. Someone could have helped her.'

Amyas gave a short laugh. 'Were you brave enough to tell her?' As Charlie slowly shook his head, Amyas murmured, 'No. Neither was I.'

The night had given way to a grey, misty dawn when Amyas knelt in front of the exhausted girl. Elena had stopped writhing now and lay on her back, her eyes closed, whimpering with pain while we watched, in horrified fascination, the growing pool of blood which trickled from beneath her across the dirt floor.

'Is that normal?' whispered Charlie.

I shook my head. 'I don't think so.' Looking at Amyas, I said, 'We have to get that child out, then we might be able to stop the bleeding' – I bit my lip, hating my ignorance and helplessness – 'somehow.'

'I'll do it,' he said, and bending his mouth to her ear, he spoke to her. The instructions he gave were in Spanish and I could only pick up the odd word, but I knew that he was urging her to make one last attempt. 'Yes,' she whispered and gathered the remains of her strength.

I knelt by her head. 'You can do it,' I smiled and held her small hands while she opened her liquid brown eyes and looked at me and then past me. They were already seeing a different country.

'Yes,' she whispered again and screwed up her face, ready for her final effort. Charlie, from where he was sitting on the trestle bed, called out encouragement and with a scream that must have been heard in the village, she pushed out her child into its father's bloodied hands. He withdrew his flick knife and cut through the cord, then took the spare hair ribbon I'd found in my bag to tie it off.

For a heart-stopping moment the infant lay limply in

Amyas's arms like a floppy doll, and I held my breath. Could it be? Had all this effort brought forth a dead baby? Then it made a sound, a tiny choking whimper at first, but as its lungs kicked into action, the small squirming creature took a breath and gave a proper cry. I'm here, it was telling us. I'm alive.

'Elena,' I said, 'you have a little girl,' and as her eyes flickered open, I took the baby from Amyas and put it on Elena's chest. Slowly, she lifted her hands and touched its face.

'So beautiful,' she breathed. The baby gave another cry and at that moment the morning sun burned away the mist and shone brilliantly into the hut. It threw light on the bloodied scene and on Elena's ashen face. She fixed me with eyes that were slowly growing dull. 'Call her Marisol,' she whispered. 'For the mother of Christ and for the sun.' Then she slowly turned her head and gazed at Amyas 'You have killed me,' she said. None of her old fire was there; only sadness. Somehow I understood the Spanish words, or maybe only the sentiment, but it was chilling, and I looked over my shoulder to see how he would respond.

But Amyas was staring at the blood running across the floor. 'Give the child to Charlie,' he said urgently, 'and help me.'

We tried. God knows, we tried to stem the bleeding. I pushed the few bits of clothing from both her bag and mine between her legs and Amyas propped them up on the orange box, but it made no difference. We couldn't save her. As the sun rose, hot and yellow into the sky, Elena's life drifted away.

Amyas and I, wasted with effort and grief, sat back

on our heels and stared at each other. It was the most terrible experience I'd ever had; far, far worse than the loss of my own unborn child, and I was shaken to my core. New life and then death in less than an hour. It was almost more than I could bear. I looked over to the baby who was lying on the trestle bed next to Charlie. He had tucked it up with a corner of the blanket and was looking at it as though it was some strange creature of which he had no knowledge.

'You have a daughter,' I said to Amyas.

'Yes,' he said. His voice was bleak. For once the usual expression of charming nonchalance had fled from his face. 'I have a daughter.'

'It'll need feeding.' Charlie's voice broke through our shocked inaction. I got to my feet, went over to the bed and picked up the baby. Her little face was screwed up in misery and she was making tiny sucking motions with her lips.

'I'll clean her up.' Using warm water from the wine bottle, I carefully wiped the blood and mucus from her sweet face and body. It had stuck in the dark hair that covered her head and I had to use more water to shift it. I took one of the cotton squares to dry her off and wrapped another one around her fat little bottom. My hands shook as I tried to put her arms into the vest that Elena had brought; I was terrified of hurting her or even dropping her. But, watched by the two men, I managed it, and afterwards, when she was clean and wrapped closely in the shawl, no one could have guessed the dreadful circumstances in which she had been born.

Amyas suddenly got up. 'I'm going to the village,' he

said, and without looking at me or the child, he walked out of the hut.

'Will he come back?' Charlie, with a hollow voice, posed the question. 'I think not.'

I didn't answer him because I didn't know how to. Amyas had left me before. Gone with an easy shrug, not even considering my wrecked emotions. Would he do it again?

Holding the baby in my arms I walked outside into the fresh mountain air and looked at the sky. It was innocently clear. A bird with a huge wingspan crossed the heavens, its head dipped down as it examined the terrain below, ready to swoop down on food for its fledglings, and I heard its triumphant cry to its mate. I saw the tips of the trees swaying in a small breeze and smelled the pine resin and the fresh green aroma of damp grass.

'This is the country of your birth, little girl,' I said out loud. 'This wild mountain place. I'll remember it all my life, even if you won't.' She made baby snuggling noises and tried to turn her head towards my breast. I loved her from that moment.

An hour later, when I was sitting on an upturned log outside the hut with the baby held close, Amyas came back. 'Here,' he said, and held out his hand. He was holding a tin of condensed milk. 'It's the best I could do.'

I put some of it in the feeding bottle and diluted it with a little spring water. Marisol took to it immediately and sucked eagerly.

When I followed Amyas into the hut I gave Charlie an 'I told you so' stare, and he shook his head in an admission of regret.

'What's up in the village?' he asked.

'They heard the screaming,' Amyas said. 'I told them that the baby was born.'

'Are the soldiers back?' I asked.

Amyas shook his head. 'No. Not so far, but I think we must go as soon as possible. The car is still in the patch of woodland where I left it. Let's get moving.'

'What about her?' Charlie pointed to the slowly stiffening body of Elena which he and I had clumsily wrapped in the blanket.

'We'll leave her,' Amyas said. 'We'll tell the priest in the village that she is up here and died in childbirth. They saw her before and they heard her scream last night. It'll be obvious to any doctor who might examine her. The locals will bury her. I'm sure of that.'

It was a cruel and horrible thing to do, but, in the circumstances, we couldn't see a better solution. There was no way that we could carry her down and then hang around to explain what had happened. I tore a page from my notebook and wrote on it, *Elena Beltrán, Republican fighter* and put the page on the blanket. I hoped that at least she wouldn't go into an unmarked grave.

There was a wallet in Elena's bag, containing a few pesetas and an address in Paris. I showed it to Amyas. 'I think it must be the address of her friends. The ones who will have the baby.' I gazed at him and he reached over and took the scrap of paper from me. After a moment he screwed it up and threw it on the embers of the fire where it slowly uncurled and started to brown. We both knew that Marisol wouldn't be going to them. There was something else in the wallet and, with some amazement, I withdrew a small gold crucifix on a golden chain. For all Elena's hatred of priests and adoration of communist ideals she had kept her cross. 'Marisol shall have it,' I said, and draped the chain over the baby's neck. 'That's what her mother would want.' It was only then that tears came to my eyes and the dreadful events of the night caught up with me and I started to cry.

'Don't.' Both Amyas and Charlie said it at the same time, and although I wanted to stop, I couldn't. The tears flowed down my cheeks and I stood, clinging on to the baby, and wept. Amyas was the first to move, taking the child from me and putting her down on the bed. Then he took me in his arms and held me while I sobbed out all the fright and surging emotions of the past few days.

'Don't cry, my darling,' Amyas crooned. 'You've been brilliant.'

'Yes, you have,' Charlie grunted. Over Amyas's shoulder I could see him standing, uncertainly, shuffling his feet and gazing at me. I knew that if Amyas hadn't been here he would have been the one to have taken me in his arms and comforted me. He was such a brick. That brought me up fast and I stepped away from Amyas.

'I'm all right now,' I sniffed, and dragged a hankie out of my pocket to wipe my eyes. 'Sorry. I don't know what came over me.' I went back to sorting out the bags, transferring the cotton squares and the couple of spare baby vests into my rucksack.

'Hey,' Amyas said. 'What's that?' He was looking at the open neck of my rucksack and the pistol which Paul had given me. I quickly explained, and he frowned. 'Is it loaded?'

'I don't know,' I answered, feeling slightly foolish. It turned out that it was.

'I'll take it.' Amyas stuffed it in his belt. 'You have the baby to carry.'

With a last look at the blanket-wrapped shape that was Elena, we set out. Charlie was much better today, stronger and able to walk the half-mile down the sheep track to the village.

People stopped what they were doing and watched us with narrowed eyes as we walked through the small main street. They saw the baby in my arms and then looked at me. They knew I wasn't the woman whom they'd seen pregnant only a couple of days ago.

'The car is at the end there.' Amyas pointed to a small copse of trees which surrounded a wooden barn. I couldn't see it. 'It's behind the barn,' he said. 'It was still there this morning.'

'Where did you get it from?'

He laughed, the old Amyas laugh. 'I acquired it,' he said. 'Get in while I go back to the church and have a word with the priest.'

'What will he say?' I was suddenly scared.

'Nothing. He'll do what I tell him to do.' I looked at Amyas in his bloodied white shirt and khaki trousers. How could he possibly persuade a man of God to do what he told him? Then I remembered. This was Amyas. People always did what he wanted, even me . . . especially me. Besides, I thought, as he walked towards the church, he has a gun stuffed in his belt.

The car was there, safe and sound, a big cream and black German car, which I think was called a Wanderer. It looked pretty new, with shiny, unmarked paintwork and pristine leather seats; so smart that it wouldn't exactly be lost in a crowd. But I didn't care, and I didn't care where Amyas had 'acquired' it. I was just relieved to get in the back and settle down. Charlie was glad too. Although he'd managed the walk, I don't think he could have gone much further.

'Where are we going?' I asked Amyas when he returned.

'Sort, first,' he said, starting the engine. 'We can get some supplies.' He looked at Marisol, peacefully asleep in my arms. 'You'll need stuff for her.' I didn't baulk at the suggestion that I was responsible for this tiny piece of humanity. I had known it from the instant I took her in my arms. 'And then,' he continued, 'I think we should head for the sea. We can probably get a fishing boat to take us around the coast to France.'

Charlie nodded. 'Good idea,' he said. 'I'm for that.'

'Amyas,' I said quietly. 'Can we go back to Ribera first and see about Paul. I need to know.'

'Do you?'

'Yes.'

'It's madness,' Charlie grumbled from the passenger seat. 'We should get away as soon as we can.' But when we set off Amyas turned back on to the road to Ribera and within ten minutes we were outside the church.

'Hold the baby,' I said to Charlie, putting Marisol into his arms, and got out of the car. I walked around the old stone building until I was at the vestry door. The door swung heavily on its iron hinges as I opened it, and I stepped into an empty room. Paul had gone.

'Is this where he was?' asked Amyas, who had followed me.

'Yes,' I nodded. 'He was on that mattress.' We stared down at the mattress which gave no sign of its ever having been occupied and my heart sank. I could only assume that Paul had died and that the priest had buried him. 'He must have . . .' I didn't finish the sentence and turned abruptly to walk outside.

'Ah.' It was the old priest, strolling around the church. I grabbed his hand.

'Father. My friend. What happened. Is he . . .'

'No, my child. The blessed Mary watched over him and he was still alive when Professor Gonzalez came. He took him in his car to the hospital at Sort. You will find him there.'

'Oh, thank God,' I said.

Amyas grinned. 'Happy? Can we go now?'

I nodded. 'Yes.' As we turned to leave the priest said, 'Another of Señor Durban's friends came looking for him.'

A chill turned my stomach to ice. 'Who came looking for him?' I asked.

'It was a man. A thin man. He came here early. About an hour ago.'

'Did he have brown and white shoes?' I didn't really need to ask.

'He did.' The priest laughed. 'Most unusual. I told him where to find Señor Durban, just as I told you.'

We returned to the car and Amyas drove back along the road. 'What happened?' said Charlie, handing the baby over. When I told him he gave a low whistle. 'Damn!'

It took us no time to get to Sort, where Amyas parked the car in a backstreet and I went into a couple of shops to find both food and clothes for Marisol. I also bought a shirt and a cotton jacket for Charlie. 'Here you are,' I said, when I got back to the car.

'Thanks,' he said, and I helped him put on the shirt. The weather was too warm for the jacket, but if we had a sea journey ahead of us, he'd need it. 'Where's Amyas?' he asked.

'Gone to find food, I think. He said we'd be too obvious if we went to a restaurant.'

'And he thinks that us driving along in this swanky car is not obvious?'

I laughed. The baby started to cry and I looked at her with concern. 'She probably wants feeding,' said Charlie. He made a show of holding his nose. 'And changing.'

Amyas returned while I was feeding the baby. He was wearing a clean shirt and had brought big rolls filled with sliced chorizo and salad, and some bottles of beer. 'The army is in town,' he said. 'We'd better go.' He drove through the hot backstreets, while Charlie and I watched through the open windows for soldiers. Several times I saw signposts announcing HOSPITAL, with an arrow pointing in the direction we were going. I half thought of asking Amyas to stop so I could go and find Paul, but I didn't. It would have been foolish. In that uncanny way that Amyas seemed to know what I was thinking, he turned his head and said, 'He'll be all right.'

Just then I saw the thin man with the co-respondent shoes walking along the road towards the hospital. 'That's him,' I squealed. 'The man who's after Paul. Oh my God!' My squeal must have been loud in that empty backstreet because the man turned his head and looked at me. A sudden breeze lifted his jacket and I saw a gun in a holster at his waist and, what was worse, I saw the instant recognition in his eyes.

Amyas jammed his foot on the accelerator and the car

burst into life – we were down the street in seconds. We rounded the corner, then drove on to the next corner and rounded that to come almost back to where we had been. Amyas drew the car into a small alleyway. 'Wait here,' he said. 'Don't leave the car.' He jumped out. 'I'll be back in a minute.'

Charlie and I waited, our eyes searching each other's faces. Was co-respondent shoes on his way to kill Paul? He could have been a friend of Guisando determined to get revenge, which was what Paul thought, or even a policeman from Perpignan, here to follow a man suspected of committing a crime. But whoever he was I was scared for Paul, and horrified that the man had recognised me. I sat, cuddling the baby, until Charlie, who had turned to look out of the back window said, 'He's here,' and the next instant, Amyas opened the driver's door and slid in.

'Now,' he said, with a rather wolfish grin, 'we get going. The sooner we're out of this place, the better.'

Chapter Seventeen

We drove through the Spanish countryside, which was hilly and steep at first as we came down from the mountains, with sheer drops at the side of the road and heart-stopping hairpin bends. I'd been scared that we would meet roadblocks, but to my relief we came across none. A few soldiers were about, lounging at cafés in the villages we passed through, drinking wine and ignoring the resentful glares of the locals. This part of Spain, Catalonia, had been Republican, but their defeated army had withdrawn to Madrid and left its supporters to the mercy of the Nationalist Fascists.

Several times the soldiers stood up to watch the Wanderer go by. It stood out as impossibly expensive and glamorous and I grumbled to Amyas that he should have 'acquired' a less obvious car. We were bound to be stopped.

'No,' he grinned. 'Just look at them. They're almost standing to attention. They think Charlie's a general and I'm his driver.'

'What am I, then?'

'You're the general's doxy,' he laughed. 'They all have them.'

After a couple of hours we reached a crossroads. A signpost pointing north read FRANCA 10 KILÓMETRO.

'Look,' said Charlie. 'France is only about six miles away, up that road.'

Amyas stopped the car. 'Should we try it?' he asked. 'It would be a hell of a lot easier than getting to the coast and finding a boat.'

'I'm for it,' said Charlie. 'The sooner we get to France, the better.' He looked at me. 'What d'you think, Seffy?'

I nodded eagerly. I'd had enough adventures in the Pyrenees and a simple car journey sounded good. 'Yes,' I said. 'Let's go.'

'Hang on.' Amyas was looking in the driving mirror and I turned my head. A truck was coming up the road behind us, and as it drew level I saw that the driver and his passenger were both in uniform. It stopped and the passenger jumped down. He was a Nationalist officer.

'Christ!' breathed Charlie. 'He's coming to talk to us.'

'Don't say anything,' whispered Amyas, getting out of the car. 'Leave him to me.'

We watched, frozen with horror, as Amyas, showing no signs of nerves, went over to the soldier. 'What d'you think he's saying?' muttered Charlie, as Amyas shook hands with the officer and jerked his head back to the car. He seemed to be laughing and at ease with the man and I knew that we had to follow suit.

'Look confident,' I said to Charlie and leant over to him and pretended to examine his wound. 'He's probably telling them you are an injured general or something. Give him a Third Reich glare.' Charlie straightened up and adjusted his glasses then stared imperiously through them at the inquisitive soldier.

The officer reached up to the cab of his truck and spoke to his driver. A map was produced. 'Amyas is asking directions,' I whispered, a nervous desire to laugh almost overwhelming me. The officer pointed to the map and then waved his arm in the general direction in which we'd been going and Amyas nodded and smiled. After another few moments of chat they shook hands again and Amyas came back to the car. He gave a sort of half-salute to Charlie and muttered, out of the corner of his mouth, 'We have to go on. Tell you the rest in a minute.'

He started the car, and as we drove away, I looked over my shoulder. The soldier was also driving away, up the road to France, and I saw with alarm that the back of the truck was full of Nationalist troops. We rounded the bend and I could feel Amyas relax. 'They're going to man the border,' he said. 'Too many refugees are trying to get through, including Republican fighters whom they are very keen to arrest and put in prison camps. I told him that Charlie is a German colonel who is in Spain as an observer, and that he was injured by a fleeing sniper so we're looking for the nearest hospital. Apparently it's in Figueres, which is on our way.'

'Wouldn't it be easier for this German to go to France?' I asked. 'That officer seemed to accept the story – wouldn't the border guards do the same?'

'No, my darling. Think. Charlie would need a German passport, which we know he hasn't got.'

Charlie shook his head. 'I don't even have a British passport now. It was taken from me at Albacete, along with all the money I had left.'

Amyas laughed rather sourly. 'And if you're his German nurse, Persephone, which I said you were, how would you explain your passport, not to mention the lack of papers for our other little passenger?'

'All right,' I said slowly. 'But why Germans? I didn't

think they were involved, apart from their air force. They don't have troops on the ground.'

'Not officially,' Charlie said. 'But Amyas is right. They do have observers and provide help to Franco.' He glanced over to Amyas, who was looking at the road ahead, efficiently negotiating the bends, his lips pursed, whistling a little tune. 'Thank you,' he smiled. 'You've rescued me again.'

I was proud of him. Proud that this brave resourceful man had chosen me. I clutched Marisol close to me and kissed her little dark head. Being with him now and then was almost enough.

By that evening we'd passed through Figueres and arrived in Cadaqués as the sun was going down. I could smell the sea through the open windows of the Wanderer and immediately my spirits lifted.

'D'you think we dare find a hotel?' I asked, as we drove slowly along the narrow winding seafront road, past dreamy white cottages, rosy-hued in the evening sun. 'I'd love a shower and Marisol needs a bath or a good wash.' We had reached the little harbour. Fishing boats were bobbing further out in the water, tied up to buoys, but the fishermen were still ashore, preparing to sail on the evening tide. It was a tranquil scene.

'I don't know,' Amyas said and nodded his head towards a group of soldiers who were gathered beside a truck. They were young, laughing and joking with each other, and didn't look in the least threatening, but Amyas was cautious. 'It might not be the safest option.' It was out of character for him and I felt nervous again. All afternoon I'd been calm and cheerful, convinced that I'd soon be back in France and safe. But now that awful squirming feeling had returned and I stroked Marisol's little hand, hoping that would settle me.

Amyas drove on to the far end of the bay and then turned away from the sea and found a track which led uphill. After a few minutes he stopped and parked the car. We were on a headland above the village and below us the ancient sea stretched away, lilac blue and gold where it caught the setting sun, boundless, beyond the horizon. Further on from where we had parked there must have been a lighthouse; I could see the beam glittering on the water and then the flash as it passed over us. I was reminded of Cornwall and the lighthouse there. Amyas and I had made love under its protective beam.

'Wait here,' he said. 'I'll go back and see if I can persuade one of the fishermen to take you. Have you got any money left, because I'm running short?'

Charlie, of course, had nothing, but I took most of the money from my wallet, leaving only enough for the barest essentials for the baby. 'D'you think this will do? If we get to a bank in France, I can have more wired over.'

Amyas counted the notes: it was a few hundred francs and might seem a lot to a poor fisherman, but was it enough to persuade him to go against an occupying army? 'Let's see,' said Amyas and made his way back along the track.

Charlie and I got out of the car. I walked up the hill a little, stretching my legs and letting the breeze blow through my hair and cool my face. I needed to take stock. I was carrying a baby in my arms who was less than twenty-four hours old. Already I thought of her as mine and felt blessed by her presence. The uncomfortable fact that she wasn't really mine I put to one side. I could think about that another time. Now I looked at the lavender sky and a pinpoint of twinkling light which was the first star and marvelled at the turn my life had taken.

I glanced over my shoulder at Charlie, who was sitting on the running board of the car. He was leaning back with his eyes closed and I realised that he didn't look well again. His face was flushed and despite the warmth of this Spanish summer evening, he was shivering. I hurried back down the hill and sat beside him.

'What is it?' I asked.

'I don't know,' he said. 'I feel a bit rough, but it doesn't matter.'

'Of course it does,' I said, and got my canteen. He drank some water, letting it run over his dry lips and down his shirt. I felt his forehead, which was hot, and when I looked beneath his bandage I saw that his wound was suppurating and the area around it burning a hot red. 'I'm pretty sure that your wound is infected,' I sighed. 'The sooner we get you to a hospital, the better.'

Charlie leant back again. 'I'm a bloody nuisance, Blake, and I'm so sorry that I got you involved. This whole idea was mad.'

'Don't be sorry, Charlie,' I said, sitting beside him. 'In a way, I've rather enjoyed it. The excitement is like a drug, even though I've been scared a hell of a lot of the time. Besides,' I grinned, 'we'll get great copy out of this.'

He gave a painful laugh. 'I always knew you were a born journalist.'

We sat together as the sun went down. The three of us, Charlie, Marisol and me, who looked like a family and who weren't, but were the closest of friends. How strange it was, but how very comforting.

I looked at my watch. Amyas had been away for more than an hour and I was beginning to worry. What if he didn't come back? He had taken most of my money and even if we had the car, I couldn't afford to fill it with petrol. And if we couldn't drive and had no money to bribe a fisherman, how the hell were we going to get away? Charlie was in really poor condition and I had Marisol to look after, so walking over the mountains was definitely not an option.

Enticing aromas of evening cooking drifted up from the village; spicy and delectable, a smell of red peppers, onions and potatoes fried in hot olive oil. I could imagine these vegetables as an accompaniment to some sort of baked fish, taken today from the Mediterranean and served on thick, brightly painted plates.

'Are you hungry?' I asked Charlie.

He shook his head. 'No.'

'Me neither.' I surprised myself by realising this, but I suppose I was too weary to eat and too full of apprehension. Charlie's head fell on to my shoulder and he slept while I fed Marisol. I had only half a can of milk left and nowhere to wash out the bottle, and I worried that I might be poisoning her with dirty milk but so far she'd appeared to be fine. The trouble was, I had no idea how a newborn baby should behave and whether I was looking after her properly.

'This is a cosy scene.' It was Amyas, strolling up the path, as relaxed and cheerful as though he'd been on a simple country walk. 'You and Charlie are getting close, I see.'

'Don't tell me you're jealous,' I laughed.

'Hardly,' Amyas scoffed. But I thought he was and hugged that knowledge to me.

'He's not well,' I said. 'He's feverish again and his wound looks horrible.'

Amyas squatted down and put his hand on Charlie's forehead. 'Mm. Not good, so it's just as well that I've got a fishing boat to take you to France tonight. In about,' he looked at his watch, 'an hour and a half.'

I took in his words. 'You didn't say "us",' I whispered, a band of longing already tying itself around my heart. 'Aren't you coming?'

He stood up and turned his back to me, looking out to the darkening sea. 'No. I'm not. I have . . . things to do.'

'But you're a deserter. It's dangerous for you to stay,' I cried. 'You'll be arrested.'

'No. I don't think so. I'll be fine.'

I was bewildered. 'Aren't you a deserter, then?' I asked.

He was silent for a moment, before saying, 'Perhaps, not really. Not as the term is understood.'

I stared at his back. At his white shirt and sandy-coloured trousers, flapping now in the strengthening breeze. He could have been on holiday, a visitor who had no interest in a civil war. Had he been telling me the truth? Had he been telling anyone the truth? It was impossible to know and I didn't question him further about it. All I asked was about Marisol.

'You have a daughter. Who's to look after her?'

He turned and came back to me. Squatting on the ground again, he took my free hand in his. 'You will, Persephone. She's yours. My gift to you. Bring her up to be as brave and forthright as you are and if she asks about her father, say he is . . .' he shrugged. 'A freedom fighter.'

I looked deep into his brown, fathomless eyes. You're not a freedom fighter, I said in my mind, you're a thief and a gigolo, just like my mother said you were, and I know you're staying behind because you can see opportunities to be either, or even both. I should hate you. But when he bent and kissed me, I held my mouth up to his willingly and took strength from him.

'What's this?' said Charlie, waking up, hot and shivery. 'Can't you two leave a man to have a bit of a peaceful snooze without canoodling over him?'

I giggled and Amyas laughed. 'Canoodling? Is that what you call it?' He looked at me and then back at Charlie with an almost sneering grin. 'Well, why not? Persephone enjoys it and, Christ, so do I.'

It was an awkward moment, even a sudden cruel show of possession on Amyas's part, after that earlier flash of jealousy. But then, just as suddenly, his normal, relaxed persona returned and he squatted down in front of Charlie.

'You're on a fishing boat in about an hour. It'll take you around the coast to . . . well, I don't know. Probably somewhere quiet. Anyway, it'll be in France. I've paid the captain and told him that he'll get the rest of the money when he comes back and when I've heard from you. That's in case he takes it into his head to throw you overboard.'

'What?' I said, alarmed.

Amyas laughed. 'Don't worry. He won't.'

'But how do we get in touch with you?' Charlie asked. 'Where will you be?'

'Well, that I don't know, but then the captain doesn't know it either. So he'll stick to his word.'

'And he won't get the rest of his money.' Charlie gave a sort of twisted smile.

'No.' Amyas gave a short laugh. 'Probably not.'

We were silent then, Charlie and I, each considering Amyas's words and actions, but then Charlie said, 'Thanks. We owe you.'

'You don't owe me anything, except . . .' Amyas looked down at the sleeping baby. 'Except to look after my daughter. That'll do.'

'I promise.' Painfully, Charlie lifted his arm and the two men shook hands in what appeared to be a rather formal contract.

'Anyway, once back in France, you can get to a hospital and have that wound looked at properly,' said Amyas, as he watched Charlie bring his arm back to his side. Pain was etched on his face and beads of sweat clung to his forehead

'I hate hospitals,' Charlie grunted. 'I make it a rule never to go near them.'

'Me too,' I added.

'Come off it, Blake. You'd just been in hospital when I caught up with you again, last November. Remember? Before we went to Berlin.' Charlie gave me a quizzical look. 'You'd been under the sawbones. What was it? Appendix?'

As I nodded, I felt Amyas stiffen and look at me, but he said nothing.

We waited for about three-quarters of an hour, until Amyas said 'Time to go' and helped Charlie get into the front of the car. I put the baby on Charlie's knee, then opened the back door ready to get in, but Amyas grabbed my arm.

'Come over here,' he said.

We walked a few steps away, on to the rocky headland. I knew what he was going to say. He put his hand on my cheek in a gesture of such tenderness that tears welled up. 'Persephone Blake,' he murmured. 'I have explored every inch of your body. You have no appendix scar.'

'No,' I whispered, dreading what would come next.

'So what operation did you have?'

I closed my eyes, remembering the hurry, the pain and the blood. 'I lost our child,' I said simply. There was no need to tell him more. 'They told me it was a boy.'

He wrapped his arms around me and held me very close. 'Will our little girl make up for that?'

'More than,' I whispered. 'Oh, more than.'

'Then I'm glad. You of all people, Persephone, don't deserve to be unhappy. You are mine, my special girl, and will be, until death. Please believe me.'

He left us at the quay, where the rotting fishing boat and its half-drunk captain awaited us. 'Remember,' Amyas fixed him with a chilling stare, 'I'll be waiting. Deliver them, or else.'

'When will I see you again?' I asked, foolishly. Marisol was wailing and the wind made the fishing boat rock fiercely on the black water.

'I don't know, my darling,' Amyas said. 'But keep watching. One day, I'll be with you.' He kissed me and held his daughter as I climbed into the boat. Before lowering her into my arms he looked long into her face and, for the first time, kissed her little forehead. 'Goodbye, my darling girls,' he called as the boatman pulled away.

And I sat, one arm around Charlie, who was struggling to stay upright, facing the shore to get my last glimpse of him.

A summer storm whipped up the sea, making the stinking fishing boat toss and roll so violently that for every minute of the five hours that it took to sail around the coast I was in fear for my life.

The captain had dismissed it as a '*tramuntana*, the wind of the north' and vowed that the worst of these winds were always in the winter so this wouldn't be bad. It felt bad to me where I sat, as instructed, in the small cabin behind the wheelhouse fighting wave after wave of nausea. Eventually, I could no longer bear the claustrophobia and the acrid smell of oil and petrol that rose from the engine room beneath my seat, and struggled up the three steps to the deck. Charlie had refused to go in the cabin. He was sitting on the wet decking boards, with his back to the wooden wheelhouse and I crouched down beside him, letting the wind slap me in the face and take my breath away. Immediately I felt better.

'How is she?' he shouted through chattering teeth. Marisol was wrapped close to my body, under my jacket and, amazingly, asleep.

'Fine,' I answered. 'She's wonderful. She's always wonderful.' My little girl, who would be mine for ever. Amyas had said so.

Towards morning the storm abated, and as a watery dawn rose over the sea we were rowed ashore. 'Francia,' the captain grunted, and without another word rowed away.

Charlie sank on to the harbour wall, muttering

incoherently. He was worse than I'd realised and I looked about me for help. I couldn't let him die here after all we'd been through. A woman, brushing the dust from her cottage steps on the road opposite the harbour, spotted us and hurried over and soon we were on a donkey cart, on our way to the police station.

'Where is this?' I asked the gendarme. 'What town?'

'Collioure, mademoiselle,' he answered, examining my passport.

'I have to get my colleague to a hospital,' I said. 'He's very sick.'

'I can see that. He, like you, is a journalist?'

'Yes,' I said. I mentioned our newspaper and the name of the editor for him to check. 'And the child?'

'She is mine.' My voice rose an octave. I was already protective. 'She was born a few days ago.'

He raised his eyebrows and gave me a searching look. 'You are well, mademoiselle?'

'Yes, perfectly. But I must get Monsieur Bradford to hospital as soon as possible.'

We were taken in the police captain's car to the hospital at Perpignan, where Charlie was urgently admitted. I found a doctor to examine Marisol, who was pronounced healthy and thriving. 'And you, madame? How are you?' he asked. 'Was it an easy birth?'

'No,' I murmured. 'It was dreadful.' I closed my eyes, remembering that awful scene. Then I picked up my daughter and said, 'The mother bled to death, but her father has entrusted the child to me.' He and his nurse watched me, as I left his office.

My room was still waiting for me at the strange hotel in Cerbère. It was an inconvenient place to stay for visiting

Charlie, but it felt comforting, somewhere to rest and get over the events of the past few days. Anyway, I'd left some of my belongings there: clothes, luggage and my beloved typewriter. To my delight they hadn't been stolen.

'You have returned, mademoiselle,' said the manager, the one who had been on duty the night that Paul and I had left.

'Yes,' I answered, my voice cold.

'And your friend, Monsieur Durban. He will return also?'

'I'm not sure. His movements were reported to someone who wanted to kill him. He was dying when I last saw him.'

The man had the grace to blush. 'How unfortunate. Is there anything I can do for you, mademoiselle? And . . .' he stared with confusion at Marisol, 'the infant?'

'Yes. I need to hire a nurse for a few days. For my baby. Can you arrange someone suitable?'

The girl he got for me was probably a relative, but she was sweet and kind and had younger brothers and sisters so was well used to handling newborn babies. 'Oh! She is *très jolie*,' she exclaimed as we put Masisol in the bath for the first time. I had bought clothes and nappies and taken the doctor's advice on the best feed to give her. She did well, putting on weight and waving her little fists in the air, as though she had been born into a privileged family in a private clinic or a grand-ducal mansion. And when I took her out, old women in the street stopped to coo over her.

Charlie was well enough to join me at the hotel after two weeks of hospital care. He was pale and terribly thin but the old Charlie was there inside. His wound was healing and the fever, which turned out to have been malaria, had gone.

'Got your typewriter, Blake?' he asked. I nodded. 'Good, then we'll get back to work.'

His wonderfully written report was filed within a week and apparently drew gasps of admiration from all who read it. I was thrilled to find that he credited me with rescuing him. '. . . a fellow journalist from this paper, Persephone Blake, assisted by another, made the dangerous mountain crossing to join me and two fellow deserters. She and another eventually got me to freedom and I am for ever in their debt. The details of our escape will be in my next report.'

'You didn't need to say that.' I was blushing with pleasure.

'Of course I did.' He frowned. 'I didn't mention Amyas by name. It might be dangerous for him, wherever he is. Although,' his frown ironed out and he gave one of his twinkly-eyed smiles, 'it'll be somewhere comfortable, I've no doubt about that.'

I had no doubt either.

We went to the English consul in Perpignan to arrange travel documents. I still had my passport, but of course Charlie had nothing. After many phone calls and telegrams, Charlie was furnished with papers which would allow him to board the plane that would take us home.

'And the child, madame?' asked the consul.

'She is mine,' I said. 'Born in Spain.' I gave her date of birth and my name as her mother.

'The father's name? We'll need that.'

I bit my lip. Did I dare to give him Amyas's name, which I knew to be false?

259

'Bradford,' said Charlie, butting in. 'Charles Bradford. Put me down as the father.'

He winked at me. 'It'll do until we get home and you get her properly registered. Then, later on, perhaps, I can be her godfather.'

I smiled. 'Thank you, Charlie,' I said and nodded my consent to the consul, before turning back and giving Charlie a kiss on his cheek. 'Of course you'll be her godfather. Who else could I possibly want?'

The consul said nothing. Like the doctor and the nurse at the hospital when I told them about Elena's death, I don't think he was particularly shocked.

We were just another war story.

Chapter Eighteen

I'd been home for three days when Jacob, with Willi tucked under his arm, knocked at my door. 'Seffy, my dear,' he said, raising my hand to his lips. 'How wonderful to see that you have returned home safely.'

'A bad penny always turns up, Jacob,' I smiled and patted Willi's smooth little head. He thumped his tail, showing approval. 'I have a surprise for you.'

'And I for you,' he laughed. He stood aside so that I could see who was standing in the corridor behind him. It was Kitty.

'Kitty!' I cried as she walked shyly into my flat, and without thinking twice, I grabbed her into my arms and gave her a hug. 'How wonderful.' I looked beyond her. 'Your mother?' I asked, but I already knew the answer and glanced over Kitty's shoulder to Jacob. He shook his head and put a warning finger to his lips.

'Mamma said she will come in a few weeks,' said Kitty, her face falling. 'Some of the girls at the school are on their own and she has stayed to care for them. Their parents have been taken.'

'Taken?' I asked.

Jacob intervened. 'That, we will talk about later. But I am happy that, at last, Kitty is here. I'm a silly old man who went to Harwich to meet her off the ferry but, somehow, we missed each other and I waited for other boats to come in. She was three days with a rabbi and his wife before I found her.'

'Well, I'm absolutely thrilled,' I said. 'Come in and have a cup of tea with me. I want to hear all about your journey, Kitty, and what you've been up to, Jacob, while I've been away.'

'But we have called to hear about your adventures, dear Seffy. It was in the newspaper, a big article. We all read it at the synagogue and again I was proud to say that you are my friend.'

I smiled and ushered them in. My flat was more untidy than usual. My travel bag was on the floor, half unpacked, and some of Marisol's clothes were hanging over the back of the wooden chair beside the window. I was learning fast that looking after a baby was utterly time-consuming. So far I'd only been out once, to buy food and various bits and pieces of baby stuff. I'd ordered a pram from Harrods, which I'd arranged to leave in the caretaker's storeroom. The cot had arrived yesterday and was installed next to my bed. Fortunately, this was a three-bedroomed apartment, so my little girl would be able to have her own room in a few months' time and so would the nanny, for whom I'd already inserted an advert in *The Lady*. As much as I loved Marisol, I wanted to work.

'You have visitors?' asked Jacob, looking around my chaotic living room. 'We should go.' He nodded to Kitty, who turned back towards the door.

'No,' I cried. 'Don't go. That is my surprise. I do have a visitor, but she will be a permanent visitor. Wait, while I fetch her.'

She was waking up when I went to her cot. My girl,

now nearly a month old and just beginning to focus on me as the most important person in her little life. She looked so like Amyas, with the same dark hair and smooth olive skin, and I knew that when she was older she would put her head on one side and give me that same amused glance. Oh, she was his all right, and as hard as I looked at her, I could see nothing that resembled her poor dead mother. Maybe I didn't want to see it.

'This is my visitor,' I announced, carrying Marisol into the living room. Jacob's mouth dropped open, while Kitty gave a delighted squeal.

'So, this baby belongs to a friend?' Jacob reached out his hand and touched Marisol's finger. 'You take care of it?'

I shook my head. 'Jacob, Kitty. Let me introduce Marisol . . . my daughter.'

The explanation that followed was brief and Jacob and Kitty listened with evident astonishment. I didn't want to go into all the dreadful events that had accompanied Marisol's birth, but even so, as I told them that her mother had died, Jacob's expression became more and more uneasy.

'This is very difficult to understand,' he said. 'How can this child be yours?'

'I've adopted her.' I couldn't help sounding defensive.

'And it is all legal?'

'It will be. The British consul in Perpignan accepted that she was mine and put her on my passport. I'll register her birth here. It will be fine.'

Kitty took Marisol from my arms and sat on the easy chair with her. They seemed to comfort each other and Jacob and I exchanged rather sad smiles. I made tea and, leaving the girls to coo at each other, we sat at the little table by the window.

'From what I read in Mr Bradford's account, you went on a dangerous assignment, yes?' Jacob looked very concerned. Sometimes I felt as though he was more of a father to me than my own had been. My father had become remote, totally absorbed in his academic research, and behaved to his daughters with the sort of careful manners one would show to strangers. He hadn't always been like that. When we were children he was full of fun, ready to play games and keen to involve himself with Xanthe and me. But something happened when we went away to school. Something between him and Mother which was so unsettling that he had retreated into his study. Now he only emerged from its comforting cocoon when Mother dragged him out in order to back up her ridiculously snobbish views. But now, I was lucky. I had Jacob who cared for me and about me. I felt sorry for Xanthe; she only had Mother.

'Yes,' I said, 'it was dangerous and I was frightened a lot of the time. But can you understand this, Jacob? It was exciting and I thrive on excitement.'

He was thoughtful. 'And this little child?'

I looked out of the window at the garden square, where summer had come to London. The plane trees were in full leaf and happy children, watched over by their mothers and nannies, were playing on the grass. The contrast couldn't have been greater. 'She was born on the floor in a shepherd's hut in the Pyrenees,' I said, 'and I watched as her mother bled to death. We couldn't save her. God knows, we tried.' My mind went back to that dreadful scene, to the blood running along the dirt and to Elena telling Amyas that he had killed her. I shuddered and Jacob saw that shudder and put his hand over mine.

'What about the child's father?' Jacob frowned.

'He was there,' I said. 'He asked me to take her.' I looked over to Kitty who was absorbed with the baby, and lowered my voice. 'He is someone I know. Someone who means a lot to me.'

Jacob looked up sharply. I knew the whole business was difficult for him; he was a man of morals and deeply held convictions. He had guessed what I hadn't said about Amyas. 'So,' he growled and Willi looked up from where he was lying on Jacob's ample lap. 'What will you put down as the father's name? This man?' His face darkened. 'This nogoodnik?'

'Please,' I begged. 'Don't judge me. I will love this child until the day I die. And,' I looked over to my little girl, 'I will love her father too, whatever happens.'

Jacob drank his tea, looking out at the sunny day, then putting down his cup he reached over and took my hand. 'Perhaps, where she comes from doesn't really matter. And you, you look different. Fulfilled. I can see that she has made you happy.'

'Yes,' I murmured. 'Very happy.'

Later, when I was giving Marisol a bottle, he asked how I was going to manage. 'You will give up your work?' he asked. 'Because, believe me, a small child can be very demanding. I know.'

'Goodness, no,' I answered. 'I can't give up my job. I've already advertised for a nanny.'

'I can help you, if you would want me,' said Kitty, her face brightening. 'I go to school in September, Uncle Jacob has arranged it for me, but for the summer, I am happy to look after Marisol.'

I smiled at her. 'That's very kind of you, Kitty, but I think I must get someone who knows more about babies than either you or I. But we'll have lots of time together. And you still haven't told me about how you left Berlin. I want to hear about that.'

'I think we must leave that for another time,' said Jacob. 'You look tired, Seffy, and your little girl needs her cot.' He squeezed my arm. 'I'm so glad you have come home.'

That night I sat in the easy chair with Marisol on my knee. My life had taken a strange turn, but despite the difficulties I could see ahead, I wouldn't have changed a moment of these last weeks. 'Where is your daddy now, little one?' I whispered into her soft cheek and she smiled as she slept, while I wondered what the next weeks would bring.

Alice Weaver was the first nanny I interviewed and I engaged her on the spot. She was just what I'd been looking for, late middle-aged, competent, cheerful and someone I could bear to have in my flat. As it turned out, most of the time she didn't stay overnight, having a little place of her own only a couple of streets away.

'My flat was given to me,' she confided, 'as a thank-you present from the family of my last but one child. It was most generous, but then, they have the brass. He has a title and you can see who he is from my references, but I don't gossip, so I won't tell their secrets, I can assure you of that. The little lad is a nice child, mind. Gone to boarding school now and doing well, by all accounts. He writes to me, quite regular.'

'And you have no commitments at the moment?'

'No,' she said. 'The last family have gone to America. War's coming, madam said. So they upped sticks and cleared off.' She gave the nearest thing to a snort before looking around the room that would be Marisol's little nursery. 'Have you got a baby bath and a nursing chair, and what about her clothes, where are they? From what I can see, you'll need one or two things.'

'Yes, I know,' I sighed. 'I've only been home for a week. The baby was born in Spain just over a month ago and, as you'll gather, I'm very new to all this.'

'Is she yours, Miss Blake?' At first the bluntness of the question seemed rather impertinent and I paused, considering what to say. But before I could formulate a reply, Alice spoke again, 'Because, if you'll forgive me saying this, you don't look like a woman who's a month on from giving birth.'

'No,' I said slowly, 'I didn't give birth to her. Her mother died and her father asked me to adopt her. He's involved in the fighting in Spain.' I was ready to tell her to go and said coldly, 'Does that make a difference?'

'Not in the least. I can see that she's loved, so I'll love her too. When d'you want me to start?'

I calmed down then and smiled. 'As soon as possible.'

'Good. I can start tomorrow. Now, you must call me Alice. I know that nannies like to play a dignified role but I'm not like that. I'm plain-speaking so if that doesn't suit, then neither will we.'

'It suits me,' I said, 'and you must tell me what I need to get.'

'Right.' She pulled down her grey cardigan over her ample bottom. 'Let me write a list.'

Under Alice's instruction, I bought furniture and curtains and pretty things for the baby. Alice's room was furnished, ready for when she would stay, and my bedroom and living room now looked beautiful. When Jacob and Kitty came round, I proudly showed them my new acquisitions. 'Ach, you have been spending money,' Jacob said.

'Yes. The flat looks better, now,' I said, looking at the new chairs and the Chinese rug. 'But it's still not as nice as yours.'

Jacob shrugged. 'That was my Leah. Such taste she had.' He raised his eyebrows as Alice walked in carrying Marisol. 'So, this is the nanny?'

I introduced them.

'Shalom, Mr Weiss, and Miss Kitty,' said Alice, handing me the baby, who was giving windy little smiles.

'Shalom, already,' said Jacob with a grin. 'Who taught you that?'

'Oh, I looked after some children in Leeds. Jewish family, they were. Lovely people. Terrible food, mind.'

I thought Jacob would be insulted, but he laughed. 'You should try mine. I'm a good cook.'

Alice chuckled. 'Could be I'll take you up on that, Mr Weiss.'

I went back to work the following week and was called into the editor's office. 'We're all very impressed with you, Miss Blake. From what I gather, you conducted yourself with what can only be described as gallantry. Charlie says that you saved his life.'

I blushed. 'I don't think so,' I said. 'There was another person who helped him. I came along later.'

'That's not what Charlie says,' Geoff grinned. 'He's told me that you were bloody brilliant.'

I didn't know what to say so just smiled inanely.

'Look,' said Geoff. 'Charlie's still not entirely fit and I need someone to cover the foreign desk. Are you up for it?'

'Yes,' I said immediately. 'Of course.'

'Good,' said Geoff. 'Things are moving on the Continent; it's all change again, and terrible for the people in Czechoslovakia. The speculation is that Poland will be next. And then France.'

I went back to my desk, happy. I was now a real journalist – at least Geoff thought I was and trusted me enough to take over Charlie's role while he was off sick. Poor Charlie, he'd still looked rotten when I'd last seen him and it occurred to me that I hadn't spoken to him since we'd landed back in England, three weeks ago.

I phoned the number of his flat in Westminster but there was no reply. I paused for a moment, thinking, then looked in my bag for the piece of paper he'd given me in Paris. It had his Dorset address and telephone number on it so I dialled it.

My call was picked up straight away, but it wasn't Charlie who answered. 'Yes?' a woman's voice said. A rather harsh, impatient voice, speaking as though the call was a ridiculous interruption in her busy life.

I asked for Charlie.

'Who's calling?' the woman demanded.

'Persephone Blake.'

There was a pause, then an abrupt 'Wait,' and I squirmed nervously in my chair. I couldn't imagine why this woman should alarm me, but she did.

Eventually Charlie came on the line. 'Hello, Blake. How are you?'

'I'm fine. But how are you? Are you recovering?'

'I'm all right. Tell me, have you spoken to Geoff? He's given you the job, hasn't he?'

'Yes, that's why I was phoning . . . in case you didn't know.'

'My idea.' He chuckled, then, 'How's our little girl?'

Our little girl? A harpoon of jealousy shot through me. How dare he? Marisol was *my* little girl. Then I remembered that his name had been given as her father and, more than that, he was present at her birth. In reality he had as much right to her as did I. 'She's lovely; growing,' I said. 'I've engaged a nanny who will look after her while I'm on assignments. I like her, the nanny, I mean, and I think you would approve.'

'Good. Look, Blake, I'm coming to London tomorrow. I'll call in. I might be able to give you some pointers.' He paused and I heard the harsh voice in the background issuing some sort of order. 'I've got to go. See you tomorrow.'

I sat back and thought about Charlie and his life in Dorset, of which I knew nothing. While we'd been recovering in France, I could have asked him, but I was so stunned by the events and so wrapped up in Marisol that I couldn't think about anything or anyone else. But then, of course, Charlie hadn't spoken of his wife. He'd offered no information about Diana. And I supposed it was none of my business. I permitted myself a small grin. She sounded an absolute harridan. No wonder he said nothing. I found myself laughing out loud and one or two people at other desks looked over and smiled. They'd been very complimentary to me when I'd come back to work, and I revelled in the unexpected camaraderie. Even

Monica, whom I'd encountered in the ladies' room, said hello in a civil manner. 'You're as brown as a nut,' she said, imagining, I supposed, that she was being friendly. 'You look like a native.'

Charlie knocked on my door before nine o'clock the next morning. I was up, making myself some breakfast, and Alice, who'd let herself in an hour ago, was in the bathroom with Marisol. I could hear Alice singing as she carefully soaped and rinsed my daughter. It wasn't a nursery rhyme, but something by her favourite composer, Ivor Novello.

'Mornin', Blake,' Charlie greeted me and gave me a peck on the cheek. He looked well, stronger and more his old self. He cocked an ear to the rich contralto coming from the bathroom. 'Is that the nanny?'

'It is.' I poured him a coffee. 'I'll introduce you in a minute. Are you hungry?'

He nodded and I put another rasher of bacon into the frying pan, while he went to sit by the window.

'So,' he looked at me. 'Excited about the promotion?'

'I'm only standing in,' I said. 'Until you're back on your feet.'

I brought our food to the table. Charlie was looking out on to the square where I could see the milk float and hear the regular clink of bottles as they were delivered to each house. It was cloudy this morning and rain was forecast. I didn't mind. I was looking forward to walking in the park later with Marisol.

Charlie made a sandwich of his piece of bacon and two slices of toast. He took a large bite. 'Mm,' he groaned in pleasure. 'This reminds me of school.'

'Don't you have bacon at home?' I was surprised.

He shook his head, blushing slightly. 'Vegetarian.'

Alice came in with a washed and powdered Marisol while we were still eating. I got up and took her into my arms, gazing into her little heart-shaped face. She had lost that crumpled, newborn look and was beginning to move her head about and to focus. 'She smiled!' I exclaimed.

Alice shook her head. 'Probably not yet, Miss Seffy, but some babies do it earlier than others.' She glanced at Charlie. 'I didn't realise you had company. I'll take baby to the nursery.'

'No. Let's have a look at her.' Charlie had finished his bacon sandwich and now came over to us. He took Marisol out of my arms and stared at her. 'My God,' he laughed. 'She's grown. Who would have believed that skinny little scrap I last saw could turn into this beauty?'

'This is Mr Charlie Bradford,' I said to Alice. 'He is . . . a colleague and,' I suddenly remembered the conversation in the consul's office in Perpignan, 'Marisol's godfather.'

'Very nice to meet you, Mr Bradford. Alice Weaver.'

'How d'you do?' He turned to me. 'Did you get her registered?'

'Oh! God. I forgot.' How could I have been so stupid?

'Right. We'll go now. Better done before you go away, don't you think?' He handed the baby over to Alice. 'We'll be out for a bit, Nanny Weaver. Take care of our girl.'

'I will, sir. And, it's Alice.'

In the taxi on the way to the registrar's office we discussed how Marisol should be registered. 'Your name as the mother, obviously,' said Charlie, 'but what about the father?'

'I could leave it blank.'

'You could but it's not fair, is it? I mean, for when she grows up. You'll have to tell her.'

I knew that in years to come I would have to have that difficult conversation, but for now? 'Well, who then?'

'Me,' he said. 'I'll be her father, and not only on paper. I promise you, Blake, I'll look after our girl for the rest of my life.'

I turned my head and stared at him. It was raining, and outside Londoners were scurrying along under umbrellas. 'That sounds like a proposal.' I said it half-jokingly.

He didn't look at me when he muttered, 'If I were free I would pursue you to the ends of the earth. Don't you get it? I'm absolutely crazy about you.'

I hadn't realised it. He'd never said anything before. Wasn't his casual flirting just the usual banter between colleagues? The sort of witty charm he displayed to everyone? Then I remembered Amyas making that slighting remark on the hillside above Cadaqués, when he'd thought Charlie and I were getting close, and realised that he'd seen what I'd missed. I took Charlie's hand and gave it a squeeze.

'You must know I can't be yours, Charlie. I'm in love with Amyas,' I whispered. 'He has been the one since the first moment I met him.'

'I know.' There was a choked sound in Charlie's voice. 'I've seen how you are with him. When he's around you take on a glow.' He stared out of the window for a while and then turned back to me. 'But the thing is,' he said, 'I'm prepared to be second best. Remember that.'

My daughter was registered Marisol Eos Bradford,

born in Spain, both parents journalists, and we came out of the registrar's office quietly satisfied. I'd wanted to keep the Greek theme of our names, Xanthe's and mine, and remembered that Eos meant dawn. And she'd been born as the sun was rising. Our girl had a surname that wasn't hers, and two parents who had not been responsible for her conception, but it didn't matter. Legally and lovingly, we were her parents.

That afternoon Kitty and I pushed Marisol through Hyde Park. The rain had drifted north and a hot late July sun glistened through the rainbow drops on the laurel bushes. 'People look so cheerful here,' said Kitty. 'Even though there is talk of war. It is different from Berlin.'

'Perhaps they were sad only in the part of Berlin where you lived. When I was there, in the city centre, everybody seemed to be excited, as though something tremendous was about to happen.'

'That is not nice,' Kitty whispered, and looking down at her I saw that she had tears in her eyes.

'No,' I agreed. 'It's awful.'

We sat down on a bench and watched people strolling by and the ducks walking along the grass next to the Serpentine. Soldiers were digging trenches on the other side of the water. I wasn't sure what they were for, gun emplacements, maybe, or for shelters in case of bombing, and the sight of them made me uneasy. How long would it be before a simple walk in a park was considered dangerous?

'Kitty,' I said. 'I want to hear about you getting out of Berlin. But before that, you must tell me. Did you go to meet me in Monbijoupark?'

She shook her head. 'I'm sorry, but we did not. I did worry that you would be waiting for us.' She looked down at her hands, they were small, still childlike, with bitten nails. I touched her arm.

'It's all right, Kitty. I couldn't shake off my companion so, although I did go to the park, it was later and I thought you must have got tired of waiting.'

'Mamma said she would come to meet you for me, because I wanted to so much, but that morning two men came to the house and said that we mustn't go. I knew one of them, Erik, he had been a student at the university until they wouldn't take Jews any more. He is the brother of one of Mamma's pupils and is working with his father now, as a butcher. But the other man, we did not know.'

I frowned. How did anyone know that the meeting had been set up? I didn't tell anyone . . . except Charlie, but that was when we were on the train home. It must have been Kitty, or her mother, who'd confided in someone. 'Why did they say that you shouldn't meet me?'

'The man said it would be dangerous for us and for you.'

'Me?'

She nodded. 'He said you were being followed and that you would be arrested if the government thought you were doing something illegal. Mamma agreed with them. It was too dangerous for us all, she said. So, we stayed at home.'

It was a confusing story. I had read a piece only the other day about Jewish children being sent out of Germany by their worried parents. It wasn't organised, but some Jewish activists were encouraging people to leave and offering help and money. Perhaps the two men were those same activists and that's how Kitty came to England. I asked her about it.

'Oh no,' she said. 'It wasn't that. We had the money from Uncle Jacob and somewhere to go. If we'd tried earlier we could have left, got the correct travel papers, I mean, but Mamma kept saying that it would be all right.'

She stared at the ducks who were squabbling over a piece of bread that an old lady had given them, then spoke again. 'Mamma was wrong, Seffy, I knew that and I think, later, that she did, but she wouldn't say. And when the man came back again last month and said that we must urgently leave, she agreed quickly. He had made all the arrangements. But then, Mamma said it was just me who was going. She had to stay to look after some of the girls who were living with us. I wanted to stay too, then, but she made me go.' Kitty's voice broke with a little sob and I put my arm around her shoulders.

'She'll come soon, Kitty. I'm sure.' I wasn't sure, not at all. But my words seemed to comfort her and she carried on with her story.

'I was taken in a car, at first, away from the city, on to country roads. I slept for a long time and when I woke up, we were in Holland. Then the man gave me a ticket to go on a train to Amsterdam and an address to go to. They were nice people at the house, very kind, and they had a daughter who was almost the same age as me. She took me into the city to show me around. I would have loved the trip, if I had not been so worried about Mamma. A week later they took me to the ferry port and arranged for someone to meet me in England off the boat. Then Uncle Jacob came.'

'It has been quite an adventure.' I smiled. 'Something you'll never forget.'

'No,' Kitty said bleakly. 'I will never forget it.'

Marisol started to cry and we got up and wheeled her back home. On the way we bumped into Jane Porter, one of Monica Cathcart's acolytes. 'Good afternoon, Miss Blake,' she simpered. 'A lovely day for a walk.'

'Yes,' I said, my heart sinking, wondering how long it would take for Monica to hear. Jane looked into the pram.

'What a pretty baby,' she smiled. 'A little girl, is it?'

I nodded and Kitty said, 'Her name is Marisol.' I think she would have said more, but I smiled our goodbyes and we walked on. Damn! Damn, I thought. When we got close to home, I asked Kitty again about her escape from Berlin. 'And you never found out who this man was, who drove you to Holland?' I asked.

Kitty shook her head. 'Not really,' she said. 'Erik called him Dov. And another time he called him der Dichter. I don't know that word in English.' She frowned 'It means one who writes, but not books, or for a paper, like you, Seffy.' Then she smiled. 'He was very handsome and he said he liked Mamma's paintings, specially the one by Charlotte Salomon. You liked that one too, didn't you?'

'Yes, I did.'

'I don't think he was German, either,' Kitty added. 'Although he spoke German perfectly. Maybe he was from Palestine. The Rabbi told Mamma that some of the Zionists were helping to get people to safety.'

'Well,' I said, as I lifted Marisol from the pram in the caretaker's room and walked with Kitty to the lift. 'Whoever he is, you should be grateful.'

'I am,' she answered wistfully. 'But I hope he goes back for Mamma.'

PART TWO

July 1939–July 1947

Chapter Nineteen

London, July 1939

I'd had a year as number two on the foreign desk and had loved every moment of it, including trips to the States and to Italy. I was learning my trade; a proper old-fashioned apprentice, as Charlie had said, and in this time of heightened tension all over Europe, I was learning it fast. Charlie had gone back to work, looking and acting his old self, flirting with the girls in the photo labs and making the new junior, who worked with Monica, blush, when he admired her hairstyle. He was constantly away, chasing up stories and coming back to the newsroom with doom-laden reports of preparations for war. All over Europe people were in a constant state of expectation. We all knew war was coming, but we didn't know when.

My life revolved around the newspaper and Marisol. She was growing into a beautiful child with huge brown eyes and softly curling dark hair.

'She's got a mind of her own, this one,' Alice would say, her tone more admiring than admonishing, and I would laugh. I loved my cheeky little daughter, enjoying her spirit and eager to show her off to all who stopped to exclaim over her when we walked in the park. Mother and Daddy are missing a treat, I thought, but I made no effort to contact them. I was finished with them.

I hadn't even told Xanthe about her when I saw her briefly for a drink at the Dorchester just before Christmas. She was on a flying visit to see our parents before returning to Berlin.

'Are you still with von Klausen?' I'd asked.

'Of course.' She sounded surprised that I would even question it. 'He's utterly spiffing.' She looked around the room, 'Oh look, there's Bella Duncan at the bar. And Gray Forbes. I've just got to have a word with them.' And she got up and left me to sit alone while she joined a group of her old friends. Eventually I went home, touching her arm and saying goodbye as I left.

'Bye, Seffy. Have a nice Christmas.' And that was it. I didn't see her again for months.

One morning in July, Geoff, our editor, called me into his office. Wondering if he hadn't been satisfied with my last article I sat, rather nervously, in front of him. He didn't speak for a moment but lit his pipe and puffed great clouds of smoke around his wood-panelled office while I waited. I knew that he had something to say to me, because he was tapping his finger on a newspaper cutting and kept glancing at me. Finally he put the pipe down on the huge glass ashtray on his desk and held up the paper. 'This is a piece from one of our rivals. It reports that some English women are enjoying themselves in Germany. Friends of the Nazi party, I believe. Some of them even titled.'

He shook his head in disgust.

My heart sank. I knew what was coming next.

'One of them pictured here is called Xanthe Blake.' He gave me a hard look. 'She's your sister, am I right?'

He put the cutting on the desk in front of me and I leant forward to look at it. There was my sister sitting on a wicker chair surrounded by a group of Nazi officers. It was a sunny day wherever that snap had been taken and the wind had blown her hair out of its usual sculptured shape and she was wearing white-framed sunglasses. And standing immediately behind her, with a hand on her shoulder, was Wolf von Klausen.

Geoff cleared his throat. 'This girl *is* your sister, isn't she?'

I nodded miserably, convinced that all the nice things he'd said about me previously were about to be forgotten and I was heading for the sack. A foreign correspondent with a notorious sister was the last thing this rather stuffy paper wanted. 'Yes,' I said desperately, 'but you must know I don't hold her views. She's got in with a terrible set of British Fascists. She's always been a bit silly.' I stood up, my heart beating fast. 'Please, don't sack me because of her.'

'Sack you?' Geoff laughed. 'Who said anything about sacking you? By Christ, Charlie Bradford would have my guts for garters if I got rid of you. No, lassie, I want you to go and see her in Berlin. Get as much information from her as possible. I believe she's very close to some high-ups in the Nazi party. Maybe she knows, or has heard, something about what their next move will be.'

I sat down again, appalled at the prospect of having to meet up with Xanthe. I didn't even know exactly where she was. The only person who would know was my mother, and she was definitely someone I didn't want ever to see again. But this was an assignment and there was no way that I was going to refuse. 'Yes,' I said. 'I'll go.'

'All right. Can you go within the week?'

I nodded.

'Good. We'll organise a room at the Adlon. You've stayed there before, yes? After that, you're pretty much on your own. Be careful. There's a heady atmosphere in Berlin, I'm told. Everybody is over-excited and has their finger on the trigger . . . so to speak. But I'm relying on you to find out what you can. Remember, it's not only this newspaper that is interested.'

It was only when I was back at my desk that I thought of that last remark, who else could be interested? Well, obviously, it was the government and I needed to discuss it with Charlie, but I'd have to call him because he'd just returned from Poland and was spending some time in Dorset with Diana. To my relief, it was he who answered my call.

'I'm going away next week,' I said.

'Yes,' he said. He sounded distracted. 'I thought you might be. Germany?'

'Yes, Berlin again,' I answered. 'To try and find Xanthe.'

'Look,' he said. 'I can't talk now, but I'll be in London tonight. We'll talk then.'

Stupidly I felt rebuffed and frowned at the receiver. Then I pulled myself together. I had to try and find out where Xanthe was. I presumed from Geoff's newspaper report that she was still in Berlin, although those pictures could have been taken months ago. Geoff seemed certain she was there, but I needed confirmation, so I took a deep breath and dialled my parents' home.

It took a long time for the phone to be picked up and I was just about to put down the receiver when my father answered.

'Er . . . Hello. Farnworth Blake speaking.' He sounded anxious, unused to answering the telephone and almost scared about who would be on the other end.

'Daddy. It's me, Seffy.'

There was silence and then, 'Seffy? Is it really you, my dear? Oh.'

'Yes.' I frowned and gazed at the receiver before putting it back to my ear and asking, 'Are you all right? You sound a bit funny.'

'Yes, yes' – now he was speaking eagerly – 'I'm all right. But you? I read about you all the time in the newspaper. You've made me a very proud man.'

Isn't it strange; that last remark from my usually distant father brought me close to tears. I could have put my head down on the desk and wept, but here, in this busy newspaper office, I couldn't, so I said, 'Are you on your own? Where's Mother?'

Another silence, then, 'She's gone. Left me, I think. Gone with some fellow to America. Says she's not coming back.'

This was astonishing news and I needed to hear it at first hand. 'Don't go out,' I said. 'I'm coming straight round.'

She had gone, about a month ago, with a man she met through Xanthe. My father seemed bewildered by it, but not particularly sad, just unsure what he should do next. The Eaton Square house was perfectly clean and tidy, the housekeeper and the maids had seen to that, and he was getting his meals as usual, but he was left without direction.

'You'll be all right,' I said. 'You can spend more time on your research. But you do need to get out a bit. Go to the British Library and to your club. And what about going to the cricket? You used to love going to Lord's.'

My father smiled and rubbed a hand through his thatch of salt and pepper hair. 'I did, didn't I? I'd forgotten about that. You must come with me, Seffy. I'm still a member, you know.'

'I will, but not yet. Look, Daddy, there are things I have to tell you. First, I've adopted a baby, so I suppose you're a grandfather.'

The bewildered look came back and I knew I must tread carefully. Slowly, and leaving chunks out, I explained the circumstances in which Marisol's birth had come about and my adoption of her, and how I had engaged a nanny to look after her while I was working.

He sat back in his leather chair and listened and I wondered how much of what I was saying had sunk in. His face was lined and tired and he looked older than his years. I glanced above him to the portrait of my grandfather, the cotton king, and saw the likeness, although my father lacked the energy and drive that my grandfather had possessed. He was a shadow of that man and so quiet that I thought I would have to explain again. I took a breath and began to speak but he put up a hand and stopped me

'I've got it. Now, what shall we do? Let's see. I'll set up a trust fund for her.' He smiled at me and I saw a flash of the happy father he'd once been. 'Can't let the poor little girl be in want, and you need your money. What's her name again?'

I hugged him, the first time I'd done that for years, and there were tears in our eyes.

So it was settled and when I took her to see him the

next day, his hankie came out again along with fifty pounds to buy her a teddy bear. 'Get her a good one; from Hamleys.'

When I asked about Xanthe, he didn't know anything. She hadn't come home, and as far as he knew, she was still in Germany.

'I'm going to Berlin at the weekend,' I said. 'I have an assignment and I thought I'd look her up.'

'Be careful, dear child, there's going to be a war.'

'I know, Daddy. It's the only thing people can talk about.'

'Do try and persuade that silly girl to come home.'

'I will.'

As I left, he said, 'By the way. I'm going to transfer ownership of the Cornish house to you. I won't be going down there again and Xanthe has never liked it. So it's yours.'

My house, I thought, as I wheeled Marisol in her pram through the busy London streets. The house by the sea, where I gave my heart away. What would Amyas think of that?

Charlie took me out to dinner the following evening to a Swiss restaurant, where we ate veal in a delicious sauce, followed by a chocolate fondue in which we dipped strawberries. It was gloriously decadent.

'So,' he said. 'Xanthe. 'You've no idea where she is?'

I shook my head. 'My father doesn't know and I've only got that newspaper report which could be months old.'

'What about your mother? She's close to Xanthe.'

'She was,' I said quietly. 'But she's gone to America. Left my father for another man.' Just saying it shocked me again. My oh, so correct mother, who lived her entire life full of concern about what 'people might think'. The mother who thought I was a trollop for falling in love with someone not in our class, but who forgave Xanthe all her adventures with married men. 'Xanthe mixes with people out of the top drawer,' she'd said, to dismiss my complaint of unfairness. 'Why can't you?'

'Wow!' Charlie gave a whistle. 'I gather that is somewhat out of character?'

I sighed. 'Completely. But it leaves me with no address for my sister and that's the whole point of this trip.'

He wiped his mouth with the back of his hand and gazed out of the window. 'Leave it to me,' he said, 'I'll get on to some of my contacts at the Foreign Office. They'll know. I bet they keep tabs on all the British nationals in Germany at the moment.'

The next day he stopped by my desk and dropped a piece of paper on to my typewriter. 'She's here,' he said. 'It's a house in one of the smarter suburbs of Berlin, my contact tells me. She's been there for a few months. He thinks she's a kept woman.'

'Hardly kept.' I shrugged. 'She's got plenty of money. We're both beneficiaries of my grandfather. Neither of us are ever in need.'

'That's what makes you so interesting.' Charlie grinned. 'You work because you want to, not because you need to.'

'Oh, I do need to.' I was serious. 'I have to prove that I'm a person, with a brain and ambition.'

'A direct throwback to the cotton king, then.' Charlie laughed. 'Don't frown, Blake. I've looked him up. I'm an investigative journalist, for God's sake.'

That was the thing about Charlie. We were on the same

wavelength and being with him was easy and fun. I didn't have to cope with overwhelming passion or the searing pain of absence and in his company I could be myself and love, yes, love being with him.

'By the way,' he said, 'I saw Paul Durban in Poland. He's very well and got me a line on Polish preparations for a German attack. Would you believe they still want to field cavalry. In this day and age?'

'How on earth did you find that out?'

He tapped his nose. 'Contacts, Blake. Something that all good journalists gather.' He scribbled something on my jotter pad. 'Here are some names and addresses in Berlin. They might be useful. But get to know people, they'll help you gather information.'

He turned to go then and I stood up and followed him out of the office. In the lift, I gave him a hug. 'Thanks, Charlie.'

'Make sure you keep in touch,' he murmured into my hair. 'Every day, remember. I'll be looking out for you to file your copy.'

I nodded and smiled. 'Bye, Charlie.'

'Bye, dearest Blake.'

Berlin, July 1939

I took an Imperial Airways flight to Cologne at the weekend and from there a train to Berlin. It was quicker than getting the ferry from Hull to the Hook of Holland and, as Charlie had said, I had to get used to flying all over the world. For people like us it was the way to go now and I was excited at the prospect of my journalistic assignment. The only problem was that I was already missing my daughter. I had no concerns for her welfare, I knew that Alice would care for her quite lovingly and that Jacob and Kitty would be popping in from time to time. I even thought that Charlie might make a visit. 'While you're away,' Charlie had said when he phoned me the night before I left, 'remember what I told you before. Put Marisol out of your mind. If you want to carry on with your job, and I know that you do, then take my advice. You've ensured that she's well looked after and that's all that should concern you. Be professional.'

I was determined to be that, at all costs, and when I was stopped at Frankfurt airport by a customs official and asked about the purpose of my visit, I was able to say 'journalistic assignment' with some pride. I watched as he took a note of my name and then, on my way out of the small airport, glanced over my shoulder to see him looking at me while speaking into the telephone.

It was early in the evening when I booked into the Adlon. In the taxi from the railway station I looked out on the familiar streets of the city centre, where people strolled along, giving no indication of the possibility of war. There was a rosy glow in the warm air as the sun went down, and stepping into the brightly lit and wonderfully polished interior of the hotel I looked about me with pleasure.

'Fräulein Blake,' said the receptionist with a smile. 'You have returned. We have put you in the same room.' Was it deliberate? A room that could be easily watched? I laughed at myself for being so paranoid and cheerfully unpacked my few belongings and brushed my hair before going down to the bar.

The Adlon was favoured by journalists of every nation and they all seemed to be drinking in it that evening. I recognised a few of them, some who had been introduced to me by Charlie on our earlier visit and others whom I vaguely recognised. One of them grabbed my arm. 'It's Persephone Blake, isn't it?' he shouted. 'Charlie Bradford's assistant?'

'Yes,' I smiled. Then I apologised, 'I'm sorry, I can't remember your name. Charlie introduced me to so many of his friends.'

'Wilf Cutler,' he roared, thrusting out his hand to crush mine in an energetic grip. He was a large mustachioed man, with bear-like arms and huge shoulders which strained the seams of his tweed jacket. 'How's old Charlie doing?' he asked.

'He's still the same, chasing stories.'

'I remember his piece from Spain.' He gave a loud guffaw. 'Just the sort of crazy thing Charlie would do. He's a real corker. One would never guess that behind those schoolmasterly specs the spirit of adventure lurks.' He guffawed again and corralled some of the other journalists to come and meet me. I found that I was quite famous amongst them and, with a drink in my hand, was ushered to a table, where I sat with four or five others discussing the present circumstances in Berlin.

'I hate this bloody place,' said one of them. 'Nothing is what it seems and nobody wants to talk.'

'Why would they want to talk to you, you miserable bugger?' another teased. 'They talk to me because I'm handsome and dashing and ask where the best bars are. I don't ask about the price of potatoes.'

In the laughter that followed, I recognised the

camaraderie of the profession I'd joined. They played hard, but only after they'd worked hard.

An older man leant forward. He was balding and had thick tortoiseshell glasses. I hadn't spoken to him yet, but I knew who he was from his name when Wilf introduced him. He was the man who'd written the article about Xanthe and the other English women. 'Are you related to Xanthe Blake?' he asked, and the rest stopped joshing with each other and listened.

'She's my sister,' I said. 'I'm hoping to take her home. To get her out of here before it's too late.'

He gave a short, rather unpleasant laugh. 'You'll be lucky,' he grunted. 'From what I saw, she's here for the duration. Completely taken in by Herr Hitler, thinks he's nothing short of a god. And of course, she's totally under the spell of that bastard von Klausen.'

'Von Klausen, the acolyte of Heydrich?' asked Wilf Cutler. The older man nodded and the discussion turned to Heydrich. I listened with a sinking heart. I'd already suspected that getting Xanthe to come home with me was going to be difficult, and it seemed that my suspicions were correct.

'Heydrich is buying up real estate, so I'm told,' said Wilf. 'Nice places where members of the SS can stay with their families. Some of them in the holiday spots on the Baltic coast, but also here in the wealthy suburbs.' He shook his large head. 'The present occupants are given little choice, I believe.'

'That's not all he's doing,' the older man growled, and I was leaning forward to listen when a hand touched me on the shoulder. I turned in my seat.

'Hello, Seffy.'

It was Paul Durban.

I jumped out of my chair and gave him a hug. 'What the hell are you doing here?' I asked.

'I am working. Like you are.'

'But I thought you were in Poland,' I protested.

'Keeping an eye on me?' He laughed.

I excused myself from my colleagues and followed Paul to another table, where we sat together, nursing vodkas. 'How are you?' I asked. He looked older. His fresh, boyish face had gone, replaced by a more serious one with tiny lines between the eyebrows and sharper cheekbones.

'All right.' He smiled. 'Happy to be out of Spain, although this place is worse, I think. But there is no fighting . . . yet.'

'There will be, although not a civil war,' I sighed. 'They all seem to be happy with the government. Most people feel no fear.'

'Most, but not all. The Jews and the mentally ill have suffered and will suffer so much more. And then there are the homosexuals. Nobody talks about their persecution.'

This last was heartfelt and I nodded, understanding him. 'Will you write about it?'

He shook his head. 'Not yet. France is a Catholic country. The subject of Jews and queers is of little interest,' he said. 'Now, let's go and get some supper and you can tell me what happened to you after Ribera. Charlie Bradford's piece was translated for one of our newspapers and I read it. I've seen him recently, but I want to hear from you.'

We walked out of the hotel and found a restaurant

with outside tables. It was a warm evening, with a bright penny moon shining out of a clear, lavender sky. 'Remember that restaurant in Cerbère?' I said. 'With the fantastic food?'

'Indeed,' he said and handed me the menu. 'This will not be as good, except for the company.'

It took a long time to tell him about getting out of Spain. I found myself talking about Elena and her death and how I had taken Marisol.

'You have the baby, still?' he asked, looking amazed.

I nodded. 'She is mine, now.'

'But her father. He was there, you say. He had helped Charlie get out of the field hospital?'

'Yes. We knew him before. I knew him very well.'

Paul wagged his head from side to side, in a very Gallic fashion. 'He is your lover, yes?'

'Yes,' I laughed, glad to be able to say it out loud. 'He was . . . is and always will be my lover.'

'So, he is with you in England now?'

'No,' I sighed. 'I have no idea where he is. He leads a mysterious life.'

'Ah. The cat that walks in the night, eh?'

The cat that walks in the night. I repeated those words as I lay in bed in my room at the Adlon later. The last night I'd been here, I'd lain in Amyas's arms in this very bed and had been transported into the enchanted land where Amyas reigned supreme. What wouldn't I have given for him to be here now . . . I closed my eyes, remembering every touch of his hands and every place where his lips had been. I grasped at the relived pleasure and when I finally drifted off to sleep, it was with a new measure of contentment.

Some time in the night I woke up. A memory of something that had been deep in my brain had come back to me. There had been another person who knew about my proposed meeting in Monbijoupark – why hadn't I remembered it before? I had told Amyas. Could it be that he'd . . . But then the sensible part of my head took over and I smiled quietly. He wouldn't have had anything to do with Kitty and her mother. That was altogether too fanciful.

The next day, after breakfast, I went for a walk along Unter den Linden to look at the shops and people and to get the feel of a city possibly preparing for war. My favourite coffee shop was bustlingly full and I had to wait to be served. The waiters seemed to recognise me but . . . was I imagining it, or was there a look of caution on their faces? The chocolate was just as good though, and when I'd finished it I walked back towards the hotel, past the bright shops, and planned to buy something pretty for Marisol before I went home. I stopped at the dress shop where I'd bought the lovely ball gown and looked in the window. I could see the shop assistant who'd been so helpful and I waved. She recognised me, as the waiters had and, like them, she was cautious and turned away. Things had changed. Now I was an unwelcome alien in this city and I wondered what Xanthe's response would be when I turned up at her door.

I'd debated with myself about ringing her first, before going, but then I decided against it. She might fob me off with some excuse, so I got a taxi and gave the driver Xanthe's address, which was in a suburb called Zehlendorf, not too far from the city centre. It was a pretty place, with large, freshly painted houses and well-tended gardens. Some of the streets were cobbled and the whole area had a sort of village atmosphere. I liked it, but, I grinned to myself, I bet Xanthe doesn't. She liked the hard pavements and bright lights of the city.

The taxi drew up at the address and I paid and got out. Xanthe's house resembled an Alpine chalet, with a steeply pitched roof and a wooden veranda around the first floor. It looked incongruous in this sunny village setting, but it was rather pretty all the same.

I rang the doorbell and within seconds it was answered.

'Ja?' It was a girl in maid's uniform.

'Fräulein Blake,' I said. And then in English, 'I'm her sister.'

'Seffy!' Xanthe careered down the narrow hallway, knocked the little maid to one side and flung herself into my arms.

Chapter Twenty

'Oh, Seff, Seff. I'm so glad to see you.'

We hugged each other, while I recovered from this unusually effusive greeting. All our lives we'd been rather at arm's length. We were so very different and as we'd grown up, we had grown even further apart.

But now, Xanthe seemed delighted to see me. 'Come in, do,' she cried and led me through the hallway into a drawing room that overlooked a flower-filled back garden. The French windows were open and I could see a little fountain, its water sparkling as it bounced into a basin held up by stone cherubs. Inside, though, the room was dreary. Dark oil paintings depicting fat maidens being rescued by Teutonic knights hung on the walls, and beneath them heavily carved wooden sideboards and bookcases, devoid of books, took up too much space. Two large sofas covered in green fabric sat opposite each other in front of the fireplace, a striped green and black rug covering the floor between them. The only brightness came from busily painted majolica lamps which stood on the carved wooden mantelpiece, and all about the room cactus plants lurked, dustily, in more majolica pots. It was a ghastly room and so unlike somewhere that Xanthe would normally enjoy staying.

'Goodness!' I exclaimed. The word sprang out of my mouth before I could stop myself. 'This is different.'

'Isn't it absolutely adorable?' Xanthe squealed. 'Wolf had it furnished down to the very last ashtray. He says it's exactly how our Führer has decorated his country home.'

'Our Führer?' I asked, amazed.

'Oh, yes,' she smiled. 'Herr Hitler. Isn't he an absolute darling? I shook hands with him once, oh, it was so thrilling. He's . . .' She put a finger to her lower lip, thinking and then beamed as she remembered. 'Magnetic, yes, that's what Wolfie says.'

I took a proper look at her. She was the same as ever, perhaps a little plumper, but she still had her angelic blonde looks. Oddly, she now wore her hair parted in the middle and fastened into little knots over her ears, as though she was some sort of country girl, and her white smocked blouse and blue patterned dirndl skirt added to the effect. These were not her usual couture clothes.

'Why are you wearing that outfit?' I asked. 'Are you going to a fancy dress party?'

She scowled. 'It's not fancy dress, Seffy, don't be silly.' Then her face brightened. 'But we are going to a party this afternoon. A picnic. Wolf says quite a few of the party members will be there. There'll be singing and dancing and we must go.' She paused as a little cloud drifted across her face, then she continued, 'He says it'll be fun and I will enjoy it. He should be home soon.' She looked at the clock on the wall and my eyes followed hers. It was a wooden clock, with dangling pendulums and carved trees and acorns around a little hut above them. As we looked, it struck the hour and a cuckoo flew out of the hut to announce the time.

I burst out laughing. 'My God, Xanthe. What the hell is that?'

She frowned and then as I continued to laugh her lips curved into a smile and she laughed too. 'It's gruesome, isn't it,' she gasped in a whisper, 'but Wolf likes it.'

'What does Wolf like?' He was standing behind us, having come in through the garden, and was just as I remembered him: tall and icy blond in his wonderfully smart black uniform with its death's head insignia.

'The clock, Wolfie,' Xanthe said, all traces of laughter gone. 'You like the clock.'

He nodded and looked at me. 'This is a surprise, Fräulein Seffy. Xanthe didn't tell me you were coming to visit.' He stepped forward and raised my hand to his lips. I suppressed the shudder that his presence always gave me.

'She didn't know. I wanted to surprise her.'

'And you knew where she lived? Perhaps she sent you a letter?'

'I didn't,' said Xanthe quickly. 'You know that I never write letters.' I glanced at her out of the corner of my eye and noticed that she was biting her lip.

'I'm a journalist. It's my job to find things out. I was coming to Berlin anyway, so I thought I'd look up my sister. And I have.'

He smiled, parting his thin lips over perfect teeth. 'Well, what a treat for her.' He went over to Xanthe and put an arm around her waist. 'Isn't it, *Liebchen*?'

She looked up at his face with glistening eyes. 'Yes, Wolfie.'

'Good.' He turned back to me. 'Your sister and I are attending a picnic this afternoon, perhaps you would care to join us?'

299

I was already going to say yes. An afternoon with members of the Nazi party would make wonderful copy, but before I could nod my head and thank von Klausen for the invitation, Xanthe grabbed hold of my arm and said, 'Oh, please, Seffy, say yes. Come with us, do. I should love that.'

'I will. Thank you, Major von Klausen. I've always enjoyed a picnic.'

'And it will give you lots to write about, no doubt. Something about the happy times we have in Germany.' He gave his chilling smile again and then said to Xanthe, 'Take your sister upstairs so she can freshen up. You could, perhaps, find her some suitable outfit.'

'I'm fine as I am,' I said firmly. I was wearing a white silk shirt and a calf-length beige gaberdine skirt. 'If I look out of place, you can put it down to my unexpected visit.'

He didn't answer, but his eyes narrowed, before he gave his polite half-bow. 'Fifteen minutes, Xanthe. I'll expect you not to be late.'

Xanthe pulled on my arm. 'Come upstairs,' she said. 'I can find you a hat, if you'd like.'

Her bedroom wasn't as dull as the living room, but it was furnished in old-fashioned tapestry-style fabrics that I thought she'd hate and when she opened her wardrobe to find me a hat, I saw that quite a few dirndl skirts were hanging next to her usual couture collection.

'What on earth has happened to you?' I asked, sitting on the bed. 'This isn't how you usually dress . . . or behave, for that matter.'

'I don't know what you mean,' she pouted. 'I like this style. It shows that I'm a true Aryan, Wolf says. Besides, this is how my new friends will dress for the picnic. We have given up the decadent style of England and America.'

This last was said parrot fashion, as though she was repeating something that had been drummed into her.

'Father wants you to come home,' I said slowly. 'I've come to fetch you.'

'Home?' She was sitting at a rickety little dressing table and looked at me in the mirror. 'What does Mummy say?'

She didn't know. I swallowed and wondered how she was going to take the news. 'Mother has left. Gone to America with some man. I don't know who. She's not coming back.' If I thought she'd be upset, I was wrong.

'It'll be Binkie Durham's uncle,' Xanthe said with a careless shrug. 'She's known him for years, off and on, and was awfully keen on him. Father is very dull, that's what she always said. He's made her life an absolute misery.'

'Well, he's the miserable one now. Quite bewildered, I'd say. But he still wants you to come home. Besides which, there's going to be a war and you can't stay here.'

'Why ever not?' She stood up and took some white high-heeled sandals out of the wardrobe. 'The Germans will be in London before Christmas. That's what I heard Wolf say. I'll go back then. With the winners.'

I was shocked. Was she really saying that Germany intended to invade Britain? Had she overheard something and given the game away? Or had she just been taken in by idle chatter? Xanthe was as stupid as ever and could have easily misunderstood von Klausen and his friends. But, at the same time, I knew that von Klausen wasn't stupid, he was just vile and he was dominating my sister. I had to try again to persuade her to come home.

'Are you happy here, Xanthe?' I asked. 'In this silly little house with these dreadful clothes? Don't you miss London? Tea at the Ritz and dancing at the Café de Paris?'

For a moment, I thought I saw a faraway glint in her eye, as she remembered the fun she used to have, but then there was a rap at the door and Wolf walked in.

'Ready, ladies?'

The picnic was held in a clearing on the edge of the Grünewald Forest, a twenty-minute drive from Xanthe's house. Von Klausen had dismissed his driver for the day and had taken the wheel of the big Mercedes himself. I was invited to sit beside him on the way there, with Xanthe relegated to the back seat.

'I understand you had an adventure in Spain,' he said. He drove very fast and I watched the road ahead in some trepidation. 'I saw an account, last year.'

'Spain?' said Xanthe. 'Did you go to Spain? How lovely. Although it's not as smart as Monte, people tell me there are some very nice places.'

'Be quiet, Xanthe.' Von Klausen frowned at her in the driving mirror.

'Sorry,' she whispered and I turned my head to look at her. She had curled up in the corner of the back seat and refused to meet my eye.

'Yes,' von Klausen continued. 'You and Mr Bradford had some narrow escapes, it would seem.'

'We did,' I agreed. 'Charlie was wounded and then he got malaria. It was bad for a while.'

'But you had help, I believe. Mr Bradford mentioned

"another" in his article. I would very much like to know who helped you.'

I laughed. 'I'm a journalist, Major. We don't disclose our sources, or those who might be put in danger. So, I can't tell you.'

'Would he be in danger?'

'He?' I wanted to spread some confusion. 'Did I say it was a man?' I could feel von Klausen's body twitching. He wasn't used to having a request refused; especially, I guessed, by a woman. But he barked a laugh.

'Still as independent as ever, eh, Fräulein Seffy?'

'I hope so,' I said, and smiled.

The picnic was in full swing when we arrived. The setting was perfect, a cleared area beside the lake, with beech trees and dense green conifers as a background. I could see an open cooking area to one side, where puffs of white steam rose from large pans into the bright summer sky. The smell of smoked sausage accompanied the steam, and looking around, I saw people at trestle tables tucking in to platefuls of those same sausages with lashings of mustard and chunks of bread.

A stage had been erected in the middle of the clearing and when we got out of the car, eight couples, the girls in outfits not dissimilar to Xanthe's and the men in leather shorts, climbed on to the stage and started to do a folk dance. Their dance included a lot of foot-stamping and the male dancers rhythmically slapping their naked thighs. I was fascinated and stopped to watch them. The music, which was blared around the area by loudspeakers, was provided by a band sitting under a canvas gazebo. The conductor kept looking over his shoulder to see who was walking across the clearing. Spotting von Klausen, he gave him a polite bow.

All around, people were sitting on the grass or at the trestles and there were smaller tables with parasols. 'We will sit here' – von Klausen indicated a small, empty table – 'and we will have drinks. Beer, yes?'

'I don't like beer,' Xanthe protested. 'Isn't there something else?'

'No. You drink beer.' Von Klausen nodded to a waitress, who went off and returned moments later with three large glasses of sparkling lager.

'*Prost!*' Von Klausen held up his glass and Xanthe and I did too.

'Cheers!' I said and took a sip. It was not unpleasant and even Xanthe took a small mouthful.

I had my camera in my bag and got it out. 'You don't mind, do you?' I said to von Klausen. 'Photographs will make a brilliant accompaniment to my article.'

He frowned and for a few seconds I thought he would make some sort of objection, but then he nodded. 'Yes, take photographs.' I stood up and snapped the dancers and the people milling about. Beside the lake, pretty, well-washed children were standing in a group, listening to a man in a brown uniform. He seemed to be telling them about his organisation, because he kept pointing to the badges on his shirt. I didn't think he was a Scout leader.

I wandered over and took some pictures of the children and then, turning round, took one of Xanthe and von Klausen sitting together.

'You must send me a copy of that,' Xanthe said happily. 'I haven't got any pictures of Wolfie and me.'

'I can arrange to have them developed, if you give me the film,' offered von Klausen. 'No cost to you, of course.'

'Well, not yet,' I said. 'I have more shots to take in Berlin. I have another few days here.'

A soldier appeared and, saluting Wolf, spoke to him in German. There was a short conversation and then von Klausen stood up. 'Chief of Police Heydrich is arriving. I must go and greet him. If there is opportunity I will bring him over. You will behave correctly.'

Both Xanthe and I raised our eyebrows at that last remark and it was the first time I'd seen von Klausen even slightly embarrassed. He'd overstepped a mark and knew it.

'But of course you will,' he said, smiling. 'You will excuse me.'

We watched him walk across the field nodding to people who half-bowed to him. I looked back at Xanthe, who was gazing at him, almost hypnotised.

'What on earth do you see in him?' I asked, genuinely puzzled. 'He's . . . scary.'

'Oh, Seff,' she sighed. 'Don't be so silly.'

I reached over and touched her hand. 'Look, Xanthe, I want you to come home, now. It's going to be dangerous for you to stay here and if you don't come home you'll be considered a traitor in England.'

She turned and stared at me. 'By whom?' she asked. 'Communists, revolutionaries?'

'No,' I said. 'By everyone except for those few halfwits you used to party with – and most of them have gone to America now. There was an article about you in the newspaper. And it wasn't flattering.'

I thought I'd got through to her, because she looked

genuinely concerned, but then she said, 'I can't go home,' and looked down at her barely tasted beer. 'Not yet, anyway. Wolf won't let me.'

'Why ever not?'

'Because I'm pregnant.'

'What?'

'I'm pregnant,' she repeated. 'And don't you look at me like that, Seffy Blake. It's only about a couple of years ago that you were too.'

I sat back and gaped at her. How the hell did she know? No one knew.

'Bella Duncan told me,' Xanthe said defensively. 'The doctor at the hospital where you went is a friend of hers. He told her and she told me. So your little secret is out. Mine won't be a secret. My child will be a proud son of the Fatherland. That's what Wolf says.'

'But he's married,' I snapped, furious with her and especially with the doctor at the private hospital. He would find a letter from my solicitor on his desk in the near future.

Xanthe scowled but I raged on. 'He's got a wife and children. You're just a mistress and nobody will accept your child. No one, that is, in the society you mix in either here or at home.'

'Wolf has daughters, he wants a son.' Xanthe looked across the clearing to where von Klausen was standing with a group of other officers. 'He's going to divorce his wife, because he doesn't need her money now.'

When I raised my eyebrows, taking in that last bit of information, she had the grace to blush. 'Christ!' I exploded. 'He's got yours, hasn't he?'

She shrugged while I simmered with rage. The bastard,

the absolute bastard, I thought, and could barely contain my temper when he walked towards us with his group of officers.

'Xanthe, Fräulein Seffy, may I present SS-Brigadeführer Heydrich.'

We stood up as a tall, severe-looking man stepped forward. He took off his cap and gallantly kissed Xanthe's hand. I was astonished to see her curtsey and determined not to be so girlish when he took my hand. All I did was nod and say, 'How d'you do?'

'Fräulein Seffy is a journalist, sir,' von Klausen murmured. 'A foreign correspondent.'

'Yes, I'm aware of you, Miss Blake,' Heydrich said. 'Von Klausen has pointed out your articles to me before. You are Mr Charles Bradford's assistant, I believe.'

'I am,' I agreed.

'And you two ladies are sisters.' He looked from one to the other of us and his stiff white face relaxed into the semblance of a smile. 'Not very alike in looks, but perhaps in convictions?'

'I don't think so.' I was being foolishly bold. 'I'm very proud to be British.'

There was a quick intake of breath from von Klausen and the little colour that he had dropped from his face, but Heydrich wasn't fazed. He looked over his shoulder to the officers who had accompanied him and von Klausen. 'You see,' he said, 'this lady is a nationalist. You, Ullmann, doubted that the English had this sentiment.' The young officer to whom he'd spoken went pink and looked down at his gleaming boots. Heydrich turned back to me.

'Quite right, Fräulein Blake. Love of one's country is

indeed something to be proud of. Even though that country is heading along a dangerous path.'

'I think we must disagree on that subject, General,' I said. My heart was thumping, but I was not going to show him that I was scared.

'Of course.' He turned to von Klausen. 'If all the English are like Fräulein Blake our negotiations are going to be difficult. I think the word to describe her and perhaps her government is . . . stubborn?'

Von Klausen gave a strained laugh. 'Yes, General.' He started to steer Heydrich away but the general stopped and turned to look at me again. 'You are perhaps related to the industrialist Blake?'

I nodded. 'Sir Farnworth Blake is our father.'

'And I believe that he has increased production at his mills recently. Is that not true?'

I shrugged. 'I wouldn't know, General. I have no involvement in the family businesses. But, of course, all factories are increasing production. Both at home and here in Germany. I've seen many reports about your steel industry.'

Heydrich nodded slowly. 'We have hard workers, dedicated to their party and their country.'

'It's a wonder,' I said, 'that you don't run out of ore.'

'Oh, we're importing it from Sweden.' Ullmann regretted those words almost before they were out of his mouth, as first von Klausen and then Heydrich gave him a horrified stare. The other officers slowly moved away from the unfortunate young man, who looked as if he wanted the earth to open and take him in.

'Sweden?' I smiled. 'How very interesting.'

'General,' von Klausen turned to his superior officer. 'The mayor would like to meet you.'

And as Heydrich turned away, von Klausen shot a poisonous look in my direction. He was furious and I was glad.

Xanthe sat down again while I took more photographs of Heydrich doing the rounds of the picnickers. Many people gave him the Nazi salute, civilians as well as military. Even the bandmaster, who paused the music to acknowledge the presence of this important man, stood straight and snapped out a stiff arm. To my eyes it looked almost like a joke, but I knew they were all deadly serious. 'I've never met Heydrich before,' said Xanthe, vaguely, watching as the dancers saluted. 'I think he's quite important.'

'He is,' I nodded. 'Very.'

I kept my eyes on the general's progress while Xanthe chattered inconsequentially in the background. At one point he was welcomed by three men who had just arrived. I knew one of them. He was a member of the House of Lords, and I swung my camera in that direction and took several snaps. Lowering it from my face I saw von Klausen looking directly at me.

I knew now that we had a short time left before Wolf returned and in those remaining minutes I sat down and begged Xanthe again to let me take her home. 'Please, come back to London with me,' I said. 'You'll be so much happier there. Even with a baby. I can help you.'

Xanthe gave a cruel little laugh. 'What on earth d'you know about babies, Seff? You lost yours. I've kept mine.'

I turned my face away. How could I tell her about Marisol? I didn't even want to think about my beautiful daughter in this dreadful place.

'See,' said Xanthe. 'You have no answer.'

'It might not be a boy. What will you do then?'

'It will be,' she laughed. 'Wolf has said so.'

Von Klausen drove us back to the Hotel Adlon. 'Come into the bar and have a drink with me,' I suggested, desperate to have another go at Xanthe.

'Oh, please let's, Wolf,' she begged. 'I haven't been here for ages.'

I knew he was going to refuse. He was clearly determined to keep her away from her old friends and I could see his head beginning to shake in refusal, so I acted quickly. I got out of my seat, went round to the rear door, opened it and grabbed her arm. 'Come on, sis.'

Von Klausen had no choice but to accompany us, and he was clearly furious. My journalist friends were in the bar and they waved to me. The older man, who had written about Xanthe and the other English women in Germany, gave her a long, calculating stare and frowned at me. Wilf Cutler bounded over to greet us. 'Seffy Blake,' he boomed. 'Now, who are these charming people that you have brought to entertain us this evening?'

I introduced Xanthe and von Klausen and they were immediately surrounded by eager hacks. It wasn't often that they got to speak to a Nazi officer who was so close to the centre of power. I thought it would only increase his anger, and that notion pleased me, but I was wrong. He turned on the charm and seemed to enjoy sparring with the reporters.

Xanthe was more animated than I'd seen her all day. With a vodka cocktail in her hand, she fluttered her eyelashes and laughed happily in the middle of the crush of reporters. 'She's stunning,' bellowed Wilf. 'How have I missed this filly?'

I laughed. 'Don't think you've much chance there,' I murmured. 'She's obsessed by von Klausen.'

'Silly girl,' he said. 'You'll have to get her out.'

'I know,' I answered. 'I am trying.'

I did have another chance to talk to her. Someone knocked the drink she was holding and it spilt down her peasant blouse. 'Oh,' she giggled, looking down. 'You can see right through it.'

'Come to my room,' I insisted. 'I'll dry you off and give you another shirt.' Von Klausen was bobbing up and down amongst the reporters, shaking his head at Xanthe, but she had her back to him and followed me to the lift without protest.

'Here,' I said, taking a clean silk blouse out of the drawer. 'Take that ghastly thing off.' As she stripped to her underwear I was astonished to see a yellowing bruise on her ribs and the evidence of fingermarks on her upper arm. Someone had grabbed her hard, so hard that at one point a small scab showed where fingernails had broken the skin. I knew exactly who it was.

'Oh, Xanthe,' I said. 'What has he done to you?'

'It was a mistake,' she said quickly. 'He was angry because I'd taken a taxi into the city without telling him. He was so nice about it afterwards.'

'D'you have to ask permission?'

'No. Well, not really. It's just that . . .'

'That you're scared of what might happen if you don't.'

She didn't answer, but looked for make-up on my dressing table. 'You haven't got much nice stuff,' she grumbled. 'Have you any scent?'

'Where's your passport?' I asked.

She shrugged, dipping her fingers into my pot of cream

and rubbing a generous dollop over her little hands. 'I'm not sure. Wolf's got it.'

'Xanthe,' I demanded. 'Get it back from him, as soon as you can. It'll be somewhere in the house. Look for it when he's out.'

'He's going away next week for a few days. He has to organise something that will happen at the end of August. I heard him on the phone talking about somewhere called Gleiwitz.'

'Where's that?'

'I don't know.' She stood up. 'Let's go back downstairs. I want another drink.'

I reached in my bag and took out some money. 'Here,' I said, pushing the notes into her hand.

She was delighted. 'Oh, Seffy. Thank you. It's ages since I had any money.' To my amazement she lifted her skirt and pushed the notes into her knickers. ' Don't say anything.' She winked, her cheeks pink. 'Wolf says I don't know how to handle money.'

They left soon after, von Klausen bowing smartly to the group and kissing my hand. Xanthe hugged me, 'Thank you,' she whispered in my ear, 'for the money and for talking to me. Come and see me again, please.'

I took a taxi to her house the very next day but she wasn't there. 'Fräulein Xanthe gone,' said the housemaid who answered my knock.

'Where?' I demanded.

She shook her head and with a nervous smile shut the door in my face.

Chapter Twenty-One

I spent the rest of the morning back in the city centre, taking photographs. There was evidence everywhere that the German people were preparing for war, just as I'd seen in London. An arrow on the Underground station pointed to the word LUFTSCHUTZBUNKER, an air-raid shelter, and in the park trenches were being dug. No matter what negotiations were taking place, I knew that the Nazi government wanted war.

As I wandered past the Kaiserhof hotel, a policeman held up his arm and I, like the other pedestrians, waited on the pavement while a small fleet of black Mercedes cars discharged groups of young officers at the entrance. They were laughing and joking, even punching each other on the arm, and I guessed that they were there for a party. In a moment another car arrived and from it emerged a bride and groom, she in a white satin dress and he in the black uniform of the SS.

I raised my camera to my eye, ready to take a photo. It would make a good shot, as a contrast to the war preparations, but the policeman put his hand in front of the lens. '*Verboten*,' he growled, and scared that he might confiscate my camera, I said 'sorry' and put it away in my bag. But it was too good to miss, so moving round through the small crowd until I was out of the policeman's sightline I took a few shots of the bride and groom.

We were kept waiting for a few more minutes until the guest of honour arrived and as he stepped out of his car an excited ripple of chatter came from the crowd. He was a plump air force officer, in a light blue uniform, and someone I recognised from the last time I was in Berlin. Amyas had been talking to him as he left the dining room that last morning.

'Hermann Göring,' someone behind me breathed, and suddenly there was a round of spontaneous applause. The Reich Minister turned to the crowd with a beaming smile and gave a wave, before disappearing into the hotel. I caught that wave on my camera and the reaction of the crowd.

Thrilled with the photographs, I walked back towards the Adlon and the Brandenburg Gate. I passed the street I'd taken to cross the river to where Sarah and Kitty lived, but I could see soldiers guarding the bridge and I walked on. On the plane I'd half considered trying to get into the Jewish sector to try and find Sarah, but this morning, at breakfast, there was much talk about one of our colleagues who had gone into the Mitte district and been arrested.

'It's not worth the candle,' bellowed Wilf. 'They're too scared to talk to you even if you can get in and then you're in danger from the SS. I mean, we've all got minders, haven't you noticed?'

I knew I had. When I'd gone up to my room last night, the man who was hovering in the corridor watched me all the way to my door and I remembered that on our last visit to Berlin I'd been followed. What if, when I went down for breakfast, somebody searched my room? I thought of von Klausen offering to get my photos developed; he wanted to know what shots I'd taken and I was sure he would destroy them if he could. With him in mind I'd used up all the film in my camera before getting into bed. Putting the exposed reels in an envelope, I slept with them under my pillow. At breakfast I'd given the reels to Wilf. 'You're going home today, aren't you?' I asked. 'Can you take this film with you and drop it in at my office? I know we're rivals but I've got shots of von Klausen and my sister and I have a feeling that he won't want me to take them out of Germany.' I didn't feel a bit guilty about not telling him that the film also contained pictures of one of our politicians as well as Göring and the Nazi bride and groom; we were friends, yes, but worked for different papers.

'No problem, dear thing. I'll get it out for you.'

There'd been no sign of Paul at breakfast and he hadn't been in the bar last night. I wondered if he'd already left, but when I came back to the hotel, at about three o'clock, he was there, standing by the elephant fountain in the lobby. He looked furtive and was obviously waiting for someone. I glanced over to the reception desk where a man loitered, reading a newspaper. I didn't recognise him as the man who had been on my corridor, so he was probably watching Paul. Suddenly Paul looked up. He'd spotted a man coming into the hotel through the main entrance. This had to be his contact. It took me no time to walk over to the reception desk and ask for my key and, retrieving it, I turned and deliberately barged into the watcher.

'I'm so sorry,' I said, bending to pick up his glasses, which had fallen off his nose, and in straightening up I managed to knock into him again. He stumbled and in that moment I sneaked a look at Paul and saw him take a scrap of paper from a man who walked past him and didn't stop.

'Are you all right, Fräulein?' The receptionist hurried around the desk. She made no enquiry of the secret policeman who was now looking furiously around the lobby for Paul. I had a feeling that despite the general acceptance of the way the Nazi government operated, there were some in this hotel who despised the fact that their guests were being watched.

'I'm fine,' I smiled. 'Just clumsy.'

I went to my room, wondering what Paul had been up to, and smiled. Nothing legal, probably. I shook my head and settled down to type up my impressions of the city and to polish the earlier article I'd started to write about the picnic. When I came down later, I found Paul waiting for me in the bar. We took our drinks to a table on the other side of the room, away from the main crush of journalists. 'Thank you,' he said when we were sitting down. 'I saw what you did. I was getting information from a contact and it would have gone badly for him if he had been seen.'

That set me thinking. Charlie had given me a couple of names and the address and the phone number of Dieter and Rachel, with whom we'd had dinner on my last visit to Berlin. I'll call them later, I promised myself. 'So,' I turned my mind back to Paul. 'You got some useful stuff?'

'Possibly,' he said carefully. 'There is an internment camp near Oranienburg, which is about twenty miles north of here. It is for political prisoners, since three years, but now the SS is stepping it up to take in more people.'

His expression changed. 'People for whom it is a crime simply to exist.'

I nodded, understanding.

'The camp is called Sachsenhausen,' Paul continued, 'and I think I might go to that area and have a look.'

'You're mad,' I said. 'You won't get anywhere near it, and if you do, you'll be arrested.'

Paul laughed, brushing his dark hair away from his face in a boyish gesture. 'It is a risk, I suppose, but these days just living is a risk and I am careful. But to be a foreign correspondent and get good information you must be prepared for an escapade. Did not your time in Spain teach you that? I know you found excitement in the mountains. Even that night in the cave was an adventure, yes?' His grin widened. 'Do not worry for me, big sister Seffy. Have another drink and relax.' He got up and, taking our glasses, wandered towards the bar.

I looked around to see who else was in the lounge. I recognised many of my colleagues who were drifting in after a day of chasing up stories. I waved to the reporter who'd pronounced that he knew where all the best bars were and was surprised to see that the balding man, who'd written about my sister, was busy chatting to a young woman. I wondered if she was another, like Xanthe, who was dazzled by the Nazi regime. Paul's watcher was sitting at another table, barely disguising who he was and what he was doing. It was the boldness and utter disregard of liberty that I found shocking about this country. While I was waiting for Paul I took out my notebook and wrote down a few key points for the article I intended to write on the subject.

'Fräulein Seffy.' I looked up, startled, to see von

Klausen standing above me. I hadn't heard him approach and I could see that he was reading my notes over my shoulder. Standing up, I snapped my notebook shut and said, 'Wolf. What a surprise.' I looked beyond him into the room, expecting to see Xanthe, but she wasn't there.

'Is Xanthe with you?' I asked.

'Unfortunately, no.' Von Klausen gave one of his icy smiles. 'She has gone with friends on a short holiday to Bavaria. The city heat doesn't suit her, so I thought a little mountain air would be good for her. But she sent her best wishes to you and I am here to deliver them.'

'She seemed all right yesterday,' I said, frowning. 'Quite well, actually and she always enjoys hot weather. I was hoping to see her again.'

'Yes, I know you were, but perhaps she didn't want to see you.'

'What?'

This time the smile was not in evidence when von Klausen, his voice glacially cold, said, 'I think, Fräulein, that you have an upsetting effect on your sister. You give her ideas. Wrong ideas, which we must endeavour to reform.'

I began to feel afraid for Xanthe. What had he done to her and where was she? I swallowed, and clutched my notebook close to my body so that he wouldn't see the slight tremor in my hands. 'Major von Klausen,' I said, putting on my most imperious tone and looking down my nose at him. 'I don't know what you can possibly mean and I insist that you give me her address. Our family in London are concerned about her, and so am I.'

'Your mother in America? Is she concerned? One would

think not.' His cold blue eyes drilled into mine and it took all of my control not to give him a slap. This monster had hit Xanthe who, despite my differences with her, was still my little sister and I yearned to hit him back. And now, added to his obvious brutality, he'd spirited her away.

'Her address, Major. I want it.'

'I'm afraid I can't give you that.' He smiled only with his lips. 'The friends she is with haven't communicated yet.'

'What friends? Who are her friends?'

'They are *my* friends.' The finality with which he said it convinced me that I wasn't going to get any more out of him. Frustrated, I picked up my bag and turned, planning to walk away and join Paul at the bar, but Paul, drinks in hand, was approaching.

'Seffy,' he said. He must have noticed my white face, for he added, 'Are you all right?'

'Yes, I'm fine. Shall we take our drinks and join the others?' The others, I noticed, had turned to look at me, seeing that there was a confrontation going on and, being journalists, eager to find out more. Paul was soon followed by one or two of the others, who had spoken to von Klausen the evening before and were anxious to continue asking questions. But I wasn't keen to make this into a general interview and took Paul's arm. 'Come on,' I urged. 'The atmosphere here is becoming toxic.' I shot von Klausen a glance as I spoke the last word.

The major interrupted with a little cough. 'Don't go before you've introduced me to your friend, Fräulein Seffy. *Mein Gott*, but you do collect young men.'

I would have hit him then, but Paul interposed his

body between us. He put the drinks on the table and held out his hand. 'Paul Durban,' he said.

'Ah, another foreign correspondent. A citizen of France and,' von Klausen looked at him with a calculating gleam in his eye, 'also one, I believe, who had adventures in Spain.'

'Yes, over a year ago.'

I was nervous for Paul, wondering how much von Klausen knew about our escape from Spain. But, it turned out, it wasn't much.

'So, perhaps you were the mysterious "another" who assisted Charles Bradford and Fräulein Seffy in their escape?'

'No.' Paul shook his head. 'I was in hospital, as, no doubt, your contacts will confirm. They will also tell you that, like so much of Spain, Sort was overflowing with reporters – it could have been any one of them. Or anyone else, civilian or military.' He grinned. 'You know, Major, we were all very anxious to report on what happened to the enemies of Franco's Fascist regime. It wasn't very pleasant. And we know that it is happening here as well, is it not, even before a war is declared.'

There was an intake of breath from the listening reporters. Paul Durban was being utterly reckless, far more so than any of the rest of us would have been.

This last remark seemed to get through, because von Klausen straightened up, adjusted his collar and said, in a voice dripping with poison, 'Perhaps, for you Herr Durban and you too, Fräulein Seffy, it's time you left Germany, unless, of course, you'd like to witness personally what happens to the enemies of our regime.' There was a fanatical gleam in his eye when he added,

'Our glorious Third Reich.' With that he turned smartly and left.

'*Merde!*' said Paul, collapsing into his chair and picking up his drink. 'That is a very frightening man.'

'Yes, he is,' I answered, scared for my stupid sister. 'Paul, you must be careful. You've made an enemy of von Klausen. He won't rest until he gets you. You should leave Berlin.'

'Should I? Should I take the easy road? Not care that men, men like me, are sent to camps, humiliated and killed?' He shrugged. 'I cannot do that, Seffy. I will bring it to the daylight. I will make an exposé.'

I was angry with him. 'Don't you care that you might get killed?'

'No,' he said simply, and drank his vermouth.

Later, I refused Paul's invitation to dinner. 'I have something I must do.'

'D'you want me to come with you?'

I shook my head, smiling. 'No, can't let you scoop me. I'll be fine.' I was planning to go and see Dieter and Rachel and I went to my room and studied my map of Berlin. It seemed that the address Charlie had given me wasn't far away, on a small street off Unter der Linden. I picked up the phone thinking I would call them first and then another thought struck me and I put it down, quickly. Maybe my calls were being listened to, I thought; it wouldn't really be surprising, so I put on my coat and went downstairs and through the lobby. My watcher followed me into a café where I bought and paid for coffee and a pastry. After a few minutes I got up and went to the toilet, leaving my half-eaten pastry on my plate, hoping he'd think I was coming back. It seemed that he did, for when I skipped out of the back door, which was beside the toilet, he wasn't following me.

I found the flat quite easily. It was on the second floor of a block and when I rang the doorbell, I felt pleased with myself. I was following up on a contact.

My ring took a long time to be answered, but eventually the door half opened and Dieter's face looked out. He stared at me as though I was a ghost.

'Persephone Blake,' I smiled. 'I'm a friend of Charlie Bradford. He told me to look you up.'

He said nothing but continued to stare at me. 'I met you and your wife last time I was in Berlin,' I said, now getting nervous under his unflinching gaze. 'Surely you remember.'

Finally he spoke. 'You were followed?' He pushed past me and looked into the corridor. There was no one.

'No. I shook him off.' I hoped that it was true, but I said it with certainty. He held the door wider and jerked his head into the hallway of his flat.

'Come in.'

The sight which greeted me was appalling. The room was a mess. Cupboards were hanging open and papers were spread all over the floor. The cushions of the sofa had been upended, a lamp turned over, and from the living room I could see through to the kitchen, which was in a similar state.

'My God!' I whispered. 'What's happened?'

'Can you not guess?' he said. 'They have been here. The security police.' He picked up a handful of papers and stood with them in his hand, looking at the destruction. 'I came home and it was like this.'

'But why?' I asked, looking around the room, at the

322

slanted pictures and the mirror which had been roughly pulled off the wall and was lying smashed in the fireplace. 'Why would they do this?'

He muttered something in German and then banged his fist against the wall.

'I don't understand,' I said.

'Because they can, because they do what they want to.' His voice was rising, getting hysterical, and I put a hand on his arm. He shook it off and looked hard into my face. 'This country is governed by evil men.'

'Where's Rachel? Where is your wife?' I asked, looking round.

'Rachel? My Rachel?' Dieter stared at me, with glittering eyes which seemed to burn in his white, distraught face. 'Do you ask me where my Rachel is? I tell you. She has gone. Taken, two weeks ago. And I cannot discover where they are keeping her.' Then, to my dismay, tears began to roll down his cheeks and he started to sob like a child while I stood, awkwardly, watching him. I didn't know what to do.

'Sit,' I said after a few moments. Putting the sofa back together, I pushed him down on to it. In the kitchen I found a bottle of aquavit. Pouring a large slug, I took it back to the living room and put it into his trembling hand.

'Excuse me,' he said eventually, blowing his nose and wiping his eyes. 'I have felt fear for many days. Going to the police station, every day, to ask about my wife and having to listen to those pigs laugh and say they are sorry for me that I have a Jew wife. "How can you bear it," they say, "how can you sleep in the same bed as a Jew?"' A sigh shuddered through him and he took a deep draught. 'Until now I keep my strength, because I need it to find her, but this . . .' He spread his hands towards the littered floor. 'Now I am broken.'

I went back into the kitchen and found another glass and, bringing the bottle with me, sat beside him. 'Tell me about Rachel.' I wondered if I was treading on dangerous territory but he seemed glad to talk about her.

'She went,' he gulped, 'to see her mother. In the Jewish sector. She has gone every week and thought that the guards would know her. I think they did, but two weeks ago she did not come home. I went to try and find her, but they would not let me through. I showed my press card, I said who I was.' He shook his head. 'It made no difference.'

'Well, where has she gone?' I asked, baffled. 'Can they take people who've done nothing wrong?'

Even as I said it I knew I was being ridiculous. Hadn't Kitty said that some of her friends' parents had been taken. What wrong had they done? 'My friend says there's a camp at Sachsenhausen. Maybe she's there. It's about twenty miles north of Berlin.'

'They have many camps!' Dieter shouted, looking at me as though I was an idiot. 'They have arrested so many people. People who have done nothing. Don't you understand? Rachel is a Jew. Do you know the hell we live in?'

If I hadn't before, I certainly did now and I was ashamed of myself for even asking the question. I knew what was going on in Germany. God knows I'd had enough examples. Charlie had told me a year ago about the arrests and my assignment in Spain had opened my eyes to the inhumanities that people can inflict on each other. There was Paul, talking about concentration camps, and Kitty and Sarah, and even Jacob. And then, on the other side, there were von Klausen and Heydrich, who were more terrifying than anyone I'd ever met. But despite all of it, I'd held myself aloof. Thinking, barely on a conscious level, that my class and money would insulate me from all of it. I was ashamed.

I looked into my glass, while beside me a man who had lost all hope wept and I had nothing to say that would comfort him except . . . 'My friend tells me that there is a Zionist group who are getting Jews out. Perhaps they can help. The rabbis know how to get in touch with them.'

'Yes, yes, we have all heard of them,' Dieter snapped, anger replacing despair. 'You have told me nothing new. These people may not be real. But if they exist they are not for the people who are already taken.' He stood up. 'You go now. I don't want you here. I don't want to answer any more of your stupid questions or hear of the few pathetic myths you have learned. Your naïvety makes me sick.'

For a moment I considered arguing with him and saying that I wasn't naïve and that I was just trying to do my job, but he had gone to the door and was holding it open. 'I'm sorry,' I whispered, offering my hand, but he wouldn't take it and I went out, my heart thumping, as the door slammed behind me.

It was a moonless night and the side street was dark and empty; I was scared and almost wished my watcher was about. My fear was mixed with anger, directed at myself as much as at Dieter. How could I have been so careless with my questions to him? So thoughtless? I knew the facts and I knew how dangerous Berlin was, but in only watching and reporting I'd taken a coward's way. Even Paul had chided me earlier about being too cautious.

As for Dieter, why hadn't he and Rachel left earlier? They knew she would be targeted, but then I remembered that she had stayed because of her parents and he had stayed because of her. As I walked back to the hotel, leaving the dark street and heading along the busy and brightly lit Unter der Linden towards Pariser Platz and the Adlon, I wondered: would I stay in a dangerous place because of my mother? The honest answer had to be no. Would I stay for Amyas? For Marisol? Yes, of course I would. The difference was love.

That night I phoned the paper and filed a report. It was brief and only said that I was returning in the morning. 'Can't say more, not here,' I said and the telephonist at the newspaper, who took my message, seemed to understand.

'Good luck, dear,' she said. 'Take care,' and that moved me almost more than Dieter's tears. I went up to bed, longing for home.

Chapter Twenty-Two

London

I flew home the next afternoon, having spent the morning shopping for clothes for Marisol, chocolates for Alice and a box of Berlin pastries for Jacob and Kitty.

'Where is she?' I cried, turning the key in my door and stepping inside. Alice, who was sitting on the sofa, listening to the radio, put her finger to her lips.

'She's asleep in the nursery. Go and see her but don't wake her up.'

My girl seemed to have grown in the few days I'd been away, and as I leant over her cot and kissed her little cheek, she moved and murmured in her sleep. 'You will be safe,' I whispered to her. 'Whatever happens I will make sure of it.'

Charlie came to the flat early the next morning while I was still in my dressing gown making tea. 'My God, you don't waste time,' I yawned.

'No, I don't, Blake,' he grinned. And while I went to get dressed, he made breakfast.

I'd sent Alice home for the day, and now I could hear Marisol chattering to her stuffed rabbit.

'Mama,' she laughed, fastening her dark eyes on me, and I bent over and picked her up. 'You're a lovely girl,'

I cooed at her, 'but I think you need a wash,' and I took her to the bathroom.

'Blake, where are you?' I heard Charlie calling.

'In the bathroom, with Marisol,' I shouted back.

He put his head around the door. 'God,' he said. 'She's gorgeous,' and he rolled up his sleeves and took over the bathing while I sorted out her clothes.

Later, I held her in my arms while we ate breakfast, handing her to him only when I got up to pour more tea. When I brought the cups back to the table, I laughed.

'What is it?' asked Charlie, who was struggling to keep his glasses out of Marisol's curious little hands. 'What?'

'We look like a typical married couple,' I said. 'Mummy, Daddy and baby.'

'I wish we were.' Charlie said the words into Marisol's cheek and stood up to take her back to the nursery for her morning sleep.

'For God's sake, Charlie,' I said, exasperated. 'You're already married.'

'Yes,' he said bleakly as he went to put Marisol in her cot.

It's time we had this out, I thought, finishing off my coffee. I have to ask him about Diana and why he doesn't seem to love her or want to be with her.

'All right,' he said when he came back. 'It's time for a debriefing.'

'Yes, I've got tons to tell you and ideas for a couple of extra articles but first . . . Charlie, tell me about Diana. You keep flirting with me and making remarks. It's not fair to her and it seems so out of character for you.' I thought back to that phone call I'd made to his home in Dorset. When she'd answered, she sounded quite harsh, as though she knew who I was and resented my call. 'I spoke to her when I called you at home. She didn't sound happy, does she know you make up to other women?'

'No.' Charlie sat down heavily on the wooden chair beside the window. 'She doesn't. She doesn't know anything. Seven years ago she was thrown from her horse and paralysed from the waist down. She also suffered some brain damage.' He gave a swift, sad smile. 'Funny thing is, she's always so happy to see me, although she doesn't really know who I am.'

'But,' I said, upset by what he'd told me and almost disbelieving, 'I spoke to her. She sounded quite sensible.'

'You spoke to Clarissa, Diana's sister. She's been with us since Diana came out of hospital and has looked after her devotedly. Clarissa runs the house, nurses Diana and cares for the boys when they're home from school.'

'The boys?'

'Yes, my stepsons. Diana was a widow with two boys when I married her.'

I put my hand across the table and took his. 'I'm sorry, Charlie,' I said. 'I shouldn't have asked, it's none of my business.'

He sighed. 'I'm afraid it is now, Blake. Now that I've told you. I'll keep coming back from Dorset and grumbling to you about the latest slighting remark that Clarissa has made. She doesn't like me because, as she never tires of telling me, I'm not a patch on Diana's first husband. Basil was my cousin, you know, but we weren't a bit alike. He farmed and rode to hounds.' Charlie frowned. 'Christ, they were all so very horsey.'

I smiled. Although it was a sad story, it made Charlie more understandable and the thought of him being part of a horsey family was funny. 'I can't think what on earth Diana saw in you,' I said. 'Or you in her, for that matter.'

'Oh, she was all right, quite sweet in many ways, and I liked the boys. I hated to think of them without a father, so, even though Diana is a bit older than me, I stepped in.'

'Like you did with Marisol?'

'No. That's different. I adore our little girl. I feel as though I could be her real father.'

I was about to pour scorn on that remark but then I realised that his emotions were no different from mine. I felt as though I was her real mother. 'We're a sorry pair,' I smiled. I thought of how I was hopelessly in love with Amyas, and Charlie feeling the same about me.

'I don't think so, Blake. I think we're lucky. Now,' he leant forward. 'Let's get down to work.'

It took most of the morning for me to tell him about Berlin and to write copy for the paper. 'This is good stuff,' Charlie said after we'd finished. 'I'll go in this afternoon to set it all in motion and, naturally, your name will be fronting it. The photographs, delivered courtesy of Wilf Cutler, have already been developed.' He laughed. 'How you charmed Wilf into bringing them to us, untouched and unpinched I might add, I can't imagine. He wouldn't have done it for me.'

'I introduced him to von Klausen,' I said. 'He got to talk to someone very close to the centre. Perhaps it was some sort of a thank-you.'

'Well, whatever, your whole piece is going to be terrific. You've done great work, especially getting close to Heydrich.'

'But you met him, remember, at that dance at the Kaiserhof.'

'I did,' Charlie agreed. 'But it was only a brief handshake before he moved on. No, Blake. I confess, I'm jealous.'

I laughed. 'That's good.'

He grinned, then looked at my notes again. 'I see you found Xanthe.'

'I did, but, Charlie, I've lost her again.' I told him about von Klausen coming to the hotel and saying that she'd gone to Bavaria. 'I don't think I believe him, but if she did go, I'm positive that she didn't go of her own accord.'

'Mm,' he nodded. 'And she didn't know anything about what von Klausen and Heydrich were up to?'

'No, not really. You know how dense she is, although . . .' I remembered the one snippet of conversation about von Klausen going away. 'She did mention a place, a place von Klausen was having meetings about and where he was going at the end of August.'

'What place?'

'D'you know, I'm struggling. I should have written it down, but at the time it wasn't possible . . . it was something like Gleiwik, or Gleiwitz, yes, that's what it was Gleiwitz.'

'Gleiwitz. Where the hell is that?'

'I don't know and of course Xanthe didn't either, but somehow I think it's important.'

'Could be. I'll look it up when I go into the office.'

I knocked on Jacob's door after Charlie had gone. I had Marisol on my arm and the box of pastries, which I'd kept overnight in my American fridge, dangling from my finger by the little cord that tied it. 'Hello, Jacob. I'm home again. I brought you a taste of Berlin.'

He ushered me in. 'Thank you, dear Seffy. It is

thoughtful of you.' He seemed rather distracted, and although I was made as welcome as usual, I could see that he had something on his mind.

'Where's Kitty?' I asked.

'Ah,' Jacob replied. 'I have arranged for her to have extra tuition to improve her English. She is with a tutor, down the road from here; she and two other children who came on the Kindertransport. I am happy for her, but . . .'

'But what, Jacob? What is it?'

Putting Willi down on his little bed, Jacob went to his desk and picked up a letter. I could see from where I was sitting that it was official. It had a government stamp on it. 'Read this, Seffy,' he said. 'Tell me what I should do.'

It was a letter from the Department of War, telling Jacob that the British government intended to register all German aliens living within the United Kingdom and that he should report to the nearest police station.

'Goodness,' I looked up at him. 'This is a bit of a facer.'

'It's like Germany all over again,' he cried, running his hands through his hair so that it stood up like a grey halo. 'Registered, counted, put on a list. What will be next? Prison?'

'It won't come to that, I'm sure. You've been here, what is it now, ten years?'

'Fourteen,' Jacob said, sitting down on his chair and beckoning Willi to jump on his knee. 'Fourteen years of paying my taxes and behaving like a good citizen.'

'Look,' I said. 'I don't think anything will come of it. Go to the police station and register. It would be better to do it straight away because that will prove that you are happy to comply with government rules. If you don't go, they might come looking for you and that would make you look guilty of something.' I had another thought. 'What about Kitty?'

'I don't know,' sighed Jacob, leaning over and taking the letter out of my hand. 'It says aliens sixteen and over. She's not sixteen.'

'Then I don't think you must tell them about her. Though they might know already, I imagine they keep an eye on German immigrants.'

'Do they? Haven't they got a quota of how many people should be allowed in?'

'I wouldn't worry about that. Some other child will have stayed behind, his parents not able to bear giving him up. You know how it is.' I tried to sound confident, but I was sure that the civil service had a very precise list of all the children who had immigrated and where they had gone and they would probably catch up with Kitty some time. 'Go to the police station this afternoon. I would.'

Willi suddenly pricked up his ears and thumped his tail, and the next moment I heard the sound of the key in the door and Kitty came in.

'Oh, Seffy,' she cried. 'You have come home.' She rushed towards me and gave me a kiss, and then after taking off her jacket she took Marisol into her arms and cooed at her.

'I hear that you are having some extra lessons,' I said. 'Do you like your tutor?'

'Oh yes, I do,' Kitty said. 'She is very nice. I have been doing a lesson this afternoon, learning . . . contractions. I can say, "I've" instead of I have and "we'll" instead of we will. Like you do.'

'Very good,' I laughed. 'It will not – that is, it won't – take you long to speak fluently. So what have you been doing besides that?'

'Yesterday I went for a walk with Miss Alice and Marisol. She showed me the Houses of Parliament and told me some history about London. She is so good like that. I love going out with her and she has promised to take me to other places and tell me stories about them.'

Jacob got up and put the letter on his desk. 'I shall make coffee to go with these pastries,' he said, leaving Kitty, Marisol and me together.

'How was Berlin?' asked Kitty. She didn't look at me, but I guessed she wanted to know whether I'd been to see her mother. I had to tell her straight away.

'Kitty,' I said. 'I'm so sorry to have to tell you this, but I couldn't get into Auguststrasse, so I didn't see your mother. The whole area seems to be out of bounds, particularly to reporters, which is what I am. I did meet someone the other evening whose wife has been regularly going in there to see her mother, but now she's been taken. To a camp, I suppose.' I took the girl's hand. 'I know that this isn't nice for you to hear but I think, I hope, you would rather I was honest.'

She nodded. I don't think she could speak, her emotions were running too high, and she rocked Marisol in her arms while my girl tried to undo Kitty's thick plait.

I cast my mind about, trying to think of something to cheer her up and then it struck me. 'Kitty,' I said. 'I'm thinking about going down to Cornwall for a few days, to the seaside. Perhaps at the end of the week. Why don't you come with me? That is, if Uncle Jacob agrees.'

'What do I have to agree about?' Jacob had come in with a tray of coffee.

'I want to take Kitty to Cornwall for a few days. Please let her come; you too, Jacob, if you would like. There's plenty of room.'

'I will stay in London,' he said. 'There are things I have to do.' He jerked his head towards the desk where the letter from the government lay. 'But Kitty, yes. It will be good for her. Thank you, Seffy.'

I turned to Kitty. 'Would you like that?'

She looked up and I could see that she had tears in her eyes. 'Yes,' she whispered. 'I would like it very much.'

So it was decided. Alice was thrilled with the prospect. 'I've never been to Cornwall,' she said. 'All over the world with some of my families, but never Cornwall. It'll be a right treat.'

I went into the office the next day and wrote my piece and took it and the photographs into the editor's office. He was sitting at his desk enveloped, as usual, in a cloud of blue, foul-smelling, pipe smoke.

'D'you mind having a look at this?' I asked. 'Is it what you wanted?'

I waited while he scanned the article and leafed through the pictures and was quite alarmed when he slapped them down on his desk. Oh God, I thought. He doesn't like it.

'You see,' said Geoff, pointing to my typewritten paper and the photographs, 'that's what the others don't get about you and I do. You always seem to be able to gain access to the right people. The pictures of Heydrich and the piece about the picnic are terrific. They give insight into the minds of ordinary Germans.'

'They're not that ordinary,' I said. 'Those picnickers were all party members. But at the same time, I did get the impression that the majority of the population, certainly in Berlin, are ready for war. They know what's coming and I think they approve.' I sighed, thinking of Dieter and Rachel. 'The minority are terrified and are being terrorised. I'll be giving you another article about that.'

He gave me an odd look. 'So, you're not thinking of leaving us?'

'No,' I said, confused. 'Why would I?'

He bashed out his pipe in the ashtray and I watched, wondering when the thick glass would break. 'Look, Miss Blake, we all know that you brought a baby back with you from Spain. There has been talk that you won't be able to manage your brief with your responsibilities at home.'

That's bloody Monica, I thought. She's been spreading the poison again. But why now?

'I do have a baby,' I admitted. 'I adopted her in Spain on our last assignment. Her mother died giving birth to her and her father entrusted her to me. And,' I said, surprised at how fiercely my words came out, 'I will never give her up, no matter what Miss Cathcart and her friends might say.'

Geoff gave an embarrassed little cough. 'I thought there was more to your adventure in Spain than Charlie put in the article. Is one to presume that the other person who helped you was this child's father? Do you have a name?'

I frowned. Our editor was a newspaperman through and through. He understood the necessity of not disclosing one's sources. And what if just saying his name put Amyas in danger?

'We can't tell you that.' I spun round in my seat. Charlie had come into the office and heard the last exchange. 'Come off it, Geoff,' he said. 'No matter how much Monica wants to know the details, neither Blake nor I will give them. Anyway, I can assure you that Miss Blake's baby is well cared for, has a proper nanny and Miss Blake will continue to be the best young reporter you have on this paper.'

Geoff grinned. 'That's all right, then. You two make a great team.' He gave me an awkward glance. 'I'm sorry, Miss Blake. Our owner had heard and was a bit worried.'

I smiled back. 'It doesn't matter. I understand what went on.' But I made a vow that somehow I'd get back at Monica. I wasn't the sweetness and light person that some thought I was.

When we were back at our desks I asked Charlie if he'd mind if I went away for a few days. 'All right, Blake,' he said. 'But only a week. Things are hotting up and I'm arranging a meeting in France with their foreign ministry. It'll probably be in about ten days' time and I'll need you for that.'

'I'll be back before then,' I promised. 'I want to show Marisol my house by the sea. I want her to sniff the Cornish air.' I had another thought. 'Charlie,' I said slowly. 'You could join us for a couple of days. I'd like that.' I was coming to the realisation that having Charlie around was a good thing. A comfortable thing. He made me laugh.

'I might,' he answered. 'It would be good to have a day by the sea. Don't hold me to it, though. If anything happens I want to be on hand and I'll want you to be with me as well.'

I gave him the address and telephone number of Summer's Rest and then, as I was about to return to the article I was writing about Dieter, he said, 'By the way, Blake. I looked up that place you mentioned. The place that Xanthe said von Klausen was going to. It's in German Silesia, not far from the official border with Poland. It's a disputed area and has been since the last war. I don't think he'd be going there unless they're up to more than we thought. I'll keep an eye on it, but maybe she got it wrong.'

'I expect she did,' I said, and that got me worrying about Xanthe again and I wondered how she was and where she was. That afternoon I went to see my father, to tell him that I hadn't been able to persuade my sister to come home.

'But you did see her?' he asked.

'Oh yes. She looked well and has a house in a nice area of Berlin.' I didn't tell him about von Klausen; that would be up to Xanthe. I didn't tell him she was pregnant, either.

'I don't care how nice the area is,' he groaned. 'She must get out of there. I've contacted the British Embassy but they have no idea where she is. How is it that you found her?'

I laughed. That was more or less what von Klausen had asked. 'I'm a journalist, Daddy. We find things out. Look, I'll give you her address and you can pass it on. They might have some luck with that. And there's one other thing. She's being very reckless with her money. Is there any way you can put a limit on her account? I know it's a trust fund but can anything be done?'

He looked up at me. 'You're trying to tell me that she's giving money to her Nazi friends, is that it?'

I shrugged. 'Possibly.'

'Oh God, that girl,' he growled. 'Nothing but trouble. Always has been.' He picked up a book from the table beside his chair and lovingly stroked its cover. It was a gesture I had seen him make so often. 'Leave it with me,' he sighed. 'I'll contact the lawyers and see what can be done.'

I had a moment of private malice. That should put paid to von Klausen. Perhaps he'd let Xanthe come home if he was cut off from her money, but I smiled at my father and said, 'Anyway, enough of her. How are you?'

He hunched his shoulders and I took a proper look at him. His face was paper white and he had dark shadows under his eyes. 'Not so good,' he muttered. 'My fellow in Harley Street wants me to go into a clinic for tests. Said the old ticker isn't working properly.'

'Well, go,' I said angrily. 'Do what you're told.'

'Yes, Seffy, dear. I will. I'm going next week.' He smiled fondly at me. 'Don't nag.'

'Have you heard from Mother?'

He nodded, miserably. 'She's started divorce proceedings and sent me papers to sign. Apparently it doesn't take all that long in America.' He flipped over the pages of the large dusty book he was reading and made a pencil note in the margin. 'I still don't know what I did wrong.'

'Nothing,' I said, upset for him. 'Absolutely nothing. It was her.'

Cornwall

It was a bright sunny day when we set off for Cornwall and all thoughts of Mother and even poor Daddy had vanished. I was excited. This time, when I arrived at the house, it would have an extra frisson because it would be mine. My property. A property that I loved and which meant so much to me, especially after being there with Amyas. I thought of him a lot on that long drive, wondering where he was and what he was doing. Nothing legal, I was sure of that.

'Why are you smiling?' asked Kitty, who was sitting beside me. Alice and Marisol had taken the back seat and were fast asleep.

'I was thinking of someone,' I answered.

'Someone good?'

'Good? Well,' I laughed, 'I don't think anyone would call Amyas good. But . . .'

'He is someone you love?'

'Yes,' I said simply. 'He is.'

'Is he here in England?'

'I don't know, Kitty. I don't know where he is. He could be anywhere.'

As we'd started off so late, and because Marisol needed to have a proper sleep, I decided to stop over at a hotel for the night in Devon. It was frustrating because I was suddenly desperate to get to Cornwall. I needed to smell the sea and walk barefoot on the beach, but in the morning, when I came to start the car, it had sprung an oil leak. The garage mechanic said it would take all morning to fix.

'Oh, God, this is ridiculous.' I looked at Alice and Kitty. 'Perhaps we should turn round and go home.'

'Oh, no.' Kitty's face fell. 'I have not been before to a beach. Please, please, Seffy, let us go.'

'All right,' I grinned and raised my eyebrows to Alice,

who was smiling too. So, after lunch, when the car was mended, we set off again and arrived at Summer's Rest in the late afternoon of a wonderful Cornish day.

Alice and Kitty exclaimed with delight over the house as, holding Marisol in my arms, I walked on to the veranda and looked at the ocean. It was smooth and calm, greeny blue and sparkling in the sun. I'll have a swim later on, I promised myself. I'll immerse myself in the water and remember the time we made love in the sea. How long ago was that? Two years? It must be. And so much had happened since.

'Your daddy was here,' I said to Marisol, who was pointing to the sea and squealing in delight. I thought of Amyas standing on this veranda and me coming up behind him and putting my arms around his beautiful, naked body. Oh, Amyas, I thought, how I want you.

'I'm going down to the village,' I said, 'to see Mrs Penney. If we're lucky she'll be able to come up and cook for us. I won't be long.'

With Marisol in my arms I walked the few hundred yards down to the harbour and to the fisherman's cottage that was the Penneys' house. She was there, brushing sand from her step, and looked at me, and particularly at Marisol, in surprise.

'Well, Miss Seffy, what can I say? Is this your child?'

I nodded. 'Yes, she is. I adopted her in Spain. Her name is Marisol and I hope you'll come to care for her as you did for Xanthe and me.'

'I dare say I will, but I'm still surprised at you, Miss Seffy. Carrying on the way you did with that man.'

'I know,' I said, 'and I'm sorry I embarrassed you. I'm down here for a week, can you come up to the house?

341

I've brought the nanny and a young friend, so there'll be the three of us.'

She gave me a screwed-up smile, from a face that had spent many days looking out to sea. 'Of course I will. I'll be up in the morning. Have you got something for supper?'

'Yes, I bought bread and milk and some eggs on the way. I'll make an omelette.'

'All right.' She stepped forward and peered into Marisol's face. 'Adopted, you say? Well, she's a pretty babby, I'll give her that. You brought a pram down here and a cot?'

I shook my head. 'I'll carry her and she can sleep on one of the little beds in the nursery until I get more organised.'

'No need,' Mrs Penney said. 'Your old cot is in the loft and there's a pram in the store shed. I'll send Penney up later to get them for you. Make do for tonight and I'll give them a good scrub tomorrow.'

'Thank you,' I smiled. Then, 'Mrs Penney, the house is mine now. My father has given it to me. I hope you'll continue with the arrangement.'

'I know it's yours, Miss Seffy. Your dad sent me a kind letter and a generous cheque.' She patted my arm. 'You were a naughty girl with that man, but I've always said you were the best of the bunch, so I'll keep on and gladly.'

I walked back up to the house, calling hello to the villagers who knew me and nodding to the summer visitors.

Kitty was waiting when I walked in. 'Seffy,' she cried. 'I have something to tell you.'

'What?' I smiled. 'Did you walk on to the beach and paddle in the water?'

'Yes. I did. How do you know that?'

'Because that is exactly what I used to do as soon as we arrived from London. Did you love it?'

'Oh, I did. But that's not what I wanted to tell you. It is a most surprising thing. I met a man on the beach. And Seffy, it was Dov! The man who came to our apartment in Berlin. It is so surprising that he is here in Cornwall. On your beach.'

I knew then. I think I'd known all along. 'Where is he?' My heart was almost bursting from my chest and I could barely get my words out sensibly.

'He is still on the beach, I think. He told me to send you down when you came home. He wants to talk to you alone.'

I had reached the bottom of the steps before I dared to look towards the sea and the figure in white trousers and a billowing white Indian cotton shirt who was standing on the shoreline. The late afternoon sun sparkled on the water and the gulls screamed as they followed in the wake of the fishing boat crossing the bay, but I had eyes only for him. As I started off across the sand the smell of ozone filled my head and my heart was beating so fast that I felt dizzy.

He turned and, as if in slow motion, started to walk towards me then stopped when we were only inches apart.

'Hello, Persephone,' said Amyas, smiling his beautiful smile and, opening his arms, he gathered me in.

Chapter Twenty-Three

Was he really here? Was I imagining it? Because even as I fell into his arms, one part of me couldn't believe it. His lips on mine and the hands which pulled my body to him could have been something snatched from my memory. That same memory of our time together, relived every lonely night; those few precious hours which sat like pinnacles of ecstasy amongst the many months of our being apart.

'Amyas?' I whispered, when I pulled my face away from his. 'Is it really you?'

'Of course,' he laughed. 'At least I hope so. Don't we always kiss on this beach?'

I laughed too but then found stupid tears in my eyes. I had wondered where he was for so long and now he was here, holding me. Loving me.

'Oh God,' I wept. 'It's so wonderful to see you. I'm so happy.'

'You don't sound it,' he said, kissing the soft skin behind my ear.

I dragged a hand over my eyes. 'Idiot.'

He put his arms around me again, holding me so close that I could feel his body through his clothes and knew that he could feel mine.

'You're thinking of us making love in the surf,' he whispered into my ear. I closed my eyes; the sensation was almost overwhelming. 'So am I,' he said, his voice choking, then kissed me again.

'Bliss,' I muttered and ran my hands over his chest pulling him harder to me. Suddenly, he gasped as though in pain and gave a little racking cough. I opened my eyes and looked at him.

'What is it?' I asked and noticed then that his face looked strained, much thinner, and that lines had appeared around his eyes. 'Amyas? What's the matter? Are you ill?'

'No. I'm fine,' he insisted, but I knew he wasn't.

'Come to the house,' I said. 'I've got people there, but it doesn't matter. It's only Kitty Goldstein and Marisol's nanny.'

'Yes,' he murmured. 'Charlie Bradford told me you were bringing them along.'

'Charlie? Why? How?' I was bewildered.

'I went to your flat, but you weren't there. The old man across the corridor with the dog told me I'd just missed you. That you'd gone away. He wouldn't say where, so I phoned Charlie. He told me.'

Poor Charlie, I thought. What must it have taken for him to say where I was and to guess that Amyas would come to find me. It was such a decent gesture, and so typically Charlie.

'Good old Charlie,' I smiled.

'Yes,' nodded Amyas, with a twisted smile. 'Good old Charlie.'

I giggled. 'Don't be mean, Amyas. And the old man is Jacob, Kitty's uncle and normally he's charming. But he's a bit frightened at the moment because there's a possibility of him being interned. And Kitty too.'

'I thought that's who he might be,' Amyas said. 'When I heard his accent I spoke to him in German: perhaps that scared him. Maybe he thought I was checking up on him.'

We were walking towards the steps and Amyas gave a grunt and staggered slightly.

'Amyas?' I grabbed his arm to steady him. 'What is it?'

'Get me up the steps,' he gasped. 'I'll be fine once we sit down.'

It was a struggle and halfway up we had to stop because he couldn't go any further. 'Wait here,' I said and ran up the remaining steps to find Kitty who was sitting on the veranda with Alice.

'Come and help,' I said. 'My friend is ill. He can't manage with just me.'

'Your friend?' Kitty looked astonished. 'How is Dov your friend?' But she and Alice followed me and between us we got Amyas up to the house.

'We'll take him to my room,' I said, ignoring the raised eyebrows of Alice and Kitty, and going in through the veranda doors, we laid him on the bed.

'That's better,' he sighed and closed his eyes.

'I'm getting the doctor,' I said, expecting him to object but ready to ignore his objections. But he said nothing and, sick with anxiety, I went out of the room to call the local physician. He was a man I'd known since childhood and over the years he had been a good friend to our family.

'Who's ill?' he asked. 'Is it you, Seffy?'

'No, Dr Jago, it's a friend of mine. I don't know what's wrong, but please come.'

'Be with you in ten minutes.' He was an admirably brief man.

When I turned away from the phone I met the eyes of Kitty and Alice. 'Explanations later,' I said firmly. Leaving them staring, I went back to Amyas.

'The doctor will be here soon.' I sat down on the bed beside him. On his shirt was a small bloodstain low down by his ribs and I gaped at it in horror. 'Let me have a look,' I said, and pushed the shirt up. He had a small dressing taped to the left side of his chest, through which blood had leaked, and around the wound a yellowing, week-old bruise told a tale of violence.

'What happened?' I asked.

'Shot,' he muttered. 'The bullet went through and out the other side but the damn thing's refusing to knit together. I think it's infected.'

'How did it happen?' I cried, gently rolling him over to see a similar dressing on his back. 'Who shot you?'

He gave me one of his familiar, careless grins. 'You don't want to know, Persephone darling. Safer not to tell.'

I could only stare at him. There was so much I didn't understand, but now I was determined to get to the bottom of it. 'You will tell me,' I said. 'But,' I could hear Dr Jago in the hall, 'after he's gone.'

Jago was brilliant as usual. 'You should be in hospital,' he said after ripping off the two dressings and examining the entrance and exit wounds, 'but I'm guessing you aren't prepared to go.' He gently pressed his fingers into the area surrounding the inflamed and puckered wound. 'And I'm also guessing that how you came to be shot is none of my business?'

Amyas tried one of his usual grins, but Jago's probing fingers had been painful and his answer came out with a groan. 'Quite right, Doctor, but I'd be grateful if you could do what you can for me. As for hospital, well . . . I don't think so. Persephone will look after me.'

'Huh,' said Jago, giving him an old-fashioned look. 'International adventurer, are you? Someone Seffy's met on her travels abroad? Well, I won't pry, but I'll dust the wound with sulpha and I'll give you some fresh dressings. Take these pills for the pain. Stay in bed for a few days, see how you do.' He stepped back from the bed, contemplating his patient. 'You know, you've been a lucky young man. Half an inch lower and your spleen would have been penetrated and you'd probably be dead by now. But even so, there's a bit of rib damage, I'd say, added to the infection.' He picked up his bag. 'I'll come by the day after tomorrow.'

'Thank you.' Amyas shook the doctor's hand.

In the hall Jago looked at me. 'Be careful, Persephone. That wound will heal, but your friend looks as if he could be dangerous.'

I smiled. 'Not to me, Dr Jago.'

He pushed a strong hand through his thick, untidy grey hair and gave me a kind smile. He had very blue eyes and a tanned Cornish face. His parents had been fisherfolk, not of the quality that Mother had preferred, but he was loved in this part of the county. 'Where's this little girl I've been hearing about all over the village?' he chuckled. 'My goodness, Seffy, you're as headstrong as ever. Taking on an orphan. I can't see your mother enjoying that notion.'

'Mother has gone to America,' I said, and then gave a

little laugh. 'So we are doing very nicely without her opinion. Anyway, my daughter is in here, with her nanny.' I showed him into the lovely white room that had been mine and Xanthe's nursery, all those years ago. After introducing them, I left and went back to Amyas. The doctor calling him 'dangerous' set me thinking. It put him in a different light and I went back into the room, ready for an explanation, but Amyas was asleep.

I made us a simple supper. Amyas was still sleeping, but Kitty, Alice and I sat at the kitchen table, and for once, we were rather nervous with each other. I knew I had to give some sort of explanation, so I took a deep breath and made an attempt. 'The man in my bedroom is a friend I've known for a while. His name is Amyas Troy, but you, Kitty, know him as Dov. He travels in the same international circles as I do when I'm working and when I was in Berlin the first time I told him about you. I think he must have got in touch with an organisation which he thought might help you. That was something I didn't know about.'

'But why is he here? Has he come to tell me about Mamma?'

'No,' I said. 'I don't think so. He came to see me. He didn't know you'd be here.'

Alice, who had steadily eaten throughout, butted in. 'Why has the doctor come?' she asked, taking another piece of bread to wipe her plate.

'Amyas has had an accident. He wasn't going to tell me, but, as you saw, he's not very well, so will have to stay here for a few days.' I reached over and patted Kitty's hand. 'That's not going to stop us having a good time though, is it? We can go on the beach and tomorrow,

Mrs Penney will be here to cook for us and if we're lucky Mr Penney will take us out on his boat. Would you like that?'

She nodded and then said shyly, 'Will you teach me to swim?'

I raised my eyebrows at that. 'I'll try,' I said. 'But we might need a bit longer than a few days. You go and have a look in Xanthe's room. She's got plenty of swim-suits that should fit you. Tomorrow morning we'll go in the sea.' Her face brightened. After all, she was still only a girl and even though her last few years had been full of worry, she hadn't lost that childlike desire to try new things.

'I'll go and look now,' she said excitedly. 'If you're sure your sister won't mind.'

'She won't,' I replied, with total confidence, knowing that if she ever came down to Cornwall again, Xanthe would throw out all the clothes she'd left in the wardrobe. 'Try everything on. All her clothes.'

When we were alone I looked nervously at Alice. Apart from the one question she had been very quiet. 'I know you're thinking something,' I said. 'What is it? Ask me.'

She put down her teacup. 'He's Marisol's father, isn't he? You can't deny it. They're like two peas in a pod.'

'He is,' I said. 'But I'm still not her real mother.'

I don't think she ever really believed me. Nobody who hadn't seen me in the previous year believed me, but I didn't care.

She got up and took the dishes to the sink. 'He means a lot to you, though.' Her back was to me when she said it and I wondered whether to keep up the pretence of mere friendship that I'd told Kitty, but Alice continued,

'I could see it straight away. You have that special look together.'

'He means the world to me,' I said. 'Do you mind?'

She turned round. 'No, Miss Seffy. I don't mind at all. I had a lover once and I'd have waded through the waters of hell for him. So you carry on.'

I gave her a hug and our real friendship started from then.

I looked in on Amyas. He was awake and seemed a bit better. 'D'you want something to eat or drink?' I asked.

He shook his head. 'Nothing to eat, perhaps some tea?'

I made the tea as I knew he liked it, without milk and with a slice of lemon, and took it into the bedroom. 'How are you feeling?' I asked.

'Better for seeing you, my darling.'

'That makes two of us,' I grinned. I wanted explanations but, as ever, I didn't really care what he'd done. I just wanted to be with him.

'Get into bed.' Amyas, moving his arm carefully, threw back the sheets. 'I want you here, beside me.'

'Yes.' And, obedient as a slave, I undressed and slipping into the bed put my head on his shoulder.

'Like old times,' he whispered, and closed his eyes.

I woke when the grey light of a new day was beginning to creep into the room, I had slept deeply and dreamlessly and now I was concerned that he might have needed me in the night and I hadn't heard him call out, but he was on the veranda, wrapped in a blanket and watching the fishing boats setting out.

'I love this place,' he smiled when I dropped a kiss on the back of his neck. 'I could stay here for ever.'

'Why don't you?' I took his hand. 'Stay with me.'

He shook his head and sighed. 'Not possible, my love. Simply not possible. Things to do. Places to go.'

I sat for a while, holding his hand, watching the light turn from grey to pale lemon and then, as the water caught the rising sun, to the sparkling blue and gold of a Cornish morning. 'You know, Amyas, it's time you told me,' I said. 'I want to know who and what you are.'

'Who I am ?' He chuckled. 'I'm Amyas Troy to you. To Kitty, I'm Dov.'

'And to your parents?' I asked quickly, knowing that he would try and skate over further revelations. 'What do they call you?'

'Both my parents are dead.' A breeze blew in off the sea and he pulled the blanket closer around his shoulders before continuing. 'My father, before I was born, and my mother when I was fourteen. I was brought up by my mother's cousins.' He gave a short, unamused laugh. 'My mother and I were passed around from family to family and from country to country. None of them wanted us, really – too shaming for a respectable group like them.'

'What shame?' I asked, puzzled.

'My father was a gangster, involved in the mob. He was executed.'

I gasped. 'What?'

He grinned and turned to me. 'No, not by the state, but by his rivals. And even though it was hushed up, my family hated to even think about it. So, I was the bastard of a poor girl who had not only had a child out of wedlock and by a thug but, much worse, outside religion.'

'What religion?'

352

'She was Jewish.'

'And your father?'

Amyas laughed. 'Who knows? She told me he was a French Catholic, or perhaps Italian, or Spanish. Even my poor little mother wasn't sure.'

The story did explain a little about Amyas; his obvious rootlessness and careless attitude towards a moral imperative, for a start. And his ability with languages must have come from living in different countries. But it seemed to have been a lonely life, even when his mother was alive. I had another thought. 'What did she call you? Your mother, I mean. Were you Amyas to her?'

He shook his head. 'David,' he said. 'I'm David da Costa.'

'But why Amyas? Amyas Troy?'

'Why not?' he replied, maddening as ever. 'Amyas denotes love and Troy, well . . . it's a good name for a poet, don't you think?'

'But you're not a poet.'

He looked back towards the ocean. 'I wanted to be. As a young man. That was the life I'd planned for myself. But then other things intervened.'

I wanted to ask more but I could hear Marisol talking and Alice moving about. Soon Mrs Penney would be here to make breakfast and I would have to explain Amyas's presence to her. 'I have to get dressed,' I said. 'And you must get back into bed. Could you eat something this morning?'

'Yes,' he nodded, catching my nightdress as I walked past him and squeezing my thigh. 'Suddenly I'm starving and no sex as an excuse. It must be all the confessions.'

By the time I was dressed Mrs Penney had arrived

and was in the kitchen with Alice. 'Where d'you want your breakfast, Miss Seffy?' Mrs Penney asked, busily frying bacon and breaking eggs into the big black pan.

'Could you lay it on the veranda, please, and I need breakfast for Mr Amyas too.' Inside I was quaking, waiting for her horrified expression and the torrent of disgust that she would surely direct at me, but she didn't turn a hair. I shot a look at Alice, who waggled her head and gave me a wink and I knew that she'd managed to talk Mrs Penney around.

'I'll put it on a tray for him.' Mrs Penney kept her back to me, but her shoulders stiffened and I knew she was holding back her temper.

Marisol was on Alice's knee, having her breakfast, and I went to sit beside them and when Alice had finished I reached over and took my daughter into my arms. 'Let me have her,' I said and looked into her little face. Oh, she was so beautiful, such a little doll.

'That little maid is the image of her father,' Mrs Penney snorted, but because I was in such a happy mood and because Amyas was here with me, I refused to take offence at her disapproval.

'Yes, she is,' I laughed. 'The absolute image.' I looked up and saw Mrs Penney and Alice exchange meaningful glances. 'And he hasn't seen her since she was born, so I'm going to take her into the bedroom. I'll let you get on. I think Miss Kitty will want breakfast when she gets up, but probably not bacon.'

'Not bacon?' I heard Mrs Penney saying in a scandalised voice as I left the room and went down the corridor.

'Look what I've got,' I said, going into the bedroom, and I put Marisol down on the bed beside him. She

354

crawled up to him and touched the bandage that was around his chest. He stared at her for what seemed ages and she looked back just as curiously; when he looked up I was astonished to see tears in his eyes. 'D'you think she'll ever know that I killed her mother?' he whispered.

'Oh, Amyas,' I said and put my arms around him. 'Please, don't think that. You gave this perfect child life and she has made me so very happy.'

'But she did say it.' He reached out to touch Marisol's hair and watched as her pink lips broke into a cheeky grin. Then he leant over and held her close to his wounded body. 'Isn't it strange, Persephone,' he sighed. 'This little girl might be the best thing I've ever done.'

Mrs Penney knocked at the veranda window. 'Your breakfast, Miss Seffy, and I have a tray here for Mr Amyas.' She came into the room and, putting the tray down on the chest of drawers, boldly took Marisol out of Amyas's arms. 'You make sure you eat your breakfast, sir,' she said. 'I'll take the little maid to Miss Weaver. It's time for her bath.'

I was astonished. Somehow Alice had persuaded her to accept Amyas and now she was being nice to him. When she left Amyas laughed. 'So me being in your bed isn't a crime any more?'

'It would seem not. I think Mrs Penney and the rest of the village have decided I'm an eccentric. There are lots of them in Cornwall, you know, so we should be all right.' I went to get his tray. 'Now eat. I want you well again and strong.' I couldn't bear to see him brought so low, low enough for tears. It was so unlike the Amyas I knew.

Kitty and I went down to the beach later that morning.

She had found one of Xanthe's swimsuits and was mad keen to get into the sea. We walked hand in hand through the little waves and then, when we were thigh-deep, I told her to lower herself in.

'Ooh!' she squealed. 'It is cold.'

'It's the Atlantic Ocean,' I said. 'Now watch me and try to do the same stroke as I am doing.' I swam alongside her and then helped her to do the same, paddling up and down, practising the arm and leg movements of the breaststroke until we were both tired. She went to lie on the beach then, smiling and happy and I was glad. Her life had been difficult for years and would continue to be, but at least this was a break from it all.

That evening, after supper, when Alice was listening to the radio and Kitty reading in her room, I went in to Amyas. He was still in bed, lying back with his eyes closed. 'I'm not asleep,' he said, when I stood beside him wondering what to do. 'I'm thinking.'

'About what?'

'Oh, this and that.'

'Whether to tell me the truth about who shot you?'

'That and other things.'

I climbed on to the bed beside him. 'First, tell me who shot you. And don't fob me off.'

Amyas frowned. 'The truth is that I don't know who exactly shot me. It was someone guarding a place I was trying to break in to. It was probably an SS soldier.'

'In Germany? Last week?' I was amazed. 'Christ, Amyas, I was in Germany last week.'

'I know,' he said. 'I saw you, once.'

'But why didn't you . . .'

'I couldn't. Not then. It wasn't safe.'

Not safe? What the hell had he been doing? I stared at him, hoping to compel him to give me answers. 'Where were you?' I asked. 'I mean, where were you breaking in?'

'A place called Sachsenhausen. It's a camp.'

'Yes, I heard about it from Paul Durban. He was going there with someone else. He asked me to come too.'

Amyas smiled. 'Did he? Well, thank Christ you didn't go. I was the someone else – me and a couple of other men.' He shook his head. 'Stay away from that young man, Seffy. I think he's got some sort of a death wish, because he shows absolutely no fear. He's as mad as a bag of frogs.'

'But why were you breaking in?' I couldn't understand. Normally people broke out of camps. 'What the hell were you trying to do?'

'Oh, God, I don't know. My colleagues thought they could get some of the political prisoners out.' He shrugged. 'It was stupid; not properly planned. When we were spotted they got away and I was the one who was shot. Paul Durban stayed behind, though, and helped me. He got me out of Berlin.'

I lay back and thought about it. Was he telling me the truth? Was he lying because, like his father, he was a gangster? What he'd told me was a fantastical story. A story with a Scarlet Pimpernel essence to it, but, then, I knew Amyas was an extraordinary man. Dr Jago had joked about him being an 'international adventurer', so maybe I could believe it. But if it was true, what else had he done and what else did he plan to do? I grabbed his hand. 'Don't do anything like that again,' I begged. 'Please. I don't care which shady organisation you're involved with. Don't let them persuade you.'

'Persephone, my love, my organisation is far from shady. And I can't say no to them. They own me.'

'Nobody owns anyone,' I asserted, absolutely sure of myself. 'You can be your own man.'

'Sweetheart, it isn't that easy.' Amyas turned and put his arm around me.

'Why not?' I cried. 'Are you obliged to someone? Mrs Cartwright?'

'Mrs Cartwright?' Amyas laughed. 'No, of course not. I used that disgusting woman to get close to the people I needed to watch. She was a means to an end.'

'You stole her jewellery and money.'

'So I did. It was too easy and I needed cash to get to my next destination in some sort of style. They can be very mean, you know.'

'Who?' I asked, now utterly bewildered. 'Who can be mean?'

Amyas started kissing my neck and ran his fingers along my breast. I could feel myself melting and knew that very soon I would be under his body and submitting myself to his touch. It took an effort to gather my senses, but pulling my face away from his I muttered, 'Who, Amyas. Who can be mean?'

'Why, the government, of course. The British government.'

Chapter Twenty-Four

The British government? I snapped my eyes open, all stirrings of passion gone, as this new revelation burst into my head. If what he'd just said was true, then that meant only one thing: he was a spy.

'Stop it,' I demanded, pushing his hands away. 'Please, Amyas, get off me. This is too important. I have to know.'

'Oh Christ,' he groaned, rolling back on to the pillows. 'This is what happens when someone demands the truth.'

I sat up and looked at his perfect face, at his neck-length black hair, which was slightly flecked with silver, and at his brown, fathomless eyes, which were now staring moodily back at me. 'The British government?' I whispered. 'You work for the government?'

'Yes.' The answer came out reluctantly. 'I do. Does it make a difference?'

I shook my head slowly, my eyes drifting towards the window, where the flash from the lighthouse momentarily brightened the sea. Did it make a difference? I wasn't sure. Did it matter that he wasn't simply a gigolo and a thief? By loving him to distraction had I imagined that I'd been reckless and daring? Secretly admiring myself for stepping away from conformity; glad to risk the condemnation of my family so that I could, for once, be more important than Xanthe. Was that what had urged me on? Had I simply been pretending?

'Persephone?'

I turned my head away from the window and stared at him, at his face and then at his bare chest with the dressing covering his wound. I remembered the nights of passion, the bliss I'd experienced under this same starry sky and the stolen nights in the narrow bed at the Hotel Adlon. I thought of the mountain in Spain and making love under the pine trees, our ardour interrupted by poor Elena's screams. That had all been real, I knew it beyond doubt. The fervour of our feelings . . . that was truth.

Yes, I had felt the rest, that sneaking, petty emotion which I had thrust in Mother's face, and enjoyed Xanthe's slight pout at my having been more daring than her. But, none of that counted, not really. Not set against the truth of what was real between Amyas and me.

'Yes. It does make a difference.' I touched his face. 'It makes me love you more.'

'Good,' he grinned, his moody face brightening. 'So, shall we carry on?' And I was once again in his arms, his mouth exploring mine as I floated on that coral boat on a sea of passion.

There would have to be more questions, but they could come later. I was in the arms of my lover and what else could possibly matter?

I asked him, the next day, when we walked down to the beach to watch Kitty practising her swimming strokes. She was joyful, shouting with the excitement of achievement when she'd swum a few yards with both feet off the bottom.

'Can you manage the steps?' I'd asked Amyas earlier, when he appeared in the kitchen, dressed and wanting to go to the shore. I was drinking coffee with Alice and Mrs Penney and I pulled out a chair for him.

'I can,' he said. 'I feel so much better today. Stronger.' He turned to Mrs Penney and smiled. 'It's because of your good cooking,' he said, and I was amused to see her blush. He was starting a charm offensive and I knew he'd win. Alice glanced at me and gave a sly grin. She knew as well as I that it was far more than the cooking that had put a spring in his step.

'I'm doing mackerel for lunch.' Mrs Penney got up and took her cup to the sink. 'So be back for one o'clock sharp. And you be careful, Mr Amyas, sir. Don't be straining yourself. It was a job getting the blood out of that shirt and you don't seem to have anything else to wear. I don't want to be washing it every day.'

'I'll be careful,' Amyas grinned. 'And thank you, Mrs Penney. I wasn't intending to stay, so didn't bring a change of clothes. I like to travel light.'

I suppressed a giggle. He knew that wherever he landed up someone would buy him clothes, just as I was planning to do. But, in the meantime, I had another idea. Just as Kitty had raided Xanthe's wardrobe I could let Amyas loose on my father's. They were about the same height, although Amyas was broader, but surely one of Dad's shirts would fit.

I mentioned it to him as we slowly walked down the steps. 'Well, I'll look,' he said, 'but I've a feeling that your father's clothes would be far too sober for me. I prefer something . . . more relaxed.' He looked down at his white cotton shirt and white trousers. 'Like these.'

'In Germany you wore well-cut suits,' I argued. 'Nothing in the least bit . . . poetical.'

'Yes,' he said. 'I was playing a part.'

'Did Mrs Cartwright buy them for you?'

He laughed. 'Of course. The old bat dragged me up and down Savile Row. Not that I minded, particularly.'

That brought up another thought but it had to be put aside, for Kitty was calling to me.

'Did you see me, Seffy?' she yelled excitedly. 'Did you see what I can do?'

'I did,' I called back. 'Very good. Try it again.'

I watched her for a few minutes and then turned my head to look at Amyas. He was sitting on a rock beside me, his eyes following the boat with the red sail as it tacked across the bay. 'Amyas,' I asked. 'Where do you live? Where are all your clothes and your things?'

'Things?' He questioned. 'I don't have things. But, at the moment, my clothes are in a small hotel in Bayswater. It's my current base.'

'You could stay here,' I said, 'or,' I was thinking hard, 'I could get a bigger flat in London and you could live there with me.'

He shook his head. 'Not possible, darling Persephone. I'm always on the move and . . . who knows, there might be another Mrs Cartwright on the horizon.'

'What?'

'It's my job, sweetheart. I have to go where I'm sent.'

'They can't make you.' I was horrified.

'Yes,' Amyas said. 'They can. Let me tell you something. When I was twenty and at university, I had a flourishing second career as a burglar.'

I looked out over the ocean. Somehow, what he was saying didn't surprise me at all.

'I had a benefactor who, it turned out, was an associate

of my father. Of course at the time I didn't know that, but this man paid for me to go to university and kept me in funds for my first year. Then he died, leaving no provision for me and, Christ, I hated being poor,' Amyas thumped his fist into his other palm, 'especially when the people I was naturally drawn to were the very rich.' He laughed. 'D'you think it sounds ridiculous? I expect it does to you because you've never had to struggle. But for me, having a ready supply of money became a necessity. I broke into large houses in Cambridge and London and took money, jewellery and anything that I could exchange for cash. And I enjoyed it. There is a sort of intellectual exercise in getting past locked doors and guard dogs and breaking into safes; in many ways it was more compelling than my studies.'

He was quiet for a moment, and I thought of my contrastingly dull years at college, when all I strived for was examination success. How boring I was, I thought. How tame. I looked at him. He had no shame about his criminal past, but then, I'd always known that shame was something he simply didn't understand.

'Weren't you scared of getting caught?' I asked.

He shook his head. 'Not at all. I planned meticulously and I was a successful thief, able to live well on the proceeds. Then something very strange happened. I broke into a house in London which the man to whom I sold my stolen goods said was owned by foreign diplomats. He said he was sure they would have items worth stealing in the safe, and he was right. As well as money, they had documents which gave the lie to what they'd been saying to our government. It was fascinating, a new opportunity for me, and I wondered what would be the best thing to

do with what potentially could be extremely important.'
He gave a brief laugh. 'I didn't have to wonder long.
Two men came to my rooms in Cambridge and arrested
me. It seems I'd been set up. The police had been
watching me for a while and now the security services
had become involved.

'They gave me an option. If I worked for them they
would keep me out of prison for ever. Of course, if I
refused, I'd go straight there. I took the job. They let me
finish my degree, even supported me, but then I was
theirs. That was twelve years ago. And, as they like to
remind me, they could still lock me up.'

'But why did they pick you?' I asked.

He sighed. 'The languages, the ability to mix with
European society, I suppose, and being able to pick locks
and break safes must have been helpful. Then there are
the Mrs Cartwright jobs. Apparently I'm what older
women are looking for.' His mouth turned down. 'Not
nice but necessary.'

'It's horrible,' I cried. 'I can't bear thinking about it.'

'Don't think about it,' said Amyas. 'Other than as
my job.'

I nodded. 'I'll try.'

We were quiet then, staring at the sea and at Kitty,
who was now sitting at the edge of the water, letting the
tide rush in over her legs and trickle out through her
toes. I remembered doing the same thing on many occasions and I was happy for her. It would be something
for her to think about during the gloomy London winter.

'You know you can't tell anyone about what I've told
you,' Amyas murmured.

'I know. And I won't. I'd never put your life in danger.'

'Well, that's all right then.' He stood up. 'Shall we go and see what Mrs Penney's mackerel tastes like?'

'Yes.'

I scrambled to my feet and walked down to the shore-line, leaving Amyas to stroll towards the steps. My mind was in turmoil. His revelations and confessions piled up, one on top of another, and I couldn't sort out what I really felt about them. I yearned to go over it again with him and to ask more questions, but I was pretty sure that he'd told me as much as he was ever going to. It would be up to me to accept him for what he was, or not. But really, there was no question.

What would Charlie think about it? I wondered. He'd be absolutely fascinated; ask the right questions and work out a way to find out more details. Should I drop a little hint? Then I was surprised and ashamed at myself for so quickly resenting the promise not to tell. I could feel my cheeks glowing in embarrassment at my disloyalty and took a deep breath. That's enough, I told myself, sternly. Just be grateful Amyas is here now and to hell with what he is.

'Kitty!' I called. 'Come on. It's time for lunch.'

We had two more days at the house. Amyas was stronger again and I could tell he was ready to leave. 'Come with us in the car,' I said, on the night before he left. He shook his head.

We were sitting on the veranda, looking up at the canopy of stars and listening to the wind. It was getting wilder and streaks of cloud were beginning to flit across the moon. Summer is coming to an end, I thought, twirling my brandy glass between my fingers. We'll have rain by morning, maybe even a storm. And soon it will be autumn and the nights will be drawing in. Where will I be going then? Somewhere with Charlie, no doubt. France first, maybe, and then Poland? He'd been talking about going there again.

'I'm not going to London,' Amyas murmured. 'Just take me to the station.'

'Why, where are you going?'

He laughed. 'It must be to do with you being a journalist, Persephone. Questions, questions, all the time. Anyway, I can't tell you.'

'All right,' I said, and had to be content.

'How's that silly sister of yours?' he asked.

'Xanthe? She's as stupid as ever.' But in saying that I remembered how worried I'd been about her. I turned to Amyas, his face strangely pale in the last of the moonlight. 'She's in trouble, I think. I saw a horrible bruise on her chest and I know von Klausen has been hitting her. He's taken her money, and on top of all that, she's pregnant.'

'Wow!' He took a swig from his glass. 'Is she still in Berlin?'

'I don't know,' I said. 'She was in a small house in the suburbs, in Zehlendorf, but when I went back to see her, they'd said she'd gone. Von Klausen said she was on a visit to the mountains with his friends. He made it plain he didn't want me anywhere near her.' I shook my head. 'My God, she's so devoted to him and to the Fatherland, she'll do exactly what he says. I got my father to close down her trust fund so von Klausen couldn't have access to it, but the trouble is, neither can she.' I sighed. 'D'you know, Amyas, you'd hardly recognise her. She's all done up in peasant blouses and dirndl skirts and looks like a waitress in a bierkeller.'

'Meow,' he laughed. 'That sounds like Xanthe speaking, not you.'

'Oh dear, so it does,' I giggled. 'But I am worried.'

He was quiet for a while and then he asked, 'What's Charlie Bradford up to these days?'

'The usual,' I said. 'Chasing up stories. There is one thing, though,' and I told him about Gleiwitz and about Xanthe saying that she heard von Klausen on the phone talking about it.

'There's a radio station at Gleiwitz,' Amyas mused. 'I wonder what von Klausen's interest is in that?'

'Apparently it has something to do with Heydrich; according to Xanthe, anyway. Mind you,' I shrugged, 'she could have misheard it. You know how scatty she is.'

'Mm.' Amyas frowned. 'Did von Klausen say where Xanthe was spending her holiday other than "the mountains"?'

'He said Bavaria.' I shivered in the strengthening breeze. 'I suppose I should go and look for her but . . . where? I'm not sure, but I think that Bavaria could be as big as the whole of Scotland.'

'Yes,' he said. 'You wouldn't have a chance.'

I sat and worried, hunched against the wind, reluctant to go in because I loved being out in a Cornish night, smelling the sea and feeling the clear air bathing my face. But soon a fat raindrop landed on my cheek, followed by another and another.

'Come on, Persephone.' Amyas stood up and took my hand. 'Let's see if we can find a way to stop you worrying.'

He did, of course. Amyas was the perfect lover,

always exciting and generous. With him, I was taken to that far border of ecstasy, beyond which I think madness lies. A madness I would joyfully embrace until it consumed my reason and entered my heart. Afterwards, when I lay in his arms, half asleep, reliving what had just passed, he said, 'I don't know what it is about you, Persephone.'

'What?' I murmured, listening to the rain pattering on the veranda chairs.

'I think you bring out the best in me,' he whispered into my cheek. 'Being with you is all that anyone could desire.'

I said nothing. Why spoil it? It was the closest Amyas ever got to saying that he loved me.

It was raining hard the next day when I dropped him off at Truro railway station. Before getting out of the car, he'd solemnly shaken hands with Alice and Kitty and touched Marisol's cheek. 'Wait for a moment,' I said to Kitty and Alice, and followed Amyas into the station. Like all stations, it was windy and this morning the wind whistled along the platforms and lifted the covers of the magazines on the newspaper rack. A train stood at the platform, steam chugging from its bowels while disconsolate holidaymakers boarded for their passage home at the end of their break.

'Will I see you again?' I asked, looking up at his face. Rain drummed on the roof and the steam from the waiting engine, combined with the mist of the day, clouded my eyes. I could smell the burning coal and oil and hear small children crying because they didn't want to go back to the city. I felt like crying too.

Amyas's old casual air was returning as the strain of

the injury faded. 'Of course you will, my love,' he said. 'You know that as well as I do.' He enclosed me in his arms. 'Somewhere, some time, you'll look up and I'll be there. It will never be the end for us.' And with a final kiss he turned and walked towards the train and I went outside and got into the car.

Kitty had taken the front passenger seat and when I started the engine she put her hand on my arm. 'Do not be sad, Seffy. You have us.'

'Yes, I know,' I said, swallowing the huge lump in my throat. 'And who could have better friends?'

I went back to work the day after we returned from Cornwall. Charlie was at his desk and I went to sit on a chair beside him. 'You didn't come down to Cornwall,' I said.

'Did you want me to?' he asked and smiled, not looking up but shuffling through the papers on his desk. 'When you-know-who was there. I presume he was.'

'Yes, he came down.' I wondered whether to say anything about Amyas's injury, but decided not to. It would only lead to further questions and I had promised, hadn't I?

'Anyway,' Charlie said, 'let's get back to work.'

For the last two weeks in August, we gathered information and planned a visit to France and later to Poland. Daily we went to government offices, hoping to get interviews with ministers, but nothing was forthcoming. Charlie's contacts gave him information off the record and it was all gloomy. 'I've had a word with one of Churchill's people,' Charlie said one evening, when we were in the Old Bell Tavern. 'Winston's in despair with

Chamberlain and his lack of preparation. He thinks that we're sleepwalking into war.'

'Hardly,' I said. 'Nobody's sleepwalking. We all know it, both here and in Germany.'

'Yes, but are we ready? Have we got enough military hardware, enough planes – enough soldiers, for God's sake? Germany has. They've been rearming for six years.'

I looked around the pub. It was full of journalists exchanging information, many of them writing their copy on the beer-stained tables. 'What sort of life will it be for us reporters during a war?' I wondered out loud. 'How easy will it be to follow the action?'

'Not easy.' Charlie took off his glasses and polished them on his tie. 'But that's not going to be my problem,' he said. 'I'll join up as soon as war is declared.'

I was astonished. News-gathering had been his life and he had an excellent reputation. Surely he would be able to stay on in his profession. 'Why?' I asked.

'Because it's the right thing to do. For me, anyway. Anyone who's been to Germany in these last few years knows what those bastards are, what they'll do. They have to be stopped.'

'Oh, Charlie,' I said and leant forward to kiss him on his cheek. 'You are the noblest man I've ever met.'

'But not the one you want to go to bed with.' He was smiling but the bleak tone in his voice gave away how he really felt. I didn't know how I felt. I couldn't imagine not having him around, there was so much we wanted to talk about, so much we had in common. We even, legally, had a child together. Thinking that, I changed the subject. 'Marisol's growing,' I said. 'You must come round and see her. She's walking all over the place and gets into everything. Alice thinks she's going to be even more of a handful when she gets a bit older.'

'Good,' said Charlie. 'We like handfuls, don't we? Much more interesting.'

'Tell you what,' I said. 'It's Alice's night off tomorrow. Come for Marisol's bathtime and then I'll give you a bit of supper. Can you make it?'

Charlie nodded. 'I'd like that.'

The next day I had a phone call at work from my father's doctor. 'I'm sorry to have to tell you, Miss Blake,' he said. 'Your father has been taken quite ill. He's been admitted to the clinic but I would advise that you see him urgently. He's entered your name as next of kin.'

I told Charlie straight away. 'You go to your father,' he said. 'I'll take over from Alice and stay with Marisol through the night.'

My father was in a room with blinds pulled halfway down the window so that he was shaded from the late summer sun. He looked shrunken, compared to the tall, rather gangly man he had been, and his face was as white as the bed sheets that covered him.

'Hello, Daddy,' I said, kissing his forehead. 'Whatever have you been up to?'

'Old ticker,' he mumbled. 'Not behaving.' Speaking was obviously an effort and he kept losing his breath. He slowly withdrew a hand from beneath the sheet and I took it in mine. I couldn't help but notice that the tips of his fingers were blue, as were his lips. An oxygen cylinder complete with rubber mask stood beside the bed and he nodded at it. Clumsily I took it and placed the mask over his face and turned the knob to send the air down the tube.

After a few minutes he pulled the mask away and beckoned me forward. 'Listen, Persephone. I've made a new will. You will inherit the family business and money. I've made provision for your sister, if she can be found, and for your little girl. Your mother is with a very rich man, so she'll be all right.'

His voice was fading, so I replaced the mask and waited until he was able to speak again. 'Lawyer will sort it all out. Don't worry.'

'You'll get better, Daddy,' I said, trying to keep the wobble out of my voice. 'I'm sure they're giving you pills that will help. Perhaps you just need a rest.'

He gave a weak smile. 'That's probably what I'm going to get.' He fastened his eyes on mine as the sister came into the room and indicated that I should leave while she attended to him. 'Persephone,' he said, as I stood up. 'You've been a good daughter. I love you.'

I sat in the echoing white corridor outside his room and wept and wished I had someone to comfort me. When I went back into his room he was sleeping.

'I think it's near the end,' the sister whispered. 'Doctor is on his way but . . .' She gave me a sympathetic smile. 'Can I get you a cup of tea?'

My father died quite soon after that. His transition from sleep to death was imperceptible to me, although the nurse and doctor who were in the room noticed it immediately.

'I'm so very sorry,' the doctor said. 'His heart was in a bad way. I told him a few weeks ago that we should be treating it, but he seemed not to care very much.'

'It's all right, doctor. I think he missed my mother,' I said it calmly, although inside I was devastated.

'I'll prepare the forms for you, if you don't mind waiting, Miss Blake.'

I nodded and sat down beside the bed again, looking at the sheet which covered my father's face.

'Miss Blake,' said the doctor as he opened the door to go out. 'I've read your articles in the paper. Your exploits in Spain and that latest report from Berlin. Your father talked often about you. I know that he was very proud.'

That set me off weeping again and by the time I got back to the apartment I was worn out by the sudden turn of events and my overwhelming sorrow. Charlie, as I'd known he would be, was a brick and sat beside me on the sofa and allowed me to cry until I had no tears left. Then he insisted that I go to bed and said he would stay.

I woke up in the night and remembered what had happened and found myself crying again. I tried to keep my weeping silent, but Charlie appeared at my bedroom door. 'Budge up,' he said and climbed into the bed beside me. 'Don't worry,' he told me. 'This is just for comfort.' I slept and when I woke again in the morning, I was calm and able to cope. I had the bed to myself.

Charlie and Marisol were in the kitchen, Charlie in a vest and underpants and Marisol in her sleep suit. 'You look a fine pair,' I smiled.

'No comment, Blake,' he grumbled. 'I'm dying for a pee but she's taking for ever over this porridge.'

I laughed. 'I'll take over. Go and do what you have to.'

Alice let herself in while I was making us breakfast. Charlie was dressed now and although I was still in my dressing gown, Alice didn't raise an eyebrow. She'd grown used to our breakfast meetings. I told her about my father.

'Don't bother about me, Miss Seffy. I know there's lots to do at a time like this, so you go and get on with it.'

'That applies to work too,' Charlie said. 'Take compassionate leave. Come back when you're ready.'

It took a few days to organise the funeral and then I went to the lawyer to get his advice about the business. 'Go and see the manager,' he said. 'Put him straight about what you expect of him. That is, business as usual. He's a good man. I don't think he'll take advantage.'

I went up north to see the mills and the clothing factory. The manager who oversaw all these enterprises was indeed a good man. 'I'm sorry to hear of Sir Farnworth's death,' he said. 'We all liked him. Now, Miss Blake, what d'you say about further expanding the uniform business? There's a war coming, and that'll mean more soldiers. We should get in on the ground floor.'

'Yes,' I said. 'I agree. And what about getting into different uniforms – nurses, firemen, all the services, military and civilian?'

'Aye, I like it. By God, Miss Blake, you're a chip off the old man's block.' He turned and nodded to my grandfather's portrait, which hung on the wall behind him. I laughed. 'Not a bad block to be chipped off,' I said.

Father's funeral was a quiet affair, but attended by a surprising number of dignitaries and one or two professors of Ancient Greek for whose departments he'd made generous provision. Of course, my mother wasn't there. She'd sent a brief telegram in response to my telegraphing her about Daddy's death. SO SORRY, it read. TO HEAR SAD NEWS. NEW YORK IS WONDERFUL.

So, in lieu of family, Charlie escorted me into the church and was invaluable at the reception we held at a hotel afterwards. He seemed to know everybody but was always there when I began to feel a bit tearful and lost. 'Come on, Blake,' he said, when they'd all gone. 'How about going to Gennaro's. We haven't been there for ages.'

I was going to say no, but he looked so eager and had been so kind that I said yes and found myself enjoying the meal and laughing at his silly jokes. That was the thing. I loved being with him.

'I'll be back at work on Monday,' I said.

'Thank God,' he said. 'I'll need you. We've got reports in that the Germans are massing on the Polish border. Something is about to happen.'

Chapter Twenty-Five

September 1939

'Read this, Blake,' said Charlie, as we stood over the Teletype machine, which was constantly clattering out news. It was a report which said that Polish troops had crossed the border and attacked a German radio station at Gleiwitz and consequently the German government had declared war.

'Gleiwitz!' I gasped. 'That's impossible.'

'Or' – Charlie tore off the report from the machine and walked about waving it in the air – 'perhaps it isn't. Could it have been the excuse the Germans have been waiting for? And the attack is not what it seems?'

I stared at him. It was too much of a coincidence, Xanthe talking about it and then me telling Charlie, and then . . . this.

'I told Amyas about Gleiwitz,' I said. 'He was very interested.'

'I bet he was,' Charlie snorted.

'What d'you mean?' I scowled at him. He always made cracks about Amyas.

'Haven't you noticed that he's friendly with the Germans. Have you ever wondered which side he's on?'

'He's on our side,' I shouted. 'Absolutely on our side. Why d'you think he had that bullet in his chest . . .' I stopped, appalled with myself for nearly giving Amyas's secret away. I think my face must have been scarlet.

'What?' Charlie grabbed my arm. 'What did you say?'

I shook my head. 'Nothing.' I knew he wouldn't let it go, he was like a terrier when it came to digging out information. I shook off his hand and in desperation walked out of the office and across the road to the small steamy café, which served dreadful tea and inedible sandwiches. This morning it was worse than ever, because it was raining outside and the steam from the boiling water machine made the windows opaque with mist. It was about half an hour and a watery coffee later, when Charlie came to join me.

'You'll have to tell me,' he said. 'It could be important.'

'It is important,' I answered, 'and I can't say anything. I promised.'

'What can't you say, Blake? That Amyas Troy, or whatever he's really called, is working for our secret service or for the Germans'?'

I stared at the coffee slopped in the saucer and at the little puddles which had dripped from the bottom of my cup on to the red checked oilskin which covered the table. I longed to share Amyas's story with Charlie, who appeared to have guessed part of it. From the first moment I'd heard it, I'd wanted to discuss and examine the implications of it. But I was held by my promise.

'Oh, Charlie,' I groaned. 'Please, don't ask me. I promised Amyas.'

He frowned and drummed a little beat on the table with restless fingers. 'Is there anything you are prepared to say?' he asked.

'I don't think so,' I said miserably. 'Only that Amyas truly is on our side, and that one day you'll find out.'

He was quiet and then he stood up. 'All right, Blake. I trust you. Now, come on. We have to get back to work.'

We returned to the office and tried to make sense of the news which was flowing in from all corners of the Continent. Every hour some new horror was reported from Poland. There were high-level meetings and telegrams flew between capitals. On the Sunday morning when Chamberlain announced that we were at war, it was almost an anticlimax.

I knocked at Jacob's door. 'Have you heard?' I asked.

He nodded. 'We were listening to the wireless. *Mein Gott*, it is frightening.' He opened the door wider and beckoned me in. 'What have you heard at the newspaper office?' he asked. 'Something more than Mr Chamberlain said?'

'Not much,' I told him. I'd been at the paper since before six, having got Alice to stay over these last few days. I had a feeling that she would be spending many nights at my flat, but she didn't seem to mind. She told me she enjoyed having a job with an employer who was at the centre of things. 'I'm only a reporter,' I protested. 'Not really at the centre of things.'

'Nevertheless,' Alice argued, 'interesting events happen around you. Makes a change from all those damn ponies that my previous families were devoted to.'

I laughed. 'I might get Marisol a pony one day.'

'I bet you won't,' she said, and grinned.

No, I thought, I bet I won't either . . . only if she wants one desperately. Otherwise I'll take her to museums and galleries and to the theatre. There's so much in London to enjoy. And then I looked out of my window and saw the barrage balloons going up. At least there was, I corrected myself. What will the next few months bring?

'No,' I said to Jacob. 'Nothing much from here, although Poland is overrun both by the Germans and the Russians. Whoever would have thought that they'd sign a pact?'

His face was sad. 'Pure evil,' he muttered. 'They are as bad as each other.' He sighed. 'All my old friends, I think of them and wonder what will become of them and, of course,' his voice faltered, 'my dear, dear Sarah. What will happen to her?'

I shook my head. Whatever happened, it wouldn't be good. 'How's Kitty this morning?' I looked around the room. 'Where is she?'

'She has taken Willi for a walk in the garden square. To keep her mind occupied. She is very frightened.'

'Well,' I said. 'Let's see what we can do about that. I've come to ask you and Kitty to join me for lunch today. Alice is cooking roast beef, the Yorkshire way, whatever that is, and she is a good cook. I don't think there'll be many times in the days ahead when we can be relaxed, so, please come.' I smiled. 'Mr Bradford's coming too, so you and Willi won't be outnumbered by females.'

Jacob took my hand. 'Thank you, dear Seffy. It will be good for Kitty, and Willi and me also.'

Even with the terrible news about the war, we were a jolly crowd at lunch. Charlie brought a bottle of whisky and Jacob a bottle of wine. Alice and I made a very English meal of roast beef and Yorkshire puddings with a plum tart to follow.

'Don't let's talk about the war,' Charlie had said when

we sat down, but we did. How could we not? We talked tactics and territories and wondered who else would join in. 'Will the Americans come?' asked Jacob.

Charlie shook his head. 'No, they won't. Roosevelt might want to, but not the American people.'

'They'll take their time, but will come to the party eventually,' Alice grunted as she dished out helpings of carrots and potatoes. 'Like they did the last time. Backward in coming forward, they are.'

'It will be no party,' Jacob sighed.

'Aye, you're right there, Mr Weiss. You must pardon me. It was just my figure of speech.' She looked at Kitty, who was hardly eating but pushing her food around her plate. 'Now then, Miss Kitty, love, I didn't cook this for you to mess it around. I've made a nice plum tart for afters and then you are going to sing for us. No, don't look like that, I've heard you and you've a lovely little voice. Give us a treat.'

'Yes,' Jacob smiled. 'My Kitty sings well.'

When we'd cleared away and Marisol was playing on the rug with the small wooden farm that Charlie had brought back for her from Poland, Kitty stood by the window and sang two German folk songs. One was about a faithful hussar, which I thought I'd heard before in English, and the other a sort of love song I'd never heard, but it was lovely. We all hummed along to the chorus and clapped wildly at the end of the performance. 'We sang that at school,' Kitty said shyly, her cheeks glowing.

'I will sing too,' Jacob said. He got up and with Willi tucked under his arm went to stand beside Kitty and the two of them sang a haunting melody in Yiddish, which lived with me for years after.

When they'd finished we sat, silent, almost stunned by the beauty of it, until Alice clapped her hands and called, 'Very well done. That was right nice.' She stood up. 'If you don't mind, I'll finish with something that would seem appropriate for this day,' and, true as ever to her beloved Ivor Novello, she sang in her deep contralto voice, 'Keep the Home Fires Burning'. Charlie and I joined in the chorus and even Jacob hummed along. Yet although that familiar melody was right for the occasion, it did bring thoughts of the last war. All day, since the declaration, I'd been anxious, but mostly, if I'm honest, excited. Now I thought of the consequences and my stomach lurched. Charlie, who was sitting next to me, took my hand and gave it a squeeze. 'Chin up, Blake,' he whispered.

Kitty sat on the floor afterwards, with Marisol, who was bashing two blocks together. Willi watched them from Jacob's knee, quivering a little at the noise. I switched on the wireless to hear if there was any more news, but there were just repeated messages about the evacuation of children and where volunteers for the armed forces should report. I looked at Charlie, remembering him saying that he would join up, but he wouldn't meet my eye.

Later that evening, when Jacob and Kitty had gone home and Alice, after putting Marisol to bed, had left too, I sat on the sofa with Charlie to listen to the wireless, which was playing popular music from the Savoy.

'The first day of the war,' he murmured. 'I wonder how many more there'll be.'

'I pray that it's not more than a couple of months,' I said. 'I hope everyone will come to their senses.'

He shook his head slowly. 'We've been to Berlin, Blake. We've seen what they're like. Do you really believe that they won't carry on until they've conquered all of Europe?'

'No,' I sighed. 'I don't believe it and I'm frightened.'

'You should be. We should all be bloody frightened.'

Abruptly, Charlie stood up. 'Dance with me, Blake,' he said. 'Let's enjoy the last vestige of normality.'

So we danced between the furniture to the strains of Al Bowlly singing 'The Very Thought of You', until Charlie held me tighter and kissed me. I meant to stop him, but I found I couldn't and didn't want to.

'I love you, so very much,' he whispered. 'I can't imagine my life without you.' The words were heartfelt and true and matched my own thoughts. It might be that I was utterly entranced by Amyas, yet at the same time I couldn't imagine life without Charlie.

'This is hopeless,' I said, looking up at him, but staying in his arms and letting him kiss my neck. 'You have a wife and I have Amyas.'

'Do you?' he said. 'Are you sure?'

The music continued but I was still thinking. Was I sure? I gazed at Charlie's kind face. A face that told of a man who would never let me down. Who, once he was in love, would be entirely faithful . . . but Amyas? No. There was no getting away from it, he wasn't like that. He was an entirely free spirit and I had accepted it. My little girl was the living proof of that.

'The truth is,' I said slowly, 'I'm bewitched by him. I'm sure that if he walked into this room now I would throw myself into his arms.'

The atmosphere changed as suddenly as if someone had opened a window and let the rain pour in. My words, although honest, had been cruel and I was sorry when I saw Charlie's face fall and felt the cold when he moved his body away from mine. I had to make it better, somehow. 'But, Charlie.' I put my hand on his cheek. 'Don't you see? I can't imagine life without you either, because I do love you, but . . .'

'But there will always be Amyas.' Charlie finished my sentence.

'Yes,' I nodded.

Charlie picked up his jacket from the back of the chair. 'One day,' he smiled, 'you'll get over him.' He went towards the door. 'One day, he'll go too far and break your heart. So I'll wait.'

Was he right? I wondered when I was alone. Will I wake up one morning and not be in love with Amyas? My mature head told me that Charlie was probably correct and that, if I had any sense, I'd stop dreaming about setting up a home with him. I should get on with my life. But when I bent over Marisol's cot to kiss her goodnight, she opened her eyes briefly and my resolve floundered. Those were Amyas's eyes, deep, enchanting pools of light, in which I had gladly drowned. I knew that I would never get over him.

I had a phone call from my solicitor the next morning. 'Miss Blake,' he said. 'I've had some correspondence from Germany about your sister, Miss Xanthe. I wonder if you can come to my office to discuss this.'

I agreed to meet him in the afternoon but we were so busy in the office that I forgot about it until twenty minutes before the meeting was due. When I told Charlie that I had to rush out and why, he said, 'D'you want me to come with you? It might be something quite difficult.'

Difficult? I was surprised. What could he be thinking of? I knew Xanthe and was pretty sure she would be asking for money. Von Klausen, furious that Xanthe's trust fund had been successfully stopped, would have made her beg for me to reinstate it. But when I looked into Charlie's worried face I began to worry too.

'Yes, please,' I said. 'I'd love you to come with me, if you've got the time.'

'I haven't got the time, but I'm coming anyway. Grab your hat, Blake.'

John Phillips, who was the son of Daddy's solicitor and had started to take over from his father, ushered us into his wood-panelled office. 'I'm glad to meet you, Miss Blake, and my father wants to apologise for not being here himself today. He's not very well, so I hope you don't mind my dealing with you.'

'Of course I don't.' I smiled, as Charlie and I sat down on the chairs in front of the desk. 'So, what has Xanthe done now?'

'The fact is, Miss Blake, I don't know. She's gone missing.'

I shot a look at Charlie, who raised his eyebrows. 'Missing?' he said. 'What d'you mean, missing?'

John Phillips lifted up a piece of paper and waved it in front of us before sliding it across the desk towards me. 'We've had this communication from a Major von Klausen, with whom I believe your sister had been residing. Apparently she disappeared from a hotel in Bavaria last week. The major wants to know if she is here in London, particularly as she is . . .' The lawyer paused, a slight flush colouring his cheeks. 'Well, apparently she's expecting his baby. He is insisting that she return to have the child in Germany.'

'We're at war now,' Charlie said stoutly. 'Von Klausen can go to hell.'

I read the letter that Wolf had written. His English was perfect, if formal, but what came through most of all was his insistence that everything should be done according to his instructions. He was convinced that Xanthe would have a son and that it was his. I tried to remember if Xanthe had told me when the baby was due, but I couldn't. Was it some time in the New Year? The war might be over by then.

'So, Miss Blake,' John Phillips looked a little embarrassed. 'What should my formal reply be? Have you any idea where your sister is?'

I shook my head. 'No,' I said. 'I saw her in Berlin in July and then the next day I was told that she had gone on holiday to Bavaria. I've no idea where she is.' I thought of von Klausen smirking when he told me that she was with his friends and that made me even more concerned. If he didn't know, who did? She wouldn't have gone anywhere on her own. Not when she was so devoted to that bastard.

'Perhaps she's trying to get back to England, now that war has been declared,' said Charlie.

'A reasonable point, Mr Bradford,' conceded the solicitor, 'but brought down by the fact that this letter was written last week before the announcement. Of course she could have known what was in the air and decided to get out.'

'Write and tell him that we don't know where she is.' I dropped von Klausen's letter back on the desk. 'Inform him that she isn't in England and should she come here, there is no question of her returning to Germany. Certainly not in the present circumstances.'

385

'Good. I'll do that and try to get my letter out through diplomatic sources. Now, while you're here, Miss Blake, there is something else.'

'Yes?'

'Your father's house in Eaton Square. Or rather, now, your house. What shall we do with it? Are you going to move in, or sell it? Put it up for letting, maybe?'

How could I have forgotten about Daddy's house? The housekeeper must still be there. Lord, was she still being paid? She must be wondering when I'd come by. 'Don't sell it,' I said quickly. I looked at Charlie, hoping he would help me decide. Should I move in?

'Why don't you leave it for the time being,' he said, 'if the housekeeper is happy to stay on and look after it. It'll be somewhere for Xanthe to live, if she comes home.'

'Yes,' I agreed, relieved. 'We'll do that.'

On our way back to the office we dropped in at Eaton Square. The housekeeper was relieved to see me and to know what was going to happen. I told her that Xanthe might come home from Germany and that she must telephone me as soon as she saw her. 'Will you do that, Mrs Cotton?'

'Of course I will, Miss Seffy. Gawd knows what your sister is doing in that place, now that war's declared.'

'Are you close to a shelter here?' We'd already had a couple of air-raid warnings, but the all clear had sounded almost as soon as the siren had stopped and nobody was really taking notice of it. Still, I felt guilty for not having been a proper employer. After all, Mrs Cotton had been with the family for over ten years.

'It's on the corner,' she smiled. 'Don't worry, we know what to do and if we haven't time to go there, we'll go down into the cellar. Mr Cotton has joined the ARP. He's a warden, got an armband and everything.'

I nodded and was about to leave when she said, 'Have you heard anything from your mother?'

I shook my head. 'She's in America. I don't think she's coming back.'

The housekeeper gave a sniff at that. 'Fancy her not coming to your father's funeral,' she said disapprovingly, and then added, 'Beg your pardon, Miss Seffy.'

'It's all right,' I smiled. 'My mother has a new life now. I don't suppose she wants anything to do with the old one.'

In the taxi on the way back to the office, I wondered whether my mother would come home now we were at war. I doubted it; she and her new husband had been almost as devoted to Hitler as Xanthe, and their opinions would now hold them up to ridicule. That brought a new thought. Had Xanthe gone to America to be with her? I mentioned it to Charlie.

'She could have,' he said. 'But surely she or your mother would have telegrammed to let you know.'

I raised my eyebrows. 'We aren't a family like that. Only my father and I were close and even that became a bit rocky in the last few years.' I turned to look at him. 'Are there such things as loving families? Or is it only in storybooks?'

'Yes,' he said. 'Of course there are. My mother and father were very close, very loving, and my childhood was as happy as anyone could imagine. I loved them and they loved me.'

'It shows,' I said, and I smiled.

* * *

The autumn weeks that followed the declaration of war were strangely quiet. Gas masks were issued and we got used to carrying them about, brown cardboard boxes with a string shoulder strap. Children were evacuated to the country from the cities but after six or eight weeks of nothing happening, many of them came home. I considered sending Marisol with Alice to Cornwall but, selfishly, I couldn't bear to be parted from her, so hung on hoping for a diplomatic end to hostilities.

With Poland overrun by both German and Russian troops, Charlie and I went to Paris twice for news conferences and to gather background information. It was difficult to know where the French stood. They were scared by the German militaristic adventures but had great faith in the Maginot Line, a series of concrete fortifications along the border between France and Germany. The British Expeditionary Force was in France too, acting as a buffer against the possible advance of the German army and I supposed that added to the rather casual air we experienced when we walked about the streets in Paris or sat in one of its many restaurants.

'Are they actually worried?' I asked Charlie, as we ate mussels in a café off the Place de l'Étoile. 'I mean, are they scared or aren't they?'

'You tell me, Blake,' he answered, tearing a bread roll into chunks so that he could mop up the last of the garlic sauce. 'Your French is loads better than mine and I've watched you chatting away with everyone. You must have gained far more insight than I have.'

I shrugged. Conversation was one thing, but understanding what people really thought about being at war was another. This was our second trip to France and I wondered how many more times we would go before peace was agreed. I said as much to Charlie.

'I don't believe that there'll be peace this year, or even in the one coming.' Charlie leant back in his chair and wiped his mouth. It was that strange week between Christmas and New Year, when people were at work, but still in a holiday mood. 'Anyway, there's something I have to tell you.'

I knew what it was immediately. 'You've joined up,' I sighed. 'You said you would.'

Charlie nodded. 'Yes, that's right. I was in the OTC at school, so I'm going straight into officer training. Next week.' He reached over and took my hand. 'Will you miss me?'

'You know I will,' I said. 'What regiment will you join?'

'Irish Guards, if they'll have me.' He took off his glasses and polished them with his napkin. 'My dad was a colonel in the Guards, that might help.'

'You could be a war correspondent. Travel with them, you know. Be in the thick of it.' I looked at him, pleadingly. 'You don't have to be a real soldier.'

'I do, dearest Blake,' he said. 'It's the honourable thing to do. For me, anyway.'

He came to my flat the evening before he went away. It was the second week in January and outside it was trying to snow. When I opened the door to him I could smell the cold air on his clothes and his face looked white and pinched. 'I've been to Dorset and said my goodbyes,' he said, flopping down on the sofa and accepting the whisky I pushed into his hand.

'How were they?' I asked.

'Well . . .' He looked into the glass and swirled the

liquid around. 'Diana didn't know me at all and I think she's quite a lot worse. Apparently she's not eating properly, although Clarissa prepares all the things she likes. It's peculiar, you know, and probably a manifestation of her illness, but she seems to have forgotten about food and why you need it. Clarissa was quite angry about me joining up . . . couldn't see the necessity of it at all. The boys were home, though, and they were impressed.' He gazed at the fire. 'Christ,' he said. 'I hope it's over before they're old enough to be called up.'

'It will be,' I said confidently. 'Stay tonight,' I said, already missing him. 'I want you to.'

He looked up at me, his eyes searching mine. 'I don't need a pity fuck.'

I gasped, surprised at the brutality of his remark. Charlie rarely swore and for him to say that to me was shocking. 'It wouldn't be,' I said slowly. 'It's two people who adore each other making love.'

'D'you mean that?' He sounded tired and uncertain, quite unlike his usual self.

'Yes, I do.' And I did mean it. I loved Charlie, he was perhaps the best man I'd ever met. And later, in bed, as we clung to each other, even the memory of Amyas flew away. Amyas was a creature of fantasy. Not of the real world.

Chapter Twenty-Six

1940

Jacob was interned in the late spring of 1940. Kitty came banging on my door one Saturday morning, her face wild with tears. There were soldiers standing in the corridor, outside Jacob's flat. His door was open wide and I could hear Willi giving hysterical little yaps.

I'd been giving Marisol her breakfast and now, with her in my arms, I came out to confront the soldiers. 'You're making a mistake,' I shouted at one of them. The other had gone inside. 'Mr Weiss has lived in London for many years. He is of no danger to anyone. For goodness' sake, he's a Jew. Do you know what Hitler is doing to Jews in Germany?'

The soldier shook his head. He obviously didn't know what I was talking about, but he did seem uncomfortable about having to take this respectable old man into custody. 'Sorry, miss,' he said. He was young, with smooth round cheeks which flushed pink when I spoke to him. 'I'm just doing what I'm told. It probably won't be for long, just until the authorities can sort them all out.'

I pushed past him and went into Jacob's flat. He was standing in the middle of the living room with Willi in his arms. A suitcase was on the floor beside him. He looked at me with a face that was both resigned and calm.

'Oh, Jacob,' I said, going over to him and putting my hand on his arm. 'I'm so sorry.'

'It was expected,' he answered. 'And I am not frightened. Do not shout at these young soldiers, dear Seffy. They, like me, have no choice. So,' he picked up the suitcase. 'I am ready. You have promised to look after Kitty and I know you will.' He gave me a kiss on the cheek before turning to Kitty and solemnly putting the little dog into her arms. He spoke to her briefly in German and gave her a kiss on her forehead, before nodding to the soldier and walking out of the door. We, Marisol, Kitty, Willi and I, watched him go, Kitty in tears and Willi struggling in her arms to follow his master.

'All right,' I said to the weeping Kitty, when we were alone in the flat with the door shut. 'We must make a plan. First, you can come and sleep in my flat. I don't want you alone here. I'll put a bed in Marisol's room, it'll be a bit of a tight squeeze but we can keep an eye on each other that way. What d'you think?'

She nodded, too upset to speak. 'Go and get your night things, and bring them over. I'll organise a bed to be delivered.'

But when we went back into my flat, Alice had arrived, and immediately changed all my plans. 'Look, Miss Seffy. Why don't I go and sleep across the corridor. I know Mr Weiss has a spare bedroom, so I can be there and look after Miss Kitty. Baby can come with me because I know you're busy at the newspaper. That way, we can all be comfortable until dear Mr Weiss returns.'

It worked out very well. Some days I was at the office

from early morning until after midnight, and had to walk home through the dark streets. We had air-raid warnings and I got to know where all the shelters were along my route, but I worried constantly that if bombs were to fall Alice wouldn't get the children to the shelter close to our flat in time and when the all clear sounded I would rush across London, my heart in my mouth.

The news from across the Channel was bad. We had already suffered a disaster in Norway and now the Germans were sweeping across the Low Countries and into northern France. Our troops were still confident that they could halt the advance and the French army were racing along the coastline towards Antwerp, ready to support the Dutch. But they had reckoned without the overwhelming power of the Panzer divisions and soon the French had to fall back, exposing Holland and Belgium to the might of Germany.

'I can't let you go to Paris again,' said Geoff, when I went into his office and proposed an assignment there. 'You have commitments at home.'

I was furious. Yes, I did have obligations to my small family and there wasn't anyone to lean on now that my father was dead and Charlie overseas with his regiment. But, all the same, I knew that if I'd been a man he wouldn't have dreamed of saying what he did.

'That's entirely beside the point,' I growled. 'I can manage perfectly.'

Geoff shook his head. 'The thing is, Miss Blake, we've managed to poach Wilf Cutler from his previous rag and I'm sending him.'

'What?'

'Don't look like that. He's a good journo; not in the

same class as Charlie Bradford and he doesn't have the feel for a place that you seem to be able to muster, but he'll do the job. And,' he put up a hand when I opened my mouth to argue, 'it's still your desk. You liaise with him. Tell him what we're interested in. Give him the names of your contacts, if you have any.'

I was outfoxed and I knew it. 'All right,' I grumbled and left his office, still smarting from the injustice of it. When I got back to my station, Wilf was perched on my desk, waiting for me.

'Dear lady,' Wilf boomed, his moustache bristling. 'So delighted to see you and, my word, you're as gorgeous as ever.'

'Shush, Wilf,' I begged, looking around the office nervously. I spotted Monica leaning over Peter Spears's desk, no doubt whispering some gossip in his ear. She looked over at me and gave me one of her horrid smiles. Lately, she'd attempted to be my friend, but I'd been cool with her. I guessed she was trying to get something useful about me to could use later on, and I wasn't going to let that happen.

'Sorry, my dear.' Wilf dragged over a chair. 'Now, what's the plan?'

In the end I was quite glad that I had someone else to discuss foreign assignments with. Beneath his bluster, Wilf was clever and totally professional. He had the situation at his fingertips and was keen to get to Paris as soon as possible. 'It'll fall, you know,' he said grimly. 'I give them a couple of weeks at the most.'

I thought of that beautiful city and how the German air force could bring it to rubble and my heart lurched. 'What then?'

He blew his nose loudly on a grey spotted handkerchief. 'Who knows? I think some will collaborate. And some will resist. It'll be the same everywhere on the Continent.'

'It wouldn't be here,' I muttered. 'I'm sure of that.'

He raised an eyebrow at me. '*Are* you sure of that?'

I thought about Binkie Durham and all the weekend fascists in his set. Then my thoughts turned closer and I swivelled in my seat and looked over at Monica.

'Yes,' Wilf murmured, for once blessedly soft-spoken, 'there are many here who would love a taste of that power.'

From Paris, Wilf sent back increasingly depressing reports. I collated them and, naming him as our correspondent in Paris, wrote pieces for the paper that went on the front page, such was their importance.

One evening, when I got home, Kitty was waiting for me, waving a letter. 'It is from Uncle Jacob,' she said happily. 'He is well and sends you his love.'

'Where is he?' I asked, taking the letter and trying to read it, but it was in German.

'He says he is in a place called the Isle of Man.' She looked at me with a puzzled expression. 'Has he got that right? I have not heard of such a town before.'

'It isn't a town,' I smiled. 'It's an island, in the sea between England and Ireland. A British island. I've never been there but I believe it's very nice, people go there on holiday, but it is cold and windy.'

'He won't mind the cold,' Kitty said. 'Berlin is cold in the winter.' She read the letter again. 'He says he is with lots of other people. Many Germans and some of them are Jewish. They are not badly treated and get food, three times a day. He's organised a chess club.'

'Does he know when he'll come home?'

Kitty shook her head. 'No. But he does say that some people have been released already, so he has hope.'

'Good.' I smiled at her. 'We'll keep our fingers crossed.'

'Fingers crossed?'

'It's just an expression . . . of hope.'

Hope was in short supply those following weeks. Our troops were retreating towards the sea in the face of an onslaught by the powerful and well-equipped German army, and one day we heard requests on the wireless for men with small boats to cross the Channel and take our men off the beaches at a place called Dunkirk. It hardly seemed possible that we could have been defeated so comprehensively, but as the news filtered through, we marvelled at the courage of the sailors of that flotilla. They had braved constant bombardment, over and over again, to get as close to the shore as possible and to pull on board our exhausted soldiers and deliver them to the larger ships lying offshore. In the end we looked on it as some sort of victory, although it wasn't. I knew Charlie had been with the British Expeditionary Force and worried constantly about whether he'd managed to get to a ship.

Less than two weeks later, Paris fell, without a bomb being dropped on its beautiful buildings, and the German army marched triumphantly through the streets, watched by stunned and sullen Parisians. Wilf got out just before all flights were halted and came into the office looking rattled. His usual bonhomie was dented.

'The French government collapsed,' he said, sitting down heavily in the chair next to mine. 'Their army was in disarray and has now dispersed.'

'What about that government?' asked Geoff who was standing beside us. 'Who's heading what's left of it now? What will they do next?'

'They're about to surrender completely. Old Marshal Pétain is convinced that signing an armistice is the right thing to do, but Laval, his deputy, wants to ally with the Jerries. I think Pétain will sack him, but he has followers. And then there are others who want to fight on. They've set up a temporary government in Bordeaux.' Wilf frowned and lit another cigarette. 'Pétain and his gang are a bunch of bloody traitors, in my opinion.'

'Yes, well . . .' Geoff chewed on the stem of his pipe. 'Get as much as you can on them, who they are, etc. and write a piece, as soon as. And, Miss Blake, I want you to find out about one of the young ministers who is opposed to Pétain. He's a general, I believe.' He thought for a moment and then clicked his dusty, pipe-stained fingers. 'That's it . . . General de Gaulle.'

I met de Gaulle a few weeks later. He'd escaped to England and was setting up a government in exile. When I was shown into the office he'd been given in Whitehall, I was confronted by a man who towered over me and appeared to be rather distrustful of the British. But he was polite and ready to talk about his plans for a Free French army and a series of broadcasts on the BBC. We spoke in French, which I think he appreciated; indeed, he complimented me on my ability. 'Most of your compatriots have no feel for our language,' he said in his sharp, northern French accent. 'The British are so arrogant they think everyone should learn English.'

I didn't answer. I could think of nothing diplomatic to say. He was possibly the most arrogant man I'd ever met.

And then, in the same week, both Jacob and Charlie came home. Jacob came first, on a Sunday afternoon, looking strained and dishevelled after an upsetting ferry crossing and the crowded train journey from Liverpool. Kitty threw herself into his arms and Willi did little bouncing jumps around Jacob's legs, yapping with joy.

'I present no danger to the British people,' sighed Jacob, sinking into his chair and taking the little dog on to his knee. 'I have been told by the authorities and have a certificate to prove it.' He rested his head on his hand and wearily closed his eyes. I noticed that the grey cardigan he wore under his jacket had a food stain down the front and that his shirt was grubby around the collar. It was so unlike Jacob, who always took such great care with his appearance.

'Jacob,' I said, moving towards the door. 'I'm going to leave you now. But when you've had a rest, you must tell me all about it. What it was like. Who was there. I'll write an article for the paper.'

He opened his eyes. 'Yes, dear Seffy. It should be told, for it was most unfair. I must tell you that I met no one who was a danger. Most of us are people who have lived here for years. Some of my companions were people who were born here. People with German names whose parents had left twenty, thirty years ago. It is so hard to understand.'

'Well, you're home now. Get used to being a free man and then we'll talk.'

Alice went home that evening, for the first time in weeks, and Marisol and I were alone. In the twilight, we sat on the sofa, she was turning the pages of a pop-up book that I'd found in the nursery at Summer's Rest.

'Be careful,' I warned. 'Don't tear the pages.'

'Farm,' she said, scrambling off the sofa, and went to play with the wooden farm, which she loved. I watched her, smiling. She'd grown into a pretty little girl with wavy, dark brown hair and enormous, brown eyes. 'Sheep,' she squeaked, standing a wooden sheep at the door of the farmhouse. 'Go inside.'

My mind drifted back to the remote shepherd's hut in the Pyrenees and the dreadful night of Marisol's birth. I thought of Elena staring at Amyas, as her lifeblood drained away on the dirt floor, and my eyes filled with tears. I got down on the rug beside Marisol and gave her a kiss.

Suddenly, our peace was disturbed by a soft knock on the door and, carrying Marisol, I went to open it.

'Hello, Blake.'

It was Charlie, in a torn and dirty uniform, leaning against the door jamb and looking as though he hadn't slept for a week.

'Oh my God,' I said, grabbing his arm and pulling him into the room. 'Charlie! Where have you come from?'

'For God's sake, Blake. Where d'you think?' He gave me an exasperated look. 'France, you idiot.'

'Yes, yes, I know that. But you missed the Dunkirk rescue. Where have you been all this time?'

'Never mind that,' he grunted. 'Give me a kiss.'

We gave each other an awkward, heartfelt hug, with Marisol squashed between us. I was overjoyed to see him and I knew that he felt the same. 'Mama.' Marisol was trying to wriggle out of my grasp and I said 'Sorry' to Charlie and broke away.

He threw himself down on the sofa and, putting

Marisol back on the floor, I hurried into the kitchen and returned with a couple of glasses of whisky. 'Here,' I said, pushing a glass into his hand, 'drink this.'

He was watching Marisol as she arranged all the farm animals in a row. After a minute, she picked up a black and white cow and, standing, walked over to Charlie and put it in his hand. 'Cow,' she said solemnly. 'For Dadda.'

He bent and gave her a cuddle, then looked up at me with eyes swimming with unshed tears. 'Oh, Christ. This is the best thing I've seen in weeks.'

After I put Marisol to bed I came back into the living room to find that Charlie had closed his eyes too and I knew that I wasn't going to get his story tonight. 'Come on, Charlie,' I said. 'Go and get into bed. You look all in.'

'I will, if you don't mind,' he muttered, dragging himself off the sofa. 'Don't think the old legs can hold me up much longer.'

He woke suddenly just after five o'clock in the morning, and sat bolt upright in bed. 'Sergeant!' he called urgently. 'Get the men . . .' His voice trailed off as he realised where he was and I put out a hand and pulled him back on to the pillows.

'It's all right,' I said softly. 'You're safe.' He turned his body into my arms and we lay, not making love but getting comfort from the closeness.

'We were cut off,' he said, after a while. 'My platoon. We were trapped behind an advancing Panzer division and we couldn't get through to the embarkation area. God, it was hell. We hid as best we could, but the land all around that area is flat and the bombardment was terrible. In the end I decided we had to try and make it by ourselves and we headed south, down the coast until we came to a fishing village.' He paused. 'D'you remember that fishing village in Spain, the place where we got a boat to take us around the coast?'

'Yes, of course,' I nodded. 'Cadaqués.'

'Cadaqués.' Charlie took a deep breath. 'I kept thinking about the white houses there and the sun going down and how it would be a great place for a holiday in peace-time and d'you know, all that time, I couldn't remember its name. Well, the village we found was nothing like that. It was barely ten houses and nobody would open the door to us. They were all terrified of the Germans. By that time my platoon was down to only twelve men. Some had been injured and we left them at a French convent; some had been captured. Anyway, in the end, we were lucky.'

'Lucky?' I queried. 'How were you lucky?'

'We met two French soldiers who said they weren't about to give up, like so many of their compatriots had done. They went down to the harbour and stole the only fishing boat that was moored. "Come aboard," they shouted and we did.' He gave a short laugh. 'The fisher-man stood on the harbour wall screaming at us as we chugged away. I didn't know what half the words meant, but the French soldiers did and just laughed.'

'When did you get home?' I asked.

'Yesterday morning, about five o'clock we landed close to Chichester. Train journey to London – which I paid for with the money I had left in my wallet, for all my men and the two frogs – then debriefing, and here I am. With you. Which is where I've longed to be for weeks.'

I kissed him and we made love slowly and tenderly, as Charlie always did. He regarded making love as an expression of just that. It was never explosive or exciting or even, as it was with Amyas, magical, but in a way it was almost better. It meant something.

Marisol woke a little later and I got up. When Alice came in at eight she was surprised to see Charlie sitting at the kitchen table, watching Marisol feeding herself cereal. She had a piece of bacon in one hand which she'd pinched from Charlie's plate.

'Home then, Mr Charlie,' Alice said, taking over the supervision from him and wiping away the dollops of milky rusk from Marisol's face.

'Yes, Alice. But I have to go, now.' He looked up at me. 'More debriefing and then down to Dorset. I'll be back in London, though, in a couple of days.'

'Good,' I said. 'We'll do a show, what d'you think?'

'Perhaps.' He pushed his chair back and stood up. 'I'd better get moving. Bye, ladies.' Marisol and I had kisses and Alice a friendly squeeze on the shoulder before he left.

'He's a gentleman,' said Alice. 'You could do a lot worse.'

When I told Geoff that Charlie was back from Dunkirk he gave one of his rare smiles. 'Thank Christ,' he said and vigorously banged out his pipe into his new metal ashtray. 'Perhaps now he'll come to his senses and settle down as a war correspondent.'

'That would hardly be settling down,' I laughed. 'It could be just as dangerous as being in the army.'

'You know what I mean, Miss Blake,' Geoff frowned.

'Don't be difficult. Now, I need a piece about the foreign royal families who've escaped the Nazis and come to Britain. See if you can get an interview with any of them.'

I left his office knowing that I was being further side-lined. Writing about royal families wasn't really what a good foreign correspondent should be doing. Geoff knew it and so did I. Wilf was gradually taking over Charlie's role and even if I was regarded as a good journalist by many people, it appeared I was only good when Charlie was around. I should have been angrier than I was, but part of me was thinking how lovely Marisol looked and I was also thinking about Jacob and how pale and tired he'd been on his return from the Isle of Man. Had I lost my desire to strive for the top? I think I had and, what was worse, I didn't really care. Still, I phoned around various contacts and spoke to the newspaper's royal correspondent and wrote up what became a much-praised piece about Queen Wilhelmina of Holland, the King of Norway and the Grand Duchess of Luxembourg. I enjoyed writing it, I loved the different stories of how they'd escaped and could imagine how, with a little tweaking, it could make a fantastic piece of fiction.

'You know, dear girl,' said Wilf, 'you're a bloody good writer. My wife said that your piece was better than any of the stories she's been reading lately. And she should know, she's never out of that damned library.'

I laughed, pleased with his praise, and didn't really mind when Geoff asked him to go to America to gauge opinion there.

When Charlie came back to London he took me out to dinner at the Café de Paris. Despite the war and the shortages that were beginning to bite hard, it was still a smart place. Those men who weren't in uniform wore dinner jackets and the women either cocktail dresses or longer evening frocks.

I found a pale lilac dress in my wardrobe, and I'd been to the hairdresser, who'd made a valiant effort to shape my hair into a victory roll, but failed dismally. Instead she found a black velvet Alice band and deftly arranged my hair around that. It looked good. Charlie had said as much when he came to pick me up. 'You're very glamorous tonight,' he grinned. 'An absolute knockout.'

'Idiot,' I frowned, but I was pleased.

Xanthe would have loved to be here, I thought, and it made me realise with a pang of guilt that I hadn't thought about her in weeks. Charlie must have thought of her too, because, as our pink gins arrived, he asked, 'Have you heard from Xanthe?'

I shook my head. 'Not a word.'

He shrugged. 'She's back with von Klausen, I'll bet. And will be despised by the Germans as well as the British.'

'I know,' I muttered. 'But then, she's always been an idiot.' I took a sip of my drink and looked around the room. 'Don't let's talk about Xanthe,' I said. 'Tell me what's happening with you.'

'The thing is, Blake, I've been seconded from my regiment. I've got a promotion to captain and I'm getting a desk in Whitehall. It's a sort of Intelligence job, which I can't tell you about, so don't ask me anything more.'

'All right,' I said. 'I'm just glad you'll be out of the fighting.' I noticed his face change, but thought he was scowling at me for being silly. Besides, I was listening to the band and looking at the dancing.

'Come on,' he smiled, getting up. 'Let's have a go.'

Later, we walked home through the dark streets, slightly drunk, but happy. There had been no air raids so far this evening, but Charlie kept looking at the searchlights which criss-crossed the night sky. 'You're waiting for a raid, aren't you?' I said.

'Mm,' he nodded. 'It's such a clear night, perfect for bombing.'

I thought of Marisol and almost ran along the pavement to my flat.

We were home just before the siren sounded and managed to get everyone to the shelter in time. Jacob and Kitty sat with us on the hard wooden bench in the cellar of a large office block and Alice held on to Marisol, who hadn't woken up. Strangely, it was Alice who was most affected by the raids. 'I hate them,' she moaned. 'I hate the Jerries.'

I held Charlie's hand. 'If this carries on,' I whispered to him, 'I'm going to send Alice and Marisol down to Cornwall. Jacob and Kitty can go too if they want.'

'Good idea,' Charlie said. 'You should go as well.'

'No.' I shook my head. 'I must stay at the newspaper.' The explosions were getting nearer and louder. People had stopped talking and now sat, looking up, as though searching for the next bomb. Suddenly there was the familiar whistle, then silence, before an enormous shattering explosion.

'Oh my God,' whispered Alice as bits of plaster rained down on us, and I heard others in the shelter murmur prayers and give little shouts of terror. What a way to end it all, I thought, strangely removed from the immediate fright, here underground, with my little family.

When the all clear sounded we made our way out of the shelter to the rubble-strewn road. Acrid smoke hung in the air and ambulances, their bells clanging, were making their way from across the river, while fire engines hosed down the smouldering buildings.

Our house hadn't been touched, nor any in the square, but we were all shaken by the closeness of the destruction. 'I'll organise it in the morning,' I said to Charlie, as we walked into my living room. 'They must go to Summer's Rest. They'll be safe there.'

'Yes,' he agreed. 'You're right.' He bent down. 'Hey, what's this?' He was holding an envelope which must have been pushed under the door. 'It's addressed to you.'

'How odd.' I took it from him. 'It must have been delivered during the raid.'

'Open it.'

Inside was a single piece of paper with two sentences written on it: '*Xanthe safe in Portugal. Meet me at the Hotel Avenida Palace, Lisbon, as soon as possible.*'

It was signed, *Amyas*.

Chapter Twenty-Seven

He was there, in a white suit and sunglasses, standing by the reception desk in the marble-floored lobby of the Avenida Palace and still so utterly and unbelievably handsome that my heart turned over at the sight of him. It was clear that in the year since I'd seen him, and despite my loving Charlie, my feelings for Amyas hadn't really changed. In a heartbeat, I could have run to him and thrown myself into his arms, blissfully ignoring any semblance of propriety. Behaving like a helpless, wanton, victim of desire.

But I was mindful of being in Lisbon, in a public place, a place which, although neutral, Charlie had insisted could be as dangerous as Madrid, if I didn't keep my wits about me. So I waited for a moment, just drinking in his beauty and remembering the nights at the house in Cornwall, where he'd taught me the intricacies of love. Or perhaps, my sensible head told me, it was only the intricacies of sex, but, oh God, I had been transported into another world. Amyas's world.

'Hello, Persephone.' He turned towards me.

'Amyas,' I said, putting out my hand. 'How very nice to see you.' I was trying hard to be calm and professional.

He looked down at me and grinned. 'Don't give me

that offhand line, darling girl. I've explored every inch of your body and will do so again.'

'Oh!' I gasped and quickly looked around to see if anyone was listening. There were other people in the lobby, men mostly, and at least two of them were watching us quite intently. But no one was within listening distance. 'Stop it,' I smiled and reached up to kiss his cheek. His face was cool and smooth, perhaps older-looking, and the sprinkles of grey in his hair that I'd noticed last year in Cornwall had spread through his temples, so that he now looked less of a dashing young man and more distinguished. A yellowing bruise painted his cheekbone and when I gently pushed up the sunglasses I could see that he had a healing black eye.

'What . . .' I started to ask, but he put a finger on my lips and shook his head.

'Later,' he whispered.

He took my arm and led me to the reception counter. 'I've booked you a room,' he said, and winking at the young, but rather smart, receptionist, spoke to her rapidly in Portuguese.

He was clearly flirting with her and with pink cheeks and a suppressed giggle she turned to me. 'Welcome, senhora,' she said and then added, in halting English, 'we have a room for you . . . on the floor . . . number one.' She clicked her fingers to a young porter, who hurried over. Taking the key, he picking up my suitcase and headed towards the lift.

'Where's Xanthe?' I asked, as we followed. 'Is she on the same floor?'

'No,' Amyas said. 'I'll tell you in a minute. Let's get to your room.'

The suite was luxurious, decorated in the belle époque style of over-the-top gold-framed mirrors and glossy marble floors, so that everything was reflected and glistening. Billowing drapes at the open windows showed that I had a small balcony. I glanced quickly outside and saw that the hotel overlooked the Avenida da Liberdade and the Restauradores Square, with its great obelisk and neoclassical buildings. I could have been back looking out of my hotel room in Berlin, except that here palm trees, not lindens, lined the streets, their flat leaves moving sluggishly in the slight breeze. Even now, in the late afternoon, it was very hot.

Looking back into the room, I gazed at the enormous bed with its carved dark wood headboard and pale rose silk spread. I took off my hat and undid the buttons of my grey silk jacket. Already I could feel a prickle of sweat on my chest. Was it the heat, or was it the presence of my lover?

'Good bed,' Amyas laughed, perhaps knowing what I was thinking. He handed the porter a few coins and waited until he'd shut the door, before taking me in his arms.

'You look wonderful, Persephone,' he breathed. 'Just as I imagine you when I'm lying in my lonely bed.'

'I bet you're never in a lonely bed,' I murmured, my face against his neck, but I was smiling. When we were together, we were lovers; apart, well, that was a different life.

'And sharp-tongued as ever,' he said, pretending to frown. He kissed me, his mouth on mine, giving and taking, until, once again, I was lost in him. His hands moved over my body and I felt myself being pushed gently towards the bed. In a moment, I would be on that beautiful silk cover and Amyas would be on top of me.

'No,' I said. 'No. Not now. I need to know about Xanthe.'

'All right,' he said and smiled at me. 'We'll leave that . . . for later.'

'Where is she?' I asked. Damn Xanthe, part of me was thinking. All I want to do is to lie in Amyas's arms, but I have to worry about her. 'Is she here, in the hotel?'

'No.' Amyas took off his white jacket and loosened his tie. He moved his arm carefully and I wondered whether he was still bothered by that chest wound. Surely it had healed by now. 'She isn't in Lisbon,' he said. 'I thought it was too dangerous, because von Klausen has men looking for her.'

'What?'

'You must know that Lisbon, being neutral, is full of agents from all sides. I had Xanthe here, in the hotel, but you know how she is.' He shook his head. 'She wouldn't keep quiet, was in the bar every night, telling her story to the world. I told her to shut up but,' he groaned, 'she's impossible. In the end, I got her out of Lisbon and took her to a place in the mountains. She's furious with me, but I think she's safe.'

I sat down on the bed. 'When can I see her?'

'Tomorrow?'

'Why tomorrow?' I was weary, but I'd made the long journey for a purpose and needed to get on with it.

'Because, my darling, I have to meet someone in about . . .' he looked at his watch, a new one, I thought and expensive, 'ten minutes.'

'What for?' I felt grumpy and heard the whine in my voice. He should be focusing all his attention on me.

'For a bit of business, but . . . you have a rest and then meet me in the lobby at about seven thirty and we'll have a drink and decide where we'll go on to eat. There's so much to talk about, why rush?'

I nodded. He was probably right. I was tired, it had been a long flight, one I don't think that I, or even the paper, could have managed to get me on.

That had been Charlie. He'd organised it.

I wondered briefly how he was and my face must have changed, because Amyas narrowed his eyes. 'All right, Persephone?'

'Yes,' I said and almost felt guilty for thinking about Charlie. 'Yes. Perhaps it is a good idea. I am tired.'

'Good. Then we'll meet in the lobby at seven thirty.'

I stood up and he put an arm around my waist and pulled me to him. 'You are lovely,' he murmured. 'I've missed you.' It was nice. It sounded as though he meant it. He picked up his jacket and panama hat and went to the door.

As he put his hand on the knob a thought struck me. 'Xanthe was expecting a baby,' I said. 'D'you know where it is?'

'Oh, God, yes.' Amyas scowled, as he went through the door. 'She's got him with her. A little boy. He never stops whimpering and she's no idea how to look after him.'

So it was a son, after all. My sister had a son. It was so unfair. After he'd gone, I lay on the rose silk bed cover and wept. How dare she have a baby when my child, my natural child, had been aborted from me in that clinic in Mayfair, where I'd been dragged by my mother.

'I want to keep it,' I'd wailed. 'It's my baby.'

She wouldn't listen to my pleading.

'If you have this child,' she'd snarled, 'you'll bring shame on the entire family.' Her words had spat poison on me. 'You went with a man who's a thief and a gigolo, who has left you and there isn't a chance that he'll come back. You've been a fool and behaved quite disgustingly, but now you have to think of your family.' She'd closed her eyes, dramatically, imagining the disgrace. 'I would never be able to hold my head up again – and as for poor Xanthe?' My mother's face went even whiter. 'Her chances of a good marriage will be wrecked.' She waited for her words to sink in, before delivering the deciding blow. 'And of course, it will kill your father.'

So I went. My baby, mine and Amyas's, had been destroyed and I was left infected, with pieces of the child still inside me, and had nearly died during the operation to correct the Mayfair butcher's work. Now I was barren. And Xanthe had her own child, which I could never have. Not a child for Amyas, nor a child for Charlie.

I cried until I was exhausted. The intensity of my distress surprised me, for I'd thought that I'd buried that horror years ago and couldn't understand why it had come back now. But it seemed that the pent-up emotions of many months had surfaced and I needed to get them out before I could move on. So I wept, until there was nothing left, then I got up and unpacked my case. I put Marisol's photograph on the bedside table and stared at it. Her eyes, those brown, mysterious pools of light, gazed back at me, loving me and telling me that I did indeed have a child. I had this beautiful, little person who kissed my face and called me Mama. How could I have forgotten? I was ashamed of myself. 'Good girl,' I said to the photograph and gave it a kiss. I felt better and by the time seven thirty arrived I was washed and dressed in a turquoise cocktail frock, ready to meet my lover.

We walked into the bar at the same time, me from the passageway from the lobby and he from the door which led to the street outside. I saw Amyas before he saw me and I noticed again that he was moving awkwardly, as though damaged in some way.

'Persephone,' he smiled and kissed my hand. 'You look lovely.'

'Thank you,' I said and allowed myself to be led to a table close to the bar, where Amyas ordered drinks and I looked around the room. It was noisy, and full of people of all descriptions. Some of the women were dressed in evening clothes and some weren't, and the men were similarly attired. Some stared shamelessly at Amyas and me, couples putting their heads together and nodding towards us.

'We're being talked about,' I said.

'Of course,' Amyas grinned. 'Lisbon has become a great big transit lounge. Everybody is on the move, or looking to see who has arrived or left. They know me, I'm always in here, but you? You're the most exciting thing they've seen all week.'

'But who are they?'

'Refugees, diplomats, crooks, journalists and, of course,' he laughed, 'spies.'

I sipped my gin. 'What do they think I am?' I asked.

'Oh, you, they know. Your entire history will have been passed around from the moment you stepped off the plane. As far as they're concerned you're a respected journalist, probably here to get information for a feature piece. The fact that you're here to collect your sister will not be known. Nobody will connect the reporter, Persephone Blake, with the blonde drunken Xanthe, because, for one thing, you and she don't look a bit alike and, of course, she is calling herself Frau von Klausen.'

'My God.' I was shocked. 'Don't tell me she's still devoted to that bastard.'

'Oh yes. And as mad as ever. Pretending that she's the real wife, and longing to get back to the Fatherland.'

I sat back. Persuading Xanthe to come home was going to be awfully difficult. 'How on earth did you get her out?' I asked.

'It was tricky. First I had to get her away from her minders and I did that by saying that von Klausen was in a hotel in Munich, but that the visit had to be secret.' He shook his head. 'She wanted to see him so much. I know she hated the people she was with. According to her, they were provincial and common and she couldn't understand why von Klausen had made her stay with them for so many months. So, one day, when they went skiing, she claimed a slight cold and stayed behind. And instead of driving to Munich, I took her into Switzerland, which was bloody difficult because she hasn't got a passport; that bastard, von Klausen, still has it.' He looked into his glass and frowned and repeated the words, 'Bloody difficult'.

'She could have flown home from there,' I said. 'Why didn't she?'

'Because she went into labour.'

I laughed. It was so typical of Xanthe to frustrate the best-laid plans. 'And afterwards, why didn't she come home? Why did you drag her halfway across the Continent?'

He sighed. 'Europe's at war, people are on edge and it doesn't take much for a suspicion to become a fatal action. I couldn't get her on a flight, especially as she didn't want to go and would have made a fuss. I was stuck with her, but I had to get to France. A little job needed doing. So I drove her there, to a place I know in Provence.' He looked at me and his mobile features changed again and he smiled. 'It's a place I wanted to take you, a beautiful perched village where the soil is red and sunflowers and lavender fill the fields. From my house you can see for miles.'

'Your house?'

He nodded. 'One day, we'll go there.' He reached over and took my hand. 'I promise you, Persephone. One day we'll drink wine on the terrace and watch the sun going down.'

It sounded real, the words more heartfelt than I ever remember coming from him, and even while I smiled at him, part of me was wondering, why is he different?

He looked across to the waiter and ordered more drinks, then stood up to shake hands with a couple who had walked to our table. He introduced them as the Prince and Princess Romanov and I shook hands with a large, heavyset, middle-aged man and a thin, sad-looking woman. When they'd moved away I whispered, 'Are they really Romanovs?'

Amyas grinned. 'Probably not, but the name does get them a decent table in various restaurants and possibly an extended line of credit. They're trying to get visas to go to America.'

When our drinks arrived I said, 'Tell me how you got from France to Lisbon.'

'Well,' he sighed. 'As you know, the Germans were moving south all the time and I was advised to get out. I suppose I could have left Xanthe there, but I couldn't. She'd have been picked up and taken back to Berlin.'

'Why?' This was the thing. Why had he taken her from Bavaria in the first place?

'Why?' He laughed. 'Why? Well, because of you, Persephone, my darling. You were worried about her and wanted her home.'

I stared at him. He'd rescued Xanthe for me, even though he didn't like her and she was putting his life in danger?

'Thank you, Amyas,' I said and, reaching over, kissed him on the mouth. It was something I wouldn't normally do in public and he was obviously surprised.

'Shall we go upstairs?' he said and grinned, his throw-away lightness of touch returning.

I shook my head. 'Not yet. I want to hear the rest of the story.'

'Nothing much more to tell. I brought her here a couple of months ago. I'd have hopped on a plane with her and the baby, the day after we arrived, but . . . there's work here I have to do. My employers made that abundantly clear. It's been hard enough keeping Xanthe's name away from them as it is. Still, she loved being in a city again, in a hotel, but was an absolute pest. In the end I had to rent a place in Sintra, which is about ten miles north from Lisbon. It's up a winding mountain road, where, once again, she's hidden from sight. A woman comes in daily, to clean and make food, but she speaks no English and you know how Xanthe is with languages. So, she's stuck for the moment. But you must get her out. There are German agents all over Lisbon. Somehow, von Klausen has got wind that she's here, and although he doesn't care for her, he definitely wants the child.'

'There's one more thing,' Amyas added, and his look was unlike anything I'd ever seen on his face before. 'Persephone, my darling girl, you'll find Xanthe changed. I don't know what's wrong with her, but she can't travel by herself, and certainly not with the baby.'

For a moment, I'd forgotten the boy. After I'd got over my weeping session, I'd tried to put Xanthe's baby out of my mind. I didn't want to think about him but now I had to. 'How old is he?' I asked.

Amyas shrugged, 'I suppose,' he frowned, thinking back, 'she had him in January, so that makes him about seven months old.'

'What's he like?'

'He's the image of von Klausen.' Amyas's mouth turned down in distaste. 'A true son of the Fatherland.'

On that sour note, Amyas finished his drink, and stood up. 'Let's have dinner,' he said.

We went to a restaurant a few streets away, where Amyas was obviously known, for the maître d' welcomed him as an old friend. 'This is the oldest restaurant in Lisbon,' Amyas said, as we sat at a white-clothed table, surrounded by gilt-framed mirrors and under a brilliant chandelier. 'The owner is a friend of mine and the best families in Lisbon come here to dine.'

'Did you bring Xanthe here?' I asked.

'Christ, no. Have you seen her eat? If she manages a

lettuce leaf it's a miracle. Drink, though? She pours it down like there's no tomorrow.'

That was worrying. Xanthe had always been a picky eater, but, from what Amyas said, she seemed to have got worse. And the drinking?

'How is she, really?'

'Oh, mad. Thin. Hysterical a lot of the time. And she loathes me. Calls me her jailor.'

'Well, I suppose you are. But thank you for rescuing her from von Klausen.'

He grinned. 'So, I'm back in your good books, yes?'

'Of course.'

'No matter what Charlie Bradford says. Right?'

I blushed, remembering Charlie speculating on which side Amyas worked for. 'He's guessed what you do,' I said. 'I didn't tell him. The only thing he doesn't know is whether you're working for us or the Germans.'

Amyas smiled. 'He won't be wondering for long. Now that he's working for SIS.'

'Is he?' I asked, trying to pretend that I already knew but was feigning ignorance. 'How d'you know that?'

He laughed and tapped his nose as the waiter appeared with our first course, a little pot of slow-cooked cuttlefish. It was delicious, as was the piri piri chicken that followed.

'Tell me about the black eye.' I wiped my mouth on the napkin and took a sip of the vinho verde, rolling it around my tongue and enjoying its slight fizzy quality. Amyas had appeared without his sunglasses this evening and his eye, although still slightly bloodshot, appeared to be healing.

'I was careless,' he shrugged.

'Don't try and tell me you walked into a door.'

He laughed. 'It could happen.'

'It's more likely a reprimand from a jealous husband.'

He grinned again, not answering me and I knew then that his injury had been caused by something far more serious.

But as we walked back to the hotel, I was happy. I was hand in hand with my lover, who had proved, by rescuing Xanthe, that he really cared about me.

In my room at the Avenida Palace, I stood nervously in front of Amyas. Our times together were so infrequent that every time was like the first time and I was shy.

'You've changed, Persephone,' he said. 'Grown up quite a lot in the last year. I almost don't recognise you.'

'I have responsibilities now.' I looked at Marisol's photograph and his eyes followed mine.

'Is that my girl?' he asked, staring at her cheeky little smile and those great, brown eyes. 'She's lovely.'

'She is. She's in Cornwall now, safe from the bombing. And, Amyas, she's so precious. If in your life you've done nothing else, you've produced the most wonderful child.'

'I know.' He gave a sudden cough and grimaced with obvious pain.

'What is it?' I asked, now worried. 'What's hurting? You've got a black eye and I could see before that you were moving awkwardly.'

'It's nothing. A couple of cracked ribs, that's all.' He touched my cheek. 'Leave it, Persephone. You know that I'm in a dangerous profession. Things happen.'

Carefully I put my arms around him and lifted up my face to his mouth, loving the feel of his firm lips on mine. We undressed slowly, me helping him with his shirt and looking, with alarm, at the heavy strapping which covered his chest. But when we were in bed, the pain from his ribs seemed not to matter, for he was as virile and as exciting as ever. I was lost again in his passion, using my hands and mouth in unembarrassed wantonness to spur him on, until we climaxed, in a fever of heaving cries.

'My God, Persephone. What's come over you?' Amyas breathed, as we lay back on the heavy pillows.

'I don't know,' I murmured, but the truth was, I did. I knew that this was going to be the last time we would be lovers. I would always adore him, but our lives were moving apart. I had different priorities now and being here with Amyas had brought me to a decision. I was going to give up my job and go home to be a mother. I would join Marisol and Alice in Cornwall. I didn't want anything else now, or anyone, except, perhaps – and here I blushed in the darkness – for dear old Charlie.

Later, he got up and dressed. 'I can't stay, Persephone,' he said. 'It would put you in too much danger, but I'll be back for you at nine in the morning. I've got a forged passport for Xanthe and, with any luck, we'll get you both on the flight tomorrow evening.'

'Are you coming with us on the plane?' I asked, but I already knew the answer.

'No. I'm going back to France.'

I didn't sleep much after he left and at six o'clock I got up, showered and dressed. I put on my khaki trousers and a white cotton blouse which I thought would be useful in the mountains. Then I sat down and wrote my notes ready for the last article I would ever write for the newspaper.

When Amyas appeared in the lobby I'd already paid my bill and my case was sitting at my feet.

'Ready?' he asked.

'Mm,' I smiled at him. 'Let's go.'

A big white Cadillac, its chrome bumpers and white-walled tyres gleaming in the hot morning sun, was parked outside the hotel.

'This is us,' said Amyas and helped me into the front passenger seat.

'What is it about you that you have to make a show?' I asked, as we drove through the city. 'Couldn't you find a more discreet car?'

Amyas laughed. 'It's very comfortable, don't you think?'

'Where'd you get it?'

'It belongs to an Austrian lady I know. A Countess Simmering.'

'And does she simmer?'

'Oh yes,' Amyas grinned. 'Quite often.'

We drove to Sintra, a pretty town with old buildings and cobbled streets. The airfield where I'd landed only yesterday was just outside the town and as we passed it, I looked at the planes lined up on the grass runway. I'd left from an airfield near Bristol on a government flight and I was going back the same way. But we headed on to the town and were soon driving slowly through its narrow streets. Looking up, above Sintra, I could see winding roads climbing the hills, and white-painted villas dotted amongst the trees.

'Is Xanthe in one of those?' I asked.

'Further out,' he said, manoeuvring the car into a tiny side street. 'We're going in here.' He indicated a café.

'I've only just had breakfast,' I objected.

'Nevertheless.'

We parked the car, then walked into the café and, with a nod to the proprietor, walked further on until we were through the kitchen and out into another street, where a black Peugeot saloon waited for us. 'Discreet enough?' asked Amyas.

'Yes,' I nodded, sorry that I'd doubted him, and we drove away, up into the mountains, where the road wound around hairpin bends, reminding me of the road in Spain which Paul Durban and I had negotiated. The trees grew denser and soon we were in cloud and the air was cold. I wished I'd brought my jacket. Finally, we turned into what looked like a mountain path and after a few minutes reached a clearing, where a Mediterranean villa stood, white-walled and flat-roofed. It was dilapidated, the walls needed a coat of paint and one of the shutters was hanging by a single hinge.

'This is it,' said Amyas and we got out.

'Xanthe!' I called, standing on the weed-covered patch in front of the house. 'Xanthe! It's me, Seffy.'

She came out slowly. A barefooted, waif-like figure, in a cornflower-blue dress. 'Seffy?' she squealed and, bursting into tears, ran to me.

Chapter Twenty-Eight

I took her in my arms and hugged her. She clung to me like a little girl and sobbed into my shoulder. 'You've come,' she wailed. 'I prayed that you would.'

'Hush, now,' I said, after she'd sobbed for a while. 'Let's go inside.' I did feel sorry for her, mostly because she was such an idiot, but at the same time I was angry. It seemed that in the last few years my life had been interrupted on too many occasions by my silly little sister. She had got herself into trouble and I resented the fact that I was supposed to sort it out. But even as I thought that, I could feel her shoulder blades poking through her dress and could see how paper white her skin was. There was no doubt about it: she needed help.

'Come on,' I said. 'Amyas and I could do with a coffee. You've got coffee, haven't you?'

'I think so.' She nodded uncertainly, and, taking my hand, led me through the front door into the square hall of the villa. It had a whitewashed interior, with a brick fireplace containing a cold stove and a pile of logs. The furniture – a chaise longue and two chairs – looked rickety and useless for sitting on, and the rug on the red-tiled floor was a cheap piece of cotton weave. I hoped, for Xanthe's sake, that the rest of the house was more comfortable.

'Are you still with him?' she whispered, looking over her shoulder to Amyas, who was following us.

'He brought me here to help you,' I said. 'Aren't you glad?'

She pouted, her lips thinner than they were before, so that her pout now less prominent. 'I don't like him. He's beastly to me and,' she shot Amyas another look, 'foreign.'

'You're ridiculous,' I snapped. 'Just be grateful that we're here.'

She took me into the small, rather grubby kitchen where a shapeless, middle-aged woman was leaning against the sink, smoking a thin cigar. 'She'll know about coffee,' said Xanthe, looking helplessly at the woman.

'Christ!' Amyas groaned and then spoke sharply in Portuguese to the housekeeper, who, with a scowl, moved the kettle to the hot part of the stove. In minutes she had prepared a tray with coffee and little cakes and had taken it into a sort of drawing room, with fabric-covered armchairs and small leather tables.

Before we'd even sat down, Xanthe snatched a cake from the plate and stuffed it into her mouth, chewing rapidly and swallowing so quickly that I was concerned she might choke. She was behaving as though this was the first food she'd had today and while I watched, she took another of cake. So much for Amyas saying she would only eat a lettuce leaf. I poured coffee and handed her à cup, which she cradled between her thin hands, and when she took a sip she closed her eyes. 'Oh, bliss,' she groaned. 'So delicious. I can't remember when I last had a cup of coffee.'

I shot a look at Amyas and he raised his eyebrows and shook his head. Now I was feeling really worried. Xanthe was plainly ill, physically and possibly mentally. I reached forward and took her hand. 'Listen, Xanthe, I've come to take you home, so when you've finished that coffee, I'll help you pack. We're going today . . . as soon as possible.'

'Home?' Xanthe looked up excitedly. 'To Berlin?'

'No,' I sighed. 'Don't be silly. We're going to England. To your real home.'

'But I can't,' she wailed. 'Wolfie is in Berlin. I have to go to him. He's waiting for me.'

'He isn't.' Already I was exasperated. 'There's a war on. He's probably away fighting. And you must come home, otherwise you'll be thought a traitor.'

She frowned. 'The war? Haven't we won yet? Wolfie said that he'd be marching through London by Christmas. I was going home then. I told Mummy ages ago. She thought it was a very good idea.'

'Mummy's in America with Binkie Durham's uncle. Don't you remember? I told you when I saw you in Berlin that last time.'

She held the cup close to her thin chest, savouring the warmth. 'I'd forgotten,' she murmured. 'Oh dear. She won't be able to meet Wolfie.'

Amyas got up and started pacing around. 'We must get a move on,' he said. 'There may be someone looking for us.'

I stood up too. 'Come on, Xanthe. Show me your bedroom and let's get you packed.'

'So we're going to Berlin, after all?' She smiled, giving a fleeting reminder of the pretty girl she'd been.

'Yes,' I lied. It was the easiest option. In her present state, she'd have no idea what aeroplane she was on. 'Hurry up.'

Suddenly, I heard a thin, little cry from somewhere

quite close. It was a pathetic sound, not the lusty yell that Marisol used to give, but a reedy wail, as if its owner had no strength. 'Is that your baby?' I asked, and Xanthe nodded.

'Where is he?'

'Umm . . . I'm not sure. He might be on the balcony. That woman puts him there sometimes.'

I followed the sound and walked through the double glass doors on to a narrow balcony which overlooked the hillside. There, lying on a rug, exposed to the mist, was a baby. A very small, painfully thin baby, who had a pinched, exhausted face and white lips.

'Oh my God,' I said, and picked him up. He was clammy to the touch and there was almost a blue tinge to his skin.

'He's freezing!' I shouted at Xanthe. 'Why the hell did you put him out there?'

'I didn't, that fat bitch did. But he cries,' she said, with the petulant note in her voice that I knew of old. 'I hate it when he cries, so I can't have him in here, with me. It wears me out.'

I was furious. How could she be so heartless, so cruel. I was ready to have a row, but Amyas took my arm. 'Get her moving,' he growled. 'I'm going to pay the woman and get her out of here. I need you and them,' he nodded to Xanthe and to the baby, who was now quiet and cuddled into my arms, 'to be in the car in fifteen minutes.'

I told Xanthe to pack her clothes while I, still carrying the baby, looked for its room. I found it down the corridor, the room furthest away from Xanthe's, a bleak space with splintered floorboards and furnished only with a dusty wicker cot. There was a small pile of clothes on the floor beside it and I searched through them for something clean to dress the child in. I took a couple of romper suits, a shawl and some cotton nappies. Gathering them up, I looked for a bathroom and there I stripped off his soaking nappy and filthy vest and washed and powdered his sore little bottom. I dressed him in a fairly clean suit and wrapped him warmly in the shawl. With the remaining nappies I went back to Xanthe.

'How are you getting on?' I asked.

'All right,' she said, gazing at me, but it was clear that she'd done nothing. Putting the baby down on the bed I dragged a small suitcase from the top of a wardrobe and shoved underwear and a dress into it. 'Have you got a coat?' I asked.

She shook her head. 'I've got a cardigan.'

'That will do,' I said. 'You can buy clothes at home.'

Her face brightened. 'Oh, lovely. It's ages since I've been to the shops.' Then the brightness disappeared. 'I haven't got any money.' She scowled. 'You took it away. Wolfie was furious.'

'You'll get it back, when we get you home. I promise.'

'Oh, thank you, Seffy.'

'Now, go downstairs . . . I'll take the case.' As she went out of the room I had a thought. 'When did the baby last have a feed?'

'Haven't a clue,' she called, halfway down the stairs. 'The woman does that.'

Amyas was standing by the car and looking agitated. 'I think I heard a car coming up the road,' he said. 'It went past . . . this place is quite well hidden, but if it's who I think it is, they'll be back.'

'One minute,' I begged, and went back inside to the

kitchen. Throwing open all the cupboards I searched until I found a baby's feeding bottle and then, in the grimy larder, found a bottle of sterilised milk on a stone slab. 'It'll have to do,' I muttered to myself, as I filled the feeder. Putting it into my shoulder bag, I hurried outside.

'Ready,' I said and got into the front passenger seat. I tried to hand the baby to Xanthe in the back seat, but she shook her head. 'Oh, no, Seffy. I'll drop it, or something. You know how hopeless I am.' She was quite animated. A little colour had come back into her cheeks. 'What an adventure,' she squealed.

I looked at Amyas. His face was set in a grimace as he swung the car out of the clearing and along the track to the road. There, he stopped for a moment, listening for sounds of another car, but I heard nothing, except for birds twittering in the trees and the occasional rustle of small woodland animals.

'It's all right,' I said. And he put his foot down on the pedal and we drove down the mountain road back to Sintra.

The car exchange went as smoothly as before and now that we were down from the mountain the mist had gone and the sun gave everything a golden glow. 'Shops,' breathed Xanthe, looking out of the window. 'Can we stop?'

'No.' Amyas and I spoke in unison.

Had I been nervous before? I realised that I had and that Amyas was still twitching.

'I'm going to take you straight to the aerodrome,' he said. 'It's several hours before your flight, but you can wait there more safely than in Lisbon. There is a café and you can sit it out in some comfort.' He turned his head to me. 'I'll have to leave you.'

I thought I heard a choke in his voice and was going to put a hand on his arm but Xanthe suddenly cried, 'Stop the car. Let me out. I'm going to be sick.'

She was sick at the side of the road. I put the baby on Amyas's knee and went to help her, but it was over in a minute. 'It was the cake,' she said. 'It just looked so delicious, but I knew I shouldn't have eaten it.'

'Are you often sick?' I asked, when we got back in the car.

'Oh yes. It's a good way to lose weight. Wolfie doesn't like me to be fat. He says I have the perfect figure. I do, don't I, Seff? I'm petite, but well formed, that's what it said in *Tatler*, when they did that piece on London society. Not like you, Seff. You're lanky, like a boy. And as for your hair, well, Mummy always said that it was quite uncontrollable.' She gave a high-pitched giggle and I yearned to turn round and smack her in the face.

'I think Persephone is beautiful.' Amyas broke his silence. 'Both inside and out.'

'Thank you,' I whispered and loved him more than ever.

'Well, you should know,' Xanthe said spitefully. 'About the inside and out.'

The aerodrome was a field with a wire fence around the perimeter. Long, low buildings surrounded the wooden control tower and I saw several cars parked in front of them and a few people wandering about. Aeroplanes were drawn up by the buildings. Two looked like passenger liners and I recognised one as the Avro on which I'd arrived. It must be the one we were going on. 'That's our plane,' I said to Xanthe, nodding towards the runway where it was standing.

'Wonderful,' she smiled. 'I can't tell you how thrilled I am to be going home to our dear Fatherland. Did I tell you, Seffy, that I saw Herr Hitler once? Oh, he was magnificent. Dynamic, that was what Wolfie called him.'

I winced, imagining what might happen if she spoke like that in London, and realised, yet again, that my troubles were really only just beginning. How could I leave her in the house in Eaton Square, with only the housekeeper to look after her? Would I have to keep her in my flat? Then I remembered that I'd decided to go down to Cornwall and to be a mother, and knew I'd have to take her with me. My heart sank.

We left the car outside the administration building. A Portuguese policeman at the door asked if we were travelling. Amyas spoke to him and produced Xanthe's passport. I saw a set of folded notes peeking out of it and then he nodded to me to show mine. To my relief, the policeman grinned and we were able to go inside.

'Persephone,' Amyas put his hand on my shoulder. 'We must say goodbye now.'

I looked up at him and saw the pain in his eyes. I stood for a moment, just gazing at him, and then I turned and thrust the baby into Xanthe's unwilling arms. Turning back I put my arms around Amyas's neck.

'Come with us,' I begged. 'You'll be safe in England.'

'I can't,' he said quietly. 'You know that.'

'I'm frightened for you.' Tears had come to my eyes and I struggled to stay in control. Even though I knew that, as Charlie had predicted, the day had come when I would move on from Amyas, he was here with me now and I wanted to keep him.

'I don't know when I'll see you again,' he breathed

into my neck, 'it might not be very soon. But I know I will. We'll drink wine on my terrace in Provence and watch the sun go down.'

'Yes,' I whispered. 'We'll do that.'

He held me very close and I felt his heart beating quite fast. 'I have loved you, my darling girl, even though . . .' He left the rest of the sentence unsaid and I closed my eyes and remembered the nights in the house by the sea, where I'd been swept away by passion. The noise of the aircraft and passengers faded into the background and all I could hear was the sound of the sea breaking on the shore of our Cornish beach.

'Remember the little church on the headland,' he whispered. 'Where we should have been married.'

'Yes,' I said, pulling back slightly and searching his face. 'What about it?'

'Bury me there.'

He kissed me hard, then, on my slightly open mouth, and immediately turned away. 'I love you, Amyas,' I said, as he walked back to his car. 'I always will.'

'And I you,' he called, as he got in. 'Give Marisol a kiss from me.'

'Every day,' I murmured. 'Every day.'

I watched him drive away, my mind whirling, full of questions, and then turned back to the door of the administration building where Xanthe had been waiting. Of course, she wasn't there. She was inside, weaving a path through the few waiting passengers to the far corner of the hall, where a small café bar was serving drinks. Her little son had been left lying on the floor beside her suitcase.

'Oh, God,' I said out loud, and picking up both him

and the bag, I followed her. 'Xanthe,' I demanded, standing behind her at the small counter. 'What are you doing?'

'Having a drink,' she smiled, holding up a glass of what looked like cherry brandy. 'First for ages. Will you pay him, I haven't any money . . . as you know.' This last was delivered with a sardonic look, and I reached into my bag and got out my wallet.

'Oh, good,' she said, 'you've got tons of cash,' and before I could stop her she'd reached over and snatched some notes out of my wallet. She held them up, counting the amount, then pushed them down the front of her dress.

'Sit down,' I insisted angrily, pointing to a little metal table and chairs beside the café, 'and stop making an exhibition of yourself. And then you can give the baby a feed.'

'No,' she said, scowling. 'I can't do that. He either won't swallow, or he's sick on me. It's disgusting.'

So I fed the little boy, slowly giving him the milk, stopping frequently to make sure that he was managing it, and then lifted him up to help him get rid of the wind. He was sick, but only a little, and when I laid him down in my arms again he gave me a drowsy smile. His face had taken on a more normal pink tinge and didn't look so pinched. I smoothed his ice-blond hair and swaddled him in the shawl. Soon he was asleep.

'He's a sweet little boy,' I said. 'What's his name?'

'His name?' Xanthe looked confused. 'He hasn't got a name. Wolf said he'd choose it.'

'Well, you have to call him something. Hasn't he been registered anywhere?'

'No,' she said. 'I don't think so.'

'Oh, Xanthe,' I grumbled. 'You are absolutely hopeless. Now, we'll give him a name. What d'you like?'

She thought for a minute and then said, 'Wolfie was talking about naming him after our Führer.' She grinned. 'I don't really like Adolf, but Wolf does. Shall we call him that?'

'Absolutely not,' I snapped, and looked around to see if anyone was listening. There was a plump, flabby man, who had come to sit at one of the other tables. His grey suit looked too tight for him and he was sweating profusely, wafting air across his face with a white canvas trilby. A newspaper lay on the table in front of him, but every so often he would raise his eyes and look over to us. It was an American newspaper, the *Paris Herald*. He must have only recently arrived here in Portugal.

'You should name him after Daddy.' Then I took a deep breath, remembering that she didn't yet know that Daddy had died. I had to tell her. 'Xanthe,' I said slowly, 'Daddy died last year. I couldn't find you to tell you, but he had a nice funeral and lots of important people were there.'

'Oh dear,' she said. 'Poor Daddy.' She looked sad for a fleeting moment and then said, 'But he had a silly name. It was after some common little mill town in the North, wasn't it? Wolfie's son can't possibly be called that. No, if he has to have a family name, he can be called after Wolf's father, Maximilian. We can name him that for now, until Wolf decides.'

Xanthe had got up to get another drink and was at the counter when the man reading the newspaper went to join her. He spoke to her and she was laughing, doing

433

her usual flirting. I watched them nervously, then got up too, when I saw him buy her yet another brandy.

'This is Karl,' Xanthe giggled. 'He's an American.'

'How d'you do,' I said briefly, and then to Xanthe, 'I think you've had enough to drink. Come back and sit down.'

'My sister is such a spoilsport,' she brayed, her voice so loud that people across the room looked our way. 'She doesn't know how to have fun.'

Karl grinned. 'I can see that you do,' he said and squeezed her arm. 'Have another drink and tell me all about yourself.' He had a strange accent, American in tone, although there was something not quite real about it.

'We're having an adventure,' Xanthe squealed. 'I'm going home to –'

I grabbed her hand. 'Enough, Xanthe.' I put as much venom in my voice as I could muster. 'Shut up and sit down.'

Karl looked as though he was going to join us but I gave him a hard stare and, getting the message, he walked away.

The situation was getting out of hand. I looked at the clock on the wall. We had hours to wait before the flight. But just then, there was an announcement on the loud-speaker and everyone looked up. It was first in Portuguese, which I didn't understand, but the people waiting in the hall were groaning and looking at each other in dismay. The message was repeated in French and I learned that due to engine trouble our flight would not take off tonight, but would be delayed for two days.

I was ready to scream. Amyas had gone, Xanthe was being a pest, and now this stranger had latched on to us. I made a decision quickly. We'd get a car back to Lisbon,

check into the Avenida Palace and I would send a telegram to Charlie.

I grabbed hold of Xanthe's arm. 'Come on,' I said
firmly. 'Our flight's delayed. We're going to Lisbon for
a couple of days.'

'Marvellous,' she squealed and eagerly followed me
to the enquiries desk. I managed to arrange a car to drive
us to the city. When we went outside, Karl was there
waiting for us. 'Off to the city?' he asked. 'Me too. I guess
you couldn't give me a ride?'

'Of course we can,' Xanthe shouted. 'What fun.' But I
wasn't having that.

'I'm afraid not,' I said. 'There isn't room, what with
the luggage and the baby. Sorry.'

'OK.' He was still smiling. 'Cute kid,' he said, looking
down. 'He's blond, like your sister.'

'It's a little girl,' I said, putting the baby on Xanthe's
knee while I got in beside her. 'And she's my daughter.'

His smile faded, but he waved a hand as we pulled
away.

'Why did you tell him that?' asked Xanthe.

'Because I don't trust him, that's why.'

'Now who's being silly,' she said, but she forgot the
conversation within minutes, as the prospect of a stay in
a luxury hotel filled her mind.

I booked us a suite, two rooms with an interconnecting
door, and I took both keys so Xanthe couldn't lock me
out of her room. I needed to keep an eye on her. 'Look,'
I said, 'if you want anything, call room service.'

'Can we go out later?' she asked. 'I'd so love to go
out.'

'Perhaps,' I answered. 'But we have to think about the

baby. We can't carry him into restaurants, can we? Be reasonable.'

She pouted again and picked up the telephone. I watched until I saw she had called for room service, then walked into my room and wondered about getting formula feed for baby Max. I'd have to go out and leave Xanthe some time, but would it be safe? From my room I could hear her on the telephone ordering a bottle of gin, and my heart sank. She'd be drunk in half an hour and I was on the point of going in to her and slamming down the phone, but then I stopped myself. She'd already had three brandies on an empty stomach. If she did get drunk, she'd probably pass out and I'd be able to get to the chemist to buy stuff for the baby.

I was right. She sat with the bottle of gin and drank it from her tooth mug, with a splash of water from the tap. I chatted to her for nearly an hour, talking about my job and asking about her holiday in Bavaria and listening to her vague replies, until her voice started to slur and she lay on the bed. 'Why don't you have a little sleep,' I suggested. 'You've had quite an exciting day.'

'I have, haven't I, Seff. I'll close my eyes just for a . . .'

She was asleep. Picking up the baby and my shoulder bag, I left the room and went down to the lobby. The smart receptionist who'd been flirting with Amyas was on duty and I asked her where I could find food and clothes for the baby. She looked at him, her mouth turning down at the sight of this tiny scrap of a child in his dirty clothes. 'Perhaps along the Avenida da Liberdade,' she said faintly. 'I know of a pharmacy.'

'Thank you.' I hurried out and, turning the corner, walked along the street until I came across the pharmacy.

They had all the provisions I wanted: formula feed, a couple of feeding bottles and some soap, cream and powder to get Max clean and comfortable. A few shops further on and I found a baby boutique and bought clothes and nappies for him. The assistant had a few words of English and expressed surprise that he was so small for his age. 'He has been ill,' I lied. How could I admit that my sister had starved him?

My shopping done, I raced back to the hotel and was just going in through the doors when I spotted Xanthe's new friend, 'Karl', standing by the reception desk. I was sure he was asking about us. Christ! I didn't know what to do. Then I walked away, around another corner and into the cocktail bar. Some early evening drinkers raised their eyebrows at the sight of us, but I walked straight through, out into the corridor and then up the stairs to our floor.

Xanthe was still asleep, which gave me the opportunity to send a telegram to Charlie, explaining the situation and asking for advice. But I knew I would have to manage on my own, so, giving Max another feed, I settled him into a drawer that I'd pulled out and went to sleep myself. And by seven o'clock the next morning I and a very hungover Xanthe were ready to face another day.

Chapter Twenty-Nine

A bell boy knocked at my door at nine o'clock and handed me a telegram. 'Thank you,' I said, and taking the envelope into the room, I sat at the table where a room service breakfast was laid.

Xanthe was sitting opposite me, chain-smoking. She had a glass of water in front of her and a packet of aspirin. She looked like hell.

'Eat something,' I'd said earlier. 'Look, there's fruit, bread and gallons of coffee. You'll feel better with something inside you.'

'I won't,' she whispered and started coughing, a rasping, racking cough which seemed to make her whole body shake.

I'll take her to the doctor as soon as we get home, I promised myself, looking at her wasted body and thinning hair. There's something awfully wrong with her.

But now I opened the telegram. WILL BE IN LISBON THIS EVENING. C.B.

I gazed at the thin paper with its stuck-on taped message and relief rushed through me.

'Who's that from?' Xanthe asked as I put the telegram in my pocket. 'Is it from Wolf?'

'No. It's from Charlie Bradford, my boss. D'you remember him? He was in Berlin when we met you and von Klausen.'

She nodded. 'I think so. He wore glasses. Wolf said he was very clever and there was something else too . . . what was it?' She rested her head on her hand, trying to remember. Her eyes were closing again.

'Go and have another lie-down,' I said. 'We'll go out for a walk when you're feeling up to it.'

'Yes, I'd like that, Seffy.' She perked up a bit. 'Can we go to the shops?'

'Yes, all right. After you've had a little sleep.'

She wandered into her room and I waited to hear her even breathing, but to my surprise, she came back.

'I've remembered,' she said.

'What? What have you remembered?'

'What Wolf said about your Mr Bradford.'

'Oh yes?'

'He didn't like him. "Mr Bradford is very dangerous," he said. "He's pretending to be a foreign correspondent but he's really a spy." I'm forbidden to talk to him.'

'That's just silly.' I frowned at her, wondering what would happen when Charlie turned up later.

'He thought you were too,' she added. 'A spy, I mean.' She gave one of her high-pitched giggles before going back to her room, where she climbed on to the bed and was asleep in seconds.

Baby Max, who had slept since I fed him at six, woke up and started yelling. His cry was more vigorous now, and when I picked him up he gave me a sweet, welcoming smile and reached out his little hand to pat my face. 'I suppose you want more food, young man,' I said to him, and using the boiled water from the jug that had come with the coffee, I made up another bottle. He sucked at it eagerly, holding on to the feeder as though his life depended on it. I suppose it did in a way, and I marvelled at the instinct for survival that he had. And Xanthe had not. She was drifting, and had lost her way.

When Max had finished I put him on the rug and let him wriggle about while I re-read Charlie's brief telegram. I was so glad that he was coming, although I was ashamed that I couldn't manage by myself and squirmed with the thought that my telegram had sounded pathetic and hysterical. What had I been expecting? I told myself severely. Xanthe to be difficult? Of course she would be, she was always bloody difficult, but I hadn't expected her to be ill and, if I was honest, I'd dismissed any consideration of the baby. I looked down at him. He was lifting his head and gazing around at the room with his fist in his mouth. I must get him a rattle or a teether or something to play with, I thought. Goodness, the poor scrap hadn't even got a teddy bear.

I got up and went to the window and stepped out on to the balcony. It was another hot day in Lisbon, the sky cloudless, but the atmosphere heavy with the threat of a storm. Delicious odours of cooking hung in the air. I looked at my watch: it was nearly midday. Alice would be giving Marisol her lunch now and then, perhaps, if the weather was good, taking her for a paddle. They'd gone to Cornwall the day before I flew to Lisbon and I longed to be with them, to cuddle my daughter, to feel the sea air on my face and swim in the fresh blue water. It was so peaceful there, far away from the clash and intrigue of war. Then I thought of my flat in London, and Kitty and Jacob. I'd invited them to go to Cornwall too. 'There's plenty of room,' I'd said. 'And I know Kitty hates the bombing. We all do.'

'Thank you, dear Seffy,' Jacob had said. 'But we'll stay. I am close to the synagogue here and, of course, Kitty waits daily to hear of her mother.'

I'd stared at him then, biting my lip, wondering how to say what I must, but he forestalled me. 'I know what you are thinking,' he smiled sadly, 'and I am prepared. But Kitty, she still has hope and clings to it. How can I destroy that?'

I turned back into the hotel room, but as I did so a figure in a white hat, standing in the square beneath me, caught my eye. It was Karl, and he was staring up at the hotel. He had a camera in his hand and as I watched, he lifted it up and pointed it at me. I stepped inside quickly. Why was I so wary of him? I didn't know, but there was just something about him that made the hairs on the back of my neck stand up.

I ordered lunch for us, grilled sardines and salad, and Xanthe woke up in time to eat. 'Can we have a drink,' she begged.

'All right, but only if you eat something.'

And she did, slowly eating a little fish and a few lettuce leaves. It wasn't much, but more than I'd seen her eat up until now and I poured her a glass of wine.

'Go and have a wash,' I told her, when we'd finished. 'Then we'll go shopping.'

'I'm ready,' she called, fifteen minutes later, walking through the interconnecting door. Her dress was creased and her shoes scuffed, but she had made an effort to comb her hair and had even painted a streak of red lipstick across her mouth. The finished effect looked so unlike her normal smart self that I couldn't help staring at her. She noticed my look and narrowed her eyes.

'You try living without money, Seff. I've been dependent on that horrible friend of yours for months and he kept me dreadfully short. Only gave me enough for food and cigarettes. And he was always leaving me alone. Said he had to go to work.' She gave a short, sour laugh. 'We can all imagine what work that would be. Mummy said he was a thief and a gigolo and even Wolf wasn't sure about him. I mean, he was supposed to be a friend of us in the party, but then he was friends with you too. Well, more than friends, really. Wolf said he was sleeping with you in Berlin.'

I froze. That bastard von Klausen, he had been watching me all the time. How dare he. I took a deep breath, determined not to rise to her baiting. 'Come on,' I said. 'Let's go.'

She didn't move for a moment. 'Is it true that you have Jewish friends?' she asked.

'What on earth are you talking about,' I said, still furious and deliberately not looking at her, but rummaging through my bag for my wallet.

'That person, Amyas, told Wolf that you went to see some Jews in Berlin. That you took a message to them. I heard them talking about it when I was on the stairs in our dear little house.'

I felt sick and for a moment the room whirled around. The shock almost made my knees buckle and I struggled to stay outwardly calm. I stared at Xanthe, who was now looking in the hall mirror and flicking at the ends of her hair. Could what she said be true? Had Amyas betrayed me in the worst way possible, and were all his declarations of love merely a front in order to get information out of me? I thought of the odd times he'd turned up, the unexplained friendships he had. Of how he shook hands with Goering and was able to travel all over Europe without any hindrance.

He'd been lying all the time. Even that story he told me about his childhood hadn't been true and Charlie had been right to doubt him. Amyas was working for the Germans, and the people he'd been scared of were following us yesterday were our agents, possibly sent by Charlie to help me.

A lump of ice settled in my stomach and in my heart. I would never trust him again. I would never even think about him.

'Well?' asked Xanthe, looking at me through the mirror.

'Yes,' I replied coldly. 'I do have Jewish friends and they are very dear to me. And if you don't like it . . . too bad. Now, d'you want to go out or not?'

I turned to the door and she followed me, but I stopped with my hand on the knob. 'You've forgotten the baby.'

'What?'

'The baby. Pick him up.'

'Oh, no,' she wailed. 'He'll be a nuisance. Let's leave him here.' She pushed past me and opened the door. Sighing, I bent and picked up Max, before hurrying after her.

I spotted Karl, on the street where Xanthe bought a dress, shoes and new underwear. He was there again, standing in the shadow of a large building when we came out of the hairdresser's, where Xanthe had insisted on going to have her thin tresses cut and styled. For a spy, I thought, he was pretty useless, but then how would I know, and, of course, there could be others around whom I hadn't seen.

I left her for a minute, looking at hats, while I went into the baby shop next door. The assistant spoke no English or French, but, with much pointing and smiling, I managed to buy a rattle and a teething ring and a small, soft teddy bear. I waggled the bear in front of the little boy and he gave a gurgle of delight, which made me laugh. How could I hate this child? My laughter, however, turned to dismay when I went outside into the street and saw Xanthe chatting animatedly to Karl.

'Oh no,' she was saying, grinning inanely. 'You've got it wrong. He's my baby. My sister is helping me with him because I've been . . . a little unwell. And d'you know, we gave him a name yesterday. He's Maximilian von Klausen. His father is a count, so his son has to have an important name, don't you think?'

He offered her a cigarette and then bent to light it. 'So what are you doing in Lisbon, Miss Blake?'

'Frau von Klausen,' Xanthe corrected. 'Well, we're –'

I stepped in. 'That's enough, Xanthe. I think you've been out too long and you do need to rest. Remember, you haven't been well.'

Karl shuffled backward and doffed his hat. 'Good afternoon, Miss Blake,' he said and I wondered how he knew our names. Almost at once I realised it must have been the hotel receptionist. Just as it had been in Spain.

'Good afternoon,' I said. 'Will you excuse us.' I took Xanthe's arm and hustled her along the pavement. Karl kept in step with us.

'Why don't you let me carry the baby,' he said. 'He must be heavy for you.'

'No!' I said rather too quickly and too loudly and Xanthe gave me an angry stare.

'There's no need to be rude, Seffy. Karl's only trying to be helpful.'

I stopped walking. 'Shut up, Xanthe,' I growled, 'and you,' I glared at the fat American. 'If you don't stop annoying us I'll call the police. Look,' I pointed across the road to where two members of the public security police, smartly dressed in their navy blue uniforms, were strolling along. 'All I have to do is yell.'

'Goodness!' Xanthe said, plainly astonished, but Karl shot a look across the road and without another word turned and walked away. I watched him until he disappeared in the crowd of shoppers and then took Xanthe's arm.

'Come on,' I demanded. 'Let's get back to the hotel.'

When we were in our room Xanthe asked, 'What was all that about?'

'I don't trust that man and you shouldn't either.' I was changing Max's nappy and showing him his new toys.

'Why?' She was bewildered and I had to make up an excuse quickly.

'Think,' I said. 'We're both well off. He could be a kidnapper wanting to take Max for ransom. Like that Lindbergh baby. Imagine what Wolf would say if you'd allowed this strange man to get at his son.'

'Oh, yes.' She looked shocked. 'I never thought of that. How frightful.' She looked down at Max as he pushed the teething ring into his mouth. 'He's quite sweet, isn't he?'

'Hold him,' I said, 'while I make his bottle.'

She shook her head. 'No. I don't think so. You're better with him. I want a drink.'

I waited all evening for Charlie to turn up and then

445

decided that he hadn't been able to make it. Earlier, I'd sent for room service and got food and more wine for Xanthe and managed to persuade her to eat a few mouthfuls of bacalhau, dried salt cod stew, and some crunchy fried potatoes. 'Not bad,' she said and even made an attempt at the sweet pancake pudding. But what she really wanted was the wine and she sat nursing a glass and smoking countless cigarettes, until finally she went to bed.

It was raining and I went out on to the balcony to feel the cooling drops on my face. So much had happened in the last few days that my mind was buzzing and I felt anxious and restless. I came back into the room and sat in front of my typewriter and, disciplining myself to do some work, I wrote an article for the paper about this strange and beautiful city. Although removed from the actuality of war, I wrote, it was full of people affected by it. You could see them in the streets and in the bars. They were watchful and anxious and eager to tell you their tale. Of course, I hadn't had actual experience of them. I would have loved to go into the cafés and bars and talk to them, get their stories and record their desperate hopes and dreams. But the need to watch over Xanthe had prevented that and stopped me from doing what could have been a truly great final piece for my paper.

At midnight I went to bed, and was lying down, desperately trying not to think of Amyas, when a quiet knock came at my door. It will be him, I thought, he's discovered that our plane didn't take off and has come back. My heart sank. How can I speak to him, knowing what he is, but when I reluctantly opened the door, it wasn't

Amyas leaning against the door jamb. Charlie stood there, in a crumpled beige suit, and I fell into his arms.

'Well, Blake,' he said, after we'd held each other tightly and I'd drawn strength from his calming presence. 'Another fine mess, eh?'

'God, yes,' I sighed. 'It's just . . .' I cast about for a suitable word but nothing would come. 'It's just a mess.'

'Tell me,' Charlie said and grinned, 'but first, is that a bottle of wine I see?'

'You're lucky,' I smiled. 'Xanthe fell asleep before she'd finished it.' And while he sat at the table beside me I told him all that had happened since I'd arrived in Lisbon.

'Xanthe's ill,' I said. 'You'd barely recognise her. She's so thin and won't eat unless she's persuaded. All she wants to do is drink and chain-smoke.'

'Not good.' Charlie took a swig of wine. 'And Amyas? What of him?'

I gazed at him, my mouth working but no sounds coming out, and then, stupidly, found myself crying. 'He's a traitor,' I sobbed, finally finding my voice, although my words came out in choking gulps. 'He told von Klausen . . . about my taking a message to Jacob's sister . . . Xanthe heard him. She told me . . . this morning.'

Charlie's eyes narrowed and he took my hand. 'You know, I always suspected him,' he said after a short pause. 'There was always something wrong about him. Too many . . . anomalies.'

I wiped my eyes and took a breath. Too many anomalies; it was true. Everything Amyas said had a catch. But only when you thought about it later. 'I loved him,' I said quietly.

'Is that the past tense I hear?' I think Charlie was holding his breath.

'D'you know, even before I learned about him betraying me, I think I'd moved on. It was what you said. One morning I'll wake up and not be in love with him any more. That morning must have come weeks ago and I hadn't realised it.'

'But he was here, the other night?'

'Yes, he was.'

God bless him, Charlie didn't ask any more and I went on to explain everything that Amyas had said, about how he got Xanthe out of Bavaria and that he'd kept her in Switzerland and then in France for months, before bringing her to Portugal. That he'd got her a forged passport and how he'd been scared that we were being followed.

'And we are being followed,' I said. 'There's a man, an American possibly, who turns up everywhere we go. On the surface he seems harmless, but . . . there's something about him, I don't know, I don't trust.'

'Describe him,' said Charlie, and when I did, he nodded. 'I know who he is. He is a German who lived in the States for years. He's low level but will be working for someone else.'

'How d'you know?' I asked, remembering what Xanthe had said about Charlie being a spy.

He grinned. 'Don't ask.'

Baby Max woke up and I went to get him out of the open drawer which I'd made into his bed.

'No mistaking whose child this is,' said Charlie, looking at him as I changed his nappy. He took him while I made up a bottle and then watched me cuddling him, while the little boy eagerly sucked on the teat.

'Isn't that Xanthe's job?' he asked.

I raised my eyebrows. There was no need for further explanation.

'So,' I asked, when Max was wrapped again in his shawl and back in his temporary bed, 'do we get the plane tomorrow?'

'Yes. We need to get you back to London as soon as possible, and Xanthe too. She has to be questioned, because, having been with von Klausen, who is close to Heydrich, she might have some bits of information we can use.'

'She won't know anything,' I shrugged. 'You know how stupid she is.'

'Just let me have a go at her. It's surprising how much you'd think has passed her by, but is stored somewhere in that silly little head.'

'You won't hurt her?' I surprised myself by suddenly being concerned for her. God knows, Xanthe had never been anything less than trouble, but I felt a protective urge to keep her safe.

'Of course I won't hurt her,' Charlie smiled.

I looked at my watch: it was close to one in the morning and I was weary. I gave a great yawn and Charlie said, 'Time for bed, Blake. Busy day tomorrow.'

'Are you staying?' I asked. I wanted him to.

'No.' He shook his head and stood up. 'I've got things still to do, but I'll be here in the morning.'

'All right.' I knew that the thought of Amyas sharing this hotel bed with me so recently was too raw for him to get over immediately and so I kissed him on the cheek as he turned to go to the door. 'Thank you, Charlie, for coming to help me.'

'You knew I would . . . if I could.'

I nodded. 'I did. I've always trusted you.'

'Even though you haven't always loved me?' He shut the door behind him while I was still thinking.

'That's where you're wrong, Charlie,' I murmured to the empty room. 'I think I always have loved you. I just didn't realise it.'

I was woken early by the sound of Xanthe coughing. I got out of bed and walked through the interconnecting door to her room. She was sitting up, trying to get her breath, and, to my alarm, I saw a spray of blood on the sheet. 'What is it?' I asked, looking at the spots. 'Where's this come from?'

'I coughed it up,' she gasped. 'It's your fault, Seffy. You shouldn't have made me eat all that fish last night. I must have got a bone stuck in my throat.'

I put a hand on her forehead; it was hot and clammy and her cheeks were quite pink. Oh my God, I thought. She's running a temperature and it isn't caused by a fish bone.

'I'll get you an aspirin.'

I went through to my room and looked in my bag. I only had a couple of pills left in the bottle and I knew I was going to need more. 'Take these,' I said and gave her the pills and a drink of water.

'I need a doctor,' Xanthe whispered. 'I feel awful.'

'I know. But I think it will be better if you can wait till you get home. After all, neither of us can speak Portuguese and it would be difficult to try and talk to a doctor here don't you think?'

'I suppose,' she muttered and closed her eyes.

I piled up the pillows behind her so that she could

sleep sitting up and then went to get dressed. Max had woken and was lying peacefully in his drawer, watching the shafts of light coming in through the balcony windows. I was sitting on the bed dressing him when Charlie knocked at the door.

'You're up early,' he smiled, brushing rain off his hair. 'I was hoping to catch you in your nightie.'

'Idiot,' I smiled back, then I grimaced and said, 'It's Xanthe. She's sick this morning.'

'What? Hungover?'

I shook my head. 'Worse than that.' I got up and led him through to where Xanthe lay against the pillows, her eyes closed.

'Christ!' he said. 'What's all that blood?'

'She coughed it up.' I looked at the drying flecks on the sheet and suddenly felt scared. How on earth were we going to get her on the plane. 'She says it's a fish bone stuck in her throat, but I don't think it's that. She's been ill since before I got here.'

Xanthe opened her eyes and squinted at Charlie, trying to work out who he was. 'Oh,' she said flatly after a while. 'It's Mr Bradford. I thought it was the doctor.' She looked at me. 'Tell him to go away. Wolf says I mustn't talk to him.'

'That's just silly,' I said. 'He's here to help us.'

'Good morning, Xanthe.' Charlie sounded all business-like. 'We're getting on the plane in a couple of hours, so I would be grateful if you would get dressed.'

She stared at him and then at me. 'Does he mean it?'

I nodded.

'Oh good,' she said. 'Home to Berlin,' and then started coughing again.

I rushed to the bathroom and, wetting a towel, held it to her face, mopping away the fresh blood and trying to cool her off.

'This is going to be so bloody difficult,' Charlie groaned. When Xanthe had stopped coughing, he grabbed my arm. 'Get her dressed.'

We made a strange group going through the glass and marble lobby of the hotel an hour later. Charlie almost carrying Xanthe, followed by me with baby Max on one arm and our bags held in the other hand. I'd paid the bill earlier and Charlie had arranged a car. I had a fleeting memory of the flashy car Amyas had arranged and was glad that the one waiting for us was a discreet black Rover.

'Get in,' he said, looking round. I looked too. It was early, before eight o'clock, but the Lisboetas were already on the streets, going to work or school and some, despite the rain, under the awnings, at the pavement cafés, having their breakfast. I knew Charlie was looking for watchers, and I examined the faces of the men and women who were walking by the hotel. I didn't know what I was looking for, so I got in the car beside Charlie, with the baby on my knee.

Just as we pulled away I saw Karl and I said his name urgently.

'Where?' Charlie asked.

'Across the road. He's running towards the phone box.'

Charlie was looking in the driving mirror. 'Right, I've got him,' he said. 'We'll be away before he gets anyone to follow us. That is,' he had another quick squint in the mirror, 'unless he's got pals on the job.'

'Are we going to Sintra now?' I asked as we drove out of the city.

'No. We aren't going to Sintra at all. I'm taking us to another airfield. A private one. It's about fifty miles north of here, so settle down.'

Xanthe and Max slept throughout the entire journey, which was a relief, because we would have had to stop if Xanthe had had another coughing spell. 'We're nearly there,' said Charlie. 'Just another few miles.' We drove through a narrow valley, where chestnut trees leant over the road and craggy outcrops cut into the stormy, morning sky. Then the terrain flattened out and we followed a curving river and I thought I could smell the sea through the open window.

'It's lovely,' I said. 'I'd like to come here when the world isn't at war.'

'Mm,' Charlie muttered, but he wasn't really listening. His eyes kept flicking to the driving mirror and I twisted around in my seat to see that a car was following us, and getting closer.

Chapter Thirty

'We're being followed,' I gasped, twisting around again to get another look at the big green Mercedes. I could see two men, a driver and a passenger, neither of whom I recognised.

'I know.' Charlie pressed down on the accelerator and the car sped up, so that after we'd rounded a bend and I looked back, the car wasn't in sight. 'The airfield is only a few miles from here,' he grunted, 'we'll be there in ten minutes.'

Suddenly Xanthe gave a cry and started coughing again. I looked over my shoulder. She had gone very white and tiny spots of blood splattered on to the window beside her. She was gasping for air and could hardly hold herself upright.

'We'll have to stop,' I cried. 'She's going to choke to death if I don't help her. Now!'

'Christ,' Charlie groaned, then, 'Hold on to the baby, I'm turning in here.' And he swung the car to the right, on to a grassy path which led through a copse. At the end of the track was a long, low, white farmhouse surrounded by chestnut trees. It was abandoned, I thought, for no one came out when we stopped.

'Go to her,' he said and I dumped the baby on his knee and jumped out of my seat. But by the time I climbed into the rear seat, Xanthe had stopped coughing and was lying back with her eyes closed.

'Can we get going?' Charlie sounded more agitated than his normal cool self.

'Yes, I think so,' I said and got out, ready to move back into the front passenger seat. I looked along the track and to my horror, through the driving rain, I glimpsed the green shadow of the Mercedes cruising slowly along the main road. 'Look,' I breathed. 'The Merc. They're searching for us.'

'Right. Get Xanthe and the baby inside the house,' Charlie said and there was no mistaking the urgency in his voice. 'I'll take the car around to the back. See if I can find cover.'

God, it was difficult dragging Xanthe out of the car. 'No!' she cried. 'Leave me alone. I don't feel well.' She opened her eyes and looked at the old farmhouse. 'I'm not going into that disgusting place. Look. The door's hanging off and . . . Oh! There's a bird flying out of the window. It's just too revolting for words.'

'You have to,' I shouted. 'The kidnappers are back. They'll take Max and probably kill us.'

'What?' she wailed, and using what little strength she had left, scrambled out of the back seat and allowed me to push her towards the building. As soon as we were out of the car, Charlie revved the engine and drove the Rover around to the back of the house and out of sight.

It was dark inside, the only light coming from the front door and the one window where the shutters had been broken. We were in a large room, with a seeping dirt floor showing through the few remaining tiles and brown, plastered walls, which seemed alive with insects.

'Oh my God,' squealed Xanthe, looking at the cockroaches which quivered their antennae menacingly before jumping from one spot to another. 'I'm going to be sick.'

'Go ahead,' I said, too distracted to care. 'Just don't make a noise.'

'I hate you,' she moaned, but I went to the window and, standing to one side, peered out. I could see nothing except for the dirt track and the trees. Perhaps, I thought, with a sigh of relief, that car wasn't following us at all and Charlie is being unnecessarily jumpy.

Max, who had been blissfully asleep in my arms, now gave a little hiccup and woke. He put his hands in his mouth and starting sucking them, and I realised that his bottle was in my bag, which I'd left in the car. If we were to be in here for any length of time, he'd need it. I'd have to leave him while I dashed out the back and looked for the car, but I was reluctant to put him on the filthy floor. I looked around the gloomy room. To one side I spotted a wooden chair. It had lost one of its arms but otherwise appeared to be quite stable and I nodded towards it. 'Go and sit there,' I said to Xanthe. 'And hold on to Max while I get his bottle.'

'I can't,' she cried. 'I don't feel well.'

'I don't care. You have to.' It was brutal of me, but I had no choice. Grabbing her arm, I led her to the chair and sat her down, then I put Max on her wasted lap. 'Hold him,' I ordered. 'And don't let him fall. Wolf will be furious if you damage him.'

'Oh,' she moaned and clasped the baby in her arms as though he was the most precious piece of china.

I saw a door in the dark wall opposite the front entrance and went to it. I tried the latch, hoping it would open easily, and to my delight it did and I walked through. I

456

wasn't outside, exactly, but in another building, a byre or animal shelter, with empty stalls and troughs and old, dirty straw littering the floor. A few farming implements lay about, broken spades and pitchforks and bins that must have once held animal feed. The far side of the building opened on to pasture, and rows of grapevines flourished in the fields beyond.

'Charlie!' I called softly, as I ran towards the opening, but there was no reply and when I got outside and looked around the corner there was no sign of the car. In the pouring rain I ran into the trees which surrounded the back of the farmhouse. There was a track through them, just wide enough for a car, but the Rover wasn't visible. I could barely believe it. Had Charlie gone on by himself?

Despairing, I ran back through the byre to the farmhouse. I was soaking, my thin silk blouse clinging to my body and my hair plastered to my head. Xanthe was still in the chair, clutching the baby, and cried with relief when I took him out of her arms. 'He's been crying,' she moaned. 'I didn't know what to do.'

'Babies cry,' I said impatiently. 'You have to get used to it.'

'I can't.' She sounded so pathetic that I couldn't find any more words to shout at her. It was pointless.

'Did you find Mr Bradford?' she whispered, in her little-girl voice.

'No.'

'Has he left us?' She started to cry and that brought on another bout of coughing; not as bad as before, but still enough to make her breathless.

'Charlie wouldn't leave us,' I said and tried to make my words convincing. 'Don't worry. It'll be all right.'

I stuck my little finger in Max's mouth and let him suck on it, while I carried him to the window. The track was clear, but suddenly, in the distance, I thought I could hear the sound of twigs snapping, or . . . my God, was that gunfire? I waited for a minute and then, unmistakably, the noise of a car engine came closer.

'Come on, Xanthe,' I hissed. 'We've got to get out of here.' I grabbed her arm, jerked her up from the chair and forced her to the back door.

'I can't go outside,' she wailed.

'You must,' I said and I pushed her through and along the separated stalls until I found one which had its three sides intact and a good covering of straw. 'Sit there,' I instructed, 'and take your son again. If you see anyone, get inside the straw.'

'Oh, God, no,' she cried, 'the smell!' but I pushed her down and put Max into her arms. Then I looked about for something to use as a weapon. Picking up a pitchfork with an absurdly long handle, I stationed myself beside the door. I thought I could do quite a bit of damage with it if someone came bursting through.

The sound of a car coming closer made my heart beat wildly and I gripped the pitchfork tighter. What if both men come at once? my head was screaming at me. What'll I do then? The car stopped and I heard the door slam. Xanthe was whimpering behind me, but Max was quiet except for the occasional sucking sound.

Footsteps sounded from the room and suddenly the door in front of me opened and I swung the pitchfork with all my might, so that it smashed against the open door splintering the ancient wood and knocking me off my feet. I heard a tumbling sound, as though somebody had thumped to the floor. Scrambling to my feet, I held my breath. Was there another person creeping towards me? The pitchfork was in two pieces, the handle broken off completely, so I grabbed the metal prongs and waited.

I heard shuffling on the floor and then a grunt, but after that, nothing.

'Have they gone?' squeaked Xanthe. 'I have to get out of this straw. Please let me. It's horrible.'

'Shut up,' I hissed, then, 'I think I've got one of them.'

'You bloody did, Blake. You nearly laid me out.' The voice from behind the ruined door was the best sound I'd ever heard.

It was Charlie, pushing past the splintered wood. Dropping the metal prongs, I rushed over to him and wrapped my arms around his neck.

'Careful,' he groaned. 'You fetched me one hell of a crack on the head.' I looked up and saw a reddened mark which would soon become a bruise above his right eyebrow. 'Thank God you missed my glasses,' he said and grinned.

'Where did you go?' I asked, moving over to Xanthe and helping her up. Charlie picked up little Max and started walking around the byre back to the track.

'Get in the car,' he said. 'I'll tell you as we drive.'

It was still raining and a mist was hovering over the trees, but when we got to the road I saw the green Mercedes and beside it, on the verge, the bodies of two men. One had a gun in his hand.

'My God,' I gasped as we drove past them. 'Did you do that?'

''Fraid so. Bad, but necessary. They would have killed you and Xanthe.'

'Who were they?' I twisted in my seat to get a look at the bodies, which we were rapidly leaving behind.

He flashed a look in the driving mirror at Xanthe, who was sitting on the back seat. I turned and looked at her too. Her eyes were closed, but I didn't think she was asleep. Pink circles flushed her cheeks and I knew she was running a temperature. God, she needed help.

'Let's just say they were friends of you know who.'

'All right,' I nodded. 'That'll do. But what happened?'

'I knew they would find the turning, so I went down that other track through the trees and came up behind them. The rain muffled the sound of my approach and they saw me too late. Horrible job, anyway, look: the airfield.'

'I love you, Charlie Bradford,' I said as he parked by a small wooden building, next to a grass runway. A plane, its engine running, was drawn up a few yards away.

'That's good,' he smiled. 'Because, despite the fact that you've nearly brained me, you're the person I want to grow old with. Now, get on board.'

Xanthe was quietly compliant, too ill and tired, I think, to make a fuss, and got on the plane without a murmur. It was basic inside, benches and canvas webbing to hold us in for the four-hour flight and we were the only passengers.

Charlie kissed me goodbye. 'Aren't you coming?' I asked.

'Got clearing-up things to do,' he said. 'But I'll see you soon.' He looked at Xanthe. 'Get her to a hospital and take him,' he nodded to the baby, 'down to Cornwall. He should be safe there with Nanny Alice.'

'I will.' I gazed at him, not wanting to turn away and

get on the plane, but he took my arm and urged me to climb the few steps. 'Bye, Charlie,' I said.

'Bye, dearest Blake.'

Xanthe was admitted to St Thomas' Hospital and, after a few days, I was invited to a meeting with the consultant. I went late in the afternoon, leaving Max with Kitty and Jacob. I'd been at the newspaper, handing in my article and explaining to Geoff that I was leaving.

'What?' he'd shouted. 'No. You can't.'

'I can, I must,' I said. 'I have too many obligations now and they'll prevent me from being the foreign correspondent that you want. That I wanted to be. I've loved this job and I'll always be grateful to you for giving me the opportunity, but now I have to be at home.'

He'd puffed furiously at his pipe for a minute, before standing up and thrusting out his hand. 'I'll accept your resignation, Miss Blake . . . reluctantly. But I will expect the odd article from time to time. You're too good a writer to lose, so don't let domestic considerations stop you from handing in a few pieces. Doesn't have to be on foreign affairs.'

'Thank you,' I said and left the office before I burst into tears. We'd had a massive bombing raid the night before and the air was heavy with the smell of smoke and the streets were full of rubble. Ambulances were still racing backwards and forwards across the bridges and past the damaged buildings.

The hospital was heaving with casualties; they lay on trolleys, or sat on chairs, or even leant against the wall. The sister in charge sat on her high chair in the middle of the room, directing the triage with firm efficiency. 'The gentleman by the door, nurse,' she called to one of her minions. 'I can see from here that he's losing blood and needs to be lying down – and get that little boy into the next cubicle. The medical student can stitch him up.'

I walked down the long corridor and into the ward where Xanthe lay. The ward sister stopped me as I went in. 'Dr McKay is in my office, Miss Blake. He'd like to see you now, before you go in to your sister.'

The consultant was past retirement age, as were many these days. The younger men were all at the front, or working at the military hospitals. 'Good afternoon, Miss Blake,' he said in a soft Highland accent. 'I did want to see you.'

'Yes.'

'Your wee sister, Xanthe, is it?'

I nodded.

'I'm sorry to have to tell you, but she is very seriously ill.'

'I guessed,' I sighed. 'She was coughing up blood and quite breathless a lot of the time.'

'Aye. Just so. Well, she has the tuberculosis. Quite advanced, I'm afraid.'

'But you can treat her?' I asked, my heart sinking as I saw the look that passed between him and the sister.

He shook his white head. 'Sadly, there isn't much we can do now, except keep her comfortable. If she'd been diagnosed earlier we would have recommended a sana-torium, where she could have lots of fresh air and good healthy food, but her lungs are dreadfully damaged. If she took a place at a sanatorium she would be going there to die and . . .' He fixed me with startlingly blue eyes that had seen too much and were too weary with overwork to be bothered with the niceties. 'And, I must

462

tell you, lassie, she'd be taking up a bed that could be used for someone we might be able to save.'

I looked from one to the other. I didn't know what they wanted me to do. 'Can she stay here?' I asked.

Sister, her double chins wobbling under the strings of her cap, shook her head. 'We're overwhelmed,' she said. 'You must have seen Casualty when you came in just now. At the moment there's scarcely a spare bed in the hospital. I think that you're going to have to take her home, or, if you can afford it, find a private clinic.'

I thought of the children. Was it safe to have Xanthe with us? 'Is she infectious?'

Dr McKay shrugged. 'It is a slight risk, but no more than you would meet on the bus or the train every day.'

'I have a house in Cornwall,' I said. 'She'd get lots of fresh air there and good food. Maybe she would get better if I took her there?'

'Did I not make myself clear, Miss Blake? Your sister will not get better. She has great black holes in her lungs which will never heal. The poor wee lassie is dying.' He shook my hand. 'I'll leave it to you to make the arrangements. Good afternoon to you.'

Sister and I watched him go and she took my hand. 'Dr McKay can be a little . . . blunt, I fear. Please don't be upset.'

I shook my head. 'Don't worry, sister. I'm used to people giving me the plain facts.' But I was upset. I'd already forgiven Xanthe for being such an idiot and often so malicious. Now I only saw her as the little sister with whom I'd grown up, played on the beach and sat next to every Christmas at the pantomime, screaming with laughter at the antics of the Ugly Sisters and Baron

Hardup. We'd had such fun together in those far-off days.

Tears came to my eyes and I searched my bag for a handkerchief.

'Let me get you a cup of tea,' said the sister, but she was looking through the glass wall of her office, patently anxious to get back to the ward.

I wiped my eyes and took a deep breath. 'No, thank you,' I said. 'I'll take her to Cornwall, but I'll need a couple of days to make the arrangements. Then you shall have your bed.'

The sirens went soon after I left the hospital. It was getting towards evening of a lovely summer day and the Luftwaffe had come earlier than usual. I, with other Londoners, hurried to the nearest shelter. In the Underground station I sat on a bench and wept for my sister, while bombs thudded and crunched down around us and white plaster sprinkled like snowflakes on to my hat.

'Cheer up, ducks,' said a middle-aged woman, who was sitting next to me. 'The buggers will be gone in a minute. The RAF will get them. Mark my words.'

I nodded and felt better even though I hadn't been crying about the bombs, and joined in the singing when somebody started up 'We'll Meet Again'.

When I got home, Jacob and Kitty, who was carrying Max, were trailing back from the shelter they'd been in. I took the little boy into my arms and he smiled. He already knew me. Kitty's face was streaked with tears and I knew she had been frightened. I wondered if my face showed evidence of my weeping and later, when Jacob knocked at my door, it seemed that it had.

'How was your sister in the hospital?' he asked, quite carefully.

I cried again and told him everything the doctor had said. 'I'm taking her to Cornwall. He said the fresh air might do her good.'

Jacob said nothing.

'I can't nurse her here,' I sobbed. 'I miss Marisol so much and I need to take Xanthe's child away from the bombing. It will be better there, even if . . .' I left the rest of the sentence unsaid and he took my hand and gave it a squeeze.

'You are doing the right thing,' he said. 'For everyone. However, I have come with a request, but perhaps now it is not possible?'

'What?' I asked. 'What request?'

'That Kitty might go to Cornwall for a little while. She is so unhappy here, she misses her mother and she is so frightened all the time. When she went before it did her so much good.'

'Of course she must come, I wanted her to. Marisol loves her and you've seen how good Alice is with her. And Jacob' – I put my other hand on top of his – 'please come too. If only for a couple of weeks. It'll give you a break, and God knows, we all need that.'

At first he refused, but after much persuasion from both Kitty and me he agreed. 'Good,' I said. 'Xanthe will be going down the day after tomorrow. I've organised a private ambulance, with a nurse to accompany her. So we'll go in the morning. It'll have to be the train, I'm afraid, as I can't get any petrol but I'm sure that doesn't matter.'

'Ah. I can help there. I have petrol in my warehouse. I was not hoarding, you understand, but it was what my

465

boy Emanuel had for driving our van around to deliver the furs. Now that he is called up and I am retired, there is no need for the van but the petrol is there. Many cans. You must fill your car and take extra for the drive back.'

'Oh, Jacob. Thank you.'

I went to see Xanthe that evening to tell her of my plans. She was sitting up in bed in a side ward and looking a little better. She had eaten some blancmange and there was a large glass of milk on the table in front of her. She had a cigarette in her mouth, drawing the smoke deeply into her wasted lungs.

'How are you?' I asked.

'This place is ghastly,' she said. 'D'you know, I asked that sister person to get me drink, a gin or a brandy, and she just laughed. "I'm far too busy to wait on you," she said. "I'm not a barmaid."'

I laughed too. 'This is a hospital, Xanthe. Not a hotel. Anyway, you're leaving here tomorrow. I'm taking you to Cornwall.'

'Oh, no,' she cried. 'I can't go there. It's awful.'

'The doctor says you have to have lots of fresh air. You can't stay here and there's nowhere else for you to go. A few weeks by the sea will do you lots of good and I'm going to be there too. We'll take Max and he'll love it.'

'But I'm not well enough to look after him.'

'You don't need to. Alice will take care of him.'

'Alice?'

It was only then that I realised I'd never told her about Marisol. At first, I'd kept the knowledge of my little daughter to myself because I knew Xanthe would say something cutting about her. Or make fun of me, and I couldn't bear that. And then I'd forgotten that she didn't know.

'I have an adopted daughter,' I said. 'She's two years old and Alice is her nanny.'

'You've adopted a child?' Xanthe stared at me. 'What does Mummy say about that?'

'I haven't told her. Have you told her about Max?'

She scowled. 'I don't know where she is. But she met Wolf and she liked him.'

It occurred to me that I should get in touch with my mother and tell her how ill Xanthe was and I resolved to write a letter as soon as I got home.

'Anyway, let me tell you the arrangements for your travel. I've hired you a private nurse.' That pleased her, as I knew it would, and she soon forgot about Marisol.

The next day Jacob, Kitty and I drove down to Cornwall with Max. It was a tiring journey, and with lots of military traffic on the road, we had to pull over continually, so it was evening by the time we got there. Kitty jumped out of the car when I parked it by the garage and called 'Alice!'

'Look what we've got,' she cried when Alice came out of the house leading Marisol by the hand.

'By God,' said Alice, gazing at Max who was clutching his rattle. 'Who's this?'

'It's Max. Isn't he sweet?'

Alice looked at me. 'You've never adopted another one, Miss Seffy?'

'No,' I smiled, wearily climbing out of the car. 'Not exactly. He belongs to my sister, who will be here tomorrow. I'll tell you all about it later on.'

'All right,' she said, and took Max out of Kitty's arms. 'He's a little lad, I see, judging by his blue frock. Does he have a name?'

'He's Max,' I said. 'Maximilian.'

'Aye, right nice name that,' she said, and bending down showed him to Marisol. 'Baby,' Marisol said, and then patted him on the cheek

I went over and picked her up. 'Hello, my little love. Mummy has missed you so much.'

Alice smiled at Jacob and was thrilled when he took her hand and raised it to his lips. 'Mr Weiss,' she said. 'I'm glad you've come down here. Away from all that bombing. You'll have a nice rest. Lovely walks, nearly as good as Yorkshire.' We laughed and she twinkled, cuddling the baby to her as she led the way into the house. 'Now come on in, everyone. Mrs Penney is in the kitchen and she's made a grand supper.'

After we'd eaten and everyone had settled down, I went into the children's room to kiss them goodnight. Alice was there, putting clothes away, and she gave me a hug. 'I'm so glad you're home safe and sound, Miss Seffy. I did worry.'

'I'm not going away again,' I said. 'I've given up my job. I'm going to be a full-time mother.'

'I'll believe that when I see it,' she said, laughing. Then, giving me an old-fashioned look, she said, 'Did you see Mr Amyas?'

I sighed. 'I did. But I don't want to talk about him.'

'Oh?'

'Leave it, Alice. But I did see Mr Charlie and I've made up my mind. It's him.'

She nodded. 'I like him,' she said. 'He'll never let you down, that one. But . . .'

'But what?'

She turned her back on me, tucking in the sheets on

Marisol's bed and adjusting the cover on the cot where we'd put Max.

'What?' I repeated.

'But Mr Amyas is who you dream of. He's part of you.'

Chapter Thirty-One

Cornwall, 1940

It was a lovely summer, that one of 1940, while London was ablaze and our young pilots daily faced the savagery of the Luftwaffe. In Cornwall we were away from the bombing but the war did affect us, with some shortages of food and fuel and sad stories of the young men from the village who were dying on land and sea.

'The Trevissick boy is lost,' Mrs Penney told me one morning, while she was cooking breakfast. 'He was a stoker on a merchant ship and them blasted Germans torpedoed him. Annie Trevissick got the telegram yesterday. She's got another boy in the Royal Navy and is in a state. I took her a bit of bacon and a few tatties last night. It'd make a supper, I thought.'

'That was kind of you,' I said. 'Are the Trevissicks the family who live in the cottages by the harbour? Near you? I think I remember one of their boys. He was a bit younger than me.'

'That's them.' She put scrambled eggs in a warming dish and stirred the pan of porridge. Alice would be bringing the children down any minute for their breakfast. 'Now, what shall I do for Miss Xanthe?'

'She'll eat some egg, I think,' I said. 'And perhaps bread and butter.' I paused. 'Have we got any butter?'

'Yes, and don't ask me how I got it. There's quite a bit in the village. We all got some.'

It was the black market, of course, and I shouldn't have had anything to do with it, but I didn't care. 'I'll give you some money, later,' was all I said.

Xanthe had been at the house for nearly two weeks now. She'd loved all the attention and had wanted to keep the nurse who'd looked after her on the journey, but, to my relief, the woman wasn't prepared to stay 'in this out of the way place', as she called it, and took the next train back to London.

Mr Penney had put a single bed in Xanthe's room, so that we could wheel it out on to the veranda and let her get the benefit of the fresh sea air. She hated it, though, preferring to stay in her bedroom, idly flicking through magazines and smoking non-stop.

'Should I take her cigarettes away?' I'd asked Dr Jago.

'I don't think there's any point.' He shook his head. 'I've had a letter from St Thomas' in London and, well, you know what they said. I knew it last week, when she first came here and I listened to her chest. Good God, it's terrible.' My face must have fallen, because he took my hand. 'I'm sorry, Seffy. There's nothing anyone can do, so let her smoke and drink, whatever she wants. We can make her comfortable, that's all.'

'I suppose so,' I sighed. 'I do understand, but some days she doesn't seem too bad, in fact she looks quite pretty again.'

'Ah,' he said. 'It's often the way with consumption. The fever-pink cheeks are charming and make the eyes look brighter. Your sister's is a classic case, but, sadly, all you can do now is love her and care for her.' He paused for a moment, then asked, 'Is Lady Blake coming over to see her? If she wants to, it will need to be soon.'

I shook my head. I'd had a letter from Mother, who clearly had no intention of braving the Atlantic, particularly since the *Queen Mary* had been requisitioned as a troopship. She'd added, 'Seeing as your father left you all the money, I do hope that you'll employ the best doctors.' I looked up at Jago and gave a brief smile. 'She won't be coming.'

We were in the hall and Alice was coming down the stairs with the little ones. Marisol, as ever, was being independent and walking by herself. Even at that young age she showed her character. Max sat happily on Alice's arm, revelling in the attention. As Alice said, nobody could have wished for an easier baby.

'My eye, those children are thriving.' Dr Jago smiled. 'Even that little boy looks well. I was quite concerned when I first saw him, what is it, two weeks ago? I feared he might be sick, like his mother.' He patted Alice's arm. 'Miss Weaver, I swear you're a miracle-worker.'

'Get away with you, Doctor,' she grinned. 'But I will say that the little one has come on quite grand. He was nothing but a soup chicken when I first got hold of him.'

Jacob, with Willi pattering ahead of him, walked into the hall. They brought in drifts of ozone and smelled of the sea. The two of them went on the beach every morning, initially for walking, but Jacob had quickly developed an interest in the rock pools and marine botany and daily brought in various seaweeds to look them up in the books in Father's study.

'Doggie!' shouted Marisol with glee, and scampered towards poor Willi who, without waiting for his master, took off up the stairs. Even his mild temperament couldn't cope with a chaotic stroking from an enthusiastic toddler.

'She's a little monkey, this one,' Alice smiled proudly and, taking Marisol's hand, she walked the children to the kitchen.

'Chess on Saturday evening?' asked Dr Jago, as he took his hat from the stand and picked up his bag.

'Yes,' said Jacob eagerly. 'If this silly old man won't be too much trouble.'

'Of course not. I'll enjoy the competition. My wife doesn't play and always does the church flowers on Saturday evening. She'll leave us a bite to eat, though.' He went to the door and called, 'Bye, all.'

In the time since we'd been down here, Jacob had struck up a friendship with Dr Jago, based on their shared love of Mozart and chess. I was pleased for him; his troubles seemed to have lessened, and even Kitty was happier. She swam in the sea and walked into the village, where she watched the fishermen bringing in the catch and chatted to the teenage girl who worked in the village shop. No one seemed to mind that she was German and I suspected that Mrs Penny had put the word around that she was a refugee. Carol, the girl from the shop, had taken her to the pictures in Truro, going to the first house and coming home on the bus.

'We saw *Rebecca*,' Kitty said excitedly. 'It was wonderful. And it is from a book. I will buy it when we get back to London.'

'You don't need to wait,' I smiled. 'I brought a copy down here a couple of years ago. Go and look in the bookcase in the study. I'm sure it will be there.'

I spent my time with the children and sat with Xanthe.

Mostly she stayed in bed, resting, as ordered by the doctors. She had little energy anyway and was eager to scramble back between the sheets after washing or having her bed made. I bought her magazines showing the latest fashions, which she examined closely, flicking through the pages in her most irritating way. She was, of course, discontented.

'I want to go back to London,' she said crossly. 'So that my friends can come and visit me. It's so boring here, with screaming children and those two people you've brought along. Who are they, anyway?'

'They're my friends. They have the flat opposite mine.'

'They're foreign.'

'Yes. You should like them. They're from Berlin.'

She turned her head, a spark of interest lighting her eye. 'Berlin? What are they doing here?'

'They're refugees.'

She thought about it for a minute and then scowled. 'Don't tell me that they're Jews. Wolf said you had friends who were Jews.'

'They are,' I said, almost happy to make her angry. 'Jacob has been in England for many years, but Kitty only came last year. Her mother has disappeared. Probably taken to one of the camps.'

'What camps?'

'Oh, Xanthe,' I said, exasperated with her. 'How can you not know? Jews are being persecuted in Germany. They're put in camps or killed. It's dreadful.'

'Well.' She threw her magazine on the floor and screwed up her face into the pout I remembered from years ago, when she couldn't win an argument. 'Wolf says they cause all the trouble. If they go to prison, it's their own fault.'

'Surely,' I said angrily, 'you can't believe that. It's monstrously unfair.'

'But of course I do.' She sounded almost bewildered by my ignorance. 'Everyone does. All my friends in Germany and here. Mummy thinks it. She told me. The Jews are not really human. They need to be put down.'

I stood up. I was shaking with anger and in another heartbeat I would have hit her. 'I'll get you a cup of tea,' I said, trying to keep the rising fury out of my voice. 'I won't be a minute.'

'I don't want tea,' she called, as I went on to the landing. 'For God's sake get me a gin.'

I stood for a minute outside her room, trying to calm down. I was desperately sorry that she was ill and I had resolved to care for her, but every single thing she said made me want to strangle her. How had she become such an unpleasant person? Was she like this when we were children and had hateful views even then? I didn't remember it that way, but then, I didn't remember her thinking at all. She'd been a terribly spoilt child – not very bright but devastatingly pretty. I remember Mother being so proud of her, pushing her to the front when we met people, and now, when I thought about it, I remembered that Mummy had a photograph of Xanthe on her dressing table. Not one of me. Nor of my father. Just Xanthe.

'The truth is, Persephone Blake,' I said out loud to the empty landing. 'You're angry because you're jealous. And always have been.'

'Now, that is something I do not believe.' Jacob was coming up the stairs, a book on marine botany tucked under his arm.

I blushed. 'You caught me talking to myself.'

He smiled. 'We all do it.' He gave me a sympathetic look. 'Has something upset you?'

I jerked my head towards Xanthe's room. 'It's her. She's so . . . unspeakably horrid at times.'

He shrugged. 'The poor girl is very sick. She cannot be expected to guard her tongue.'

'Oh God, Jacob,' I sighed. 'You don't understand. She says terrible, anti-Semitic things and I think of you and Kitty and poor Sarah. I remember my friends, Dieter and Rachel, in Berlin and all the terrifying stories that Charlie collected.' I put my hand to my mouth to stop myself from swearing, I was so incensed. 'How can she speak like that? I truly think she must be mad. And now, I have to do her bidding. Get her a drink and go back into her room as if nothing has happened.'

He was thoughtful for a moment, then he put his book down on the lamp table beside Xanthe's door. 'Get the drink. I'll take it in to her.'

'No!' I was shocked. 'She'll be hateful to you.'

'It doesn't matter. If she wants to say these things, it's better she says them to my face. Go, I'll wait here.'

When he went in with the drink, I stood outside her door, ready to rescue him, and heard her say in a horri-fied voice, 'What do you want?'

'I've brought your drink. Pink gin, I believe.' Jacob sounded very calm.

'Leave it and go,' Xanthe snapped. 'I won't have you in my room.'

'All right,' said Jacob, mildly. 'But first, I'll pick up this magazine, which has dropped on the floor.' There was the noise of paper rustling and then Jacob said,

'Ach, this sable coat in the photograph here. It is of inferior quality.'

'What?'

'Poor quality. This company. They do not buy well.'

'How d'you know?' I could hear that Xanthe was intrigued.

'How do I know?' asked Jacob. 'You ask how do I know, young lady. I tell you. Because dealing in furs is my business. Haven't I bought sable from all over Russia? This,' I heard the sound of a hand slapped against paper, 'is schlock. Rubbish.'

'I'm going to buy a sable coat, when I get better.' Xanthe was quieter.

'So,' said Jacob, 'go to a good shop. Buy the best. Here, your drink.' He walked out of her room and gave me a wink as he went downstairs.

Astonished, I followed him and, leaving him in Father's study, went out and down the steps to the beach. Alice and Kitty were there with the children. Kitty was holding a sleeping Max, while Alice danced Marisol through the little waves on the shoreline.

'Max, he is a good baby,' said Kitty, smiling down at the little boy's face.

'Yes,' I answered. 'Surprisingly good, considering the circumstances . . .'

'The circumstances of his birth?' Kitty looked up at me. 'Or that his mother is so . . . I shouldn't say this, Seffy, but I will. His mother is so bad.'

I sighed. 'Xanthe is not a nice person,' I agreed. 'And she has some evil views, but . . .' I looked at Max, who opened his eyes and smiled up at Kitty, 'it's not his fault.'

'No,' she said and bent her head to give him a kiss. 'I

love him and Marisol.' Then she asked, 'Is his father a good man?'

I shook my head. 'No. I'm afraid not. If anything, he's worse than Xanthe and we mustn't let him take Max away.'

'Oh!' Kitty looked at me. 'Does he want to take him?'

'Yes, he does. But he's a Nazi officer and there is no way he can get to England, so Max is safe with us.'

Kitty looked both horrified and relieved, then, after a moment, she put Max in my arms. 'I'm going for a swim,' she said, 'and then, after lunch, Carol, from the shop, and me are going into Truro on the bus. You don't mind, do you?'

'Of course not,' I smiled. 'Go and enjoy yourself.'

I watched her in the calm, blue water. She was getting to be a strong swimmer, trying new strokes and yearning to be proficient enough to swim across the bay, like I did. Her time in Cornwall had done her good, and Jacob also. 'Stay longer,' I'd said to them one day. 'You don't need to go back to London and suffer in the bombing. Besides, I love having you here. We're like a family.'

'I will stay,' said Jacob after a few minutes' consideration. 'But only if I can be of use. The other evening I saw you looking at the books from the factories and shops that your manager sent. Perhaps another eye, cast over the figures, might help?'

I could have hugged him. 'Oh yes. Thank you, Jacob. I have no idea what I'm looking at.'

'So,' he said. 'First, I will look and then we will look together, so that I can teach you. Then your business will truly be yours.'

My business. It was often the last thing I thought about,

but I realised, once again, that I had to take a serious interest in it. It was the basis of my fortune and I knew I couldn't be like Daddy and retreat from the world. I had to learn how it worked and what I needed to do to keep it going. I leant against a rock, with Max lying peacefully in my arms, and thought about my life. How different it was from two years ago. So many things had happened, I had a daughter, I was responsible for Max, my mother had left and my father had died. And now Xanthe was dying. It was almost too much. It left no time for me, for love.

I thought about Charlie then and, with a catch in my heart, wondered where he was. I hadn't heard from him since I left him at that airfield in Portugal. My mouth was suddenly dry and I prayed that he was safe.

Geoff had asked about him that day when I went to give him my resignation. 'Seen old Charlie, lately?' he asked, but I'd shaken my head.

'Not since before I went to Lisbon,' I lied.

'God, I wish he was still writing for us,' Geoff groaned. 'Wilf is good, I won't deny that, but' – he waved his pipe towards the pieces of writing that littered his desk – 'Charlie was something special. He made foreign news come alive.'

'I thought so,' I agreed. 'But he'll be back, after the war.' He didn't say anything. Soldiers were dying every day.

Surprisingly, Monica had asked about him too, as I cleared my desk. Where was he? she asked, because he didn't seem to be in the regular army any more.

'How would I know?' I shrugged.

'Oh, I just thought you might, seeing as how you're

so close.' She tapped a red-painted talon on my desk. 'It's a surprise that you're leaving,' she said. 'But I suppose you have so many other calls on your time. I know you don't need the money, but with your little girl to look after, as well as your sister . . .'

'What about my sister?' I'd looked up sharply.

'Oh,' she flushed. 'I understood that she wasn't well.'

'And who did you understand that from?' I glared at her.

'I don't know.' She looked suddenly nervous. 'I heard it somewhere. But, if I'm wrong, I'm sorry.' She waited for a few seconds and then glanced at me with narrowed eyes. 'Am I wrong?'

I ignored her and left the office. Thank God, I thought, as I walked down the stairs, I never have to see her again.

Now, sitting on the beach, I thought about that conversation. How on earth did she know that Xanthe was sick? It was very strange. Then I remembered that, as a gossip columnist, she had a web of informants everywhere, in all the police stations and possibly in all the hospitals. Someone at St Thomas' had probably contacted her and, in exchange for a few pounds, given her the name of a notable patient.

'Penny for them,' said Alice, coming to sit beside me. Marisol was on the sand in front of us, putting shells and shiny pebbles in her tin bucket.

'Not worth a penny,' I smiled. A fishing boat was setting out from behind the headland and I watched it, and watched Kitty as she walked out of the sea and picked up her towel.

'Thinking of him?'

'Charlie? Yes, I was, as well as other things. I was praying that he's safe, wherever he is.'

'I'll join in that prayer,' Alice nodded. 'I'm right fond of him, but that's not who I meant.'

She meant Amyas and he was someone I refused to think about. He was a traitor.

'No.' I didn't realise that my voice sounded so cold until I saw the change in Alice's face.

'I'm sorry, Miss Seffy,' she said. 'It was wrong of me to be so forward.'

'It doesn't matter,' I answered. 'Now, come on, we must go up for lunch.'

August melted into September and the sunset came earlier every evening, but we lingered, not yet ready to leave this beautiful place. I thought that I would never leave. Why should I? I was happier here than anywhere. But then I thought of Xanthe, who was getting weaker, and knew that soon she'd have to go into hospital. Back in London, I supposed. But the peaceful surroundings had, like a drug, invaded our senses and none of us was ready to return.

A strange routine had developed, and with it a stranger friendship. Every lunchtime Jacob would take Xanthe a pink gin and talk about his business of buying furs. He'd expanded from which furrier was the best, to telling her about his travels in Russia and Canada and how he'd chosen the pelts. She seemed fascinated and listened, lying back on her pillows, while he spoke of mink and ermine, silver fox and his and her favourite, sable. But one day, he brought up a book with her drink. 'Today,' he said, 'I think we have learned enough about fur. I shall read to you.'

I was listening outside her room, still nervous because she hadn't lost her ability to be spiteful. Indeed, if he was a second late with her drink, she would ring her bell and demand the presence of 'that old Jew', whose name she never learned; nor did she think for an instant that her offensive nomenclature would stop him from coming to her.

'A story? What story?'

'A romance,' said Jacob. 'About a princess and a commoner and a fight for the throne.'

'All right,' she said reluctantly, and lay back while he started to read *The Prisoner of Zenda*. She loved it, listening intently for the half-hour that he spent with her and eagerly looking forward to it the next day. When that was finished, they went on to *King Solomon's Mines*.

I listened to the radio all the time. The news was terrifying. I heard about the non-stop bombing raids on London and listened while the announcer calmly listed the number of planes which had been destroyed. He always said 'planes', never pilots, but I thought about the families who would never see their young men grow to maturity. When I took Kitty to the cinema one afternoon we saw a newsreel of the destroyed buildings in London and the stoical people carrying on their business in the midst of the rubble. I thought briefly of my flat and my father's house and wondered if they'd been damaged, but I guessed not. Someone would have told me.

Then, different pictures came on, of the King and Queen and the two princesses, who always seemed to wear matching jumpers and skirts. They were shown walking through a garden, the princesses hand in hand and with little dogs jumping around their feet. The cinema audience gave little mutters of appreciation and

Kitty whispered, 'They look nice. Not like very important people.'

Finally, in the middle of September, we heard the gravelly voice of Winston Churchill announce that the Battle of Britain was over. The Luftwaffe had been defeated and the threat of invasion diminished. Jacob and I looked at each other after hearing it.

'This is not the end,' said Jacob. 'Far from it.'

'But it is a victory. Let's celebrate that.' I poured us a couple of whiskies, and when Alice came down, I poured her one as well.

'I think about those young men who are dead,' said Alice. 'Only slips of boys, they were. It's very sad.'

We were quiet then; a celebration didn't seem right. Finally Alice said, 'Mrs Penney says there's a barn dance at the church hall on Saturday night. Why don't you go, Miss Seffy? Take Miss Kitty. You too, Mr Weiss.'

'I am too old for dancing,' Jacob chuckled. 'No, I will look after the children and Xanthe. You go, Miss Weaver. You, Kitty and Seffy. Who knows? You may catch the eye of a fine young man.'

'Catch his foot, more like,' Alice laughed. 'But, if you're sure you don't mind, I would like to go.'

On Saturday, I helped Xanthe eat some supper and then took her to the bathroom. She was very weak and quiet.

'I'm going out to the village for a couple of hours,' I said when I'd got her back in bed and put on her bedside light. 'Jacob is staying in the house and all you have to do is ring your bell if you need something. He says he'll come and read to you.'

'All right.' Her breathing was quite shallow and I could

483

hear her chest rattling. She didn't seem to have enough energy to cough and I was relieved. I was terrified about what would happen if she did.

All the village was at the barn dance and as soon as we got into the hall, Kitty darted off to find Carol, while Alice and I stood by the door, feeling rather awkward. Not for long, though. 'Miss Weaver.' It was one of the fishermen that Alice spoke to when she'd walked the children by the harbour. He was in a tight suit, with a sprig of gorse tucked into his buttonhole and gave Alice an awkward little bow. 'It's a Valeta waltz,' he mumbled. 'D'you know how to do it?'

'I do, lad.' And she followed him on to the floor and cut a fine figure in her chartreuse frock and high-heeled shoes. I'd never seen her wear them before and worried that she'd fall over, but she was very graceful.

Dr Jago took my hand for the Dashing White Sergeant, whirling me round until I felt dizzy. 'My God,' I said, after the music stopped, 'I haven't done that since I was at school.'

'You haven't lived, Seffy,' he laughed. 'You should give up London and come down here permanently. Make a life for yourself.'

'I'm thinking of it,' I grinned and followed him to the trestle table where the fruit punch was being served by his wife.

'Hello,' she said. 'I haven't seen you for ages, you're all grown up.'

'I'm heading for thirty, Mrs Jago,' I protested. 'I've been grown up for years.'

'There's grown up and then there's grown up,' she said, giving me a friendly smirk. 'It's time you got married.'

484

I laughed and wandered over to where Alice was deep in conversation with some of the village matrons. In the months that she'd been here, she'd made many friends, and had become part of the local scene. I envied her.

It was hot in the hall so I went outside to breathe in the cool air. The lighthouse beam was flashing over the village, lighting up the granite stone cottages and the white-painted façade of the pub. The sea slapped against the harbour wall and clouds were flitting across the golden harvest moon. The good weather was about to break, I thought. Things were changing.

I was about to go back inside when the beam from the lighthouse illuminated the pub again and, in that instant, a familiar face stared down at the cobbled square from an upstairs window.

It was Monica Cathcart.

Chapter Thirty-Two

For a second I froze and then, before the lighthouse beam could come my way again, slid back into the shadow of the village hall, trying to collect my thoughts.

Monica Cathcart?

What the hell was she doing here? Nothing good, I was sure.

I looked again at the pub, its Lobster Pot sign swinging in the strengthening breeze, and then looked at the cars parked around the side.

I spotted Dr Jago's Sunbeam and the van that Mr Penney used to take the catch to market twice a week and one or two rusting old vehicles, which surely belonged to the young farmers who had come along to the dance, but there, amongst them, was a newer car, a gleaming maroon Bentley, which had attracted a few curious villagers. People glanced at it as they walked towards the hall and a couple of youngsters, bored with just staring, had climbed on to the bonnet and were daring each other to stand up. Some of their less daring friends and older lads, who were smoking outside the hall, were watching and calling out encouragement. A door opened and Alan Williams, the landlord, came out of the back of the pub, carrying a crate of empties.

'Clear off,' he shouted, dropping the crate. 'You young

buggers! I'll be on the blower to your pa, Johnny Roche, just see if I don't.'

The youngsters scampered away and when the older boys drifted back to the dance I took the opportunity.

'Mr Williams,' I called.

He looked around and then spotted me as I stepped, momentarily, out of the shadow.

'Miss Blake?'

'Can you come over here for a sec,' I pleaded. 'I don't want to be seen.'

He didn't question me, but wandered over as though he was going to look in on the barn dance. When we were side by side in the shadow, he said. 'Well now, Miss Blake. What is it?'

'That car,' I said, pointing to the Bentley. 'Did it bring visitors to the pub?'

'It did,' he nodded. 'Two ladies. A Miss Cathcart and a Miss Porter. Mind, they didn't drive. A man drove them, but he's not staying. I don't know where he went.'

He stared at me with some concern in his pale blue eyes. 'They asked about you, Miss Blake. Wanted to know where your house was.'

'Oh my God,' I breathed.

'I didn't tell them, so don't you worry. I said I didn't know. You're one of us, aren't you, and anyway I didn't like the cut of their jib. Especially that Miss Cathcart.'

'Thank you, Mr Williams,' I said. 'They're people I want to avoid.' I looked up at the window, where I'd seen Monica. 'I saw Miss Cathcart looking out just now but I don't think she saw me.'

'She's taken a bottle of gin up with her and I dare say

she won't be awake for long. You go back to the dance and enjoy yourself.'

'Thank you, Mr Williams.' But I knew I was going home.

'I'd watch out, though,' he said, as he turned to go. 'It won't take them long to find you. Not in this village.'

I slipped back into the hall and found Alice. 'I'm going home,' I said. 'D'you mind walking Kitty back when the dance is over?'

'No, of course not. But shall we come with you? Are you not feeling well?'

'It's not that. I'm a bit worried about Xanthe, but you stay and enjoy yourselves.' I saw the fisherman with the sprig of gorse in his buttonhole weaving his way through the crowd. 'Your beau's on his way again.'

'I'll give him beau,' said Alice with a rueful grin. 'He's full of beer and acting the giddy goat.'

I walked home quickly, up the steep lane from the village, using my torch to light the way. For some reason that I couldn't work out, I was frightened. Monica Cathcart was a horrible woman and a dreadful gossip and I knew she'd been keen to find out about Xanthe. She'd obviously come down here to learn more. But why bring her pal Jane Porter, and who was the man who'd driven them and wasn't in the pub?

A weasel suddenly ran in front of me, scaring me senseless, and the torch clattered from my hand and fell into the undergrowth on the edge of the road.

'Damn,' I said, scrabbling around in the grass and weeds to retrieve it. The bulb had broken so I had to walk the last few yards without a light. Rounding the final bend, I saw the house, a chink of light showing from the hall window where the curtains hadn't been pulled close enough. Then, with a gasp, I stopped, for in the driveway, beside the garage, was the shape of a man outlined against the white-painted doors and caught in the light of the moon, as the clouds raced by. I knew him. It was Karl, the American from Lisbon. Now I was really terrified.

I slipped back along the lane, until I got to the fence which surrounded our garden and hoisted myself over it. I ran back to the house and, as I'd done often as a child, climbed up to the veranda via the ironwork trellis which supported it and stood outside my bedroom window.

The house was dark and silent, almost as if it was empty. Quietly I opened the long window and slid in, walking quickly across the room. I stood beside the door for a moment, listening for sounds of life. There were none. Taking a deep breath, I opened the door to the landing. The lamp was on and, softly, I walked along the corridor until I came to the nursery and pushed open the door. I could have wept with relief when I saw the two children safely asleep in their cots, Marisol on her side with her toy rabbit clutched to her face and Max on his back with his arms flung out.

Thank God, I breathed. Now for Xanthe.

Her door was open. Looking in, I saw she was sitting up against her pile of pillows, her head turned to one side and her eyes closed. Jacob was in the chair beside her, a book on his knee. They were both very still. My heart was beating so loudly that it surely could be heard. Jacob looked up and put his finger to his lips.

'She sleeps,' he whispered.

I beckoned him with an urgent gesture, and Jacob, survivor of an internment camp, asked no question, but followed me down the stairs.

In the hall, Jacob looked at me. 'What is it?' he asked. 'You look worried.'

I didn't know what to tell him. Karl could still be outside, or could even be breaking his way in, to take Max. I gave an involuntary shudder and Jacob reached out and took my hand.

'Tell me, Seffy. I can see that something bad has happened.'

'I think we could be in danger,' I said. 'I saw a man outside who may be trying to take Max, and two women have come to the pub. They might be involved.'

He frowned. 'This sounds very strange to me. Who might want to take Max?'

'I'll explain later.' I looked at the door and wondered if Karl was about to break in. Jacob saw my face and walked towards the door.

'Don't open it!' I hissed and he paused.

'So,' he said. 'We act. First we lock all the doors and then we telephone the police.'

How strange, I hadn't thought of that. Previously, my adventures had all happened in countries where help from the police had not been an option.

'Yes, of course,' I said, and went to pick up the phone. I called the police and after briefly explaining the problem and being reassured that they were on their way, I took a breath and tried a different number. It was the one which Charlie had given me for his office in Whitehall. The switchboard operator told me that Captain Bradford wasn't there and that she couldn't give me any further information.

Jacob and I waited for the officers to come from Truro and when Alice and Kitty came home I told all of them what had happened in Portugal. I hated telling Jacob that Max, whom he loved, as he loved Marisol, was the son of a Nazi who delighted in persecuting Jews. 'Major von Klausen wants his son and I'm sure that the man who followed us in Lisbon was his agent.' I swallowed. 'I saw him standing outside this house.'

They listened with growing alarm.

'But you told me it would be all right,' said Kitty, her face pale. 'You did tell me that Max's father wanted to take him. But you said he could not, because he is in Germany.'

'I think he has friends here.'

'Oh!' She looked frightened and Alice put an arm around her shoulders.

'Look,' I said, trying to reassure her. 'There are four of us. We can easily protect the children and each other.'

'Quite right,' Alice said stoutly. 'I'm going to sleep in the nursery. Just let that bugger try and get past me.'

It was hard to explain the seriousness of the problem to the policemen from Truro.

'Major von Klausen is an important SS officer, with links to the highest command of the German government,' I said. 'He has no male children and he wants his son. I think he has organised a group here, in this county, to take him.'

The inspector looked astonished. 'And your sister was married to this man?' He raised his eyebrows to his sergeant who stood by the door, and the sergeant shook his head in disbelief.

'No,' I confessed.

'She was his mistress?'

I nodded, hating the distaste in his voice. 'But she isn't well,' I added. 'You can't question her.'

'She has TB,' said Jacob firmly. 'And has not very long to live. You must not upset her.'

The inspector glanced at Jacob. 'And who, exactly, are you, sir?'

'Inspector,' I said, my voice louder than I'd intended. 'Has someone looked for the man who was standing outside and has anyone gone to the pub to question Miss Cathcart? She is a fascist, you know. Before the war she was very much part of that movement.'

He frowned. 'Many people were followers before the war. It wasn't a crime.'

'It is now!' I shouted, and Jacob put a restraining hand on my arm.

'The man outside?' he asked. 'Have you captured him?'

The inspector shrugged. 'No sign of him . . . if he was ever here, and yes, Miss Blake, I have sent an officer to the pub. Miss Cathcart is being questioned even as we speak, although I don't know what good that'll do.' He looked around the kitchen, at the dresser with the fine china dinner service, which had been in the house since my grandfather's time, and then up to the pulley, where the children's clothes were drying. He directed his gaze back at me. 'I understand, Miss Blake, that you are some sort of a journalist. A writer. D'you not think that this could be . . . something from your imagination. I mean, spies? In Cornwall?' He grinned at his sergeant, who joined in with a chuckle.

'No,' I said coldly. 'It is not part of my imagination. And I do request that you leave a constable here overnight to guard us.'

'I can't,' he said, standing up. 'I haven't the men. But I will make further enquiries when I get back to headquarters. In the meantime, I suggest you all get some sleep.'

We were left alone, my urgent request for help put to one side.

'I'm still going to sleep in the nursery,' Alice snorted, and taking her mug of cocoa, which I'd made while we decided what to do, made her way upstairs.

'Go to bed, Kitty,' I said. I felt utterly drained and desperately needed to be on my own. 'You too, Jacob. There's nothing more we can do tonight. Tomorrow, I'll try phoning around; my solicitor, for one thing. He might know who to contact.' Of course, who I really wanted was Charlie. He'd know what to do.

Xanthe's bell was ringing and I went to her room. She was sitting upright against her pillows, her eyes bright and her cheeks suffused with the shell-pink glow from her bedside lamp. I paused, just to look at her. She was so beautiful that if it hadn't been for the thin dribble of blood at the corner of her mouth, she could have been a glamorous model from one of her magazines.

I took a cloth from her washstand and wiped the blood away. It was fresh.

'Have you been coughing?' I asked.

'Just clearing my throat,' she whispered. 'I think a man was in my room. A man in uniform.'

'Yes,' I said. 'It was a policeman. We thought we saw a prowler, but he's gone now. It's all right.'

'Oh.'

I waited for her to make a fuss, but she didn't seem interested. 'I'll get you a drink,' I said. 'What would you like?'

493

'I don't know.' Her voice was fading and her eyes wandered around the room. 'Is Wolf downstairs?' she said. 'Will he come up to see me?'

I didn't know what to say. She was obviously confused, the fever was taking over. 'You do seem awfully warm,' I murmured, and wetting the cloth again wiped her face and neck. Then I squeezed it out and laid it over her forehead. I'll get Dr Jago out in the morning, I told myself. A decision had to be made about Xanthe's care.

'That's lovely,' she whispered. 'The temperature here in Berlin is stupidly hot. I'm going to ask Wolf to take us to the seaside. Monte would be good, or perhaps Biarritz. Yes.' Her eyes shone. 'Biarritz. The wind comes in off the sea there and it would be wonderfully cool. It's just as smart, really. Royal families stay there, some even live there. And it has a casino. I went there once, with Binkie.'

I sat in the chair beside her, half listening, as she prattled on, until eventually she dropped off to sleep again and I closed my eyes.

I was woken at seven o'clock by Jacob, who gently shook my shoulder and put a cup of tea on the table beside me. He looked critically at Xanthe, who was lying low in the bed and breathing hoarsely.

'I think she is worse,' he said quietly.

'Yes.' I got up, and gently taking Xanthe under the arms lifted her upright. She weighed nothing.

'Mrs Penney is in the kitchen,' Jacob said. 'Shall I fetch her?'

I shook my head. 'Let her get on, I'll see to Xanthe and then I'll phone Dr Jago.'

It was odd that I didn't mind carrying out the most

intimate care for Xanthe, this little sister whom I'd despaired of and even loathed for a good part of my adult life. Again I remembered her as a child, a child who'd held my hand when we'd walked by the sea and who wanted me to tell her not to be afraid. Love and sympathy were my abiding emotions that morning, as I gently washed her and put her into a clean nightdress. She woke up and smiled sweetly at me.

'Are we having a fitting for new clothes,' she whispered, as I lifted her wasted arm into the sleeve of her nightdress. 'Oh, I do hope so. I like pink. Tell Mummy I must have pink.'

'I'm going to get you a cup of tea and some bread and butter,' I said, after I'd combed her hair. 'Then Dr Jago will come to see you.'

'All right,' she nodded and gave a bubbly little cough. I held my breath, watching her, but her cough was so weak that only a small trickle of blood coloured her lips and I wiped it away with the flannel.

'Here,' I said, putting the bell into her hand. 'I won't be a minute.'

Mrs Penney was in the kitchen.

'How is she?'

'Not good,' I sighed. 'I just telephoned the doctor. Can you get me a tray with tea and bread and butter?'

'I will. Then you must tell me what went on here last night. I hear that the police were at the house.'

'I saw a prowler, but they wouldn't believe me. There was a man standing in the front garden when I came home from the dance. I think he was connected to the two women staying at the pub.'

'The police might not believe you, but I do.'

I glanced at Mrs Penney, who continued, 'There are two great big footprints in the flower bed under the window. I noticed them when I walked up to the house.'

'Oh,' I said and paused, wondering what more to say. 'The thing is, Mrs Penney, and I can't tell you how I know it, but I think the man and those two women may be after Xanthe's little boy.'

She gasped and quickly looked over her shoulder as though Monica and Jane might be about to burst through the door.

'Don't worry.' I tried to reassure her, showing a confidence I didn't feel myself. 'We'll keep a lookout and now that the police have been told, I'm sure they'll investigate.'

'Well,' she gave herself a little shake. 'I'll tell 'em in the village to watch out for those people. We won't let them get up here, if we can help it.'

'Thank you, Mrs Penney. Now, I'll take that tray.'

Dr Jago came upstairs while I was feeding Xanthe. She'd managed a few sips of tea and, with encouragement, took a bite of bread and was mechanically chewing it. 'I'll wear my Schiaparelli tonight,' she said.

'Will you?' I stared at her. 'What for?'

'The Embassy ball, of course, you dolt. What are you wearing? Something dull, I expect. You have absolutely no idea how to dress. For goodness' sake, Seffy, go and buy a new frock.'

Once I would have scowled at her and told her to mind her own business, but now, realising sadly that she was drifting in and out of confusion, I simply chuckled and was glad to see her smiling too. When Jago came in, he grinned. 'What's this?' he said. 'Two sisters lazing

496

around inside when it's a lovely day. It's time you got better, Xanthe Blake.'

'Hello, Doctor,' Xanthe murmured. 'Have you trans-ferred to London now?'

He raised his eyebrows and looked at me. I shook my head.

'Well, Xanthe.' He took out his stethoscope. 'Let's have a listen.'

She fell asleep before he'd finished examining her and when we spoke on the landing, his face was sad and serious. 'I won't dress this up, Seffy. Your poor sister hasn't long now. Her heart is failing, she's confused, and she's bleeding from her lungs. It'll be a day, two at the most. You must prepare yourself.'

'I am prepared,' I muttered. 'As much as one can be.' He heard the catch in my throat and put an arm around my shoulder.

'I'll come back this evening,' he said. 'Go and have a cup of tea or coffee now, you look all in. I've heard about the excitement last night from Mr Weiss. Are you still worried?'

I nodded. 'I am, but the police don't seem to be. They think I'm imagining it.'

'And you don't think it's because you're upset about Xanthe? Are things getting on top of you?'

'No, they're not,' I said firmly.

'All right.' He walked to the staircase. 'I believe you. I've read enough of your articles to know that you've been in danger and do recognise it when you see it. I know a few people in Truro. I'll get in touch with them. Now, I must be off. See you this afternoon. It'll be about five.'

It occurred to me after he'd gone that I hadn't seen

the children that morning, so I ran downstairs. They were in the kitchen with Alice and Mrs Penney, having their breakfast. 'It's a lovely day,' said Alice. 'Quite warm for the time of year, so I think I'll take these two on the beach this afternoon. It'll give you a break and maybe you can have a sleep.'

'Yes, good idea.'

I took over helping Marisol with her bowl of porridge and warm milk and she rewarded me with a bright, cheeky smile. I laughed and gave her a kiss and then dropped one on Max's blond head. 'Is Kitty up yet?' I asked.

'Yes,' Mrs Penney said. 'She's gone down the village to get some messages for me. And,' she looked at the door to see if Jacob was about, 'I did hear that she was dancing with the same boy most of the evening. Joe Feather's lad, he is. On leave from the navy. But don't worry, he's a nice boy, or was before he went away.'

I looked at Alice and she shook her head. 'Miss Kitty's growing up. What is she now? Fourteen, fifteen? There's nothing much you can do, but I'll have a word with her, if you like.'

'Oh, thank you,' I sighed.

Before lunch I took the children in to see Xanthe. She was awake, staring out of the long windows, which I'd opened earlier to try and cool her down. The nets were dancing in the slight breeze and the smell of the ocean filled the room.

'I've brought Max and Marisol to see you,' I smiled.

Slowly she turned her head towards us and looked at the children. 'How sweet,' she said. 'Are they from the village? Did Mrs Penney bring them?'

'No,' I said. 'These are our children. This is your little boy.' I put Max on the bed beside her, where, stronger now, he sat up with his thumb in his mouth.

Xanthe looked down at him and then gave a weak grin. 'Silly Seff. How could I have a little boy? You're playing a prank on me.'

'I'm not,' I said. 'Don't you remember. You and Wolf. You had his baby.'

'Wolf?' She looked away to the window. 'I think I met a Wolf once,' she murmured vaguely. 'He had a nice uniform. It was black. Was he at Monte?'

Her eyelids were drooping and I took the children out of the room. A thought occurred to me then. When Xanthe died, who would be the legal guardian of baby Max? As far as I knew, von Klausen was still alive, but, then again, Max hadn't yet been registered. I held him close. He would be mine. He and Marisol. Brother and sister.

The telephone was ringing when I came back downstairs after leaving the children in the nursery with Alice. 'Hello,' I said wearily, too exhausted to care who was calling.

'Hello, Blake.'

'Charlie?' My heart did a few somersaults and I grasped the receiver more tightly as though I was holding on to his lapels. 'Oh, Charlie,' I cried. 'I can't tell you how I've longed to hear your voice.'

'That's what a man likes to hear.'

I pictured the grin on his face and laughed. 'Oh, God, I've wondered every day where you were and if you were safe.'

'I'm back in London and quite safe, dearest Blake. But listen, I haven't much time, I'm getting the train down to you; I'll be in Truro tonight. We've heard about your visitor and that bloody Monica and her pal are with him. We're taking it very seriously. You should see the police back at the house within the hour.'

I felt tears coming to my eyes. 'Thank God,' I whispered. 'And, Charlie; Xanthe's dying.'

There was a short silence, then, 'I'll be with you, Seffy. I'll hold your hand. I'm yours, for ever.'

'And I, yours,' I breathed.

When I went into the kitchen, Mrs Penney told me that there was a policeman standing by the front gate. 'I'm glad to see him,' she said fervently. 'I'll take him a sandwich and some tea.'

Xanthe slept through lunch and I didn't bother to wake her. I stayed in her room, reading a book and listening to her laboured breathing, occasionally standing up and walking through the long windows on to the veranda. In the afternoon Alice took the children down to the beach and I watched them. Max was so much livelier now, banging a little shovel on a tin bucket, while Marisol toddled down to the sea. A white motorboat was cruising slowly around the headland and into the bay and I watched it for a while and then went back in, to Xanthe. She was coughing, too weak to empty her lungs, but the constant racking motion produced larger and larger trickles of blood.

'I think I've got summer flu,' she gasped, before suddenly closing her eyes. I held my breath, staring at her. Oh God, I thought. Is this it? Has she died? But no. Her chest was rising and falling jerkily and I saw that she was only asleep. It was almost too much to bear and I walked back to the veranda and looked out again to the beach.

It was different. The motorboat had come closer in, rocking at anchor on the far side of our small bay and now there was a dinghy near the shore. A man was standing beside it. I frowned. Who dared come on to our beach? Couldn't they see the 'Private' notices?

I looked for Alice and the children and after a few seconds saw Alice between the rocks, close to the steps. She'd obviously strolled up there ready to bring the children in for their tea, but now she was lying down, with Marisol sitting beside her. Marisol was banging her little fists on Alice's chest and then turning to point down the beach. I followed her hand and choked back a breath. Monica Cathcart was walking quickly along the shoreline with Max in her arms.

Chapter Thirty-Three

I ran. Off the veranda and down the stone steps to the beach. I was racing so fast that that I nearly fell, just managing to grab the railing with one flailing hand to stop myself tumbling over and on to the rocks at the bottom.

'Jacob!' I screamed as I ran, 'Mrs Penney! Get the policeman!' I didn't stop to see if they'd heard me. I leapt off the bottom step and ran to where Alice was lying, unconscious. Marisol, tears streaking her face, held her arms up to me and I knelt down and picked her up.

'It's all right,' I crooned, holding her close. 'Don't cry, sweetheart.' I looked at Alice. She was beginning to move, moaning with pain, and when she struggled to sit up, I saw a bloodied gash on the back of her head.

'My God,' she groaned, putting a hand up to her concussed head. 'It hurts.'

I looked along the beach. Monica had seen me and was trying to run towards the dinghy. Max's thin wail echoed back, sounding like that of the seagulls as they followed the fishing boats. I had to get him.

Jacob was at the top of the steps, on his way down, and I thrust Marisol into Alice's arms. 'Hold her,' I said, 'Jacob's coming to help.' Kicking off my shoes, I started after Monica and my little boy.

She was a city person, not used to running and her

steps were short, sand clogging in her high-heeled shoes, and stride by stride I began to near her. The man suddenly looked up and I realised it was Karl. Swearing, he turned round and shoved the dinghy back into the surf. Monica glanced over her shoulder, her face white and terrified to see what had caused this, and so did I. The policeman was running down the steps, followed by Kitty and another officer.

'Wait for me,' she screamed, but Karl had his hands on the oars and was beginning to dip the blades into the water. 'Wait!' she cried again, and then, in a horrible act of panic, dropped Max so that he fell, face down into the little waves that were breaking on to the shore. Ignoring him, she waded into the sea, desperately trying to get to the dinghy.

My heart couldn't pump any harder than it did in the seconds it took me to reach Max and scoop him up out of the water. He'd stopped crying, his eyes were closed and his face was covered in sand. I wiped away the sand with shaking hands, a million unsaid prayers running through my head. Then he wriggled, and opening his eyes gave an indignant yell.

I wanted to weep with relief and hold him close, but I hadn't finished with Monica and Karl. 'Sit there, Max,' I said, putting him down, further back up the beach. 'Kitty will be here in a minute.' Then I waded into the blue-green sea.

The tide was coming in with the familiar strong Atlantic swell I'd known since I was a child. I'd swum in these waters for years, but Monica, used only to the country house pools of her wealthy friends, was struggling. She had started to swim, frantic to get to the dinghy, but the tide was overwhelming her, forcing her backwards, so that she was getting nowhere and was soon exhausted.

'Karl,' she shrieked, 'help me!' But Karl, just as desperate to escape, ignored her. Inexpertly plying the oars of the dinghy, he was heading for the white motorboat.

I swam, my strong, practised strokes quickly taking me to where Monica was thrashing her arms in the water, gasping and choking as the sea streamed into her nose and mouth.

'Help me,' she screamed, 'please,' before her head went under and then bobbed up again. For the merest second, I considered it, but images of the children came into my head and I grunted, 'No,' and saw her sink once more beneath the blue swirling water, before I set off after Karl.

He hadn't reached the motorboat, as his hands kept slipping on the oars, making the dinghy bounce on the swell. Unable to speed through the water, he watched me swim towards him. I saw him drop the oars and reach into his jacket and then, in a split second, a gun was pointing at me.

I heard the shot as I dived beneath the waves, then another as I swam underwater. When I came up I was on the far side of the dinghy and Karl was standing up, facing away from me while he searched the water, ready to take another shot.

Bastard, I thought, and heaved myself up against the side of the dinghy. It rocked violently and sent Karl tumbling, headfirst into the sea. The gun went flying. He won't be able to swim, I thought, as I climbed into the boat. He's too fat. But I was wrong. He came up a few yards away, water streaming from his hair and face, and swam strongly towards the dinghy.

'Bitch,' he shouted, and reaching the boat grabbed on to the side. Now, for the first time since I'd plunged into the sea, I was scared. He meant to kill me. Never mind the consequences.

I think adrenalin took over as I pulled on the fingers of one of his hands, trying to tear it from the side of the boat, but he was strong and his grip was relentless. Suddenly he let go and his hand shot out to grab my arm.

'No,' I screamed and writhed in an effort to force his fingers to give way, but he was slowly pulling me to the edge of the boat. If he got me into the water it would be the end. I was sure of that, but I thought of the children and knew I couldn't give up.

I reached behind me with my free hand. My fingers touched an oar and without really thinking, I wrested it out of its rowlocks and with a strength that emerged from some primal force, I lifted the oar and smashed it down on his head.

'Aagh,' he gasped. Letting go of my arm and the side of the boat, in one dramatic movement he went down beneath the surface. I waited, horrified, gripping the oar with both hands now, until he emerged, a bloodied mark on his head and his fingers reaching for the safety of the dinghy. I didn't think twice: I swung the oar with all my strength, crashing it into his face, hearing the bones shatter.

Seconds later he was floating, face up to the blue Cornish sky, just another piece of useless flotsam, as the swell slowly took his body towards the beach.

I lay in the dinghy, catching my breath, and gazed at the shore. Jacob and Kitty, with my children in their arms, were standing like statues, obviously horrified by what they'd seen. One policeman had dragged Monica to the beach, where she lay like a malevolent devilfish. He was trying to revive her and I watched, hoping she was dead.

After a while I sat up and waved to Jacob and Kitty, who called out in relief, and then, taking the oars, I rowed slowly to the shore where a group had gathered.

'Oh, Seffy,' said Jacob, tears flowing freely, 'thank God, you're safe.' And Kitty joined in hugging me so that Max, who was squeezed between us, gave another indignant yell.

Marisol reached up and patted my face and then grinned. 'Mama wet,' she said.

The policeman who had been bending over Monica stood up and came over to me. 'Are you all right, miss?' he asked. His shirt and trousers clung wetly to his body and his dark hair dripped water down his face. I guessed he'd gone into the sea to save Monica.

'Yes,' I nodded. 'I am now.'

He looked out to sea where the dark shape of Karl bobbed on the water. 'Is it worth while me going in after him?'

'The tide will bring him in,' I said. 'All you have to do is wait.' If my voice sounded dismissive and cold, I didn't care and, it seemed, neither did anyone else.

More policemen arrived as the afternoon turned to evening. Monica was taken under guard to the hospital in Truro, but Alice refused to go.

'You've got concussion,' said Dr Jago. 'That damn woman fetched you a hell of a crack. What was it? A piece of rock?'

'It was.' Alice repeated the tale she'd told the inspector

half an hour before. 'She said they were planning to have a picnic on the beach and did I know somewhere she could get water for her kettle. I told her it was a private estate and she would have to leave. I do apologise, she said, as nice as pie, and turned as if she was going back to the dinghy. I turned also, to take the children up the steps, and that's when she must have picked up the stone and hit me.' She took a sip of hot tea. 'I was a fool, you know. I never thought it could be the woman that Miss Seffy had warned me about. After all, she was well spoken and well dressed. It's not what you'd expect. Anyway, Doctor, I'm not going to hospital and that's flat.'

Jago grinned. 'I'm not going to argue. I wouldn't dare.' He turned to me. 'How about you, Seffy? Any problems?'

'I'm all right,' I said. 'In fact, I'm better than all right.' I was still buzzing with the adrenalin and finding it difficult to come down. 'I'm going up to Xanthe now.'

'Yes,' said Dr Jago. 'I'll come up too.'

She was awake, her fingers clutching the edge of her sheet and a bewildered look on her face. Mrs Penney was sitting beside her with a bowl of potatoes on her knee and a peeler in her hand. She looked up at me, her face sad, but her voice belied it and was full of her usual bustle.

'Don't you worry, Miss Seffy,' she said. 'I'm going to stay on this evening. I'll make you all a hot meal, because I know you'll need it.' She patted Xanthe's arm. 'I've done a nice bit of soup for Miss Xanthe, with jelly to follow.' She smiled at her. 'You'll like that, won't you, my lovely?'

Xanthe nodded. 'Thank you.' Her voice was tiny and breathless. 'Are we going to the pantomime?'

Mrs Penney, shaking her head, picked up her bowl of potatoes and went out of the room, and Dr Jago got out his stethoscope and listened to Xanthe's chest. 'Well, young lady, this cold is persisting. We might have to think of some different treatment.'

Xanthe coughed, struggling to bring up the phlegm that was blocking her airway and a spray of bloody mucus peppered her face and shot across her sheets. I got the cloth and gently cleaned her up. 'I'll change your sheets in a minute,' I said. I wanted to speak to Dr Jago, so I followed him out of the room.

'What's this new treatment?' I asked.

He sighed. 'Nothing really, except . . .'

'What?'

He wouldn't look at me, but stood examining a seascape which hung, with others, on the wall. 'This isn't going to end well, Seffy,' he said. 'Xanthe will have one big cough and a major vessel in what remains of her lungs will burst and she'll drown in her own blood. I've seen it before and there's nothing I can do except . . .'

There it was again. The except.

I took his arm. 'Tell me,' I begged. 'What can you do?'

'I can give her a big dose of morphine, now. It'll send her to sleep and she won't wake up.'

He was proposing killing her. I stared at him with my mouth open. The adrenalin which had fizzed around in my body for what seemed like hours had dispersed and I felt flat and weary. In the distance I heard a car drawing up on the front drive and thought it must be more police arriving, and wondered if I was going to be questioned about what I'd done to Karl. I'd killed him, hadn't I? I'd swung an oar at his head so that it burst like a pumpkin and I'd been glad. And what about Monica? Hadn't I left her to drown? I was guilty of murder and attempted murder.

There were people in the hall and Dr Jago stopped contemplating the seascape and turned his head to the stairs. I did too and then my heart did its familiar jump, for there was Charlie, racing up the stairs and taking me in his arms.

'Well, Blake,' he murmured. 'I hear you're the heroine of the hour.'

'I'm not,' I sobbed into his uniformed shoulder. 'I'm a murderer.'

'From what I hear, you killed a man who was trying to kill you. A German spy and someone who deserves no sympathy. And as for Monica.' He pushed away from me and, with his thumb, gently wiped away the tears on my cheek. 'It's a pity she didn't drown.' And he grinned and hugged me again.

'I gather this gentleman is a friend of yours, Seffy.' Dr Jago smiled and thrust out his hand. 'Peter Jago.'

'I am a friend,' said Charlie, for I was still mopping up my tears. 'Charlie Bradford.'

'Ah, the famous Charlie Bradford, whose excellent articles I've missed this last year. Captain now, I see.'

'Yes, sir. I'm working in Whitehall at the moment.'

'Well, I won't ask about that.' He turned to me. 'Seffy, I'm going home now to have my supper, and then I'll come back. Think about what I said and make a decision. Either way, it won't be long now.'

Charlie and I were alone on the landing where the only light was from the lamp on the half-moon table. I could hear Dr Jago calling goodbye to Jacob and then the sound of Jacob closing the door of Father's study. Alice was in the nursery at the far end of the corridor with the children, so when Charlie bent his head and kissed me, we could have been the only two people in the world.

'Oh, dearest Seffy,' he murmured. 'I do love you.'

I kissed him again, loving the strength of his arms around me and the feeling of security that he gave. When Charlie was around, I didn't have to think everything out for myself. We were a team and I wanted to be in his arms for ever. But then I heard Xanthe coughing.

'I've got to go in to her,' I said. 'Oh Charlie, she's so near the end.'

'Shall I come with you?'

'Please,' I nodded. 'But . . . don't be shocked by what you see or hear.'

I opened Xanthe's door and walked quietly to her bedside. 'Hello, Xanthe,' I said and picked up the glass of water that was on her table and gave her a little sip.

'I've brought Charlie Bradford to see you,' I told her and motioned Charlie to come closer.

She flicked her eyes up to him. 'He's a soldier,' she whispered and gave a little smile. 'Did you meet him at the Guards Ball the other night? I danced with the general. He said I was the prettiest little filly he'd ever seen.' She gasped a small, tinkling laugh. 'Silly old booby.'

'Let me lift you up,' I said. 'You're falling into the bed and that's not good for your chest.'

'My chest hurts,' she sighed. 'And it feels so tight. I've tried to cough up what's stuck there but I can't. If you bang me on the back, maybe that would work.' She looked at Charlie. 'Let him do it.'

'All right.' Charlie moved forward and prepared to bend over her.

'No!' I said, quickly, stepping between them. 'He's too strong,' I said to Xanthe. 'He might hurt you.'

'I wouldn't,' Charlie whispered.

'Leave it,' I whispered back and got the cloth and wiped her clammy face. Suddenly she started coughing and blood bubbled up between her lips and trickled down her chin. Within seconds she was gasping for air and her face was going blue. Terrified, I forced a finger in between her teeth and managed to pull out a viscous trail of bloodied mucus and a tiny grain of something more solid. She took a rasping breath and colour returned to her lips but tears were welling up in her eyes and tipping down her wasted cheeks.

'I want my mummy,' she wailed. 'Where is she?'

It was heartbreaking and I had to swallow the lump in my throat before I could speak to her. I looked at Charlie. He was shocked; pity was etched on his face. I sat down on the bed, beside my poor little sister. 'Don't cry, Xanthe, darling,' I said, putting my arm around her thin shoulders. 'Dr Jago is coming back here in a minute. He says he's got something that will make you feel better. You close your eyes for a few seconds and have a little sleep.'

She was asleep in a moment and I sat and held her hand while I made up my mind. Charlie perched on the end of the bed and reached over to stroke my arm. 'Christ,' he whispered. 'This is awful.'

'I know,' I said, 'but not for much longer.' I had decided.

Mrs Penney brought up a tray with soup for Xanthe

and offered to feed her, but I told her not to bother. 'Let her sleep,' I said. 'She's too ill to eat.'

'Well, I'll bring a tray for you and the captain,' she said. 'You need something solid inside you, Miss Seffy.'

When Dr Jago came back, he beckoned me out of the room and raised an eyebrow. 'Have you thought about what I said?'

'Yes,' I answered bleakly.

Charlie had followed me out. 'What?' he asked, quietly angry. 'What are you making her think about? Seffy's had a dreadful day and Xanthe is . . .' He shrugged. 'Well, you know how Xanthe is.'

'Tell him,' I said, fixing Jago with a long stare. 'We have no secrets between us.'

The explanation was brief and to the point and Charlie pushed a hand through his thick fair hair and gazed at me. 'What d'you think?'

'I think,' I said slowly, 'that Dr Jago is going to give Xanthe the morphine. She's in agony and the next coughing bout will finish her, but in a horrible way. So,' I nodded firmly to Jago. 'You go ahead.'

'Good girl,' whispered Charlie. 'It's the right choice.'

She was still asleep when Dr Jago opened his bag and got out the small bottle and a syringe. He drew up a dose and glanced at me. 'Ready?'

I held Charlie's hand and nodded.

Xanthe died half an hour later, without waking up, and I remained calm when I kissed her forehead, before drawing the sheet over her face. Then it hit me. My little sister was gone, and I was the last of the family. I broke down and wept into Charlie's shoulder, letting all the terror of the day, mingled with the loss of Xanthe, pour out of me.

'You are the bravest woman I've ever known,' said Charlie softly. 'And, remember, you aren't the last. You have the children. And you have me.'

'I know,' I said. 'And I will love you always.'

Jacob and Kitty, followed by Alice and Mrs Penney, came up to pay their respects to Xanthe and then we all went downstairs to the kitchen. 'Whisky, I think,' said Charlie, taking charge, and we sat around the table, drinking whisky, but not really talking.

Mrs Penney left before ten o'clock. 'I've made up a room for Captain Bradford,' she said as she put on her coat and gave me a meaningful look. I ignored her. I was going to spend the night in Charlie's arms. 'Anyway, the village will want to hear about Miss Xanthe. Poor girl,' she added and blew her nose. 'I'll be here at half seven in the morning.'

That night I cried again and Charlie held me close, allowing me to sob myself to sleep. When I woke it was early, before six, and I lay looking out of the window and reliving the previous day's events. It was almost too much, too much life and too much death, and I shuddered and wanted to forget.

Charlie stirred and in his half-sleep reached out and held me. I looked at his broad square hands and at his arms with their faint covering of blond hair. His face, without the perpetual glasses, seemed younger and less academic. Solid and dependable, like the faces of the young farmers who came into the village with their hessian sacks of potatoes and fresh-cut winter cabbage. I knew he would never let me down and would be a good father to the children, and yet . . .

The morning breeze blew through the open window,

sending the nets into a wild dance, and I thought of Amyas, of those magical nights when he'd first come to my bed, when it seemed that he and I existed in a different reality. How I had adored him, how the merest touch of his fingers on my body had transported me to the realms of ecstasy, so that I forgot everyone and everything. A tear squeezed from my eye and I sighed. That feeling would never return, I knew it.

'Awake, Seffy?' Charlie's voice was muffled and I looked down. His face was nestled in my shoulder and his arm lay across my breasts.

'Mm,' I agreed and turned to him. Making love with Charlie was wonderful, satisfying, and provided what I needed most. Comfort. And afterwards, when he sat up and looked around the room, I was suddenly thrilled that he was here, in my house by the sea. The place that I loved more than anywhere else.

'I don't know how you can ever bear to leave here,' he smiled. 'It's a fabulous house.'

'It is,' I agreed, 'and I'm not going to leave it ever again. I'll live here, with the children. I've got the businesses to see to, but we've got competent managers and Jacob is helping me with overseeing the books. The fact is, Charlie, that I've had all the excitement I could ever wish for. Now, I'll settle for dull.'

'And dull includes me?'

I laughed. 'You could never be dull. But what I'm saying is that from now on I'll be satisfied to get my excitement second hand, through you.'

'That's all right, then. Glad to oblige.' He sat up. 'I have to get going. Monica is being transported to London this morning, along with her stupid friend, Jane Porter.

We picked her up in Truro station, where she was trying to get on a train. I think she'd got in too deep and wanted out. Anyway, we'll question them.'

'What'll happen to Monica?'

He shrugged. 'A lot of interrogation, to get as much from her as possible, and then, who knows. It's up to the prosecutors. I think she'll be spared the rope, if she gives us enough info. But it'll be years in prison.'

'Good,' I breathed and thought of Max. 'You must see the children before you go.'

'Of course I must.' Charlie dropped a kiss on my cheek. 'And we have to decide about Max. That little boy needs a birth certificate. Are we heading to the register office again?'

I grinned. 'Yes, we are. You're about to become the proud father of another son.'

'I'm delighted,' he laughed. 'Now, where's the bathroom?'

We had breakfast on the veranda, in coats because the weather had turned colder and dark clouds were gathering on the horizon. Charlie had walked around the house and looked down at the beach and decided this was where he wanted to live too.

'How's Diana?' I asked. He hadn't brought up the subject, but I thought one of us should.

'Oh,' he said, looking out at the ocean, his face not betraying his feelings. 'She carries on, more confused now, and doesn't know me at all. Even Clarissa is a stranger to her, a kind stranger, though, who is greeted every day as though it's the first time they've met. In a way, I feel sorrier for Clarissa. She's quite broken up about it.'

I nodded. 'It's terrible for everybody.'

'And are you prepared to wait for me?'

'Of course I am,' I said and gave him a kiss. 'Never doubt me in that.'

He went back to London, promising to return for Xanthe's funeral, which was held the following week.

It was a quiet business, laying Xanthe to rest, in the little graveyard overlooking the sea. The weather was cloudy and a few spots of rain fell on us as Xanthe's body was lowered into the freshly dug grave. Those were the war days, when youthful death was a common part of life and so, although I mourned and the villagers expressed their sorrow, it didn't affect me as much as I suppose it should have. Charlie held my hand during the service, and Alice stood on my other side, a stout, reliable figure. Jacob and Kitty stayed at home to look after the children, and I understood. This was not their religion and it would have been difficult for them no matter how much they had become part of my family.

A few days afterwards, Jacob announced that he and Kitty were going home. 'I have loved my time here,' said Jacob. 'My new friends I will keep until the end of my life, but Kitty needs her education and I need to re-acquaint myself with the synagogue. Not going there every week has left a hole in my life, which I do need to fill.' He clasped my hand. 'Do you understand, dearest Seffy?'

'Yes,' I said. 'But, Jacob, I'll miss you terribly.'

'Ach, I'll feel the pain too, I know it. For you and the little children. But, if you will permit it, we will come down to Cornwall often. Kitty has made friends too and it is so good for her. She has become a girl again.'

'Of course.' I could feel tears pricking at the corners of my eyes. 'Your rooms in this house will always be ready for you. And your papers will be safe in the study.' I smiled. 'I'm looking forward to your book on Cornish seaweeds.'

After they'd gone I spoke to Alice. 'I know that being here wasn't what you signed up for when you took on the job,' I said. 'Am I making life difficult for you?'

She shook her head. 'Why would I want to go away from this place?' She laughed. 'It's a little bit of heaven.'

So we were left, Alice and I, with the children, who grew stronger and happier with every day that passed.

Chapter Thirty-Four

Soon after Xanthe died I went to London and Charlie came with me to the solicitor's, where we discussed how to register Max as my son.

'You are Xanthe's next of kin,' said the old lawyer, now returned to harness after his son had been called up, 'and there isn't any documentary proof that Major von Klausen is Maximilian's father. In the absence of a marriage or birth certificate, or even a will, it would appear that you are his legal guardian. And, if you want, we can start proceedings for a formal adoption.'

'Thank you,' I smiled. 'Please go ahead.'

So Max became my son and Charlie's name was given as that of his father. We went for a drink and a meal afterwards in one of Charlie's great little places. It was a tiny Greek restaurant in Soho, where the white tablecloths bore evidence of other diners and the elderly waitresses argued with each other in the back room. But we drank ouzo and ate a dish of pork marinated in vinegar and herbs.

'I'm going away at the end of the week,' Charlie said. 'Don't ask me where.'

I nodded. It was wartime, men went away. And came back, or didn't. I held his hand. 'Try and be safe,' I said and that was enough. It had to be, so I went home to Cornwall..

Somewhere, deep inside me, I did have an idea of what he was doing, but we never talked about it. On his infrequent periods of leave, we spent time together at the house and with the children. He loved Cornwall almost as much as I did and soon became a well-known and well-regarded visitor to the village. Mrs Penney kept hinting that we should get married, but all I did was grin and tell her that I wasn't in the mood to give up my freedom.

The children adored him. They called him 'Papa', much to his and my amusement. I suppose Alice had introduced the word and they kept to it, until they got older and he became Pa. He played games with them on the beach and spent hours on the floor in the nursery and the living room, building towers out of wooden blocks and making dens with the aid of old curtains. When Charlie was with us, we were a proper family but, of course, the war intervened and he had to leave us.

I started to write, as a hobby really, and then it became an addiction that had to be satisfied every day. I wrote first one and then another long novel set in the Victorian era and populated by strange, high-minded characters, who strived to improve the world by distributing wealth to men with ideas. Reading the pages back one day, I realised how ridiculous and boring it was and put the manuscripts into a chest in the loft and resolved to give up this new-found hobby. But, one day, I began to write an adventure story, set during the reign of Good Queen Bess. It worked and when I showed it to a publisher, he took it on.

'Can you write another,' he asked, 'in this vein?'

'I can try,' I said, still bubbling with excitement.

'Because, you know,' he said, 'people need to be taken out of themselves. Five years of war and they're exhausted by day-to-day reality. Something like this,' he waved my manuscript in the air, 'full of dashing courtiers and back-stairs intrigue, will be like a tonic.'

I went home from London on the train, grinning like a fool and surrounded by bags and packages. In my excitement, I'd used my coupons to get new clothes for the children and something smart for myself. I'd bought Alice an astrakhan hat, to go with her Sunday coat. I knew she'd love it.

I wondered what Charlie would say. He'd laugh, but would be encouraging.

'Go for it, Blake,' he'd say, and grin. 'Although why have you made Sir Walsingham look like me?'

'Because he was a spy?' I'd joke and I laughed out loud in the crowded train, imagining the conversation. I missed him, though. He'd been away now for months and Marisol kept asking, 'Where's Papa?' and Max would say solemnly, 'Papa gone.'

They were there, waiting for me, when the taxi dropped me at the house, my two little monsters, sitting on the stairs. It was past their bedtime but they'd persuaded Alice to let them stay up for another few minutes.

'Mama!' they squealed as I walked in, and threw themselves on me. They were allowed to stay up a little longer, as they opened the packages of new clothes and toys. Marisol had a wooden bagatelle game, which she loved, and I'd bought Max a little Bakelite telephone, which looked exactly like the one we had in the hall. There was such excitement that Alice and I had a job getting them up to bed, but, eventually, after a story and kisses, they were asleep and we came downstairs for a bite of supper.

'Here,' I said to Alice, opening the cardboard box with which I'd juggled all through the journey. 'This is for you.'

'Oh!' she said, exclaiming in delight as she drew out the astrakhan hat. 'It's right nice, that. You shouldn't have spent your money, but it's lovely.'

Mrs Penney had left us a fish pie, which we ate in the kitchen, with a glass of cider to wash it down.

'Did you see Mr Charlie when you were in town?' Alice kept glancing towards the hat, which she'd left on the dresser. She was dying to try it on.

'No,' I sighed. 'He's still away. But I did see Jacob and Kitty. They're well and send their love. Kitty has started at university and she suddenly looks so grown up. I know we saw them only a month ago, but somehow she seems different. Not so frightened now. New friends, I suppose.'

'She'll do well, that young lady,' Alice said. 'She's got a clever head on her shoulders.'

'I know,' I said. 'And she's still living at home, so Jacob and Willi aren't lonely. Jacob's coming to stay here in a few weeks' time, he says he misses the sea.' I smiled. That was exactly how I felt these days, when I was away from Cornwall.

'What about the flat?' Alice, carrying the dishes, followed me into the scullery, where I was pouring water into the sink. 'Are you thinking of letting it?'

'No, not the flat, but Father's house in Eaton Square has been requisitioned. Apparently it's being occupied by some American Embassy people. The housekeeper has stayed on to look after them.'

'I suppose that's all right. It was lucky to escape the bombing – and your flat, for that matter. All of us, indeed.' She bent down and riddled the Aga and then reached for the bucket of anthracite. 'What's it like in London? Still a mess?'

'It's better, I think. Not so much bombing now and the cinemas and theatres are all open.'

She went to the sink and washed her hands and then put the kettle on to boil. 'We're better off here, and no mistake. Now, a nice cup of tea, then off to bed, Miss Seffy. You look all in.'

A few days later Charlie rang.

'Oh, Charlie,' I gasped. 'How wonderful to hear you.'

'And you, Blake,' he answered. 'You can't know how much.' There was a little catch in his voice, which I put down to excitement, but then he said, 'Diana's dead.'

'I'm so sorry,' I said, but I wasn't really.

'Actually,' he continued, 'she died in March, six months ago, from measles, of all things, but I didn't know. I only came home the other day. Look, I'm getting a train tomorrow morning and I'll be with you in the evening.' There was a pause and then he said, with that same catch in his voice, 'If you still want me.'

I was puzzled. 'Of course I still want you,' I said. 'Nothing's changed.'

But the man I picked up from the railway station at Truro was a shadow of his former self. 'Charlie,' I called, running forward through the steam to the army officer standing next to the rear carriage, and then my steps faltered. He stood, holdall in his right hand and the sleeve of his left arm neatly pinned up.

'Oh, God, Charlie,' I breathed, almost to myself. 'What happened?' And I walked slowly towards him.

Charlie looked at me, despair and apprehension mingled on his face. 'Hello, Blake.' He sounded exhausted. 'Here I am.' He swallowed. 'Not quite the same as before.'

I looked into his tired blue eyes and felt a surge of

love overwhelm me. 'You are exactly the same as you were before,' I said.

'Even with this?' He jerked his head to the empty left sleeve.

I nodded. 'Even with that.' Then I grinned. 'I love you, you dolt. Don't you see? Nothing else matters.'

'Oh, thank Christ,' he said, tears glistening in his eyes and we clung to each other, while the train shuddered and steamed and the other passengers walked away.

At home, after greeting Alice and Mrs Penney, who had stayed on to make us a meal, he told us what had happened. 'It was a grenade,' he said and did a typical Charlie rueful grin. 'Got too close.'

Mrs Penney gave him a suspicious look. 'You said you worked in an office and the most dangerous thing you ever encountered was a letter-opener.'

'Did I?' He smiled. 'Well, they can be very sharp.'

Alice raised her eyebrows at that and then smiled. She touched Charlie's shoulder. 'I'm just glad to see you home, Mr Charlie. And I know the little ones will be too.'

His face fell a little at that and he flashed a quick glance at me.

'It'll be all right,' I said.

When we went to bed I asked him, 'Was it really a grenade?'

'Something like that. I'll tell you, one day.'

I watched him from the corner of my eye, wondering how he would manage to undress. He was slow, struggling a little with his tie and then the buttons on his shirt.

'Can I help?' I asked.

'No,' he shook his head. 'I can do most things, now,

except tying my shoelaces, but, Seffy, I'm nervous about you seeing my stump. It's pretty gruesome.'

'I'm nervous too,' I said, 'but, come on. Get that shirt off.'

His arm had been removed just above the elbow and the skin pulled down over the bone and puckered together in a rough fashion. I knew that the operation must have been performed in difficult circumstances and my stomach turned over at the thought of the pain he must have suffered. It wasn't nice to look at, but I bent and gave the remaining part of his arm a kiss. 'There,' I said. 'I've seen it now, so let's get on with our lives.'

He nodded, too full of emotion to say anything.

When the children raced in the following morning, Marisol, the leader, skidded to a halt when she saw Charlie's head on the pillow beside me. 'Papa!' she shouted, joyfully. 'You've come home,' and she launched herself on to the bed.

'Careful, sweetheart,' I warned, grabbing her around the waist. 'Papa's been hurt, so you mustn't be rough with him.'

'Where?' she demanded, furiously, her dark curls tumbling about her face. 'Which part can't I touch?'

Charlie had both arms in the bed, but, after a nod from me, he sat up and showed Marisol and Max the stump.

'Oh!' wailed Marisol, staring at it with horror, while Max sucked his thumb harder. 'Poor Papa. Did a naughty German do that to you?'

'Yes,' said Charlie, 'but I'm all right now, and despite what Mama says, you can be as rough as you like. Come on, give me a hug, and you too, Max. And take that bloody thumb out of your mouth.'

I left them tumbling over in the bed and listened to

the squeals of delight as I went into the bathroom and then down to make tea.

Later that morning we all walked on the beach. It was a cool, late September day and the sea was busy and rippling, working itself up into an autumn storm. The children had gone on ahead, Marisol, shoeless, dancing in and out of the surf and Max, ever the quiet one, collecting shells in his tin bucket.

'There's something I need to ask you,' Charlie said. He looked better today, not so tired and with the wind whipping through his hair and bringing colour to his cheeks, almost boyish.

'Oh, yes. What is it?' I was watching Marisol, making sure that she didn't get her dress too wet.

'It's this,' he grunted and when I turned to look at him I was astonished to find he had one knee in the sand. 'Seffy Blake,' he said. 'Will you marry me?'

I paused for the merest second. I knew I was going to say yes, but I wanted to preserve the moment so that in years to come, if someone asked me where Charlie proposed, I would be able to close my eyes and examine my picture of the setting. The beach, the restless waves topped now with white horses, and the sky. The hazy, blue sky, full of lumpy white and grey clouds, which scudded inshore on a strengthening wind.

I looked down at him, his face stiff with anxiety, as he waited for my answer and I got down on my knees in front of him.

'Of course I'll marry you, Charlie,' I whispered, taking his hand. 'And gladly.'

We kissed then and laughed. 'Shall we do it as soon as possible?' he asked.

'Yes.'

Spots of rain were beginning to fall and the children were running back towards us. 'Charlie,' I said, pointing to the headland. 'The little church above the sea, where Xanthe's buried. Can we have the service there? Then at least one member of my family will be somewhere close.'

'Yes,' he smiled. 'I'd like that.'

We told Alice and Mrs Penney when we got back to the house and got kisses from both of them. The children jumped around, joining in with the excitement, although they didn't really know what it was about. Still, they understood that everyone was happy.

That evening I phoned Jacob to tell him the news and to ask him if he would give me away. 'I know it's not your religion, Jacob, but you are as close as a father to me and I would love it if you could.'

'Ach,' he said and I heard the smile in his voice. 'Sometimes these differences in religion do not matter. Yes, dearest Seffy, I would be honoured to be your father for the occasion. And my Kitty will be so pleased. You are marrying a good man. A man I respect.'

The night before the wedding Charlie and I sat out on the veranda, wrapped in blankets, for it had turned much colder. He was going to stay that night at Dr Jago's house, for convention's sake, but we'd had supper at home and were now watching the lighthouse send its beam across the sea. All the preparations had been made and Jacob and Kitty established in their rooms. We had another visitor. Christopher, Charlie's younger stepson. The older boy had been killed on the beaches at Anzio, a fact that Charlie bore stoically although I know it distressed him. But Christopher had come to join in the celebrations and

I liked him straight away. He was a nice boy, in his last year at school, and eager to join up.

'Go to university, first,' Charlie had begged, when the subject was discussed over supper. 'For God's sake, get an education. The war's nearly over and we'll need bright people after it because there'll be so much to do.'

Christopher had grinned but said nothing. He was a young man who would go his own way.

'I like your boy,' I said to Charlie, as we sat and nursed glasses of brandy. 'You should have brought him here before. And Kitty is quite awestruck.'

Charlie laughed. 'Jacob would have something to say about that.' He looked out to sea and then took a gulp from his glass. 'Seff, there's something I have to tell you. I must say it now, and then if you want to call off the wedding you can.'

I gaped at him. 'What?' I asked, shocked. 'What on earth could be so bad?'

'It's about Amyas.'

I think my heart stopped beating. I'd tried not to think about Amyas for so long now that to hear his name mentioned was almost like hearing a forbidden word. Amyas, about whom part of me still dreamed. 'What about him?' My voice was no more than a choked whisper.

'I told you he was a traitor, or rather, I let you believe he was a traitor. That isn't true. He works for us. Has done all along.'

I looked away from him, to the dark sea. There was no moon tonight, not even the faintest glimmer, so beyond the regular beam from the lighthouse and the dim swinging light on the veranda, all was blackness. I could hear the surf crashing through the rocks on the edges of the bay and from behind me, the faint sound of conversation, as Alice and Jacob caught up with all the news.

'Say something . . . please.' Charlie's voice was hollow.

'Amyas told von Klausen about me taking a letter to Sarah. I know he did. Xanthe heard him.'

'Yes, he did,' Charlie confirmed. 'But von Klausen knew it anyway. He knew you'd been there, you were followed all the way, and informed on by someone at the girls' school in Berlin.'

'They wouldn't,' I gasped. 'They were all in danger.'

'Precisely. And that's why they would turn informer; to save a child, a parent, a husband, who knows? It's a sad fact, but it does happen.'

'But Amyas did tell him.'

'He dripped out information, useless stuff, generally, just enough to keep his cover intact. He knew that you were being watched, because he was their main watcher. And when von Klausen wanted to arrest you . . .'

'What?' I was shocked again.

'Oh yes, that was the plan, but Amyas stopped them. He said you were useful and would lead them to others.'

I sat back in the chair and thought about Amyas telling me the story of his childhood. 'He told me he was black-mailed by the British government into being an agent.'

'Did he?' Charlie shrugged. 'That was before my time, but I wouldn't be surprised. He was a thief and utterly amoral.'

I knew that, I thought, but I didn't care. Not when with one look he could compel me to follow him to the ends of the earth. Or could he? Hadn't I lost that feeling? Decided that I had grown beyond him and resolved to put him out of my mind when Charlie said that he was a traitor. I turned my head to look at my soon-to-be husband.

'Did you know that he was a double agent when I told you what Xanthe said?'

Charlie reached out his hand and took mine. 'I suspected it, but . . . I wasn't entirely sure and there was another thing.'

'What? What other thing?'

'Oh God, Seffy, you know what.' He sat up and glared at me. 'I was jealous, for Christ's sake. I've adored you for years, loved you . . . ever since we first met, but you didn't love me and I tried to live with it. In a way I'd accepted it, because how could I have competed with Amyas Troy? Look at me, I'm an ordinary bloke, interesting perhaps and with an interesting job, but compared to him in looks and fascination, nothing . . . but then there was a chance, and I took it.' He groaned. 'And now, this,' he looked down at his pinned-up sleeve. 'I'm in second place and always will be.'

My mind went back to that hotel in Portugal. How he'd paused before telling me that he'd always suspected Amyas and convinced me that he, Charlie, was the person I should be with. He'd lied to me and I should hate him. But I didn't.

I snatched my hand out of his and even as his face fell, I put both my hands on his shoulders. 'You listen to me, Charlie Bradford. As far as I'm concerned, you're in first place with me and always will be. I love you, with or without that bloody arm.' And I bent and kissed his mouth with as much conviction as I could muster.

'And Amyas?' he muttered.

I thought for a few seconds before replying. 'Amyas

is in the past . . . or no, not in the past, really. It's as though he doesn't actually exist, except in dreams. He's a fantasy, a fairy tale. And like a child who grows out of fairy tales, I've grown out of Amyas.'

'Oh, thank God,' Charlie sighed, and kissed me again. He didn't ask me if I still had those dreams.

And so, the next day, we married at the church on the headland, in front of our two children and our close friends. The sun came out and sparkled on the sea and gleamed red and gold on the autumn leaves. People from the village clapped us as we walked back to the house and I threw the place open for them to have a celebratory drink with us. Geoff, who had come down from London, gave me a kiss on the cheek. 'I've been dying to do that for years,' he said. 'I always thought you were the most charming girl ever to work at the paper. And a bloody good writer too. The job's open, whenever you want to come back.'

I shook my head. 'Thanks, but no. I've got a job, bringing up these children and being a wife.'

'Oh, well,' he sighed. 'I'll just have to settle for Charlie, I suppose.'

Charlie, glass in hand, came to join us. 'What's this?' He grinned. 'You expecting me back at my desk?'

'Of course,' said Geoff.

''Fraid not, chum. Not yet anyway. I'm in the army. I might be a bit damaged, but I've still got a brain and they want me to carry on.'

I squeezed his arm. He was going back to London in a week and although we'd miss each other, I knew that he'd be safe, or at least safer, given that we were still at war. No more missions to occupied countries.

We went to a hotel on Dartmoor for a couple of days'

honeymoon, but after one night away, we came home. 'Your house has spoilt me for other places,' he said.

'Me too,' I laughed, then gave him a fierce look. 'And it's *our* house.' I paused, then said, 'Maybe, when the war is over, we'll go abroad again.'

'Yes,' he nodded. 'Perhaps to that place in northern Spain, um . . . can't remember its name.'

'Idiot,' I grinned. 'Cadaqués. Why is it that I keep having to remind you? All right, that's where we'll go.'

But it wasn't the first place we went to when the war ended. We went to Germany, with Jacob and Kitty to look for her mother. Of course, we didn't find her, she had gone, murdered, along with her pupils in an extermination camp.

'I can't bear this place,' I whispered to Charlie, while we stood, waiting for Kitty and Jacob in the bleak office where the lists of the victims were being compiled.

'I know,' he said. 'It's hellish.'

We were learning every day of the numbers who'd been killed, and every day seemed like another nightmare. But Kitty had grown up and was made of stronger stuff than me.

'I'm going to stay on here in Germany for a while,' she said, when we returned to the hotel. 'They need people in the displaced persons camp. I have languages, and I can help. If I can't find my mother, I might find someone else's.' She looked at us, defiantly. 'I'm going to try, anyway.'

'You're a good girl,' said Jacob, wiping his eyes. 'And I think you do the right thing. But I will miss you.'

We came home to a quieter life. Charlie left the army and went back to the newspaper, but spent half of his time with us. He travelled abroad sometimes, managing well and continuing to write carefully researched and insightful articles.

My novels continued to sell – as my editor said, people needed to be taken out of themselves – and life continued without disturbance, until one day when Mrs Penney knocked on the study door. I was busy, checking through my latest chapter.

'Yes?' I said, not looking up.

'There's a gentleman to see you, Miss Seffy.'

'Is there?' I asked. 'Who is it?'

'A Mr Beaumont.'

'Do we know him?'

Mrs Penney shook her head. 'No, Miss Seffy, but there's something, I don't know . . . something about him that I almost recognise. Perhaps I saw him, a long time ago.'

I gazed at her and suddenly felt dizzy. Could it be? 'Show him in,' I said, with a dry mouth, and stood up.

It wasn't him. The man who came into my room was my age, thin and slight with a balding head and a livid scar across his face, which dragged his eye down so that he was almost unrecognisable. But I knew him.

'Percy?' I asked, walking towards him with my hand outstretched.

He gave a crooked smile. 'Yes, Seffy. How very nice of you to know me.'

'I remember everything about that summer,' I said. 'It will live with me always.'

'I thought it might,' he nodded. 'And that's why I've come. Amyas needs you.'

Chapter Thirty-Five

Provence, July 1947

I looked through the car window at the fields of lavender and sunflowers which spread in a glorious patchwork across the landscape. Earlier we had driven past acres of vineyards, their regimented rows in full leaf, and I watched men and women stroll between the lines, tying the vines in place and hoeing out the weeds. Closer to the city of Avignon, orchards of peach and apricot, their blossom finished now, flourished in the balmy weather. It was exquisite countryside, rich with all the beauty and promise of bounties to come.

I rolled down the window, allowing the sweet-smelling air into the car, and closed my eyes to let the perfume bathe and calm me. The nerves which had tingled for days now were jangling at full pelt and I wondered, yet again, if it was wrong of me to travel here. I should be at home, in Cornwall, with my husband and my children, in a place that could rival Provence for its scenery.

Oh, certainly Cornwall was beautiful, but that beauty mainly came from the sea, the ever-changing sea and the fresh ozone-filled air, which made you feel alive and excited. I never tired of it. But here, it was different; a painted landscape, dreamlike and magical.

'Nearly there,' said Percy, and, opening my eyes, I

saw that he was smiling his crooked smile at me. 'The house is up here.' We were winding up an empty road towards one of the *villages perchés*: exquisite fortified villages built on top of small hills of white bauxite or red clay, where houses clustered around a castle and a church and small lanes led you from one fantastic view to another.

'Are we going into the village?' I asked.

'Not quite. We live just outside. More private.'

I nodded. Amyas would like that. He'd teased me about having a private beach in Cornwall, but he'd loved it. But then he'd loved everything about Summer's Rest. The white-painted rooms, the blue hydrangeas in the garden, the veranda where we sat and looked out on to the bay and my bedroom where we'd . . . I caught my breath. Now wasn't the time to be thinking of that.

But ever since Percy had walked into my study two weeks ago I'd thought of little else.

'Needs me?' I'd taken a huge breath and clasped my hands together to steady them. 'Why does he need me?'

'Because he wants to see you before he . . .' Here Percy's voice faltered.

'What?' I asked but I knew the answer.

'He's near the end.' I could see tears in Percy's eyes.

'I don't understand,' I said, my voice choking. 'What illness does he have? Can't it be cured?'

'I've promised not to say.' Percy frowned. 'Don't ask me, Seffy, but please, I beg of you, come and see him. Soon.'

'But where is he?' Could he be in London? I wondered. A train ride away? Been there all this time, while I'd lain beside dear Charlie and tried not to remember?

'He's at his house in France. I'm going back tomorrow,

but if you'll come, I can meet you in Avignon and take you to him. Please, Seffy. He wants to see you, so much.'

His house in France. He'd told me about it and how we would sit on his terrace and watch the sun go down. I tried to remember where we'd been when he'd told me. Was it here? No. It had been in the hotel in Lisbon, when we went to rescue Xanthe.

I gazed at Percy, my mind full of conflict. Amyas needed me, Percy had hinted that he was dying. I felt rather faint and sat down suddenly. 'I will try to come,' I said, my voice low. 'But it will take me a couple of weeks to make the arrangements. Besides, I have to talk to my husband first.' Charlie had a right to know.

He was home that weekend. He'd been in Greece, reporting on the civil war, and looked dirty and exhausted when I picked him up at the station.

'It's terrible,' he said. 'Civil wars are so much worse than wars between nations. Everyone hates and everyone lies.'

'Who'll win?' I asked, driving swiftly through the country lanes. It was May and the hedges were bright with white blossom, and as we got closer to home tantalising glimpses of the sea sparkled on the horizon. The sun had come out to welcome Charlie home.

'I don't know,' he sighed. 'It depends on whether America will support the right-wing forces. And, anyway, it'll go on for two or three years yet. Nobody seems ready to give up.' He sighed and looked out of the window. 'Don't let's talk about it, now. Tell me what you've been up to and how the children are.'

'The children are fine. Marisol is doing tests at the moment to see if she will be able to take the exams to go into big school. She will, of course, and Charlie, that's something we have to talk about. Are we going to send her to boarding school? And if we are, which one?'

'Well, you went, and I went and it didn't do us any harm. But, Seff, I don't want to send her to some boring place where all she'll learn is how to be a lady. She needs to have her horizons widened, then she'll fly.'

'Yes,' I nodded. 'I want that too and I saw a newspaper article about a school in Somerset; it's co-ed and very sporty. She'd love it. She could have a couple of years at the high school here first, so that she can keep all her friends and then go on there.'

'And Max?'

'Well he could go too. He's awfully bright, Charlie. The teachers can hardly keep up with him.'

'Doesn't take after his mother,' Charlie laughed, and I laughed too. But that meant that he took after von Klausen and I gave myself a little shake. Since the end of the war I'd been increasingly concerned about him. He'd disappeared, even though he'd been on the Allies' list of wanted men. What if he'd survived and came looking for his son?

Charlie put a hand on my thigh. He knew what I was thinking, he always did, it's what made us who we were. 'Don't worry, Seff. We'd have heard from him by now. And there's nothing he can do, anyway.'

I wasn't so sure.

After supper I told him about Percy's visit. 'He came here once, before war, and was talking about going to Spain. Do you remember him?' I asked. 'He was there, when you joined the Republicans.'

Charlie shook his head. 'People did speak about him, but I never met him.' He sat back and thought. 'He joined the regular army, when we declared war. I often heard his name mentioned, a brilliant tactician, ended up a colonel, I think.' He turned to look at me. 'What did he want?'

I took a deep breath before saying slowly, 'He wants me to go to France, to see Amyas.'

There was a long silence and then Charlie got up and walked on to the veranda. After a minute I went to join him. He was sitting, hunched up, on one of the chairs, watching the silver moon rise over the sea.

'I thought we'd finished with Amyas Troy,' he muttered. 'My God, Seffy, are you never going to be free of him?'

No. Oh God, no, I wanted to shout. Don't you understand? I'll never be free of him. He's part of me.

But I didn't voice any of that. 'I think we will be finished with him soon,' I said slowly. 'Percy more or less said that Amyas was dying.' I paused, waiting for the fluttering in my stomach to subside. 'He wants to see me before he . . .' I couldn't finish the sentence.

'Why?'

'I don't know.'

Charlie got up. 'I'm tired,' he said. 'I'm going to bed.'

After a few minutes I went to bed also and turning my back to him gazed out of the window at the moon. I didn't know how to handle the situation. The last thing in the world that I wanted was to hurt Charlie, but I knew I was going to France. Nothing would keep me away.

His voice came out of the darkness. 'Where is he?'

'In Provence,' I said. 'Near Avignon, apparently.'

'When are you going?'

I sat up. 'How d'you know I am?'

'We both know you are,' he muttered. 'Nothing will keep you away.'

I touched his shoulder. 'Come with me? Please?'

'Why would I want to see you with your lover?' Charlie's voice was muffled as he dug his face into the pillow. 'You must be mad.'

It was a long night and I stayed awake for most of it. I was angry with Charlie for not understanding that I had to go to France. And how could he call Amyas my lover? I hadn't seen him for seven years and in that time I'd been entirely true to Charlie. But Amyas wanted me and I had to go.

I got up at dawn, even before the children were awake, and went down on to the beach. It was ages since I'd swum across the bay and in that misty half-light I took off my nightdress and started out. It was a foolish thing to do, really, but with every stroke I felt stronger and calmer. Amyas and I had been together here, and made love in the surf afterwards. The memory was very strong, and I smiled as I swam through the flat green water.

When I walked out of the sea, Charlie was waiting for me, holding out a towel. I wrapped it round me and we sat on the rocks at the bottom of the steps. I was cold now and Charlie put his arm around me.

'I'm jealous,' he said, simply. 'I always will be. No matter what you say, I know you still think of him, still imagine that it's him, not me, beside you.'

So I lied. 'You're wrong,' I said. 'I told you three years ago that I'd got over him and that I love you. Nothing has changed.'

'But you still intend going to him?'

I nodded. 'But, come with me, Charlie. You matter to me far more than he does.'

'And if I said I didn't want you to go, you'd stay at home?'

I held my breath. 'Yes,' I nodded. The thing was, I knew him. Charlie would never forbid me from doing anything.

He groaned. 'I'm not going to stop you, Seffy. You know that. So go. But come home, to me.'

I went to France and put up at the Hôtel d'Europe in Avignon. After I'd settled in I phoned Percy and told him where I was.

'Oh, Seffy.' His voice at the end of the phone sounded more relieved than welcoming. 'I'm so glad. He's waiting, but I won't tell him. I'll let it be a surprise. I'll come for you at midday tomorrow.'

I changed my outfit twice the following morning; I, who normally didn't care about clothes, was determined to look my best. The weather was so much hotter than at home and I finally settled on a pale green cotton blouse and a stone-coloured skirt. The green picked up the colour in my eyes and brought out the copper in my hair, and I stared at my reflection in the mirror, wondering if I'd altered over the years.

I waited anxiously in the lobby, too twitchy to read the newspaper, and when Percy came in, I jumped up. It was strange of me to be so nervous and so eager, but I couldn't help it and gabbled stupidly about my journey and the hot weather, anything really, as he led me to the door. When we got outside I had a surprise. The car parked at the front of the hotel was one I recognised.

'Oh!' I said. 'I've been in this car before.' It was the cream and black German Wanderer, in which Amyas had driven Charlie, Marisol and me to the coast, in Spain.

'Have you?' asked Percy, surprised. 'Amyas is very fond of it. He says he bought it in Spain.'

'He stole it in Spain, more like,' I laughed. 'I remember shouting at him for having such a flashy car, when we were trying to escape.'

Percy grinned. 'That's Amyas,' he said, but the grin turned into a frown and then to a face full of sadness.

'How long have you been here?' I asked, as we manoeuvred through the broad streets of Avignon.

'Oh, since the end of the war. Amyas and I have been in contact for years, in Spain, and all through the war. Both my parents were killed in the Blitz, so there was nothing left at home for me. Not even the home. Then, out of the blue, he invited me to come and stay and I've never left.'

'His illness,' I ventured. 'What is it?'

'Let him tell you.'

He would say no more and I was left wondering.

I could see the villa ahead of us, white and low, with archways opening on to terraces. We pulled up in front of stone steps and Percy jumped out. Walking around to my side, he opened the door for me. 'Come on in,' he said and led the way up the steps.

Now my nerves were really tingling and I could barely put one leaden foot in front of the other as I walked into the cool expanse of Amyas's house. After the brilliant light outside the interior seemed dark, and it took a moment for my eyes to adjust. Gradually, I could make out that the room I was in was beautiful. Furnished with comfortable chairs and sofas, and with *objets d'art* scattered around – porcelain and silver vases, small bronze figurines. The walls were covered in paintings of different styles and different eras but all . . . wonderful. My eyes went straight away to one painting, which, when

I moved closer, I recognised immediately. It was a picture of a young woman, sitting on a bed, looking as though she was waiting for someone. That painting, by Charlotte Salomon, had hung in Sarah Goldstein's flat in Berlin.

'Recognise it?'

I closed my eyes and waited until my heart calmed before I turned around. He was there, beautiful as ever, with his amused dark eyes smiling at me. Now, his hair was completely grey, but other than that . . . No, not other than that. My eyes trailed down past his white suit. Amyas, my Amyas, was in a wheelchair.

I didn't rush towards him, but walked, until I was standing in front of him. Then I knelt down. 'Hello, Amyas,' I said.

'Hello, darling Persephone.'

No more words would come and I wrapped my arms around him, while he bent his head and kissed me. Nothing had changed, his kiss was the same, strong and probing, and in that moment he still had the power to transport me. I had surrendered again, to that bringer of magic.

After a while we both drew back and stared at each other. 'Percy thought he'd surprise me, but I knew you'd come.'

'I knew I would too.' Then I laughed and he laughed as well and kissed me again.

'D'you like my house?' he said.

I looked around. 'I've only seen this room, but it's lovely. You have so many beautiful pieces.' I paused. 'I won't ask how you acquired them.'

'Best not, darling girl.' he laughed.

I looked at the Salomon painting. 'That was in Sarah Goldstein's apartment, in Berlin.'

'Yes,' he nodded. 'I think her girl should have it.' He frowned. 'I can't remember her name.'

'Kitty.'

'Yes, Kitty. You must take it to her.'

Percy came in then. 'Lunch is ready. Shall we eat?' He grabbed hold of the handles of Amyas's chair and pushed him through the long windows on to the terrace. For a second I watched them, my heart breaking at the sight of that exciting, vital man confined in such a cruel way, but then, biting my lip, I followed them through the windows. We ate on a shady terrace at the back of the house with its broad expanse of red-tiled floor and white-plastered arches. The view through the arches was breathtaking. All the countryside lay in front of us, fields and vineyards and distant villages of red-tiled houses. There was a lake, surrounded by trees, and on the horizon the blue Luberon hills rose into an azure sky.

'Oh!' I said, entranced.

'Like it?' Amyas grinned.

'Yes,' I breathed, stunned by its beauty.

A woman brought a platter of charcuterie and a bowl of salad to the table. She was about my age, small, dark-haired and rather pretty. I noticed that as she passed Amyas, on her way back to wherever the kitchen was, she put an affectionate hand on his shoulder. He saw me looking and gave a grin.

'It's not entirely gone,' he said.

'What hasn't?' Now he was going to tell me why he was in a wheelchair.

'The ability to . . .'

'What?'

'To recall a memory, perhaps.'

I looked at Percy, who was opening a bottle of wine and deliberately not looking at us, and then to Amyas. This couldn't go on. I had to know.

'What is it, Amyas?' I asked. 'Why are you in that chair?'

'Because, my darling Persephone, I can't walk. My back is broken.'

In a way, I was relieved. Terrible though his words were, he hadn't announced a death sentence. He didn't have some devastating illness, in which he had to count the days. I'd seen men coming home from the war paralysed, in wheelchairs, but beginning to make a new life for themselves. But then I remembered Percy begging me to come here, with tears in his eyes. There had to be more.

I reached out and took Amyas's hand. 'I'm so sorry,' I said, looking into his eyes.

He gazed back at me, searching my face, and I saw the heartbreak that was washing over him. We had to talk, but later, when we were alone.

'This looks delicious,' I said brightly, putting a few slices of garlic sausage and a spoonful of cold, sautéed peppers on to my plate.

'It will be,' Percy said, pouring wine into my glass. 'Claudine is a good cook. Just wait and see what she's made for supper.'

As we ate, I talked about the children. I had photographs of them, and went to my bag to get them. 'Look,' I said. 'Here's Marisol, on the beach.'

Amyas looked at the picture for a long time. 'Do you remember that night?' he murmured.

'How could I ever forget it? But, as you see, she's brilliant.'

'How old is she?' asked Percy, unaware of the nuance, taking the black and white snap and studying it.

'She's nine,' said Amyas.

'And the image of Amyas,' Percy laughed. 'I'm afraid there's nothing of you in her face, Seffy.'

Amyas and I smiled at each other. 'No, there's nothing of me in her,' I agreed.

'And who's this young man?' He was holding a photograph of Max.

'He's my sister's son. My sister died and I adopted him.'

'Was his father killed in the war?'

I took a gulp of wine. 'I don't know. He was a Nazi officer. And not a nice man.' I sighed. 'I worry that he'll come and claim Max.'

'He won't.'

I stared at Amyas. 'How d'you know?'

'Because he's dead. I shot him, in . . .' he tapped a finger on the table, thinking. 'It was in about 1944, I think. He'd worked out who I was, what I was. So I killed him, in his house in Berlin.'

'Oh, thank God.' It was as though a huge weight had rolled away. 'Charlie will be so relieved.'

Amyas gave a short, rather sour laugh. 'I didn't do it for him,' he said. 'The man with the ready-made family.'

'But he will be glad,' I said sharply, scowling at him. 'And he's a wonderful father.'

After we'd enjoyed the fruit and cheese and the little cups of strong black coffee that Claudine brought in, Percy took Amyas away and I sat on the terrace and looked at the view. I had a lot to think about and so many questions to ask. How had he got his injury and

544

why was Percy so concerned? What more had I to learn?

It was late afternoon and the sun was quite low in the sky when they returned, and Amyas and I were alone at last. I studied his face and saw that beyond his still handsome features some other emotion looked out at me. It was as if . . . and here, my mind went back to that day in Cornwall, when he'd first left me; it was as if he'd already moved on.

'How did you get your injury?' I asked. 'Tell me honestly, it's too important for some throwaway remark.'

'Oh, here we go,' he grinned. 'The investigative journalist is still lurking in that brain, despite the new-found concentration on popular novels.'

I blushed, wondering how he knew I wrote novels, and then sighed. Of course he knew. 'Never mind that. Tell me,' I demanded.

Amyas looked away from me, out to the landscape, golden now with the hot, late sun gleaming on the fields and picking up glittering reflections from the little lake. 'I was shot,' he said slowly, 'by a firing squad.'

'But why aren't you dead?' I was astonished.

'The officer sent to perform the *coup de grâce* thought it wasn't necessary. I suppose I must have looked dead. Then, after the soldiers went, my friends rescued me and brought me to a doctor in the village.' He sighed. 'I was not paralysed before the doctor's attentions, but I was after. He wasn't good, and perhaps was drunk. We all drank too much then.'

'But he saved your life.'

Amyas shrugged, slowly, as though this movement

545

was a new ability or perhaps painful. 'Is it a life? I think I should have died.'

'It is a life,' I insisted. 'You have money, people who care for you, and this lovely house. There are so many things that you can enjoy.'

He shook his head. 'No. I don't want to live like this.'

Claudine came on to the terrace with a bottle of wine and some glasses. Amyas turned his head and watched her. 'Look at her,' he said angrily. 'She should be in my bed, like she was when we were fighting. Now she can only make me food and wash me. No, Persephone. This is not a life.'

I began to get an inkling of why Percy had come for me. I was here to cheer Amyas up, to make him see that this was a life worth living.

'You have a daughter,' I said. 'A wonderful, beautiful daughter. I would love to bring her here to see you. Of course, she doesn't know about you, but, when she's older, I'll tell her.'

'No,' Amyas shook his head. 'I think it might destroy her. You and Charlie are her parents. Leave it at that.'

He took my hand. 'Are you happy, Persephone? You and Charlie and the two children? Do you ever think of the old days?'

'I am happy,' I said. 'Charlie is a good man and I do love him.' I had a sudden thought. 'He lost his arm, did you know that?'

Amyas nodded. 'I knew. He and I worked for different branches of the same organisation and I was told he threw himself on top of an injured comrade when they were ambushed. Very noble of him.'

He said that last very coldly and I was suddenly

546

furious. 'Stop it, Amyas.' I said. 'Charlie is decent, always has been. He's made me very happy and secure. Why are you so jealous?'

'Why? You ask me why?' He threw back the rug that covered his legs and I saw that he was wearing shorts and that his thighs were withered, the muscles gone and the skin mottled and blue. 'You know why.'

'No,' I groaned. 'That's not why. You were jealous years ago. And so is he. You're as bad as each other.'

Amyas looked down at his lap, then back at me and said, 'Not any more.'

'Don't go.' I tightened my hand around his arm and tried to pull him back from the doorway through which he was staring. 'Please,' I begged. I didn't mind the tears that were running down my face. 'Stay. Stay with me.'

'No.' He shook his head. 'This is something I have to do. So let me go.' He gently pushed me away.

I got up then and left him on the terrace while I walked into the house and out through the front door. I wanted to leave, to go home to Cornwall, to my family. I couldn't bear to be with this shell of a man who had not only lost the ability to walk but who had lost the most vital thing about him. His charm had withered along with his legs.

Percy came to find me where I was sitting on the stone wall which surrounded the house. The sun was sinking into the mountains and I could hear the cicadas in the oleander trees beginning to chirp their evening chorus.

'Has he upset you?' Percy asked.

I nodded.

'He does that. Often. But not for much longer. Come on in. He wants to say goodbye to you.'

How strange, how sad, I thought, as I trailed reluctantly

back into the house, that it should end like this. Hating each other.

He was where I'd left him, a glass of white wine in his hand, but, when he looked up at me and grinned, he looked different. The old Amyas was back, in charge of life.

'Darling Persephone,' he said. 'I've got something for you. There.'

On the table was a notebook and I reached for it. 'Don't look at it yet,' he said. 'It's for when you leave.'

'What is it?'

'My poetry, of course. Remember I said that I wanted to be a poet. Well, these poems are for you.'

'Thank you,' I said and felt tears pricking at the corners of my eyes. 'Are you feeling better?'

'Yes.' He nodded slowly. 'I've decided to take charge again.'

'Good,' I smiled. 'Like the old Amyas.'

'Like him.' He stared out at the landscape, which was slowly dissolving in the blue mist. 'Persephone, my darling, which do you think was the best time for us? The first, at your house on the beach – or in the wood in Spain? The hotels?'

'The best time? God, Amyas,' I murmured, 'every time I'm with you is the best time.'

'Even now?'

'Even now.'

'Then I'm happy.'

We sat holding hands as the night descended. We didn't speak any more and when the glass dropped from his grasp and the empty bottle of pills slid off his lap, I still didn't move.

Epilogue

Amyas was buried in the graveyard of our little church above the sea. He had arranged it all, entirely confident that I would comply with his desires. He'd even written to the vicar and got permission.

I didn't go to visit him often and Charlie never, but now and then, when a restless mood came upon me, I would set off and walk along the headland until I came to the church. And, passing by the old stone building, I would wander through the cemetery, pausing for a while by Xanthe's grave, before walking on to the plain headstone that stood close to the wall. From here you could gaze out to sea, watching the boat with the red sail tack across the bay and, if you turned sharply, you could see my house.

In my fanciful moments I wondered if Amyas sat on the wall and waited to see me walking on the beach or swimming across the bay. Did he see his daughter? Admire her spirit, which was so like his, and be proud of her beauty?

I brought the painting back to Kitty, explaining that the man who had saved her had also saved the picture and wanted her to have it.

'I must thank him,' she said. She was home on leave from her work with the Displaced Persons Commission, looking so grown up that Jacob and I barely recognised her.

'You can't,' I said. 'He's dead.'

Was there a catch in my voice? I think there must have been, because she took me in her arms and hugged me. 'Don't be sad, Seffy. You've got us.'

Jacob put his head on one side and smiled at me. He was holding a dachshund puppy, Willi Two, who was a handful. Old Willi had died in the winter and although Jacob had said he was finished with dogs, I'd ignored him and bought the puppy for his birthday.

'I'll be in Cornwall next week,' he said. 'Max said he wants to learn German. Ach, he's a clever one that boy.'

'Goodness, he's already got me teaching him French and he badgered Charlie to teach him his times tables,' I said. 'Well, we'll look forward to seeing you. Alice too.' I smiled when his cheeks went pink.

I went then to see my lawyer. It was the son, happily returned from the war, unscathed and eager to relieve his father from work.

'The new property, Mrs Bradford, in France. It is, as you know, a bequest, but there are entails. Colonel Beaumont has a lifetime right to live there, but he can't refuse you a visit.'

'I know,' I said, 'and Colonel Beaumont is a dear friend and I can foresee no problems.'

'On the colonel's death the property will revert entirely to your daughter, Marisol Bradford.' He gave me an enquiring look.

I trusted him. 'Marisol was Mr Troy's daughter.'

'All right,' he nodded, content and not inclined to pry.

'Now,' he said. 'Do you want me to pursue Max's claims to his father's estate? Major von Klausen was a wealthy man and there is still money; in Switzerland and estates in Argentina, to where his wife and daughters have emigrated.'

'No,' I said it firmly. 'There is no need. Absolutely no need.'

With that, I left the lawyer's office and went to pick up Charlie from the newspaper.

'All done?' he asked, and I nodded.

'All right. Now, let's go and eat. I've heard of this great little restaurant. It's French, Provençal, but not one of those fancy places. It serves the real, rough, country food.'

'Sounds wonderful,' I said, and smiled.

So we sat down and started with stewed red peppers and charcuterie, which immediately took me back to Amyas's house in Provence. In my bag I had the first copy of his book of poems, which I'd had printed, and I kept touching it and letting my fingers stroke the title and the author's name. When we get back home, I told myself, I'll go up to his grave and show him. Maybe I'll read one of the poems out loud.

It was a bright summer afternoon when I walked along the headland to the cemetery. I stroked my hand over the headstone, tears coming to my eyes as I re-read the inscription. It never failed to move me. AMYAS TROY, WHO LOVED THE DAUGHTER OF ZEUS.

Then I read his poem:

All of You

Some of you,
Or part of you,
Or most of you, is not enough.
I want all of you,
Your body and your soul
Your heart and your five senses,
Your love, your hope, your trust
And your desire too.
I want all of you.

When I Was Young

Mary Fitzgerald

**'When I was young the war started.
When I was young my father was a soldier.
When I was young I went to France and fell in love.'**

1950

Eleanor is seventeen when she goes to stay on a vineyard in the Loire Valley. But the beauty of her surroundings is at odds with the family who live there. It is a family torn apart by the terrible legacy of war, and poisoned by the secrets they keep.

Despite his forbidding manner, Eleanor is drawn to Etienne, the dark and brooding owner, though his wife's malicious behaviour overshadows everyone's lives. But when death comes to the vineyard, Eleanor finds her faith in her new-found love is tested to the limits.

arrow books

The Love of a Lifetime

Mary Fitzgerald

Sometimes love is not enough

From the moment Elizabeth Nugent arrives to live on his family's farm in Shropshire, Richard Wilde is in love with her. And as they grow up, it seems like nothing can keep them apart.

But as World War II rages, Richard goes to fight in the jungles of Burma, leaving Elizabeth to deal with a terrible secret that could destroy his family.

Despite the distance between them, though, Richard and Elizabeth's love remains constant through war, tragedy and betrayal.

But once the fighting is over, will the secrets and lies that Elizabeth has been hiding keep them apart for ever?

arrow books

THE POWER OF READING

Visit the Random House website and get connected with information on all our books and authors

EXTRACTS from our recently published books and selected backlist titles

COMPETITIONS AND PRIZE DRAWS Win signed books, audiobooks and more

AUTHOR EVENTS Find out which of our authors are on tour and where you can meet them

LATEST NEWS on bestsellers, awards and new publications

MINISITES with exclusive special features dedicated to our authors and their titles

READING GROUPS Reading guides, special features and all the information you need for your reading group

LISTEN to extracts from the latest audiobook publications

WATCH video clips of interviews and readings with our authors

RANDOM HOUSE INFORMATION including advice for writers, job vacancies and all your general queries answered

Come home to Random House

www.randomhouse.co.uk